MW01286058

Spellmonger

3rd Print Edition, 2013, 2016

ISBN-13: 978-1522975038

ISBN-10:1522975039

The Spellmonger Series

Novels

SPELLMONGER

WARMAGE

MAGELORD

KNIGHTS MAGI

HIGH MAGE

JOURNEYMAGE

ENCHANTER

Other Spellmonger Works

The Road To Sevendor – Anthology

The Spellmonger's Wedding – Short Story

The Spellmonger's Honeymoon – Novella

HAWKMAIDEN – Cadet Novel

Spellmonger

Book One of the Spellmonger Series

By Terry Mancour

"Magic is merely the beginning of the vocation of the spellmonger; far more important is the ability to know a community, see to the things it needs that no one else sees, and ensure its safety and security. Trying to get paid for that is the real trick.*"*

Master Faran, the Spellmonger of Idris

Dedicated to my Parents,

Irving and Andrea Mancour

Who never stopped encouraging

me to be a writer, no matter what

kind of crappy job I had.

Not *once.*

CONTENTS

Acknowledgements

I would like to gratefully acknowledge the assistance, encouragement and inspiration provided by **Emily Harris**, my long-suffering editor, **Janet Sawyers**, my post-production specialist, **Lance Sawyers**, my art director, **Tim Faherty**, my volunteer copywriter, and all of my fans who have enjoyed the series and given me encouragement.

Northern Steppes

Duchy

of

Alshar

Boval Vale

Duchy

of

Castal

Duchy of Vore

Ducby

OLD IMPERIAL MAGOCRACY

of

Remere

Duchy of Merwin

The Five Duchies

Farise

Chapter One

The Bell Of Minden's Hall

"The westlands of the Alshari Wilderlands are a remote region filled with a robust people, brave and strong; yet they are a peaceful folk who have seen little of the feudal struggles of the eastern duchies. Apart from issues of dynastic dispute or the occasional territorial disagreement, there is little for them to fear in their rich mountain freeholds."

— Roadbrother Ostus,

Wandering The Wilderlands Of Alshar

I awoke with a hangover to the unpleasant and unwelcome sound of the village bell.

You'd expect a bell to tinkle merrily. There was no merriment in this toll – this bell was a locally produced, crudely-forged iron affair that lived in a rickety rough stone bell tower in the middle of the tiny mountain hamlet that was my home. It had a forlorn, off-pitch ring that you could hear for miles throughout the vales. This close, with this much of a hangover, it sounded like a particularly sadistic demon pitifully calling my name . . . *Min . . . Min . . . Min . . .*

For a bare, confusing instant I thought I was back in the jungles of Farise during my stint in the army, except that I wasn't pouring with sweat. A misty mountain chill enveloped me instead, and the smells weren't the pungent aroma of rotting vegetation and continual rain, but the relatively clean smells of mountain grass and damp thatch afire.

As I emerged from sleep, my mind still foggy from the previous evening's excesses, I finally realized that the demon of my dreams *was* actually the bell, and I blearily realized the implications: *the village bell only rang when there was a fire or other emergency requiring everyone's attention.*

I groaned miserably into my warm, welcoming pillow, preferring the smell of the sweet mountain herbs and goose down to the odor of burnt thatch, as I struggled to marshal my resources. If there was a bell, I reasoned, that meant an emergency, and almost every emergency would call for the assistance of the trusty village Spellmonger.

That was me. I needed to go to work. *Damn it.*

Once that thought occurred, my feet – still in my boots (it had been *that* kind of night) swung over the side of the bed of their own accord and hit the floor in a manner that was entirely offensive to my head's delicate condition. My feet had better sense than my head, it seemed. An emergency at this time of night was almost always a summons for fire duty or some medical issue or a missing favored goat or something else important to the local peasants. I had spells for that.

I encouraged my protesting head to work properly as I rose and shook myself awake. I could smell smoke. So it *was* probably a fire. The fire would have to be one of the close-by farmsteads, too, I reasoned, because I had spells on the village as a whole to prevent such things within the bounds of the hedgework. But *which* farmstead? I tried to clear my head for a moment and summon the energy to do a simple detection spell.

It took a moment to happen – magic and alcohol don't mix well. This sort of spell is easy, and it doesn't take much energy, thank Ishi, because at the time I didn't have much. It's the sort of minor spell or cantrip I did all the time – and fire is a lot easier to detect than lost goats. I held my hands about two feet apart and a rough mental map of the village swam before me for my inspection.

It was an image in three dimensions, it could only be seen by employing magesight, and it was a spell that had become a familiar tool during my six-month tenure in the rustic mountain hamlet of Minden's Hall. The preparation had been intensive. It had taken weeks of constant study when I had first set up shop, walking every inch of the tiny village and meeting every person who lived within, but when I was done the resulting map the spell manifested was as complete a representation of the village as I was capable of crafting.

Fire is the easiest element to detect, and my wards were a point of professional pride – I'm really good with fire spells, so there should *be* no fire. While my protection runes were loosely wrought enough to allow for *some* flame (else nothing inside the village would ever get cooked) the wards should have quickly extinguished any serious-enough unauthorized fire with the intensity necessary to burn damp thatch.

Unless something had pushed *through* my wards.

That thought sobered me another measure, and I wisely decided to investigate a bit before plunging headlong into the night. My stomach lurched unpleasantly as I studied the spell and it only got worse the longer I took. My inspection of my wards in magesight was clear: there were *several* areas of excitement that should not have been there, had my wards remained intact.

Before the dire implications of *that* really set in, I heard the first of the screams: a high, panicked, girlish voice – that stopped abruptly.

I had heard screams like that before, in the jungle villages of Farise, thousands of leagues south of here. A scream of fear and panic and terror, of being woken up in the middle of the night to the sight of violence and blood. The first time I'd heard it, it had been when I'd helped raid a village of peasants whose lords were on the wrong side of the war. You don't forget that sound.

My feeble brain knew it was unlikely to be bandits. The village of Minden's Hall lays within Boval Vale, as peaceful a domain as I'd ever seen, high in the western Minden Mountains and remote from the trade routes that bandits were traditionally attracted to. Any self-respecting bandit wouldn't starve here, but he wouldn't prosper. There just wasn't enough coin in a primarily barter economy. The local people had little more than cheese and cattle to steal.

Professional soldiers or unemployed mercenaries were also unlikely. It wasn't unknown for mercenary companies between engagements to occasionally sack a village out of boredom and need for loot, but there weren't any mercenaries closer than the next barony, or the town of Tudry, leagues to the east, as far as I knew.

I quickly dismissed the idea of an inter-house war as well. The local lord, Sire Koucey of House Brandmount, was a kindly, mature nobleman who didn't seem to *have* any enemies that I could tell. He and his younger brother, who held the smaller portion of his domain, got along like brothers were supposed to. Nor was the distinguished old knight engaged in a feud, his borders were unthreatened by his noble neighbors.

That left two possibilities: a peasant uprising (which seemed just as highly unlikely – I'd never seen peasants so pleasantly free and content as those in Boval) or . . .

Oh, crap.

There was only one other reasonable possibility. I cursed savagely and reached for my weapons belt as the magemap dissipated from my attention. And I was suddenly very much awake.

I hadn't touched my weapons harness in months. The last time was to move it from the foot of my bed to a peg on the wall, and I hadn't even bothered to draw my sword back then – a slender, utilitarian army-issue mageblade. I drew it now and then pushed it back into its scabbard. It was even getting a little rusty. A spellmonger in a remote mountain village just doesn't have occasion to use a warmage's tools. That's why I was way the hell up here in the middle of nowhere in the first place.

As impressive as a warwand or mageblade might be to the rubes, as tools they were rarely useful for removing warts, discouraging rats from nesting, or finding lost livestock – which is how I spent most of my professional time these days.

If I'd had my way, the harness would have stayed on the wall until the spells faded away and the leather rotted. But the leather slipped easily over my shoulders, and I could feel the tingle of magic from the warwands like I was back in the army again.

I *hated* that feeling. I moved out to the country in the first place anticipating a long, boring, prosperous existence capped with a peaceful and dignified death in my sleep, surrounded by my adoring, weeping descendents. I'd had enough excitement in battle for two lifetimes, already, and I'd come to Minden's Hall seeking boredom by the fistful. *Not* ringing bells, burning thatch and screams of terror.

As I buckled the belt I shouted into the darkness for my apprentice, my head painfully regretting rousing him even as I did it.

Tyndal was a good lad, a local boy I'd discovered working in a stable when I'd first arrived here. He was quite Talented at the art of magic for his age, but he was *completely* inexperienced at this kind of thing. Indeed, at fourteen summers, he was completely inexperienced in *most* things. But I knew that if I didn't put his idle hands to work doing something useful he would feel obligated to rush outside to defend his village, and probably get himself killed in the process. And since I had just started getting him trained up decently, that would be a horrible waste of an apprentice.

Considering his weight and size, he was also at least as drunk as I was – a local farmer, Goodman Tilleb, had paid me three big earthenware jugs of the local hard cider for enchanting his scarecrow to repel cornworms as well, and I had quite generously shared the take with

Tyndal. Three quarters of a jug had passed our lips and inspired a long and witty debate about a subject that I could not seem to recall (although I clearly recall being witty about it) before sleep took us just a few hours before. We were paying for it now.

Tyndal sputtered and waved pointlessly at the air before the wiggle of my toe succeeded in bringing him back to the land of the conscious. He rose from his cot (still dressed and wearing *his* boots, I noted), his eyes bleary with sleep, but with expressions of confusion, excitement and fear vying for victory on his face.

"The . . . *bell?*" he asked, unsteadily. "Is that the bell?"

"Tyndal, get *up!*" I whispered harshly. "But *quietly!*"

He smelled the smoke, too. "Fire? There's a *fire?*" he asked, his eyes swimming with confusion and alcohol.

"Not a fire – not a serious one, at least – I checked. But fire is involved. *Some*thing is happening outside, something unpleasant." There were more screams in the distance to helpfully punctuate my report. They did nothing to help my poor head.

But it was time to go to work, so I got to work. Damn my commoner's work ethic . . .

I crept over to the window and cautiously peered down from the second story of my shop, out into the uncobbled dirt track the locals insisted on calling a street. I saw menacing shadows moving through the moonless night, and heard growls, shrieks, and more muted screams peppering the cool, damp air. I employed the magesight spell again, which had the useful effect of letting me see in the dark – though not nearly as well as real daylight did.

I could see the shapes below were moving with organized menace, creeping quietly from house to house, weapons in hand. There were a *lot* of murky shapes down there, lurking in the darkness. I counted ten before I stopped, and from the screams there were many more. I repeated my earlier curse in a whisper and fell back before any of them could see me. I had to think.

"The village is being attacked," I pronounced. "We'll have to do something about that."

Tyndal was crouched nearby, wide-eyed with a fear that was magnified by drunkenness and compounded with confusion. I nodded reassuringly to him, and he relaxed a bit. Then he got nervous again when I pulled a spare warwand from a sheath behind my back and tossed it to him. He caught it automatically, and stared at it as if it were a foreign thing.

"It has four charges. If you need to defend yourself, just point it and say the command word: *guerestra*. It's Cormeeran for 'camp follower'," I explained. "Nothing you can't handle. But you're going to have to *mean* it, if you want it to work. Don't hurt yourself with it. Can you use a bow?"

"Huh? Attacked? Who is it? What is it? *Bandits?*" he asked, alarmed, ignoring my question. He crawled over to the window and peeked out himself, but without my stealth. That was not the smartest thing to do. I should have stopped him, I suppose, but I was too busy getting myself armed. I shook my head as I crept over to one of the trunks I kept along the walls of my chamber.

"Not likely," I responded in a quiet whisper. "We're too remote for any serious bandit, or even an amateur, much less a band of them. I think it's more likely that it's—"

"*Goblins!*" my apprentice shrieked far too loudly, his voice breaking unexpectedly and his eyes white with fear. He had reached the same conclusion as I by the simple expedient of looking out the window. "Master, a whole *army* of 'em! At least *thirty!* They're attacking everyone and burning—"

"*Keep your fool voice down!*" I commanded, reprovingly. "And get away from that window! Goblins might be poor shots and unused to archery, but your fat head will be too big a target to miss!"

He dropped down below the sill, breathing heavily, his eyes wide with fear and excitement and his knuckles white as he clutched the warwand with renewed energy. "*Can you use a bow?*" I repeated as I took my short bow out of the trunk and began stringing it.

The boy nodded, wide-eyed. I figured he could, but I'd never asked him. From what I had seen the Bovali peasants as a class were well-acquainted with the bow, if not universally adept. Most lads up in the mountain reaches spent their summers among the pastures, keeping the cows in order and keeping the wolves at bay with some variation of the long Wilderlands bow. There was some incredible hunting this deep in the Wilderlands (if you like that sort of thing) and the famed Wilderlands longbow was a notoriously powerful and accurate weapon in the hands of someone who had the strength and skill to wield it.

I handed him my recurved war bow, much shorter and lighter than the local standard, and pushed the quiver after it. He seemed a lot more comfortable with it than the warwand.

"Goblins!" he repeated, shaking his head, his young voice a dazed, disbelieving whisper. He hung the quiver at his waist and strung the bow.

"Yes," I agreed, grimly. *Goblins.*

Around most places in the West, particularly the Wilderlands regions of Alshar and Castal, the peasants called them "goblins." In other places where their race interacts with humans they're known as "scrugs," "hairy folk" or most commonly "mountain folk." To the ancient Imperials they were known as the *casadalain*, the "Low People of the West." They call themselves simply *gurvani*, "the people."

Standing no more than four or five feet tall, these little furry black creatures live a crude tribal existence, traditionally inhabiting caverns or crude settlements in remote mountain valleys or stony barrens in the Western Wilderlands – like the one I lived in – and to a lesser extent, the mountain chains of the northeast, the Kuline range to the east, and the jagged central peaks of the Farisian peninsula to the south. They will sometimes move into arable land no humans are using to practice some very primitive horticulture, but they hunted and gathered and mined more than farmed. Goblins do not favor grains as much as meat.

Ordinarily they keep to themselves, rarely leaving their vales and caverns except to hunt and trade, or for serious goblin business, whatever that might happen to be. Mostly they leave us bigger and stronger humans alone.

Occasionally, however, some tribal leader will get them roused up enough to stage raids against human settlements for cattle and swine and loot. *Very* occasionally, a strong enough leader has risen to lead confederations of tribes against humans in force. And they knew how to fight, after a fashion.

The series of conflicts known locally as the Goblin Wars, which ended almost two hundred years ago, was the last time that sort of thing had happened. Since then they hadn't been much of a threat to anyone. Most folk in the East consider them little more than talking animals, if they think of them at all.

Despite popular opinion, however, goblins are easily as intelligent as humans and some even have a surprisingly strong talent for magic. I had witnessed the power of gurvani shamans the Duchies had allied with a few times in the mountains of Farise, back during the campaign. They weren't slouches when it came to practicing their own type of magic, and some were as deadly in battle as a human warmage.

I prayed to Ishi and Briga and Trygg that I would not be facing one tonight, hung over and tired and unprepared. The gurvani style of magic is crude, by ancient Imperial standards. So are the iron maces they carry. Both are also extremely effective.

It wasn't that I wasn't confident I wouldn't prevail against a shaman. I just wasn't in the *mood*. I just wanted to go back to bed or throw up, the cider in my stomach protesting all this vigorous activity.

I threw my mantle over my harness and then I took only a few more moments to locate the box of knives, darts and daggers that completed my arsenal. I kept imagining my Training Ancient was screaming in my ear as I did so, yelling about how slow I was and how many people were dying because I wasn't moving my arse with more alacrity.

I tried to ignore that bitter memory (no one likes the Ancient who trains them) and the rising pain in my head and focus on what I was doing.

There was no time to distribute my weapons properly, so I pushed a sack of iron spikes into a belt pouch, tucked a dagger behind my back, and tossed a gaudy foot-and-a-half-long Farisi war-knife I'd acquired as a souvenir to Tyndal.

He looked nervous and scared as he automatically caught it, but he was ready to follow his fearless master into the night, where the screams were picking up in frequency and volume and the demon disguised as an alarm bell was ringing ever more frantically.

It occurred to me that an apprentice who was frozen with fear and ill with drink would be little use in his first fight, and likely be among the first casualties if I sent him to war thus handicapped. There isn't much I can do to bolster the resolve of someone else before battle, outside the magical equivalent of a pep-talk, but I could at least mask more of the symptoms of his drunkenness.

I grabbed his face, looked deep into his eyes, summoned a little more power and whispered a charm over him. His eyes came into focus and color returned to his cheeks. I included myself in the charm and immediately began to feel better. It didn't exactly get rid of our hangovers, but it did make us not notice them so much. I added a spell of alacrity for myself, on the premise that I would need quick wits and sharp reflexes before dawn, while the magic influenced my apprentice. Tyndal looked relieved. He was still scared – Briga, so was I! – but he was less likely to pass out, now.

When I turned toward the door I once again realized that I was a bit drunk myself as the room swam. I was just feeling better about it. I almost took the time to do a more thorough job on myself, but I didn't want to waste any more energy than necessary. This wasn't the first time I would fight hung-over. I kind of think it gives me an edge. I could be fooling myself, too.

"Thank you, Master," he said gratefully. "What should we do, now?" Tyndal asked, his voice breaking and his eyes darting around wildly.

I looked at him oddly. "Goblins are attacking our village. We go fight them, of course," I said as I threw open the door to the stairs below. "Let's go!"

As I left the bedroom I held out my hand and called my staff and it floated obligingly to me. It's a built-in spell that takes hours and hours to do, requires a ridiculously expensive piece of yellow knot coral to work, but the effect is *incredibly* impressive to the average ignorant peasant.

Most magi carried a staff – it's a symbol of our profession, much like our silly pointed hats – and most spellmongers keep a useful array of spells hung on them for emergencies. Being a former warmage, mine had more nastiness than most, including a number of useful defensive spells. I hadn't bothered to refresh them recently and wondered idly if the spells were sour yet. Like bread, magic can go stale. I could always hit someone over the head with it, I decided.

The two remaining wands on my weapons harness were far more deadly than my staff. I took just a moment to make certain they were there and at the ready. One slim willow wand, about fourteen inches long, stained dark with linseed oil and sweat and covered in carefully-inscribed runes, was capable of launching at least a score of slender bolts of magical force (about the size of an arrow, with similar effect) against which few mortal armors were proof. The thick oaken wand on the other side of my belt could deliver a massive wave of force akin to being struck by a kicking horse, and could do so two dozen times before it was exhausted.

I hadn't used either one in over a year, but the magical tingle I felt as I drew the willow wand from its scabbard told me that time had not dimmed their effectiveness much. If magic can go stale like bread, then war spells are more like hardtack than a soft loaf.

We paused by the door to gather our wits and draw weapons – Tyn clumsily nocked an arrow and I took an instant to caress the cloth-wrapped hilt of my mageblade – *Slasher*, I had named it – across my shoulders and adjust the harness. I noted that six months as a well-fed village Spellmonger seemed to have caused my harness to shrink a bit, something I could reflect on later. Then I opened the door and we pushed outside to defend our home.

All was chaos. I've been in better-organized riots.

People screamed in terror at shadows, and the shadows screamed fearlessly back. Fires were starting to erupt from a few of the homes, despite my carefully-laid spells, as people panicked and spilled lamp oil or dropped torches in flight. And *something* was still pecking relentlessly against my warding spells, I could *feel* it.

As we burst through the door and into the street, wands blazing and arrows flying, we did not hesitate to start fighting. I elected to toss my staff like a spear into the back of the head of a passing gurvani, his club raised angrily to the height of my heart. There were others around us. I grabbed a wand as I felt an arrow whiz past my shoulder. The willow crackled and hissed in my hand as it sent two invisible bolts into the furry pelt of the next goblin I saw, half-turned in surprise at our sudden and unexpected appearance.

Nor was he alone. Tyndal's first shot had caught one in its narrow jaw, a painful and annoying but not mortal blow, and he was screaming like an injured child at the shaft protruding from his cheek. He dropped his weapons while he clutched his small hands at his spurting wound, which made him an easy enough target to finish off. The third goblin looked at me, dumbfounded, surprised by the sudden assault. He and his mates were crouched over the body of someone on the street before we interrupted, probably looting it. I hoped that's all they were doing. The gurvani had been known to occasionally eat human flesh.

I took two steps toward them and nearly slipped. When I glanced down I saw the body of Goodman Horlan, a local cheese buyer and merchant, separated by a few feet from the top of his head. I had skidded in his brains. It took me a moment to realize it, and by that time – luckily for me – my body had already taken control before my stomach could react to the mess. Army training was good for that.

I had helped Horlan unload a few blocks of salt just this morning, discussing a fee he owed me. Now I was treading on his brains. For some reason I was really angry about that.

Our invaders proved just as angry, as a few more darted from the shadows and attempted a countercharge toward us.

Automatically I dropped the willow wand and drew my blade as I "called" my staff back to my hand to throw a defensive spell – nothing serious, just a *"you stay away!"* type of thing. It's not a battlestaff, after all. But even noncombative wizards like to enchant some common offensive and defensive cantrips in their staves in case of bandits, beggars, or irate clients, if they're wise. Being a former warmage, mine were just a little more . . . *thorough* than most. My spell at least slowed them down long enough to let me draw my mageblade.

It wasn't enough to stop their charge, not really, and they came close enough so that I was soon fighting hand-to-hand. My sword clanged on the iron haft of the first goblin's little weapon, and before I knew it I was face to face with my small black-furred attacker.

The specimen in front of me was about four and a half feet tall, naked save for a leather belt and iron ornaments, covered in a coat of thick black hair that was glistening in the firelight with fresh human blood. His face was full of fangs and rage as he growled savagely at me, and his eyes glowed like a madman's. He gripped a roughly-forged iron mace in his furry little fingers which he threw over his shoulders as he stopped my blade. A skillful twist brought it toward my face in a swift overhead swing. He was clearly intending on braining me as he had my late neighbor who owed me money.

Slasher, thirty-eight inches of enchanted government-issued high-carbon alloyed steel and mediocre enchantment stopped his attack in turn, and for a few seconds I remembered everything my swordmaster ever told me. Or at least my muscles did. With a twist of my wrist I passed the razor-sharp tip cleanly through his throat. I felt a wave of revulsion roll over me as his blood (darker than a human's, but no less red, hot, or sticky) splashed over my hands and clothes.

It occurred to some part of my brain that less than five minutes ago, I had been *peacefully sleeping* – this was *not* my preferred way to wake up. I gave the blade a horrible twist to make sure *he* wouldn't wake up and we were out of immediate foes. Three gurvani corpses lay between Horlan's body and his head.

"Where do we go now, Master?" Tyndal asked, looking around

frantically with dazed eyes. There was blood and black hair on the long Farisi knife in his hands.

"The bell tower," I grunted commandingly, scanning the area with magesight to be sure there were no more goblins lurking in the shadows. "We'll take action along the way as needed. But we head for the tower," I decided. "If for no other reason than to *silence that godsdamned bell!*" The tower was the village's rally point for fire or other disaster, and that's where all the able-bodied men should be gathering, called by the frantic ringing. It still hurt my head like a demon, and I wanted to put an end to the annoyance. Tyndal nodded and followed me as I plunged into the darkness.

Bodies were starting to litter the street, I saw. I passed a few more former neighbors and a few more former goblins as I headed toward the next spot of commotion.

The problem was, even with magesight working for me, these little bastards were *sneaky*. They kept popping out of nowhere and had I not been prepared, careful and lucky I would have had my head bashed in (or at least a kneecap) more than a few times. I slew two more gurvani with Slasher from behind and smashed another one between the eyes with my staff (he rushed me while I was stabbing his comrade) while Tyndal put an arrow into a fourth before we ran into the first live human we'd seen, Goodman Miklo, the village barber.

He was holding a wooden stool in one hand and a butcher knife in the other as he fended off two of the creatures, his back to his shop and a savage, desperate grimace on his face. A third goblin on the ground at his feet told me that he had been luckier than poor Goodman Horlan. I couldn't help but notice that he fought pretty well for an untrained barber, but I knew that he couldn't hold out for much longer against the pair, who were swinging those little clubs in a flurry against his stool. He had a wife and three young daughters to protect, though, and I knew he'd go down in their defense before he'd retreat if I didn't intervene. Besides, we'd need his medical skills for the wounded – if any survived the night.

I decided it was a pretty good time to *announce my presence with authority*, the way they taught me to at War College. Warmagi love that sort of thing, as the sudden appearance of a spell-casting warrior can affect the morale of both sides of a conflict. I raised my staff and sent a very pretty and barely destructive wad of magical sparks at Miklo's two attackers. It's a flashy bandit warding spell I'd hung on the staff almost two years ago. Seconds later the unprepared gurvani were writhing on the ground in agony while their nervous systems fired randomly. It would only last a few seconds, but it was enough time for Miklo the Barber. He didn't hesitate. He carefully stabbed both of them through the neck with his knife, and then smashed the second one in the head with his stool for good measure when having his throat cut didn't stop his movements.

"Well struck!" I complimented him, automatically.

Miklo stared at me in wonderment as he surveyed the dead bodies, the bloodied stool still in his hand. He was a barber, no stranger to blood, but not blood extracted by violence. I nodded reassuringly, made sure he wasn't wounded or going into shock, and encouraged him to join me.

He nodded firmly in return, relieved once he saw someone else was in charge, and said something to his family behind the door. I heard the heavy bar being lowered behind it. Miklo stooped to pick up a longish curved blade from the twitching gurvani's dead hands. Despite the smaller handle, it was longer and had more heft than a butcher knife, which he passed back inside to his terrified wife.

Poor Miklo moved as if through an unreal dream, his face blank. I've seen that look before – the expression of someone who has never seen violence suddenly thrust into a violent situation. I wore it myself, once.

I stopped long enough to put a cantrip – that's a small, simple, easy spell like lighting a fire or heating up water or something that you've practiced so often that you can almost do it in your sleep – that would make it nearly impossible to open his door.

"To keep your family a little safer," I explained, when he asked. "Let's collect some more of our folk and head for the bell tower," I ordered. Miklo hefted his new dagger and battered stool and followed dutifully behind Tyndal.

We collected Goodman Brunan, who we found standing at the door of his harness shop with a long cheese knife freshly stained with dark blood held menacingly in his hand. Bru wasn't in a daze – he was fighting mad. He holds a reputation in Minden's Hall for hard dealing and a quick temper, and he was full of both tonight. He happily joined us, and we continued toward the village's bell tower.

We saw plenty more bodies of both species along the way. I stepped over them as casually as I could – I'd learned to cultivate an indifference to casualties in Farise – and continued on, while my fellow villagers took turns crying and vomiting when they weren't fighting for their lives. I let Tyndal try to comfort them. I was searching for more allies, and found them.

Arstol the Saddlemaker joined us next, armed with an antique rusted sword, and then the five of us took on a large knot of the invaders who were just leaving the house of Jowdi the Jolly. They had blood on their fangs, and I didn't want to think about what they had been doing to the friendly family inside the silent home. My imagination of those events inflamed my attack.

We blindsided them with a force and ferocity one might not ordinarily expect from normally peaceful mountain villagers. I had to stop my little band from continuing to pointlessly punish the gurvani corpses and encourage them to move on to more productive work – there were others to be slain that night, no need to linger over the dead of either species. We couldn't waste time on idle vengeance any more than we could waste it running up to the castle to ask for its protection. This was our home. We made for a woodshed behind a cot which gave us the illusion of cover and the time to pause for a moment to get our bearings.

I could hear all of "my" men breathing heavily from the exertions of the fight and the growing cloud of smoke as I again brought my magemap into view, and noted that the largest concentration of the gurvani was actually *around* the bell tower, where we were headed. There were plenty of stray goblins between them and us, but there were plenty of people, too. If we could convince the latter to battle the former, we might stand a chance by the time we arrived at the stone tower.

Two more villagers came up behind us (and were almost accidentally shot by Tyndal) while we waited, Goodman Guris and his son Gusdal. Both held powerful Wilderlands bows and carried hatchets at their belts. They slapped the others on the back and turned to me – for whatever reason – clearly expecting orders.

So I gave some. No one told me not to, after all, and no one seemed to be actually in charge. But I kept it short and simple. "There are two more around this corner," I reported, "then three in the house beyond that. We go as a group, and we don't leave anyone behind. Archers shoot over our shoulders, and pick your shots. Rally anyone else you see to us. Keep your eyes open for shadows. Let's go!"

The next ten minutes turned into a frantic, confusing, running house-to-house battle, and thankfully we were victorious in each encounter – as a group, we were starting to out-number the little bands of three or four who were raiding and pillaging. Better still, along the way we picked up another four men who were willing to fight. All of a sudden we were a military unit of irregular light infantry and I found myself elected Captain. I was admittedly the most qualified, but I dearly wished someone else would come along and take over.

But while we were winning the individual engagements, my men were taking wounds that real soldiers would have avoided – like Gusdal hacking into his own leg accidentally with his hatchet and Bru's hand getting opened up by a goblin's rusty iron dagger. We were almost feeling victorious about the evening as we approached the commons, but then, by the light of our burning homes, we saw a horrible sight.

The bell tower was the scene of the real siege, though it was more riot than an organized battle. There were about a hundred gurvani tribesmen in the square, throwing stones and javelins at the handful of people who'd managed to make it inside the rough stone building before getting cut off.

As a fortification, it was a poor choice. It was only a three stories tall, of undressed local stone, and there wasn't room inside for more than a dozen folk if they were really well-acquainted. But it was also the only reasonable choice, as it had stout walls and a thick oaken door bound in iron to keep the village urchins from ringing the bell out of mischief. At least one of the besieged was hanging on that bell rope for dear life to summon help. Mothers screamed for their children, children screamed for their parents, and some screamed for their lives as goblin maces smashed at the knees and feet of those brave or desperate enough to try to escape.

Occasionally, the men would throw the rocks and javelins back down at the invaders, and someone with a bow in the tower was making good use of it . . . but mostly the villagers just hid and screamed in terror.

My little band halted by the edge of the village square and I motioned for them to take cover behind a barn while I took stock of the tactical situation. I had never expected to use that term again, but my time in the service of the Duchies had made me automatically think of such things at a time like this.

It was amazing – I hadn't been in pitched battle in two years, yet it all came flooding back to me as if I'd just mustered-out. The constant looking around, the attention to arcane detail, the purposeful extension of awareness . . . all of the warmagi's tools came to me so easily. Too easily.

Well, at least I was in command this time.

I had maybe six or seven men and a few boys, mostly with improvised weapons and no combat experience. Oh, each had trained in the village "militia", of course, but in this remote province that was as much social ceremony as it was training for war. These men were shopkeepers and artisans, not warriors. They were running on fear, anger and adrenaline, which are not the best ways to approach the pragmatic realm of combat. Several of them wanted to go ahead and attack the large band of goblins right then, but I urged them to be calm . . . and Ishi's tits, they actually *listened.*

While attacking the foe in the rear sounds glorious in theory, the goblins outnumbered us significantly enough that our glorious gesture would be futile and as short-lived as we would be. Even warmagic wouldn't turn the tide against such odds, not by myself. I could drain my wands and staff at the brutes and there would still be more than enough of them to defeat us. The best we could do was pick off stragglers and wait for help. Help I was dearly hoping would be forthcoming.

The local lord of the valley, Sire Koucey, had built his castle only three or four miles away, and the bell – which continued to ring desperately – could be heard from there. True, he and all of his gentlemen men-at-arms would only add a dozen and a half defenders to the fray, but they were a dozen and a half well-trained, well-armed and mounted Wilderlords. Compared to the few shopkeepers and craftsmen I was leading, that was as good as an army. Wisdom dictated we sit tight and wait for reinforcements. Only nobody wanted to be wise that night. People were getting hurt. And dying.

"That's Lida!" Gusdal shouted, spotting a girl he fancied screaming on the second floor window of the bell tower. He started toward her automatically, but his father restrained him before I could.

"Enough, lad!" the elder whispered harshly to his son. "We'll get them all back proper – if we keep our heads! Rushing in there will just get you *both* killed. Let's wait and see what the Spellmonger has up his sleeve!" he said, hopefully.

He wasn't the only one who was eager for that. I was kind of curious what I'd do, myself.

"What should we do?" Arstol asked in a whisper. Confused faces looked around for an answer and then they all looked to me – the relative stranger with the sword – for leadership. And hells, *I didn't know what to do.*

While I was trying to figure it out we were joined by another small group of three – local farmers with pitchforks and axes – and again a moment later by four more with mauls and picks and other improvised weapons. They were making all manner of unlikely suggestions for taking the attack to the enemy, and I foresaw a lot of stupidity and quick deaths as the likely outcome. If left to their own devices the untrained men would get themselves killed.

It was time to be a leader.

"Pick them off," I said confidently, smiling and trying to look bloodthirsty. "Arstol, you take three axe-men and go to the other side of the barn. Snipe at them until they notice you and pursue. Kill any of them that try to get around our flank that way. In fact, I'm going to try to lure a few your way. When they get to that side, come out screaming like Korbal himself was chasing you. The rest of you wait until they turn – and they will – and then hit them from behind. *Hard!*" I emphasized, hoping my desperation would sound like confidence.

It sounded like a good plan to them only because they knew nothing about warfare. Still, any plan, even a poor one, was better than this chaos.

I stuck my head back around the corner and reactivated my magesight to see them in the dark. Most were clustered around the bell tower, a few were guarding strategic points to head off any stragglers, but a few were just standing around, watching.

I picked out a small group of goblins on the edge of the larger mass, slightly separated from the others as they guarded the gateless entryway through the hedge that surrounded the village. Just the sort of unit who would be looking to respond to organized resistance. They looked bored with what they were doing, so I gave them something else to think about.

"The rest of the archers with me!" I commanded, rounding up the few bowmen, including Tyndal. "Listen carefully. I'm going to count to ten. I imagine you all can count that high. On three, step out into that space between the barn and the house – that will give you a field of fire on the largest group of them, the ones guarding the gate. Try to keep to one straight line. On Five, nock arrows. On Seven, fire. On Nine, you turn and come back here. Very simple. Ready? One!" It was basic volleying, using a wall of arrows to more devastating effect than picked shots. Not the sort of archery these men were used to, but easy enough to figure out.

As I chanted the numbers my archers performed more or less as they were supposed to, although their timing was not the best. Still, they managed to send a flight of shafts at our foe at the same time I opened up with both wands. At least half of them hit, from the screams. By "ten" we had retreated to safety in good order and awaited a reprisal.

Sure enough, a band of ten or so dark furries loped across the commons toward our position. When they were out of sight of the rest of their brood, Goody Arstol and his axe men leapt out at them, bellowing at the top of their lungs. Half the crew panicked immediately and turned to flee. The other half was paralyzed enough by the confusion to get caught by the mob of villagers at my command. They might have been novices at volleying, but they knew how to hunt. The archers didn't let anyone escape.

"Ten down, ten *times* that many left to go," I said, grinning. "Alright, let's see if we can do that again. This time fire and then charge with hand weapons – quietly! We only want a piece of them, not the whole army! I'll lead, the rest of you do what you did last time." With that I sheathed my wands and brandished my staff as I slipped around the corner.

Now, my staff is not a warstaff, as I have said. It is a perfectly ordinary magical tool that is very useful for making a light in the dark, judging the depth of puddles, and impressing the locals with my mystical wisdom. One doesn't go to War College, though, without picking up a little of the rampant paranoia that flies around so liberally there. While the tool wasn't a full-fledged warstaff, I had put a few special enchantments on it. The current situation justified my efforts. I had the perfect spell.

This spell was fairly subtle, and I was unsure if it worked on gurvani, but it was worth the attempt and I honestly didn't have any better options. Upon my silent command it releases a tendril of magical energy that gets into the target's brain and tells them *"hey, there's something over here that needs to be looked at!"* It's technically a distraction spell that we used in the jungles of Farise to eliminate sentries or remove pickets from their posts.

As it turns out, the goblins were just as susceptible as the Farisi had been, and a largish clump of eight or nine got caught in it. In moments they were shuffling towards the far side of the barn with what I expect were the gurvani equivalent of blank looks on their faces. Just what we wanted.

I took my place with the main force and waited. As the last of the gurvani passed the edge of the barn, all three axe men launched themselves at their backs, Arstol in the lead with his rusty old broadsword. It was enough of a distraction to break the distraction spell, but by that time the goblins were whirling confusedly, trying to figure out just why they were there in the first place – which gave my belligerent shopkeepers and artisans an opportunity to lay into them.

We managed to slaughter all of them with only two minor injuries. The townsfolk were elated at the victory, and I had to keep them from cheering too loudly lest they alert other foes we were behind them. I would have felt better about it if we had taken care of more than a drop in the bucket we were faced with.

But our melee attracted attention from both the gurvani and a few other straggling townsfolk, which was helpful. The archers picked off another three goblins as they tried to figure out what was happening, and we collected three more men, another one with a bow, who had been on the other side of the tower. That heartened me – with our smaller numbers, more missile weapons would be welcome.

Which got me thinking . . .

"Arstol, good work! Now, take your axemen and as many volunteers as you can find and make your way around to the other side of the bell tower. These fellows will show you the way. Kill anything that has more hair than you do!"

That brought a round of laughs and catcalls – Arstol was a hairy, hairy man.

"Once you get to the far side take up defensive positions – behind buildings, through windows, whatever – just make sure your backs are covered. Collect whoever else you can along the way. You, archer! Goodman Henir? Stay here with Tyndal; I'll need you two to cover me. When your men are in position, Arstol, give a shout. I'm going to get these bastards riled up, and then I'm going to scare the shit out of them! Make ready to slay as many as possible."

Arstol nodded like he knew what I was talking about (when I wasn't particularly certain myself) and started picking volunteers. Nearly everyone wanted to go. That was fine. My whole point of sending off the erstwhile "taskforce" was to get them out of the way and keep as many of them as possible from getting hurt.

A few stayed with me, and we kept ourselves busy by ambushing whatever gurvani nosed around the side of that barn. The archers and I took turns sniping, they with their bows and me with my warwand, while we waited. Eventually I heard the shout from Arstol, and I prepared my spell.

It was sheer bluff. My warwand was running out of power and my staff only had a few useless enchantments left on it. But the rank-and-file gurvani aren't too bright, as a rule, and I was counting on this. I had the archer, Henir – a lad of sixteen, the son of the town weaver – tie an oil-soaked cloth to an arrow and send it sailing to the near edge of the invader's siege. It stuck there, unnoticed except for a few curious goblins, and burned pitifully. The poor quality oil we'd tapped from a lamp wasn't letting it burn very bright or very long.

But it lasted long enough. I summoned as much power as I could, draining every reserve in my staff, and fed oxygen to that little flame until it was consuming the entire arrow and the leaves, litter and debris around it – just what I was looking for. I started altering the flow of power to craft an illusion. Before three deep breaths had passed, a "fire giant" nine feet high had sprung into life behind the gurvani troops, lighting their hairy backs with a bright yellow flame.

It was a crude illusion -- I was expending control of detail for size – but it was effective. Fire is the easiest element to sculpt, after all.

One moment the tribesmen were wailing against a few miserable peasants in a rickety stone tower, the next they were being "attacked" by a flame demon from some forgotten hell. The light from my illusion illuminated the village square and banished the shadow, and for the first time I saw the true numbers of the invaders. Somewhere around a hundred and fifty, I guessed. As most gurvani bands numbered a few dozen, this was almost an army.

Though I was nearly at the end of my power reserves, it was a fairly simple cantrip to add a loud voice to the fire giant. Unfortunately, I knew only a few phrases in gurvani, none of which were appropriate to the occasion. But I also knew that many of the little buggers also spoke a debased dialect of the language of the Tree Folk, with whom they were known to trade. And I happened to know a few dramatic phrases in that tongue.

"*Sala vadu nestu kala!*" I shouted through the spell, my voice amplified by the cantrip. *I come as Death to defilers of my people!* It was a line from the Tree Folk epic *Kaladarbu*, which I doubt any of the gurvani had read. Hell, few humans outside of my profession or the scholarly nobility had read it. It doesn't translate well, as the Tree Folk only use writing to humor us. Mostly they just memorize stuff that's important.

The effect, however, was beautiful. The Tree Folk language immediately caught the attention of every goblin who hadn't already been staring at my spell, and they suddenly looked concerned, if not frightened.

One gurvan with more courage than sense ran at the "demon" with his little axe, swinging mightily. He overextended himself and landed in a heap on the other side, his fur smoldering from the encounter and his iron helm askew. A few javelins passed through the figure, leaving it likewise undamaged. It's hard to damage magically flaming plasma with iron.

I willed my creation to take a step forward, knowing that it wouldn't last much longer. But the attack on the bell tower had all but ceased. The mass of black furry faces looked up at the illusion in terror, and a few openly broke and ran away as I added a few more visceral growls through the spell to intimidate them.

"Send a few shots at the front of the group," I whispered to Henir. He nodded and launched four arrows in rapid succession against them. Three hits, one probably fatal, and the other archers were taking advantage of the distraction with similar effect. Seeing the giant and their fellows falling from the ragged volleys was enough to convince a few more to run toward the hedge – but I'd hoped for more. The rest stood near-paralyzed by the sight. I could almost feel their fear preying on their minds, encouraging them to run away, back to the holes that spawned them. I wished that I knew a spell that could do that without the dramatic expenditure of power I figured it would take. Gurvani prefer to fight when they have the clear advantage, and the confusing response to their raid had made them doubt themselves.

But there always has to be a hero in the crowd. A large gurvani, clothed in black leather armor (which was unusual) and wearing some fanged animal's skull for a helmet, leapt in front of the crowd and yelled something in their gibbering tongue. I didn't know exactly what, but I guessed it was something along the line of "*Don't run away you cowards! It's only a fire demon!*" Like I said, I don't know much gurvani, but there were enough Tree Folk cognates to give me the gist.

Tyndal took the opportunity to put an arrow into his thigh just as struggled to make the flame man reach down and "grab" the leader. To his credit he did not bolt from either the arrow or the fiery giant. He swung his war club bravely at the thing's "head" instead, ignoring the sudden pain from his punctured thigh as he passed his weapon through it.

For a moment, it might have worked. He had the attention of the gurvani and was proving that a little illusion was nothing to be afraid of – even if arrows were. That picked up their morale. They started growling and chanting and waving around their weapons, even as their war leader's pelt began to burn. I was expending every last ounce of energy I had to keep the illusion going, and was about to run out. The fire giant was losing stature and cohesion as it ran short of fuel and arcane energy. Between the effort and my hangover, I was feeling about as poorly. Collapse wouldn't be far behind.

Then the cavalry rode over the hill. Literally.

The Wilderlord knights of Sire Koucey had arrived in the proverbial nick of time, some two-dozen strong, stout lances and long swords flashing in the light of my fading illusion. Just as my fire-beast dispelled, the first horseman – Sir Cei, the Castellan of Boval Castle I recognized by the badge on his broad shield – rode bravely into the midst of the goblins, skewering the leader on his lance with deadly efficiency.

I watched with professional respect as he dropped the spear with the still-writhing gurvan on its tip and drew his sword while his warhorse reared and began stomping on screeching furry bodies. I'm not a knight and never wanted to be one – I'm smarter than that – but it was undeniably impressive to watch a man work his trade like that. Especially when he was saving my ass.

The rest of the troops, each bearing the white bull on a green field on their shields and banners, followed closely behind in a rough wedge formation. Seeing their salvation at hand, my stupid villagers, eager to participate in the coming victory, decided to wade into the rear of the invaders' chaotic formation swinging their farm-implements as effectually as possible. I considered drawing my own blade and wading in, but I had seen enough blood today. My body and mind were exhausted, and I dearly wanted a nap.

That's when it got my attention. There was a feeling I'd had since I'd arrived at the square, and it suddenly got stronger.

I eschewed magesight and just tried to reach out with my mind . . . and sure enough, I felt something . . . *there*. At the far end of the mass of fur, blood, and bodies was a single gurvan who seemed undisturbed by the rout that was taking place in front of him. Instead he was waving his arms like he was swatting flies.

Sighing tiredly, I reactivated my magesight . . . and he lit up like a beacon.

A shaman. And by the amount of magical "glow" he gave off, I could see he was a potent one, perhaps the most powerful one I'd ever seen. Powerful enough to make me reconsider that whole nap idea. That at least explained how the gurvani managed to sneak through the wards that surrounded the village without detection. I'd placed the wards myself, and they would have been sufficient against your average bandit, but not much more. I had not thought we needed a more rigorous defense against a real magical attack.

A good shaman, or even halfway decent hedgemage, for that matter, could cut through the ordinary wards like harp strings, if they're good enough, just by throwing power at them until they overload and collapse. This shaman was at least that good, and I could tell by the obscene amount of power he was drawing that he was preparing a nasty surprise for Sire Koucey and his iron-clad boys.

It was time for some action, I realized. The cavalry were fighting against the warriors, but ignoring the shaman who was muttering, not murdering. This was a job for a warmage.

"Henir, Tyndal, quickly, loose every shaft you have against that one goblin . . . *there.* The tallest one. Don't wait for the command, just do it, boys!" I shouted as I prepared myself. Their arrows were probably going to be ineffectual, I realized, but it was possible that they could distract the shaman long enough for me to do something useful.

I had just a few arcane tricks left up my sleeve. My warwand was effective against non-magi, but magically defending against such a straightforward attack was pretty easy if you knew it was coming, and the shaman could not have failed to realize the basic nature of its attack. I could counter, if I had time and had something nasty prepared, but I didn't and I didn't. Anything potent enough to finish him off would require real power, and lots of it, I realized, and I had blown almost all of my reserves on that fire-giant illusion.

It dawned on me that the only thing left to do was…

Shit. I'd thought I'd never have to do *this* again when I'd retired.

When most people think of a warmage (those who actually do think of such things that is) they think of a regular wizard throwing spells in combat. That much is true, of course, but our training at the War College was a lot more extensive than that. We learned wards to guard camps, spells against detection, scrying spells to scout the enemy from a distance, and a lot of other warmagic useful on the battlefield.

We were also taught how to be effective combat soldiers in our own right, to keep from needing infantry bodyguards while we were in battle, and to give us more of an offensive punch when we attacked. In particular the arcane warmasters at Relan Cor had taught us certain special spells that we could use on our *own* bodies to make us more efficient for the kind of hand-to-hand fighting that could break out at any time in a combat situation.

The techniques are complex to learn, mentally exhausting and sometimes physically painful over time – not everyone's body and mind could take the stress of basic warmagic– but once you learn the spells they become second nature. Most warmagi who aren't masochists only use them if absolutely necessary.

Now seemed like a good time to indulge.

I said the appropriate mnemonic trigger words, drawing on every last spark of power left at my command, and suddenly everything around me was in slow motion, as if the combatants and their victims were mired in glass. In fact it was my perceptions and my reactions that had speeded up. My head hurt from the effect, and my stomach desperately wanted me to throw up what was left of last night's cider, but I didn't take notice of my body any more, except in passing, when the warmagic spell was activated. I was more than mere flesh, for a few glorious seconds. Pain and fatigue become something to note, not something to suffer.

But the spell wouldn't last long. I had to take advantage of it.

I dropped my staff and sprinted towards the shaman, moving three times faster than I could possibly have hoped to un-augmented by the spell. Slasher came to my hand automatically, adding the little power stored in the blade to the magical field that fueled my body, and a wordless battle-cry erupted from my lips of its own accord. I noticed in passing one of Henir's arrows in flight, hanging in the air like it was taking a leisurely stroll. Few among the foe even noticed me as I raced among them toward the shaman. A gurvan warrior who tried to interpose himself between me and my prey raised his club high over his shoulder, but then Slasher slashed. I left him behind me clutching the stump of his hand in shocked amazement while I faced the real threat.

The shaman saw me coming, of course. No doubt his own magesight was up, in this chaos, and I would be difficult not to notice. He shifted his beady gaze toward me even as he prepared to release the spell he had hung, a defiant grimace on his scarred black lips.

I guess he thought I was either a knight with some spark of Talent, or a hedgemage with a sword, but he definitely did not expect or knew how to contend with a fully-trained veteran warmage, or else he would have shifted his spell to a defensive one. They taught us in War College that the all-out offensive attack has a better chance of succeeding than a more cautious approach in such situations, and I was testing that theory. With my life.

I could feel the power surge from his hand and couldn't help stealing some to keep my own spell going. He seemed lousy with it, and as he jutted one fist at me the arcane power leapt from one hand to the other. Quickly tapping into that unguarded stream was easy, particularly because he wasn't (or didn't know how) to defend against the effort. That gave me enough of a jolt to follow-through with my attack. When the power rushed over me I realized too late that it was far more than I'd even been able to manage. My reserves weren't exactly full, but I felt better than I had since the damn bell had awakened me. Well enough to eliminate this ugly goblin.

As I slid to a stop near him with a twist of my wrist I sliced at his left knee, right shoulder, left side, and his neck in rapid succession while my other hand worked a distracting little flash cantrip to keep him distracted from defending properly.

It was a partial success. He blocked the first blow with the haft of his club, and part of the second, as I circled around his body with preternatural speed. He was still trying to block the third in precisely the wrong place when my thin mageblade passed horizontally between his shoulders and his head, severing the neck neatly. He died before he was aware of the fact ... and as happy I was about that, suddenly I was faced with a dilemma.

Magical power that is summoned and not used can either dissipate slowly, or it can release explosively, depending upon the vessel and a host of other factors. That was what had killed the Mad Mage of Farise during the final assault during the war. He had built up power, tremendous power, to counter our attack during our siege. Then Orril Pratt, half-mad in his grief and defiant rage, had been deprived of his release mechanism at an inopportune moment and it overloaded his brain – at least that's what the gossip said.

But there are important laws in magic, laws which can rarely be violated. All of that power *must* be expressed somehow, and in the absence of a powerful mind to control it, magical energy can be volatile. When the Mad Mage finally blew apart against the greatest warmagi of the day, he had taken a good portion of the tropical Citadel with them.

When I realized just how much power the gurvan had summoned I knew that I was in a similar position. It was also likely to take out me, most of the surviving goblins, all of Sire Koucey's cavalry, and probably half the village unless I could channel it away somehow. It was happening too quickly for me to form an *apis*, or other thaumaturgical construct to absorb the power. I had to *channel* it. I still had the remnants of the fire illusion hanging around, and that seemed to be the most convenient thing to do, so I sent it all into one big fire-illusion spell and directed it straight up.

The result was spectacular. A fountain of fire nearly a mile high, and twelve feet across, bursting at its apex in the biggest firework I had ever seen. It lit up the entire village like it was daylight, and it could be seen for miles around. It was so terrifying to the normally nocturnal gurvani that those who were not already retreating bolted and ran as fast as their hairy little legs could carry them.

Me, I collapsed in a heap next to the recently living body of the shaman. I stayed there, catching my breath and waiting for the spell to diminish, until Sire Koucey himself, jingling with every step in his armor and spurs, shook me back to consciousness.

"Excellent job, Spellmonger," he said, a grin dividing that gray-white mustache and beard, when I regained my senses. "We've got them on the run. My knights are chasing them back to their damn holes, but that would have been difficult going without . . . whatever it was you did. Well done!"

I stared up at him for a moment while I tried to make sense of what he said. This seemed to be an occasion that called for a grand and noble gesture. I had just been honored by the lord of the domain, after all. It seemed a good place for ceremony, a gesture, or at least a few thankful words.

When speech was available to me again, I managed to mumble, "Thank you, my lord," before I bowed . . . and vomited used cider and bile on his boots.

Chapter Two

My History . . . And A Frightening Discovery

"From ignoble seeds do mighty trees grow, just as from the plainest stations in life arise the most wise and most valiant of our society."

— *Archmage Ricard II*

Once upon a time, in a tiny village called Talry on the bank of the great river Burine, in the Riverlands Barony of Varune, the Duchy of Castal, a Great and Powerful Mage was born unto a common man and his wife.

I'll spare you the suspense. It was me.

The place I grew up was a nice, quiet little river-village, where most of the people farmed or fished, a few sold goods and services to those who farmed or fished, and even fewer lived off the taxes paid by those who sold goods and services to those who farmed or fished. It was a pretty little village on the west side of the river, only six miles from the looming Castle Talry, where Baron Lithar made his home.

My father had the baking license for the river village of Talry-on-Burine, and was viewed as a master of his craft by his colleagues as far away as Dretsel. His bread was always smoother and tastier than any the farmwomen made, his pies were counted as having no equal, and the fruit-and-honey-cakes he made for holidays were the stuff of legend.

He supplied bread not only to most of the village and the barges that traveled the river, but the Baron's castellan also sent to him for special dainties that the castle bakery couldn't produce as well as he could. He was particularly good at berry pies, and as a kid I made a small fortune selling "reject" pies out of the back of the shop to my peers.

In any case, due to my father's incredible ability to take flour, eggs, yeast, milk, and such and transform them into the best breads in the Five Duchies, he thrived. He married my mother, daughter of the miller in Poom Hamlet, upriver fifty miles or more, got his master's license, secured a grant from Baron Lithar, and began a long lifetime of raising bread and kids in relative prosperity.

As his fame and recognition as a baker increased, so did his fortune, until he had the third largest house in town, a small stable of his own, and the exclusive right to make sweet pies and pastries for a five-mile radius of his shop. He was blessed with a beautiful, hard-working wife and many children.

All girls.

When my eldest sister was born, my mother says he was as excited as any new father. When my sister Litha was born two winters later, he feasted his neighbors on her name-day and spoke expectantly of the son his wife was sure to birth next. Six years and three more daughters later, he had become something of a town joke. With each new pink healthy daughter my mother presented to him, it added to his despair.

Don't misunderstand – he was a doting father to all of his children, loved each of my sisters dearly, and never once griped about their dowries. But he wanted a boy to pass his craft to. He envisioned a dynasty of great bakers.

He tried everything, to hear my mother tell it. He consulted the Baron's wizard, the local hedgemage, itinerant witches, birthsisters, and every granny within twenty miles seeking a sure-fire way to ensure male conception. He went so far as to sponsor a festival in the village to Trygg, the Mother Goddess, ostensibly to celebrate my eldest sister's coming of age, but in reality as a means of begging her priestesses for a boy.

After a decade of nonstop procreation I finally arrived. My father was so happy he could have burst. My mother was just *relieved*. Six healthy children is a lot to expect from a woman. Not that she minded the attempts – I get my lusty nature from her – but by the time I came along, she was ready to lapse into the role of grandmother.

They named me Minalan, after my maternal great-grandfather, and proceeded to spoil me only as a boy with five older sisters could be spoiled. My childhood was cushy, comparatively speaking. My sisters took turns babying me and torturing me, depending on the sister, her mood, and the position of the stars. Mama was strict but benevolent (she had raised five spirited daughters, so I didn't get away with much), and Dad tried to be stern but usually ended up being as indulgent to his only son as he was to his daughters.

He did make me work hard, though; running a bakery is hard work in the best of times, and no hands ever went idle. Father worried initially that the over-dose of female attention would soften me, but by the time I was five it was clear that I was as sturdy as hardtack and had the spirit of a spicy pepper roll. Dad relaxed. He had his heir. Until that fateful day.

*   *   *

When one of the village men shook me awake the next morning, I had been dreaming about Talry and my parents. The sun was well on its way toward noon. Tyndal was snoring beside me, almost as tired as I was from an evening's work that had not ended until dawn. It was a mark of how exhausted I was that I had not responded to the wards that should have alerted me to his presence the moment he crossed my threshold.

"Begging your pardon, Master Minalan, but Sire Koucey and Sir Cei would like to see you. They're in Micit's barn," he said when I finally came downstairs. With that the villager, whom I didn't recognize (a thick man wearing a brown woolen cap and tunic that was the unofficial uniform of the Bovali peasants) turned and left. He also wore a thick leather coat over his tunic and carried a five-foot spear like it was a hoe, so I assumed everyone was still on alert from the attack.

I glanced at my snoring apprentice and decided to let him keep sleeping. There was no reason we should both be falling off our feet. I quietly picked up my weapons belt and tip-toed down the stairs, where I took a moment to put myself in order. I put on my 'business' cloak, a dark blue woolen mantle that I had paid a local lady to embroider with stars and moons and all sorts of meaningless arcane symbols.

I also grabbed my hat, the standard four-pointed affair that had been a fashion rage three hundred years ago. It was now the unofficial headgear for professional spellmongers and other magi. Three of the points were smaller than the last, and were sewn to the conical center. I felt a little silly wearing it, but the more important the man, the sillier the hat, my father always told me.

I grabbed my staff from where I had dropped it last night and decided I was ready to meet the lord of the land. I tiredly tripped over the threshold as I left the shop, so I stopped and hung a cantrip that would make me appear alert, awake, and refreshed, in utter contradiction to the way I felt. It used nearly every scrap of energy that a few hours of sleep had restored, but I couldn't appear before His Excellency, Sire Koucey, Lord of Boval Vale and Liege of Brandmount looking like a wastrel.

I was greeted along the way with solemn nods and grateful smiles, and even a bow or two. There was a new respect in the eyes of my neighbors, thanks to my efforts in the attack. Several made a point of thanking me.

Yay, I'm a hero, I thought dully, trying to ignore the wailing cries of those who had lost family in the night, or the moans of the wounded where they suffered from their beds. I saw several men who had fought the previous night, and made a point to nod back to them – they were the ones who deserved the praise.

It's easy to take a man who has been trained to fight and put him in danger. It is much harder to rise to the occasion when the toughest fight you had ever been in had ended with a mug of cider and nothing more serious than bruises. The thirty-odd victims of the gurvani had been a severe blow in a hamlet so small, but they carried on as if it was the day after Market Day. The stoic mettle of the Bovali impressed me. Many of these sturdy mountain people were going about their business as if nothing had happened at all.

A knot of men-at-arms in the livery of the Lord of Boval Vale – a white cow on a green mountain – were loitering around outside, and I nodded sagely to them as I passed. I was surprised when they snapped into a loose approximation of attention. I just didn't warrant that kind of thing.

I saluted automatically, and then grinned self-consciously at myself when they returned the courtesy. It had been a while since I had done that.

Lord Koucey and his dour Castellan, Sir Cei were inside, puffing away on their pipes while they looked over the stacked bodies of the raiders. There was a nasty, cloying odor of death, blood, and burnt hair that was truly nauseating. Live gurvani smell fairly pungent, and death does little to help matters. I understood immediately why they were smoking so early in the day. I bowed to the gentlemen before quickly moving to light my own pipe.

"Master Minalan," the Lord of Boval said around his pipestem in his high, reedy voice. "My thanks for your expert work last night. Had you not rallied the people and plied your magics as you did, I would have found Minden's Hall a smoking ruin and been shy several tenants here this morning." He bowed his silvered head in a gentle salute, revealing the beginnings of a thin patch in the center of his pate.

The Lord of the Vale was a short man, but well-muscled, and he had seen at least fifty summers in this valley. He had sharp, penetrating eyes that held equal measures of intelligence, wisdom and wit. He was also an adept warrior, good with a lance or sword, and an excellent combat leader.

When I had first met him during the Farisian Campaign, he also proved an excellent drinking companion in addition to being a competent officer and a fierce fighter. His men, mostly doughty archers and tough country knights, likewise impressed me both in battle and in camp. He had brought two hundred, mostly peasants retrained as infantry or archers. He had brought more than half of them back from that hellish province, which is more than many commanders from that bloody campaign can say.

When I took him up on his invitation to settle in his remote little valley I became even more taken with the man as a liege. He proved to be a good overlord in peacetime as well as being a good war leader. His people didn't quite love him, but they did accord him far more respect when he was out of earshot than most nobles warranted from their subjects. In the six months that I had lived here as village Spellmonger, I had witnessed him dispensing judgment and making shrewd decisions that convinced me that he had the best interests of his people and his lands in mind, not his own aggrandizement– a rarity among the nobility anywhere.

Sir Cei, on the other hand, was a tall, hulking, sulking, bitter-faced man of thirty summers or so, a distant cousin of Koucey's from Gans. Sir Cei was typical of many of the "country gentlemen knights" of the Alshari Wilderlands in most ways, but he had a flair for organization. He was an excellent manager of his lord's estates despite his famously sour disposition.

He hadn't accompanied Sire Koucey to Farise (someone had to stay home and tell the peasants what to do, I guess) and I could see now why Koucey had been so jovial on campaign. He may have been an excellent Castellan, but having Sir Cei around was much like being a teenager under the eye of a matronly and disapproving aunt.

"It was my duty and pleasure to serve, my lord," I said, lighting my pipe by flashy cantrip, and then bowing. That sort of thing impresses the layman, you know. "I am only sorry I could not have saved more of your people." Almost two score of his subjects were dead, and twice that many were egregiously wounded.

"I blame them, not you," he grumbled, kicking a black furry corpse with his pointed horseman's boot, causing his spurs to jingle. I winced when I noted that there was still a large splotchy vomit stain on it. "Particularly that witchdoctor. He was quite potent, it seems, to do so much harm so quickly – though not as tough as our Spellmonger!" Koucey laughed, slapping me appreciatively on the back. I didn't think it was that funny.

"He was the most powerful mage I have encountered since Farise, my lord," I said, seriously. "You recall we encountered the gurvani in the jungles of Farise," I said. He nodded. He never tired of mentioning the war and the grueling campaign, although he saw it a damn sight more loftily than I recalled. "Their shamans were good, but not nearly *that* good. That shaman was handling far more power than any single mage in the Duchies. I cannot tell you where he came by it – perhaps he was just brimming with Talent – but that kind of power would have almost classed him as a Master Mage. . ." I trailed off as a horrifying thought suddenly occurred to me.

Farise.

"Quickly, where is his body?"

"Over there," Sir Cei grunted. "The men wanted to start lopping off heads for warning spikes, but I insisted that all bodies be thoroughly examined first." Probably for loot, though he was too darn noble to say it. Cei likes being thorough, but he's also utterly incorruptible. When anyone is watching.

"Excellent," I muttered absently, and began the unsavory process of hunting through body parts and disemboweled, furry little corpses.

I was looking for one particularly gruesome limb. Thankfully it didn't take me long to find it. I pulled a leathery black fist, severed midway between elbow and wrist, from under a pile of other discarded body parts. The cut was clean and sharp, which meant it was most likely the one I was looking for. The axes of the villagers and the lances of the horsemen made wounds far less neatly than Slasher.

Carefully I pried the stiff, cold fingers apart. At the center, as I expected and feared, was a centimeter-wide stone of bright milky green, like an emerald only far deeper. It was smooth around most of its diameter but had a rough backside.

I exhaled slowly, and backed away a step. Sire Koucey and Sir Cei had crowded around me, and when I stepped back they jumped as if bitten by the thing. Then they relaxed when it didn't do anything in particular. Of course, if they knew what it was, they would have headed for the horizon as fast as their feet could carry them.

*   *   *

I never wanted to be a wizard – indeed, the thought had never occurred to me.

My plans around adolescence centered on finding some way to get Hedi the Miller's daughter alone and up her skirts and eventually inheriting the shop some day and baking bread for the rest of my life. Noble goals, these.

But Fate, or Luck, or the Gods had other plans, and about the time I started growing hair in unlikely places and cracking my voice, things just started *happening*.

I began learning the basics of professional-class baking as soon as I could knead dough. I had a perfectly common boyhood for the first twelve years of my life as my father's apprentice. Nothing more extraordinary than fights and stolen kisses ever happened, and if I blackened more eyes than I received it was probably because I ate too many cookies and was strong from toting too many bags of flour. And cutting too much firewood.

You might not appreciate just how much firewood a good-sized bakery requires on a daily basis. Dad's ovens were *huge*. Between the needs of the castle and the village and the regular contracts for journeybread Dad had with barge captains, he had two large ovens that rose above the roof of our house, and one small one that was still pretty damn big.

They were rooms unto themselves, large enough for a man to crawl into to clean (and guess who got that job?).

They dominated the rear of our house, great pregnant-looking domes constructed of wicker and river clay. Dad had painted them the traditional red, of course, and you could see them for almost a mile downriver.

Every morning he (or one of his apprentices) would get up long before dawn and start the laborious process of feeding the fires, banked the previous day. Every third day someone (*always* one of his apprentices – rank hath its privileges) would climb in with a broom and spade and excavate the mounds of ash before they relit the fire and began stacking wood upon it. It took half a chord of wood to re-heat the large ones back to baking temperature and another half to keep it going all day. We used a lot of wood – Dad employed three families of woodcutters to supply him.

I started toting wood from the shed to the ovens as soon as I was old enough to walk. At first it was fun. Then it was work. Then it was torture. By the time I was twelve I had lugged whole forests of trees into the gaping maws of the ovens.

While I didn't know it at the time, my magical Talent (or *rajira,* as the old Imperials call it) was starting to come out.

It was little things, at first, things I didn't even notice back then. During hide-and-seek I could always find everyone, no matter how cleverly hid, or hide myself so well that I'd never be found. While playing ball games I always knew when and where the ball would be before it got there. Perfectly normal "childhood" magic, the kind that every kid everywhere thinks that they can do.

But in late winter of my thirteenth year things came to a head. I'll never forget that day as long as I live.

I had spent most of the night fuming about a fight with my youngest sister. Urah and I had always been at odds, largely because we were closest in age. In truth she was no better or worse than my other sisters when it came to alternately teasing and spoiling me. But Urah had a temper, and she often took it out on me when she was fed up at being the youngest girl but not the youngest child.

We fought often, over stupid things, and sometimes it escalated beyond reasonable sibling rivalry and came to blows and nasty tricks. I don't remember what the particular offense was, but I do recall that she got away with something big and blamed me for it.

As a result, Dad had given me punishment detail for three weeks. In our house there was only one punishment: *feed the ovens*. That particular day I had gotten up way too early, gulped a cup of hot milk, and stomped out into the late fall chill to begin my torture. I fumed at Urah the entire time.

I stomped my way back and forth between the shed and the ovens, a journey that I had long ago calculated to be twenty-three steps both ways, and on each trip back I held almost as much wood as I could carry. Every step of the way I cursed Urah under my breath. Not a good idea in front of the oven, which is also a shrine to Briga, the Fire Goddess (in Boval they call her Breena, other places Breega, but in Talry she was Briga), but I was pissed off at my sister and figured the goddess would understand.

By trip six (it took nine trips for enough wood to get the fires started) the exercise had warmed me up. By trip eight I had loosened my jacket, and my boyish curses had become audible. At the end of trip nine I stacked wood as if every piece was aimed at my sister's head. I had worked myself into such a frenzy that I didn't even realize that I had started a fire.

With magic.

I stood and gaped in horror as the dry poplar and oak sputtered into flame. In moments a roaring fire was making my face uncomfortably hot. Smoke poured out of the oven's mouth, as it normally did. The fire was spreading evenly from place to place. It was a perfectly laid fire. But I knew for a fact that I hadn't started it. The spill I would have used was inside the house on the hearth altar yet.

Had Briga heard me? I wondered, horrified that I might have just doomed my sister to a premature and fiery death. I dropped the rest of my wood and started to run away, when I ran smack into my father's rotund belly. I looked up at him with tears in my eyes, and he looked down at me, concerned.

"I saw the whole thing," he said, softly. "Get your cloak on and go out to the shed, to my workroom. There are some things you and I need to discuss."

I nodded, and then remembered my chores. "What about the oven?"

"I'll get Urah to do it. She should be up by now, anyway. She'll never catch a man if she stays lazy like that." I grinned at him, relieved that he wasn't angry at me.

I grabbed my heavy wool cloak and trudged outside to the woodshed. When you think woodshed, you probably think of a tiny shack just big enough to store a half a chord or so. Perhaps if we were a simple farmstead; my Dad burned so much wood that he required a huge shelter for it.

The entire right side of it was full of firewood, while the left side held my Dad's workbench and tools, as well as a few extra bags of flour and salt and such. Behind that was Dad's workroom. Mama may have run the house and shop like a Duchess, but the shed was my Dad's domain, a place of refuge from his wife and family when he craved solitude.

I was almost as shocked by the invitation as I had been by the magical fire. Dad's workroom was Forbidden Territory, inviolate, his inner sanctum. It was where Dad kept his records and did his accounts – my father was proud of his literacy and secretive about his money. I found out later that he kept his secret recipe book there, too, the one he claimed didn't exist, in a brick-lined safe under the floor. *Mama* never even went in there.

To be caught anywhere near it was grounds for a switching. An invitation within had never been extended to any of my kin that I knew of. I waited outside until Dad showed up, not able to bring myself to enter alone. He didn't speak, just laid a fire in the tiny stove, and poured water into a small tin kettle on top. Two mugs were set out, and I could smell the crushed *kafa* leaf in their bottoms.

"Well, son," he finally began in his deep baritone, "it looks like you broke the egg basket on this one."

"Dad, I don't know what—"

"What happened? I think I do. But I'll need a little help to explain it," and with that he reached up on the top shelf and took down a small, pint-sized earthenware jar.

I knew about that jar. Just about every kid's dad in the village had one of those jars stashed somewhere where their wives wouldn't find it. It contained a very powerful distilled liquor that Opa the Woodcutter made to supplement his meager income (regular spirits were available to the folk of Talry, but they were taxed heavily. While Opa's brew was untaxed and, therefore, illicit, I don't think the baron or anyone else minded his discreet trade).

Opa brought a new pint every week when he made his regular delivery. Sometimes when Dad had friends over, he'd take them out back to "show them something in the shop," and they almost always seemed friendlier when they returned.

He pulled the cork and took a deep sip, then handed it to me. I was in shock. This meant I was a man, by the unsophisticated standards of village artisans, and I swallowed repeatedly before I could bring myself to take a drink of the liquid fire. I coughed and sputtered, but Dad expected this and was ready with a cup of water. When I had calmed down (and warmed up significantly) he had me tell him everything I could about the event.

When I was done he took the jar back and stood up, sighing. I sat there silently and watched him putter around, looking behind books and under papers for his pipe and herb pouch. I found watching him comforting. He seemed so calm, and the shock of the earlier event was starting to fade into a dreamlike unreality.

Armed with pipe and pouch, he sat back in his chair and began the ritual of packing it. He also began telling me about my family, on my mother's side.

Mama's people were from Poom Hamlet. Twenty-miles upriver and inland another six. But they weren't from the Castali Riverlands originally. They had re-located there about five generations back from someplace up north, around the Kuline Mountains.

Family history said that they were nobility – legend said royalty – from some long-forgotten petty-kingdom in Wenshar, on the outskirts of the Magocracy. The name Manuforthen was somehow attached to the legend, though if that was the name of an ancestor or the name of the kingdom, no one was sure.

What was whispered, though, was that our ancestors had been magelords, potent magi who had left the borders of the Imperial lands in the East to strike out on their own, away from the power of the Archmage. When the Narasi tribes that were my father's ancestors swept down from the steppes on the decadent Imperial lands, Mama's ancestors had fled south. Some of them fled to Poom Hamlet, where they settled down, forgot about magic, and ran the mill.

Dad had never thought anything might come of it – all of Mama's kin seemed normal enough (except my Uncle Clo, but that's just the way he is), having intermarried with Narasi over the generations until there was no trace of their Imperial past in their features. No one else seemed to show any signs of magic in their blood – but the *possibility* was always there, Dad explained. It had always been there, but he and Mama hadn't taken it seriously. Until now.

*   *   *

"What in six hells is it, Spellmonger?" Sire Koucey demanded at my gape-faced stare. "It *must* be magical. And deadly. You look as though you've seen a ghost."

We were among the pile of bodies the surviving peasants had gathered for disposal, with their dead kin and neighbors arrayed respectfully on one side of the barn, the black and furry foes piled up unceremoniously on the other. As soon as it was light enough to do so I had tracked down the corpse of the shaman, and then spent more time seeking his shattered hand among the stiffening limbs of dead gurvani. The little black fingers still clutched it tightly in the rigor of death, but I had pried them open and revealed his treasure.

"Not far from it, my lord," I answered, breathlessly, my heart sinking a foot a minute. "*That,* Sire, is something I haven't seen since the Farisian campaign. It is something that most wizards live a lifetime and never get to see. The one I saw there was half this size and in the hand of a master sorcerer."

"It is an enchantment, then?" he asked, having no real idea what he was asking. I answered him as he wanted.

"It is *all* enchantment, my lord," I whispered. "And it means trouble for your domain." And my livelihood, but that wasn't what I was focused on. I had bigger things to concern me than my clients – indeed, my worst possible fear was realized.

The Imperials called it *irionite.* My people, the Narasi, called them witchstones. It's a type of green amber found, it is said, in some mountain streams in the Kulines and Mindens. But this innocuous looking little translucent rock was mightier than the foundations of the strongest fortress.

It made a dent in my mind, like a magical fire whose flames warmed the part of me that does magic. These stones were once only nearly-mythical devices. Now they were almost unheard of. Historically, they were extremely important. Witchstones were the source of power that propped up the ancient and creaking Magocracy for centuries against the onslaught of my barbarian ancestors, after all. And for centuries, it took little more than that.

Irionite magnifies a mage's natural expression of magic a thousand fold or more, providing an abundant font of arcane energy to those attuned to them. No one knows how, or why – the few specimens that have popped up have presented an irresistible lure to the magi who found them, and all study on the matter is a closely-held and highly-regulated secret under the Bans on Magic– but the barest amount of that translucent green stone was enough to amplify the powers of the dullest mage. A simple flame cantrip, such as I use to light my pipe, can be turned into a raging inferno with a witchstone. Spells that would ordinarily take hours of preparation and concentration could be done with little effort. Or so I had learned.

Wars had been fought over the stuff. A lot of them. And recently. The Mad Mage of Farise had killed thousands of soldiers and sailors from the Duchies with a mere *sliver* of it. To see that green pebble in a black and furry hand made me so frightened my bowels turned to water.

"This is going to complicate things." I said in a voice that was almost a whisper.

*   *   *

For those of you who weren't fortunate enough to get an Imperial education in the Art and Science of Magic – and I assume that is most of you – the story of irionite is intrinsically intertwined with the history of the Magocracy, and, by extension, that of the Five Duchies and of all Callidore itself.

The Magocracy evolved on the lost island of Perwyn, a mountainous subcontinent located somewhere in the Eastern Ocean. It was alleged to be the Birthplace of Man, though there are other places that claim to have human settlements at least as old, and most legends say we were spawned from the Void above. But when we arrived, we knew little of magic. The Tree Folk taught us.

The First Archmage, Cordan, legend has it, united the various tribal magi of Perwyn under his banner at the city of Nomaowi and fighting against the original despotic rulers there. While he was consolidating political power he also established in writing the basic principles of Magic, convened the first Privy Council of Magi, and founded the first Imperial Academy of Magic. He also fought a successful war against his competitors using his cabal of magi liberally against them. Eventually, through war and negotiation, he dominated the other non-talented factions on the island, and handed his successor a tidy, unified and well-run little kingdom.

He is also, hagiographically speaking, credited with receiving from Yrenitia, Goddess of Magic and Science, the three Great Gifts of Perwyn. The first was the Periodic Table of the Lesser Elements (the *Perada*, in Old Perwynese); the second was the Twenty Principals of Magic and the Physical World (the *Perinsi*); and the third was the basic symbolic system for shaping and channeling magic, which are still in use to this very day (the *Padu*, for those taking notes). What exactly he did with these gifts is still debated in the rarefied chambers of academia and religion. But whatever he did, the man got results.

For almost a thousand years human civilization flourished on Perwyn. Dynasties of Archmagi ruled (often benevolently) over the island and its associated mainland colonies. Masters of politics and diplomacy as much as magic, they ruled by guile and wit, shrewdness and calculation.

They ruled with the backing of the Dabersi Guards, the elite warmagi who were the Archmage's personal army. They ruled by maintaining control of the sea-lanes against the pirates of Farise (who were troublesome even when they were a "loyal" province of the Magocracy), the corsairs of Cormeer (who didn't much like the Old Magocracy) and the navies and leviathans of the non-human Sea Folk (who had little enough use for humans at all transgressing in their sea lanes).

But mostly they ruled because of magic. Using irionite, few non-magical forces could stand up to the Archmagi. Where did he get it or the knowledge of its use, when humanity had no previous understanding of the art? The most accepted historical theory implicates his alleged involvement and research with the Tree Folk of the Continent.

That ancient race had contact with the coastal colonies that later grew up to become the Greater Magocracy and then the Five Duchies. It is said that they even helped establish humans on the continent, lending their expertise with plants and soil to us to make the land a viable home. The First Archmage was said to have been shipwrecked near one of their settlements in his youth. Some stories say he stole the first nine witchstones, from them, others say that they were given to him. Either way, the First Archmage of Perwyn, Cordan I, reigned and ruled with those most potent of artifacts in his hand. Later he placed all nine in the Emerald Staff of the Archmagi, and that just made him and his successors more powerful.

The nine stones of the Staff weren't the only witchstones to be used by the Magocracy. Over time new stones were discovered or obtained by other means by prominent families of magi, but compared to the powerful array of them in the Staff even these wonders were relatively powerless.

The Staff could do all sorts of wondrous things, such as raising or quelling storms (useful for controlling the sea lanes) and laying waste to enemies with bolts of Blackfire (handy for quelling the occasional rebellion or coup attempt). It was said to have had a voice of its own and was free in offering wise advice to the reigning Archmage – in some cases, the legends and histories hint that the Staff itself played an active role in the scheming politics of Perwyn.

The power was put to the test many times, including the construction of the Twin Towers of Nomaowi, the creation of the Spire of Perwyn, changing the course of the River Ilnoy, and the reclamation of the Samprinso Bay from the sea some three centuries after the first Archmage died in office.

That last one was notable because of both its scope, which was godlike, and its failure, which was catastrophic.

For four short years Kephan the Damned, the thirty-second Archmage of Perwyn, basked in the glory of his greatest magical achievement, growing the island's limited arable land by almost a third. Unfortunately, something went wrong and eventually nearly the whole island plunged back into the depths, leaving only a tiny archipelago of mountaintops to mark the site of the great civilization. After the Inundation the Spire of Perwyn, an ancient gray tower that had been built on the highest point of the island, was the only remaining sign that a civilization ever existed there.

When the survivors regrouped on the mainland, the Staff had been recovered, and the first Archmage of the Later (or Greater, depending upon your view of history) Magocracy began the long slow process of unifying the coastal colonies and rebuilding them into a shadow of Perwyn's lost glory. Irionite became the means by which the barbarian hordes (my ancestors) were held back, irate nonhumans and rebelling peasants were kept in line, and politics were dominated. The Palace of the Archmagi was built in Reymes using irionite.

It was also the means by which the first of the Mage Wars were fought.

If the old Archmagi of Perwyn had used the stones to unite an empire, they were used by the Magelords of the Later Magocracy to nearly tear one apart. Noble houses of magi had conserved their own stones and taken advantage of the loss of Perwyn to build their own bases of power. A score of feuding houses, descendants of Perwyn's displaced nobility, spent two hundred years or so laying waste each other's holdings in an attempt to grab power from whomever was perceived to have had it.

For a time the stones were plentiful, it seemed, and nearly every mage of any significance had one. Factions allied against other factions while entire villages were destroyed in the orgy of bloodshed. Great magical weapons of devious and deadly design were used to wipe out whole districts. It was a dark time in history, broken only once the sitting Archmage, an impotent snot of a magelord named Sinfineer, quit sitting on his hands and began using the Staff the way it was supposed to be used.

He finally put together enough of a coalition to defeat his opponents, then brought his allies to heel. He made all irionite the property of the Imperial House and had it collected from friend and foe alike. In an act of great charity (according to the official historians) or of great desperation (according to his critics) he had the bulk of it taken to sea and dropped ceremoniously into the depths where Perwyn once lay.

That made him enormously popular with the common people, who were tired of magical death descending upon them without notice, and extremely unpopular with the nobility, who were almost powerless beside the strength of the Staff. But it did bring peace and centralized authority to the land.

Four hundred years later that peace and stability was abruptly overthrown by the invasion of the Empire by my ancestors, vicious horseback barbarians from the steppes of the North. Our priests were no match for the Imperial warmagi, but we had a huge army, inspired leadership, and faced inept military commanders and a relatively weak Imperial army.

Too late did the Archmagi realize their folly, and the last few did their damnedest to defend their tattered Empire. The remaining stones on the Emerald Staff were cannibalized to create Androbus, the great Sword of the Empire, a last-ditch attempt to save the Magocracy. (It failed, by the way; the sword was lost when the Imperial capital was taken by King Kamaklavan and his five sons.)

The brutal oppression of the Imperial nobility and all things magical began almost immediately after the creation of the Five Duchies, King Kamaklavan's attempt to divide his realm to his heirs equally. He instituted the Bans of Magic to control the arcane forces, founded the

Royal Censorate of Magic to oversee the conquered magelords of the Empire, and nearly oversaw them out of existence. The empty staff still sits today in the old Palace at Reymes, guarded by the monks who live there now, a gilded and bejeweled and utterly impotent relic of more powerful days.

Since then, there has been no irionite to speak of in the Five Duchies. Few modern magi have heard more than legends about it. Those who have dared to use it are quickly destroyed by the ruthless warmagi of the Censorate. Much of the lore about it was lost during the invasion. While it is rumored that some of the old Imperial families managed to preserve some within their secret cabals, the green amber itself was nearly mythical until a decade ago, when the Mad Mage of Farise used a tiny chunk of it to start sinking Ducal warships and upsetting the lives of thousands of Ducal citizens (myself included) in a nasty little war.

Now a goblin shaman had gotten a hold of a witchstone more than *twice as large* as the Farisian fragment. The gurvani didn't have all of the noble and idealistic restraints on its use that the Magocracy or Farise had – and even less reason to like us, after the Goblin Wars. If there were more stones like this from where the shaman came from, there would be more trouble. A lot more. Trouble we were not prepared to handle.

I tried to explain what I had found to Sire Koucey and Sir Cei as well as I could, but the understanding a country knight of the Wilderlands has for such esoteric matters is minimal. Koucey looked thoughtfully at the stone while Sir Cei prepared to dispatch scouts into the mountains, searching for any more signs of gurvani activity.

Very carefully I reached down and scooped up the stone in a cloth. What little is known about the stones suggest that they have a kind of sentience of their own, or at least a magical connection with their wielder. It seemed imprudent to allow my bare skin to contact it. I carefully wrapped it and tucked it into a pouch on my belt.

Koucey looked confused and disturbed, as he should have been. "What is such a potent implement doing in the hand of a goblin witchdoctor? Surely those beasts don't know its power."

I shook my head. "My lord, the gurvani have inhabited these hills long before our ancestors came here. And it is said that the reason that the Duchies, and the Empire before them, have produced so many magi while other lands have but few, is that the forests and mountains where these creatures live have some magical essence that flows downstream with the rivers, and thus invigorates the natural talents of our people. I grew up on a riverbank myself, though there didn't seem to be anything particularly special about it."

"Yet despite all his power you slew this one without too much difficulty." He said it as if it settled the matter.

"No, my lord. I slew him because I took him by surprise, and he was not expecting a trained warmage to attack him, only helpless villagers running in fear. Had I been a second later, or even a little less aggressive, he could have erased this village from this valley like a child stomping on an anthill."

Sire Koucey looked down at the shaman's corpse with new respect, and not a little fear. He sighed heavily.

"I feared that the goblins had been stirred up. There have been signs. It happens every few decades, or so. Usually a few raids are sufficient to convince them to keep within their holes and away from our frontiers. I never heard of them attacking in this strength, nor this deep into our country. What is *your* advice, Master Minalan?" asked Sire Koucey calmly, as if we were discussing cattle over a beer in the market.

"I would like to think that this is a mere raid for food or treasure, but the evidence here doesn't support that," I said. "This looks more like a war party scouting our defenses, not a chicken-stealing adventure. It is unlikely that this was an isolated event, as much as I would like it to be so. My lord, if the gurvani are on the move, and they have more of these witchstones, then all of your people are in peril. I would look strongly to their defense."

That settled the matter in the lord's mind. "Sir Cei," the old knight snapped.

"My lord?"

"Prepare the castle for siege. Send word to my brother to do likewise at Brandmount, and dispatch riders to the Towers to make ready. Summon the militia to service, and break out the armory for immediate drill. Have sentries posted at each village, and send a message to the Lords of Presan and Gans informing them of the situation. They will send word to Count Ramoth and the Duke."

"Aye, milord."

And, just like that, we were at war.

"Minalan, I am going to ask you to investigate this matter on your own. You seem to know what you are doing," he added, with restrained confidence. I couldn't disagree, except for the part about me knowing what I was doing.

"Yes, Sire. I shall begin at once. I shall take the stone back to my laboratory for further study. Perhaps some answers may be gleaned from it. And under the circumstances I feel a trip to the north of the valley would be wise."

Koucey looked startled. "You mean to involve the Tree Folk?"

"The Tree Folk are involved only in what they want to be, my lord," I reminded him. "I merely wish to put a few questions to them and take advantage of their wisdom, if they allow. Their long acquaintance with the area might prove useful."

"As you wish," the knight said, slowly, scratching his bald pate. "Though I don't know what kind of help *they* can provide." The dismissive and somewhat wary tone intrigued me. The Lord of Boval Vale largely ignored the colony of non-humans in his domain. They weren't in the habit of paying tribute, after all.

"Something, perhaps, some clue. They are wise and have long haunted these vales. *If* they will treat with me, they may shed some light on this. I dearly hope so, or we are likely all doomed."

Chapter Three
The Shard of Irionite

"The use of the mineral known as irionite shall be limited in the extreme; no unqualified mage shall seek to explore the mysteries of this most potent of devices save that they are fully trained and qualified by the Censorate to do so. Improper use of irionite shall impose the harshest of penalties upon the transgressor."

– The Royal Bans of Magic

I sat and I stared at the little green stone like it might bite me. It didn't; it persisted in lying there on the little pillow of silk and pretending that it was just an innocent, pretty little piece of harmless rock. I knew better. I took a deep breath and let it out.

Irionite. The stone of fable.

It is at once the most dangerous and most useful substance in the world. It is said to be rarer than diamonds, more precious than gold, more powerful than any known magical component. It had been mentioned in universally reverent tones by my instructors at the Academy.

My own experience with the stuff was less than helpful. All I can remember about irionite was that miserably stormy night in Farise, when my unit raided the palace of the Doge, fighting against his professional army and his sorcerous lackeys. I still wake up screaming, dreaming about that night.

Orril Pratt, the Mad Mage of Farise, had used a piece of irionite in crafting the deadliest magical weapon since the Magocracy, and he wasn't prepared to come quietly. He hurled bolts of death at us that blew holes in the streets and started raging fires so hot that they burned the masonry. He made the heads of my squad mates explode and sent huge chunks of ruined city flying out to smash our siege engines. Had it not been for superior planning, pure desperation, and more luck that we were probably entitled to, it's quite possible that that little green chip of stone would have defeated us.

The one in front of me was twice its reputed size. It had been taken from the hand of a simple goblin shaman.

I stared at that damn stone for hours before I got up enough courage to probe its arcane depths. I'd done what research I could first, of course. I am a Thaumaturge, among other things, after all; I knew the basics of the study of the science of magic. So I approached my investigation like a school project. It hadn't taken me long to exhaust my tiny library for references on the subject. I had learned a little more than I thought I would, which only made me more afraid of what we were facing.

Jarik's *Metaphysical Reality* had a small listing for irionite, and said it originated in the loamy meadows of mountain valleys of the Minden Range (where I was standing), although it was often found more rarely in the Kulines. Apart from a few minor pieces of folklore and obvious lies, the Sage of Sherbrook had little else to say on the manner.

Koval's *Talismans and Sigils* had a more complete listing, and included an account from an even earlier epoch that declared that the Magocracy had stolen its powers from the gurvani and the Tree Folk when they came to this land. Koval made some astute speculation that the powers that they stole were in the form of irionite gems, and mentioned a few lost and obscure references that I wasn't familiar with to support his claim.

Lister's *Magical Miscellany* described a little of the stone's use in the Magocracy, including some theories about their origin. This last entry was by far the most helpful – and the most frightening.

Lister wrote of several accounts of the stones being used for phenomenal feats of magic, including the destruction of whole towns, freezing of rivers in the middle of summer, animating armies of the dead, that sort of thing. Lister's theory about the origin of the stones was interesting and made a great deal of sense. Irionite was not a mineral, he contended; it was an *organic substance*. He theorized that it was a type of amber, possibly from the sap of the *kellesarth* tree.

Kellesarth, as Lister explained, is an evergreen shrub whose berries are rich in a substance that was named *kellan* by the sages of antiquity. *Kellan* has the effect of temporarily increasing the expression of potential magical talent in a mage, which is why a distillation of the berry is sometimes used in the early days of an apprentice's training if he is having a hard time producing power.

Sometimes the distilled essence will allow the pathways used for magical work to open up more fully and less painfully than if left to develop on their own. It has been used to varying degrees of success to treat a few of the rare magical ailments that our profession is hazard to. The book also mentioned that some mountain peasants eat the raw berries before orgiastic fertility rituals, as it increases their awareness.

(That last one I doubted. I had been in the mountains for over six months, now, and if someone was having orgiastic fertility rituals they had failed to invite me.)

Prolonged use, however, can be addictive and toxic, causing madness, gradual degeneration of nerve control, and eventual death. *That* part wasn't in dispute. There is even a fringe element of my profession that perpetually seeks to discover a way that *kellan* can be used safely. They haven't had much luck, and you can find the poor, palsied bastards hanging around the Academies sometimes, begging their wiser colleagues for money for more "research."

Kellesarth was not uncommon in the lowlands, where it often made a fragrant and decorative shrub around manor houses and old Imperial buildings. When found there, it usually isn't potent enough to produce *kellan* in any quantity. And while it is a bit sappy, I couldn't imagine a single bush producing enough sap to solidify the kind of volume I assumed it would take to form a witchstone. Botany is not my strong suit, but the *kellesarth* shrubs I had grown up around simply don't *get* that big.

However, in the few months I had been in the mountains I had noticed that the *kellesarth* grew much larger and more robustly at this altitude. Until now it had merely been a curious footnote of botanical lore for the book I would someday write in my dotage. If those more robust *kellesarth* trees produced a significant amount of sap, then it was only logical that the magical properties of the plant were present in stronger quantities – enough to produce a kind of amber, perhaps, over a few centuries.

It also explained why the rivers that were spawned from these hills produced a bumper crop of magi in the valleys below: particles of irionite or *kellesarth* sap would have washed away into creeks and streams with the rain. Water runs downhill. People drink water. Therefore, *kellesarth* particles became infused in the tissues of future magi. Like me. It was a compelling theory.

The gurvani have inhabited these mountains far longer than humans, and they must have come into contact with both the tree and the rock, I reasoned, the same way that we had. Despite prejudices to the contrary, the average gurvan is not any more or less stupid than your average human peasant. In fact, from what the lore masters at the Academy taught us, there is evidence that the gurvani once had a vibrant, if primitive, kind of nascent civilization in the lower valleys . . . before humans showed up and shoved them back up into the hills.

I knew that there were ruins of pre-Imperial structures that seemed to be of gurvani manufacture, and not the far more sophisticated Alka Alon. While their magic differed greatly in form from Imperial or Tree Folk styles, it has proven to be potent in the past. It was almost a certainty, then, that the Mountain Folk had knowledge of irionite, and were now using it.

That begged a couple of pressing questions: Was this raid a fluke, a one-time occurrence by an opportunistic leader? Did this particular tribal shaman luck onto this mammoth chunk and decide to vent his rage on our village? That seemed the most plausible story. But why now and why here? The shaman was dead, and I didn't know a lick of necromancy to ask him. Too many questions, not enough answers. But they had to be there, and I had to find them. Quickly.

So I stared at that little chunk of pretty rock and I tried to muster up the courage to delve deeper into its mysteries. I studied plenty of Thaumaturgy ("the science of magic", technically) and knew how to begin, at least in theory.

After five hours, with sweat pouring off of me like rain, I finally gave up. There was just too much I didn't know about it, and what I did learn was tantalizingly incomplete. As far as I knew, there were *no* magi who specialized in this field of magic – hard to do when it's proscribed by law and punishable by imprisonment or death. In fact, as far as I knew I had in my possession more irionite than any single mage in the Five Duchies had ever had – me, a village spellmonger in a backward little mountain hamlet.

I needed help. Magical help, and Inrion Academy and all of my professional colleagues were leagues and leagues away. Not that they would have been any more help than my rustic neighbors when it came to figuring out the mysteries of the shard – most of my old masters hated even mentioning the stuff, feeling the unseen eye of the Censorate on them.

Indeed, there was only one place I knew of where I might get knowledgeable advice on such short notice. But that would mean a short journey, one I had been eagerly anticipating since I arrived in Boval Vale.

"Tyndal!" I hollered finally, not tearing my eyes away from the stone. I didn't have long to wait – the boy was rarely out of earshot.

"Yes, Master?" he said, eagerly appearing at my elbow.

"Pack our things. Cloaks, supplies for six days, travel clothes, blankets. Then run over to the stables and have Karres saddle up Traveler and see if he'll rent a horse for you, as well. Then find one of the village boys who wants to make a penny by running a message up to the castle. You got that?"

"Pack, horses, message. Got it!"

"Good lad," I said, taking down a piece of parchment and an inkpot from the top shelf. Trying to remember my best court manners, I penned an ass-kissy letter to the local lord explaining what I was doing, out of courtesy.

To Sire Koucey, House of Brandmount,

Lord of Boval Vale, Liege of Brandmount,

I bid you greetings.

My Most Gracious and Puissant Lord:

After due and serious consideration concerning the Object which was discovered in the hands of the goblin shaman, I have come to the conclusion that, indeed, further research will be necessary to ascertain the nature of the Threat with which we are faced. To this end, I shall depart from the Village of Minden's Hall this very morning with my apprentice on a journey that should last no less than six days and no more than nine. During my absence I beg that you station at least a brace of your good gentlemen here, lest a similar misfortune befall the Village before my return. While I think such an attack is unlikely, it is nonetheless a prudent course of action under the circumstances.

I also urge you to continue your preparations as if for war, for I fear that this raid was but the beginning of a conflict that could embroil all the lands along the Western March. Drill the militia, make a good store of provisions and arrows against the necessity of siege, and take especial care to patrol the frontiers of your lands against a similar incursion. I will do my best to discover the nature and the extent of the Threat to our peace.

May Trygg and Luin Bless Your Reign,

Master Minalan the Spellmonger

By the time I had completed the message, sanded the ink dry, rolled it into a tube, and sealed it with my overly-gaudy-but-impressively-mystical-looking seal, Tyndal had returned with a boy of about nine in tow.

"Horses are saddled and ready, Master, your bags have been packed. This is Ulne. He will bear your message to the castle."

I handed it to him gravely. "Do not show this to anyone," I said, seriously, "and defend it with your life against goblins, do you hear, lad? Make certain that it finds its way into the hands of Sire Koucey, or one of his trusted ministers. Fail me, and I shall turn you into a chicken!"

The boy's eyes became a big as dinner plates as I fixed him with my best serious stare. He nodded vigorously, took the tube and the penny I offered him, and ran off like demons were chasing him. As soon as he was out of earshot I had to laugh.

"Was it really that serious a message, Master?"

"No, Tyndal, or I would never have trusted it to a boy of his age. But if he thinks it's that serious, he will make certain that it finds its way there. Now, while you load our baggage I'm going to get some other items we might need."

"Yes, Master. May I ask where we are going?"

I considered. My own masters, back at the Academy, would have scornfully reproved any apprentice who had the temerity to ask such a question. I liked Tyndal's native curiosity, however – it made for a good mage – and I never was much for pointless discipline, anyway. Pretending to be infallible just wasn't my style. "I can't figure this thing out, so we're going to ask for help from the Alka Alon."

"The Tree Folk?" he asked in an excited whisper.

"The very same. Now move quickly and we can camp on the other side of the Ro tonight."

With a grin so wide it nearly split his head, he complied.

*　　　　*　　　　*

Let me tell you about where I lived. Boval Vale sits just behind the first ridge of the Great Minden Range, which runs north to south along the western edge of the Five Duchies, in the depths of the Alshari Wilderlands.

It is a smallish valley, only fourteen miles long, north to south, and six miles wide at its widest point, but it is deep and sheltered and abundantly fertile. The small Ro River runs like a spine through its center, fed by innumerable mountain streams, and it eventually empties at the north end of the valley through the Mor Pass and into the Morifal River.

The sheltered nature of the place kept the vicious Minden winters from being prohibitive, and the fact it was so easily defensible from aggressive Wilderlands neighbors kept everyone secure and happy. Boval is a valley of beautiful green meadows and heaths, of pleasant groves and beautiful streamlets. And it has lots of cows.

That's where it got its name. *Boval* means "Valley of Cows" in one of the ancient tongues of the pre-Duchy tribesmen of Alshar. The sweet grass, the altitude, and the livestock produce an abundance of rich milk and cream. And the particular mixture of mold spores in the air up here allow the Bovali to produce a very tasty and delicate cheese that is in high demand in the east. That's the Valley's chief export.

There were six villages or estates worthy of the name dotting the valley. Minden's Hall is the second largest, next only to the small town of Hymas. The vale's only real municipality sat on the shore of the small lake of the same name that the Ro turns into before it continues its northern journey.

Sire Koucey's castle lies three miles from Minden Hall and four miles from Hymas, at the southern end of the valley. To the far south is the estate of Winakur, and to the north there was another smaller, older fortress called Brandmount (Sire Koucey's family's ancestral home) which protected and was served by the village of Malin. A tower guarding the Mor Pass through which the Morifal River runs called, of course, the Mor Tower.

Duke Joris II of Alshar granted his family the valley over a century ago as a reward for the Brandmounts' service in his wars with the Duchy of Castal (where I'm from) and the Goblin Wars. Since that time, the Brandmounts have been virtual kings of this secluded little land, enjoying more power over their folk than most lowland barons do. Indeed, counting the smaller pockets of fertile land in the hills around it, the Boval Vale was at least twice as large as most lowland domains, even if it didn't have near the population. All told, there were only about six or seven thousand people making their living farming, hunting, fishing, and making cheese here.

Of course, they weren't the first inhabitants of the Vale.

At the extreme northwest end of the valley, up a little hollow ringed on three sides by steep mountain cliffs, is a forest grove that is the home to a reclusive clan of Alka Alon, the Tree Folk. The Bovali had little interaction with this remnant of that once-great race – they settled in the more fertile cattle country in the southern end of the vale – but it was known to happen.

The diminutive arboreal race was legendary to the local peasantry, and any encounter was seen as a sign of favor. Occasionally one or two would venture out of their forest enclave and wander across the fields, playing their tiny flutes or singing with voices like crystal bells as they hunted birds and small animals with their bows. It was considered a sign of extreme good fortune to spot one in your fields, and some farmers even went so far as to leave little offerings of milk (which I knew the Tree Folk did not drink) or cakes or such to try to lure them.

They seem so childlike, standing just above waist-high on a grown man; yet their large, soulful eyes and pale skin make them seem wise beyond the abilities of mortal men. Legends about them interacting with humans eye-to-eye seem to be misplaced, because I'd never seen one over four-foot-ten. No doubt those tales were crafted by those so enamored of the species that they wished to grant them a larger stature.

The Alka Alon also have forgotten more about magic than any human ever will know. Including irionite.

To children they were granters of wishes and playful spirits. Tyndal, little more than a child himself, was eager to meet them for the first time. He asked me a hundred questions before dusk about my few brief encounters with them, and he dragged out of me every scrap of information I knew about their habits – which wasn't a lot.

We know that the Alka Alon are related distantly to some of the other nonhumans: Mountain Folk (*Gurvani*), River Folk (*Hoylbimi*), and Iron Folk (*Q'zahrai*), Stone Folk (*Karshaki*) and others are all probably kin, but probably not the Sea Folk or the human- looking-enough-but-damned-strange Valley People. Yet apart from stature and build they resemble the other races very little.

They are purported, however unlikely, to be immortal. They are certainly extremely long lived, by human standards, with lifespans measured in centuries, not decades. Their long, nimble fingers seem out of proportion to the rest of their bodies, and their greenish-black hair and slightly mottled skin gives them the ability to fade into the foliage and virtually disappear. I suspect their magic may aid in that.

They are beings of innate mystery and wonder. Their very presence inspires a religious-like awe in most people. Magi are even more entranced, since the simplest Alka magics are surpassingly elegant compared to the Imperial method of doing magic. In fact, the Alka Alon enclave in the northernmost reaches of this valley was one of the things that initially attracted me to Boval.

Every wizard dreams of learning from the Alka Alon. The Tree Folk are unparalleled masters of magic. Their music-based arcane style is almost incomprehensible to an Imperially-trained mage, even though our system is reputedly based on theirs, according to the lore. It is written that to the Tree People, every song is a spell and every spell is a song; considering how much they like to sing, it's no wonder they enjoy this reputation.

It is also written that they knew everything there was to know about witchstones, which is why I was *very* anxious to confer with them.

Their culture is elegantly primitive. They eschew the written word in favor of memorization and oral history. Their mastery over and fascination with trees is famous (hence, their name). They can do amazing things with wood, growing a tree into whatever shape they desire, it is said.

Their poetry is magnificent, what little we know of it. They are adept musicians, and though their style of music is utterly inhuman it is beautiful beyond mortal invention. No human could sing as sweet. They have a four-octave range, although it's on the upper end of the scale, and they can sing for minutes at a time between breaths.

It is said that the Tree Folk have no separate word for *music, story, history, spell,* or *record.* It's all covered by a single word, *kala,* which just means "song." They didn't seem to use writing until they learned it from us, and then they only use it to humor us. They just remembered everything. Useful, that.

While generally peaceful, we know they war among themselves and with other races. We know that they once had a great civilization before we came here, the ruins of which still dot the Duchies. Whatever happened to it they have retreated to their treehouses and given up iron and steel, kingdoms and conquest. They don't really need it. Their enclaves are nearly impossible to enter by force. If anyone has ever done it – Archmage, god, or demon – I've never heard about it. *No sane person attacks a Tree Folk clan.*

They use no gold or other precious metal to trade – they abhor worked metal at all, preferring to shape their tools out of wood and stone – so they have nothing worth stealing. They use small bows and tiny arrows tipped with a wide variety of poisons that can either make you go into a peaceful sleep for a few hours or die horribly and painfully over days. Their skill at archery is legendary. But if you made war on the Tree Folk you probably won't get close enough for them to use their bows anyway.

They are sneaky buggers who use magic like we use pots and pans. They know you are coming long before you get there, and when you do show up they can make you blind, throw up illusions to perplex you, cause your horse to rear in confusion, make you lose direction, make you forget you were looking for them, or infest you so badly with biting insects that you would just rather go home.

They were once masters of this world, they have told us, and we suspect from their own sagas they have shared with our loremasters. One legend says that they were overlords of the other races in ancient times. They are still held in respect, if not god-like awe, by most of them to this day. Long before Man came to these shores from Perwyn they were overthrown (says one theory) or secluded themselves voluntarily (says another), abandoning their high civilization and retreating to their forest fortresses to enjoy lives of quiet contemplation.

No one really knows how, when or why the Tree Folk gave up their great civilization and went back to their trees, but speculation has been rampant in academic circles for centuries. When asked directly they are annoyingly silent on the topic. Whatever their mysterious past, they now interfere little with the affairs of the world beyond their trees, though they still can have an effect on the larger world when they choose. When the Tree Folk appear in our own legends and histories, it is usually in the role of wise observer, divine avenger, or mysterious magical benefactor.

It's interesting. The Alka Alon and the gurvani had a roughly similar level of technology. Both lived by primitive agriculture and hunting and gathering, and both dealt in rudimentary trade with us and each other. Both used magic, had laws (after a fashion) and practiced religion. The gurvani even had a slightly higher level of technology than the Tree Folk, from our perspective, as they used primitive metallurgy while the Alka Alon abhorred using iron.

The goblins also wore clothes, after a fashion, while the Tree Folk ran around wearing only the occasional belt or harness for carrying tools and pouches or a reed flute or whatever else they want to carry, and left their privates exposed.

I met my first Tree Folk in the jungles of the Farisian peninsula, during that bloody campaign. They were never treated well by the remnants of the old Empire (*my* people saw them as semi divine, but then again we rarely had congress with them up on the northeastern steppes). That adoration and awe after their conflicts with the Doge made them delighted to help our army through the jungles and mountains, including providing us with supplies and the occasional dry place to sleep.

I was impressed by their hospitality, back then. I was even more impressed by their culture. Their babies are always happy, their elderly are respected and admired, and their clans were models of both efficiency and aesthetics. If there was ever a bad-tempered Tree Folk, I'd never heard about it.

The gurvani I had met on the campaign, by contrast, seemed to have a more brutal culture by human standards. After a short infancy, children are expected to viciously compete for resources, and the weak and sickly are given no favoritism: if they die, then the tribe is stronger for it. Tribal leaders rule by strength of arms and come to power in individual duels. Shamans are forged by cruel trials that are both physically punishing and mentally challenging, and many do not live through the ordeal. Those who do are extremely powerful and often serve as tribal leaders or advisors to war chiefs.

They use writing much like we do. The gurvani written language, if you can call it that, is a hieroglyphic system that contains only around sixty symbols. To their credit, it is their own invention, developed long before humans came to this part of the world. You can still see gurvani hieroglyphic inscriptions on stones in Boval and far out into central Alshar. Locals call them Goblin Stones.

While not overly warlike (despite folklore to the contrary and recent events, the gurvani rarely attack human settlements) they do have an elite warrior society, quasi-religious in nature, whose job it is to defend the tribe. Their favorite weapons are the javelin and the club (either wooden or iron), although tribes who live closer to humans have picked up the bow and sword, and use them quite effectively. They use magic, after a fashion, though their murky system is unlike either the Imperial or the Alka Alon in most ways. They feud against each other, indulge in jealousy and hatred, and use force to settle most disputes, not negotiation.

In short, the gurvani are a lot more like us than the Tree Folk are. Perhaps that's why we dislike and fear them so. And *vice versa*.

The Alka Alon, not the gurvani, are the undisputed masters of magic on Callidore. It is said that even the gods seek their help when it comes to the Art. Their spell signature is so distinct as to be unmistakable, and so efficient that some fairly minor Tree Folk charms have lasted well over a thousand years.

But finding them these days is hard. Their enclaves are found in rugged, inaccessible places remote from dense human populations – places like Boval Vale. Some claim that they have enchanted forests and glades even in the middle of our civilization, but seeing how difficult it is to find one, that could easily be myth or wishful thinking. But we knew they were out there, among our lands.

Ranging from small settlements of a few hundred to living cities of thousands, they are content to sing and grow wood and wander aimlessly through their own lands, unmolested by the outside world. The settlement at the northern end of the valley was reportedly a large one, and had been here since before any human had trod these vales. While I hadn't visited there yet, this seemed as good a time as any.

The Tree Folk were sure to know something about the gurvani raid, I figured. Whether or not I could get them to tell me was another matter.

* * *

The massive bulk of Boval castle loomed ahead on the road East, as we hurried along on horseback, high on a promontory that gave it command of the surrounding vale. I was no stranger to military fortifications, and this one was unusual for a region so remote in the Wilderlands: a castle large enough for a prosperous Baron or even a Count, perched on a prominent hill in a mountainous valley far from the nearest human foe. That's what Wilderlords usually defend their territory from: other Wilderlords.

That elaborate pile of gray stone represented a tremendous expense of resources. Yet Boval Vale had no natural enemies here in the mountains. Even goblin raids were a rarity. So how was so great an expense justified? And, more importantly, where did Sire Koucey find the treasury to have it built? Not by taxing the cheese trade, that was certain. While it was definitely a strong part of the lord's income, it would have taken five centuries of merciless cheese taxes to raise enough to build Boval Castle. Another mystery of this beautiful valley I wanted to know the answer to.

My young apprentice's initial excitement about the trip wore off by noon, though he continued to be interested in seeing the scenery and being seen on horseback by farm girls. Tyndal had been born on a dirt farm a few miles south of the castle, so he wasn't yet in unfamiliar territory, but he had any kid's interest in the countryside.

After peppering me with questions for fifteen minutes I decided to use the time for something a little more constructive, instructing him in Magical Theory, specifically Enchantment – a subject vital to developing beyond the hedge-mage level of practice. He settled down when I began lecturing, eager to pick up a new skill or two.

That afternoon, as Tyndal and I crossed the ford at the Ro, I could tell my apprentice's head was buzzing with questions that his mouth didn't have the courage or words to ask. I let him stew for a while, to see how long it would take, and I was rewarded when we halted to let our clothes dry in the quickly fading sun. It gets dark a lot faster here than in my native land.

"Make a fire," I commanded, as I unloaded the horses. "And I don't want to see a tinderbox in your hand, either."

He grinned, and went to gather wood. He hadn't used a tinderbox to start a fire since he learned that simple ignition cantrip, one of the very first he was taught. When he returned and started laying the fire, the dam broke and the questions started coming.

"Master, why have the goblins attacked us?"

"Tyndal, they are the Mountain Folk or the gurvani. Only the ignorant and superstitious call them goblins."

"Master, why have the gurvani attacked us?" he repeated.

Good question. I wished I knew.

"Well, I think it has something to do with that green stone the shaman was using. I think he found it somewhere, and then he used it to influence a whole tribe to attack the village. With that kind of power it would be easy to influence the weak-minded."

"Do you think there will be more attacks?"

"It's hard to say," I admitted. "The gurvani aren't exactly peaceful, but they aren't usually so aggressive. I think it will depend on whether or not they get their hands on more Irionite."

Man for man, a gurvan cannot stand up to a well-armed human. It is only in large groups under a fearsome leader that they can have an effect. "From what Sire Koucey says, they do make raids every few years, and I guess it's about time for them to do so again. Who knows what enmity they hold for humans?"

My apprentice looked thoughtful. "It is said that they inhabited this valley, once, and that Sire Koucey's great-grandsire finally drove them back up into the hills," he mentioned.

"Perhaps they want it back, then."

"They want it . . . *back?*" Tyndal shuddered, pulling his light mantle around him. The night attack had left a mark of trauma on him, I could see. Of course, no one likes hearing that his home is coveted by another. He built up the firewood into a stack while he thought. With little effort he then ignited the wood with his cantrip, using dry leaves he had found for tinder. As the fire belched smoke into the air, I noticed a sudden change in his expression, from fear to determination.

"It's a possibility. As motives go, it's a fairly common one. And you know, that's probably not too far from wrong," I admitted.

"Well, then, perhaps you should teach me how to *fight,*" he said, trying to hide his eagerness and fear.

I kept my face stern, but inside I couldn't help but laugh. It seems every boy imagines himself as a great warrior. If they only knew the truth about war . . . .

"Perhaps I should," I finally murmured, reluctantly. "Swordplay, however, is difficult to master. You should learn the rudiments with a staff. The bow you are familiar with, though you're a bit young for a great Wilderlands bow.

"But the easiest weapon for a mage to learn is the warwand. I will teach you how to make one, I think, and we'll leave more . . . *robust* training at arms for a later time. It is hardly more difficult than a cantrip, and you have mastered each of the requisite techniques. Enough for a simple essay into the craft, I think," I decided. "First, fetch a willow branch, as straight as you can find it, the length of your arm from wrist to elbow."

He dug around in the firewood he had gathered first, and finding no such stick he trotted back into the copse to search. While he did so I began preparing dinner by toasting sausages over sticks and slicing cheese. He returned a few moments later with a stick that I examined very carefully, while I explained how vital it was to check the wood for arcane flaws. Not every branch was up to the charge of power it took to make a wand. Using a poorly-suited stick for a warwand is generally a bad idea.

I then made him use magesight – a spell he had only recently learned – to discover any hidden weaknesses in the wood. He spotted the one I had seen toward one end, which pleased me, and it took him little time to whittle it away and re-inspect the wand.

"Good," I said, when he finished. "Now, dry the wand in front of the fire after you have stripped off the bark. While it is drying, I want you to build up power, as much as you can, and hold it. When you can hold no more, construct in your mind the *kaba* form and fill it."

The *kaba* is a thought-form, a psychological construct that most Imperial Tradition wizards use to contain raw magical power. Depending upon the mage's skill, a *kaba* can contain a tremendous amount of pent-up power and it is often the starting point for powerful spells. Tyndal had successfully constructed a few of them over the last month, with increasing facility, and he'd been practicing the skill.

Using magesight I could see the blue cube he was building spinning slowly in front of him. Without magesight it merely looked like he had a bad case of indigestion. Perfecting the *kaba* is one of the hardest, yet most essential, techniques a mage must master, especially for enchantment. His progress was adequate, even advanced, for his age and experience, and I was proud of him.

After twenty minutes of filling the cube, he looked up at me, sweat beading on his forehead, and nodded that he had finished. I checked it, and it was indeed full.

"This will be the most basic form of warwand," I warned. "Not the sort of thing a trained warmage would use, but effective enough in its simplicity. Take up the wand in your hand, and take your second knife out. Inscribe the glyph for 'holding,' the *ygra*, about an inch from the base of the wand." I waited for him to do so. "Now inscribe the directional marker pointing from the *ygra* to the operational end of the wand. Then, inscribe the *selan* rune, the Rune of Release, as the old sages called it, at the end of the directional marker.

"Good, good, now carefully transmit the power of the *kaba* into the *ygra*." I watched him struggle to do this. Tyndal had only learned how to transfer power very recently, and this was a difficult step for him – kind of like directing the course of a river by using just your hands. It took another twenty minutes for him to manage, and at the end of it he was out of breath and sweating profusely. Those who say "it's as easy as magic" don't do a lot of magic.

"Now inscribe a binding rune – make it a simple one, like *bela* or *jagth*. Those are the best when dealing with raw power. You can use *goromon* or one of the other complex ones if you wanted the power to convert to, say, fire or frost or something. This basic warwand is just pure arcane power."

I watched proudly as my apprentice finished one of his first enchantments, and then I took the wand from him and examined it carefully. It was actually better than *my* first warwand, which bode well (and which I neglected to mention). It was brimming with power, and tightly contained. I handed it back to him.

"Excellent work," I praised. "Now, every time we stop for the night, I want you to put another charge on it. The wood is strong enough to handle four or five without burning out, unless I miss my guess. Each time you add another, simply inscribe another *ygra* and add a point to the *bela*. Understand?"

"Yes, Master. Shouldn't we test it?" he asked, eagerly.

"In due time, Apprentice. I have passed it. One does not discharge a warwand lightly, especially when there might be foes about – or friends, for that matter. They are dangerous to those unshielded."

"Yes, Master," he said, his eyes focused on his creation. "You will teach me how to shield, then?"

"In due time, boy. You've done very well, here. Now eat up, I know you're tired. Magic improves both hunger and desire for sleep. I'm going to set the wards for the evening. I'll tell you what, though, we'll stick around long enough in the morning to both add a charge to our wands before we continue our journey." He looked like he felt a little more secure about that. Heck, I'm sure I did too. It was all an illusion of safety, but we humans cling to such illusions tightly.

As we settled into sleep, safe within the wards, I felt a twinge of sympathy for the boy. Had someone attacked *my* home village, I would have been eager to strike back, myself, at his age. Even though I hadn't grown up here, it *was* still my home of six months, and I still felt a sense of violation as I recalled the attack – and the number of dead neighbors it left behind.

*   *   *

After our morning mediation and wand-charging we were on our way down the road to Hymas, the largest town in the Boval Valley. Where I'm from it would hardly qualify as a large village, but here it was an urban center of sorts.

Hymas is the central market for all of the villages in the populous southern part of the Vale. As cities go in the far west it is large, nearly two thousand souls in and around it. The shops and houses are all made out of the abundant local gray stone foundations above exposed beam frames covered with wattle-and-daub. The roofs were of thatch or tile (if the owner was affluent), and everyone had brightly-painted wooden shutters.

The four main avenues are all paved with cobbles and define the city-limits nicely. There is no city wall – the idea of such an expense for such a small town is laughable with Boval Castle only a few miles away – but there are small stone watchtowers scattered throughout the town, providing light and security through the night as well as a good view of the forests around it. Fire is more of a threat here than foes.

Hymas sits just half a mile from the shores of Lake Hymas (or Hyco, depending on your accent) where a tiny fishing village of the same name provides fish and eels to supplement the beef, poultry, barley and wheat (and, of course, the famous cheese) found in the market.

The market, just off of the main square, was elaborately decorated with hanging posts and little shrines to the gods, especially to the important deity Bova, the cow goddess, as well as Trygg and Ishi, but to the others in the Narasi pantheon as well.

(It was an interesting point about Boval Vale that it had no real temples to the gods, something I found very strange in a domain this size. In most Alshari towns larger than five hundred people you can almost always find an enterprising landbrother, herbmother, or birthsister who has set up a temple or at least a shrine– but not *here*.

I tried to find out why when I first arrived, and the rumors varied from Sire Koucey's desire to keep his people's money in their pockets (or his) to the whisper that the valley was cursed and no priest would try to sanctify ground here. That didn't mean the gods weren't' worshipped or prayed to, just that they had no place to live in between prayers. The tiny shrines in the market, tended by lay societies devoted to particular deities, were the extent of organized religion in the region. Except for the religious festivals where ordinarily-virtuous women found religion and drink a heady enough combination to lay aside their virtue for an evening, I can't say I missed it much.)

About half of the population fished the waters of Lake Hymas and traded their catches with the other half of the population, which farmed the loamy soils around the lake. There were plenty of artisans for a town of its size. Hymas was practically a metropolis, compared to the other villages, having two blacksmiths, a large stable, a sprawling market area, potters, cobblers, wainwrights, carpenters, masons, barbers, several cheesemakers, flax weavers, and even a glass blower.

The market was comparatively quiet that day, but with autumn already hinting its arrival, there was a small but steady stream of merchants preparing for the caravans that would soon come to buy the cheese made over the summer.

We skimmed the edge of the quiet confusion, dodged a few porters and waited for a cart to turn around before we found the house we were looking for.

Just off the main square on the affluent northern side of the town, tucked in between the apothecary shop and the glassmaker, was the residence and laboratory of my biggest competitor, a self-important little twit with the pretentious and unlikely name Garkesku, self-styled "Master Garkesku the Great."

He was the only other Imperially-trained mage in the valley, though some of his techniques seemed closer to hedgemage styles than the Academy classics. He had been practicing here in Boval for about ten years, and had a decently prosperous urban practice and three long-suffering apprentices. His position so close to the market kept business coming to his door. His prices had kept those in serious need coming to mine, the cause of some professional friction between us.

His shop was well-kept, but his entryway was cluttered with many mysterious looking objects of no real magical value. So was mine, but his just looked *tacky*.

I wasn't fond of Garky. He was just the kind of pretentious ass my profession can do without. Condescension and pretense dripped off of his tongue like honey, and he frequently resorted to vague threats of "the Higher Powers" and "Unclean Spirits" during fee negotiations.

He did quite a bit of oracular business, which most Imperially-trained magi shun, as well as the usual sorts of love and fertility charms that are every spellmonger's bread and butter. He skirted that line between legitimate practice and hucksterism as closely as any professional mage I'd ever met. Only someplace like Hymas could he get away with it.

Garkesku built his practice on impressing the bumpkins with his greatness and magical power, and until I showed up he half pulled it off. His bearing was haughty and supercilious. He dressed in outrageous costumes, many with colored feathers or brightly-colored silks, including a truly shocking rendition (in black velvet and cloth-of-gold) of the traditional four-pointed mage's hat.

From the moment I met him, I knew I could compete successfully against him and have a lot of fun doing so. There's an old adage that a spellmonger practicing in a village will starve to death . . . until a second one moves in, whereupon they will both prosper from their clients paying to fling spells at each other.

We hadn't actually flung spells at each other yet, but there was definitely some lively competition between us already.

He was terribly polite to me when I first showed up, and even *graciously* offered to allow me to apprentice with him for a year or so before setting up, say, at the far *northern* end of the valley (where his previous biggest competitor lived before his death a few years before). I politely declined. I hadn't ever *been* apprenticed, I was academy trained, but I had studied for months with some of the better Alshari spellmongers in Tudry and the outskirts of Rolone. I didn't need his help, or his hand in my purse.

When I told him I had taken a shop in Minden's Hall, the tiny hamlet in the west, he had a very hard time controlling the level of his vitriol. I found out later that he had bought the old bookseller's shop across the street from his own – at great price – on the misplaced rumor that I was planning on setting up there. To keep *me* from having it.

But my choice was still far too close for his professional comfort. Minden's Hall might as well have been across the street, not half-way up a mountain, as far as he was concerned. I would be just as available as he to the rural clients, and Minden's Hallers wouldn't be coming his way, anymore. Folk from Winakur wouldn't mind the extra few miles of travel for quality service, and some of his regulars had already shown an interest in changing their trade.

Garky viewed the competition as a subtle personal attack. It wasn't, but he was the kind of mage who made everything personal. I tried not to antagonize him, but it was hard, sometimes.

Don't get me wrong. I have nothing against a little harmless self-promotion in the course of performing your duties as a spellmonger. When I took up residence in Minden's Hall one of the first things I did was dress up the reception area of my shop with dark fabrics painted with glowing runes, added a few animal skulls and other revolting stuff, put out a few impressive-looking books of poetry (almost no one in Minden Hall could read, anyway) and always kept some incense going on the brazier, just to add to the spooky atmosphere. It contributes positively to a spellmonger's reputation, and even in a town where there is no competition, a wizard's reputation is still worth quite a bit.

I won't go as far to say that everything I did was quackery – far from it. But the locals feel better about plunking down their hard-earned silver (or a chicken, a wheel of cheese, a sack of potatoes or whatever else they have to trade) if they get a bit of showmanship along with the spell.

After all, removing warts is a pretty simple affair. If I just walked in, did the spell, and walked out, it would do little for my reputation. So I add a few nonsense words, wave my arms about vigorously, and burn some nasty smelling incense before I complete the spell. It keeps my customers satisfied that they're getting their money's (or their chicken's) worth, and every wizard and spellmonger I've ever known does the same thing.

Garkesku, though, took it a bit far. He had apprenticed to the former court wizard of the Duke of Alshar (well, the *former* Duke of Alshar, since Duke Lenguin had assumed the Coronet a few years before Farise) who had served as a baronial court mage at the time, and to hear him talk it might as well have been Yrentia herself who schooled him.

He used the title "Master" though I knew he had no more than a journeyman's letter tucked into his papers. He had never been to any of the Academies – he had never been anywhere south of the northern Riverlands – and was slightly scornful of me the first time I met him and mentioned it.

Hymas was *his* town, he made clear, and he didn't need any fancy Academy-trained mage to mess up his business. Garkesku had a corner on the magic market in the southern part of the Vale for a decade, now, and to prove how powerful he is he stopped riding about on a horse, like a normal person. Instead he had a Remeran-style litter built, and he hired four big strapping farm boys to haul his lazy ass around town when he needed to go somewhere. He looked ridiculous, and the people said so behind his back, but I had to admit it did get folk's attention. That's just Garky's style.

Around forty-five years old, two decades my senior, he regularly wore the most garish purple silk robes I've ever seen. He treated his hair with lime (an old magi trick) and he weaved bleached horsehair into his beard to appear much older . . . and presumably wiser.

To complete the picture he wore the professional hat in the old Imperial style – centuries out of date and completely ridiculous looking, with gold tassels sprouting from every peak and two long firebird feathers poking out at odd angles. The three surrounding points weren't even sewn to the cone, they flopped around his ears like a beaten dog.

Garky hobbled around on a staff he didn't need for support to make himself appear more venerable. Before I showed up, it had been working. People paid him a fair amount of respect for the comparatively simple work he did, and didn't complain about it until I began undercutting his high prices and providing better, more practical spells. Had he chosen to work (or even travel) anywhere outside of Boval, any serious professional wizard would have laughed him out of the country.

Now that I was around he had lost all the business he used to have from Minden's Hall and quite a bit from Hymas. But he was also wary of me, once he learned I knew warmagic, too. Every now and then he tried to sully my good name without *seeming* to do so; but he wouldn't challenge me directly, as he knew I was a warmage and in any magical duel I'd win, no question about it.

Mostly, I ignored him, and occasionally sent some of my sillier or more annoying clients to him as referrals to keep him from getting *too* nasty. Every wise tradesman needs a rival he can pawn the worst of his clients off on. My dad taught me that.

I didn't really want to spare the time, but I felt obligated to warn him about the irionite in gurvani possession. As the second-best mage in the Valley (Okay, maybe *third* best – Zagor the Hedgemage up in Malin was actually pretty good at most practical kinds of magic, for a self-taught fellow, and he didn't take himself *nearly* as seriously as Garky did) I thought he deserved to know that the possibility of serious magical attack existed in our quaint neighborhood.

I had Tyndal take the horses down to the market stables to be watered and rested while I reported to him. Tyndal was eager to comply, just to see the big stables. The boy has a great understanding and appreciation of horses. In fact I'd discovered him doing simple wild magic in a stable.

I didn't bother knocking at 'Garkesku the Great's' ornate and ostentatious shop. I went right in and immediately felt the pull of a minor door-warding spell that obviously alerted Garkesku – a pointless expenditure of magic. A bell would have worked as well.

His reception area made mine look barren by comparison. He had an entire stuffed Wenshari catbear in one corner, its glass eyes glaring balefully down at his visitors, and there were three times the number of skulls, musty books, bizarre looking rocks, and dead things in jars of alcohol sitting around as I had on display. The reek of cheap incense was overpowering.

From behind the curtain, in the bowels of his shop, I heard his voice, augmented magically by a cantrip to inspire fear and excitement. It's a cheap gimmick.

"Who hath dared disturb the work of Garkesku the Great, mightiest wizard of – Oh, Minalan. It's *you*. Good day."

"And good day to you, too, 'Mighty Wizard,'" I said with just a trace of smirk. He suppressed a scowl. He looked down at my road-stained clothes and my well-worn weapons belt and suddenly became afraid. His hands disappeared in his robe.

"Uh, what can I do for you today, Master Minalan?" he asked nervously. "Perhaps there is some service I can perform for you?" I could feel a flit of magic brush up against me.

"No, you can't. And knock off using the Soothing Voice spell. It doesn't work on me, and you should know better."

"If this is about Vano's bull, let me first tell you that Vano is a well-known liar. I—"

"It's *not* about Vano's bull, but now you've intrigued me," I said, crossing my arms in front of me. "Pray tell, what would Goodman Vano be lying *about?*"

Vano ran a prosperous farmstead just outside of Boval Castle, and his kin were the envy of the Valley. I'd treated his prize bull for lazyfoot, a common disease of mountain cattle, just a few weeks before, and he had seemed quite satisfied at the time. Apparently Garky hadn't been able to master the malady, despite three visits, each more expensive than the last. Obviously, Garkesku was telling tales behind my back. Not that I was worried – I do good work, and the farmers knew that.

"Oh, nothing, nothing," he assured me. "Merely a misunderstanding with a client. Now, I'm *sure* you didn't come all this way to discuss mere cattle, Master Minalan. What may I do for you today?"

I ignored the jibe and delivered my news. "You may not have heard, yet, but the night before last Minden's Hall was attacked by goblins. And killed almost *forty people.*" That got his attention.

"Forty? Slain by goblins? That's horrible!" he said, and honestly looked horrified. I could almost hear what he was thinking, too: *Forty clients killed! That's horrible!* He caught himself, as something occurred to him. "Wait. Wasn't the village *warded?*"

"Of course," I answered, evenly.

"Ah," he said, condescendingly, "the farmers up there are a sturdy but stubborn folk, with little mind of such arcane matters. The value of quality oft escapes them in their ignorance. But no doubt they will reconsider their wards when they are done burying their dead." He tried to suppress a small smile, and almost succeeded. "Well, that *is* unfortunate. I've always been rather adept at wards, myself. *Years* of practice, you know. Practical experience you just don't get in the Academies. Perhaps I can spare some time if you'd like to study with me about some of the more *advanced* functions . . ."

"Damn it, Garky, those wards were *perfectly* sound, and would have stood up to even the likes of you," I said forcefully. It had become a sore point in our strained relationship when the village elders voted to let me provide the wards on the village for free, when winter broke, instead of paying Garkesku to do his usual half-hearted job. "My wards are *twice* what yours are, and you know it. They were military grade. And they were sliced through by the gurvani shaman."

"*My* wards would have stood up to the primitive attacks of the tribal casadalain," he sneered, openly this time, arrogantly using the proper Imperial term for the gurvani to put me in my place.

"Not a primitive casadalain armed with a bloody *witchstone*," I pointed out, flatly. "Not unless you've gotten *significantly* better at your craft in the short time I've known you."

"*What?*" he asked, alarmed.

"The shaman had help. He had *irionite*." I almost enjoyed watching the blood drain from his face at the news.

"*Witchstones? He had irionite? A goblin witchdoctor?* How do *you* know?" He was scared, but his first impulse was to challenge my veracity. Idiot.

"Because I took it off of his body . . . after I slew him," I said, trying to sound casually dangerous. I suppose I succeeded, because Garky's face turned even paler at that. If there was any doubt before about who was the superior mage, it was gone now.

Still, he tried to turn this to his advantage. That was just his nature.

"So you have this . . . *witchstone*," he said, softly, his eyes shifting rapidly with opportunistic thought. "Well, such things are exceedingly *dangerous,* as I'm sure you've heard. Not to mention prescribed. They shouldn't be tampered with lightly. A young man such as yourself may not understand the subtle dangers of such powers. Why don't you leave it here with me, where it's safe, and perhaps I can study it and find a way to neutralize its power--"

"Not in *a thousand* years," I said amicably. "I have had some personal experience with irionite, if you recall. In the hands of the Mad Mage of Farise. He was an Imperially-trained Adept-class mage, too, not a rustic village spellmonger, and even then the power drove him mad. I have no desire to turn it over to *you* and risk the safety of everyone in the Vale."

"But Master Minalan—" he began to object, his tone turning from arrogant to obsequious. He did both quite well, I had to admit.

"I shall keep it, for the moment. As a matter of fact, I'm on my way to the north end of the valley to talk to the Tree Folk about it. I'm hoping they can shed some light on this disturbing attack.

"But the important thing – the *only* important thing – is to be ready against another attack. If the gurvani have stumbled across a cache of irionite, our lives aren't worth a broken wagon wheel. There are *dozens* of gurvani tribes in the hills to the west of us. If they ever got organized, with irionite behind them, they'd be unstoppable. And we would be destroyed."

"So why have you come to *me*, if not to enlist my aid?" he asked, sniffing haughtily.

"Professional courtesy," I said, emphasizing the word 'professional'. "And because I have a feeling that Sire Koucey will retain you to build up the defenses of Hymas, so I thought you'd like a little advance warning, enough time to make some preparations."

Garkesku looked like I'd kicked him in the metaphorical groin, an expression of anguish and despair that would have been funny under other circumstances. He could see his shop in flames, his clients dead, and himself a poverty-stricken refugee in the eastlands, competing against serious magi for the first time in his life. The thought terrified him.

"I'm sure it was just a simple raid," he tried to dismiss. Even he didn't believe it.

"It was a large, well-organized group. My professional opinion tells me it could be a scouting force for a much larger attack. In that case, Sire Koucey will have to prepare a defense, and will likely be sending for you soon to assist. I would impress upon you the importance of *strong* wards in such a case, Master. Your *strongest* wards, and no cheese paring." That was a local expression – when cheese merchants made the rounds of the creameries in the Vale, it wasn't unheard of a farmer to trim the cheese lightly after it was weighed and neglect to inform the merchant.

"Wha-? Oh, of course, I--." He looked like he swallowed a spinefish. "Wait! You said you . . . *did* recover the piece?" he asked. "Intact? A witchstone?" He looked around, as if there were Censors hiding behind every door. "Can I see it?"

I almost said no, but I could understand the irresistible allure. And yes, I felt like showing off to a barely-respected professional colleague, because I am not without an ego. I nodded, reluctantly, and pulled out the pouch. Never taking my eyes off of him I displayed the rough chip of green amber. His eyes nearly blazed at the sight of it. He swallowed several times before finally pulling his gaze away.

"My goodness, this is an amazing find!" he whispered. "Absolutely amazing! A thing of such power . . . you know, I really do think it best if a mage of more experience than one so young should be the one to explore its properties—"

"*Stop it*, Garky." He *hated* it when I called him that. "As far as the Censorate is concerned, possession of irionite is *illegal*. Since there isn't a Censor in five hundred miles, I'm going to overlook that . . . but I'm not about to give it to *you*. The stone is *mine*."

He shifted from obsequious to haughty in a heartbeat. Clearly he felt that such a young mage, a foreigner and budding competing tradesman should submit to his age, wisdom and experience. He got angry, and his nostrils flared.

"By *what right*—" he sputtered, throwing up his hands in frustration as I put the stone away.

But I wasn't a peasant to be bullied by this tepid spark. "By right of *single combat*," I said in my best commanding voice, "to the *death*. I stood toe to toe with the shaman and bested him, spilled his blood and took it from his dead hand. Do not try my patience right now, Garkesku, I've seen too many corpses since last sunrise and that makes me irritable. I stopped by to tell you this out of professional courtesy, to warn you to prepare yourself. Not because I like you, not because we're friends, but because that's the kind of man I am."

He wasn't about to let it go. "I still think that my experience and unique perspective as a long-time—"

"Enough!" I finally demanded, all shreds of civility tossed aside. "The stone is *mine.* Look to your spells and defend your people or flee like a coward, it's your choice. I am going to consult the Tree Folk, and I'll tell you what I learn. But *don't* try to wheedle this jewel from me again," I said, tucking it away inside my shirt. "I don't trust you or the strength of your mind to bear its power without any kind of oversight.

"But if it makes you feel better, I don't trust my own strength of mind yet. I've studied it, but I have not dared to use it, yet."

"That's uncommonly *wise* of you," he said, sinisterly. He wanted it. He lusted for it visibly. Hell, *any* mage would. But letting him play around with it would be a waste of a witchstone. I decided to point that out.

"Besides, where would you begin your study, Master Garkesku? I had no idea you were trained a thaumaturge. . ."

"My master concentrated on far more *practical* concerns," Garkesku said, sourly.

Of that I was confident. Thaumaturgy – Magical Theory, that is – is rarely taught with any vigor out in the provinces, to apprentices who are expected to earn real coin with their art. Only Imperial magi with wealthy patrons had the time and energy necessary to study it in any detail, and even fewer magi had the brains for it. Or the need for it.

"Luckily, I did. One of the first rules of *practical* thaumaturgy, Garkesku, is *not to poke your mind into strange artifacts*. Until I know more about it, it is a very dangerous, very expensive jewel, nothing more.

"One more thing," I said, enunciating each word as I turned to go. "If, upon my return, I discover that you *have* suddenly taken a holiday with your Great Aunt Bufi in Remere, I'll *find* you, Garkesku. I'll hunt you down like a wounded rabbit. You have a *responsibility* to these poor folk that you've been cheating all these years. They are *your* people, now, like it or not."

"I assure you—" he began indignantly. I stopped him. I didn't want his assurances, and wouldn't have believed them if he'd voiced them.

"This attack may have been an isolated incident – I surely hope so. If it isn't, though, then you, me, our apprentices, Zagor, and even the Boliek sisters in Roby Hamlet will have to stand up to them, because swords and lances aren't going to do *squat* against gurvani combat magic with witchstones!"

I'm sure my eyes were blazing, because I was livid at the thought of this little worm trying to slink off into the night while his clients and neighbors were slaughtered by bloodthirsty goblins. The *least* he could do was stand and die with them. He looked at me, his head bowed slightly, and he sighed. Then he surprised me. He conceded.

"You are right, my friend. I will prepare what defenses that I can. You need not worry that I shall try to escape."

"You'd better not," I warned, leaving his shop.

*   *   *

When I returned to the square (which was much more of a proper town square than Minden Hall's quaint commercial district) I treated my apprentice to a well-earned meal at the only decent inn in Boval Vale. I'd been looking forward to it since our paltry meal on the road the night before.

The *Lakeside Inn* was a small, ramshackle building that served what little traffic passed through Hymas – mostly cheese merchants from the east, itinerate clergy, and tinkers, and such. I'd stayed there only once, when I was first came to Boval looking for a place to settle but I'd been impressed by the place. The innkeeper was a large, friendly woman named Mother Breda who treated everyone who crossed her threshold like family.

That isn't always a *good* thing.

Her four grown sons helped her run the place. Whether it was cooking, slaughtering a goat, bringing up beer from the cellar, splitting firewood, doing laundry, or changing the straw in the mattresses, the four boys (I use the term figuratively – the eldest was over thirty and the youngest was seventeen) scrambled around hectically while their mother sat on the stool by the fire that was her unofficial throne and yelled orders.

I don't mean that she casually shouted, like Mama would occasionally do. I mean this woman *screamed* her desires at the top of her lungs. From anywhere within a half-mile radius of the *Lakeside Inn* you could hear her bellow.

When I say she treated everyone like family, that meant that she felt free to shout at *you* as if you were one of her boys. If you were actually in the same room with her it was deafening. Concerned that she was going a little deaf herself, I'd casually checked her hearing and such a few months back and found her in perfect health. I guess she just liked to shout.

We were among only a few guests that day. There were a small number of peasants from Winakur in town on business, stopping in for a pint of ale before they made the long walk back home, and there was a single packtrader who lingered over a bowl of stew, but that was it. I ordered from Mama Breda – who bellowed the order back to her youngest son –and then joined Tyndal at one of the trestle tables.

Tyndal was hacking into an excellent hunk of bright yellow Boval cheese and a half of a loaf of her bread (not as good as Dad's, but whose is?) and was waiting for a bowl of the stew that was bubbling over the fire and filling the air with such gastronomical promise. He had thoughtfully ordered a tall mug of ale for me already, which I used to wash the road dust from my mouth while I was waiting for my own lunch.

"How did Master Garkesku take the news, Master?" he asked between wolfish bites.

"With his customary grace," I said, making a sour face. "He tried to convince me to give him the stone. I tried to convince him that he needs to prepare for a war."

"Do you think it will be war, then? The goblins – gurvani – have always been peaceful. Since we took the valley away from them, that is." He looked worried and scared and excited all at the same time.

"Yes, well, apparently at least a few of them want it back. Did they look particularly peaceful last night?

"Not really," my apprentice admitted between bites.

"If this band wasn't alone, then this could be just the opening move in a larger conflict," I warned him, depressed at the prospect.

"Then we'll be ready for them!"

Tyndal tried to sound savage and brave, and might have, if his voice had not chosen that moment to break an octave. I grinned and then fell to eating when the stew appeared. It was three-meat, three-bean stew cooked *for days* with wine and vegetables. Wholesome and hardy, and with the cheese it was exquisite.

"Do you really think the Tree Folk will be able to help us, Master?" Tyndal asked me again, after his mouth cleared.

"Honestly, Tyndal," I confessed between bites, "I'm mostly going to the Alka Alon to see what they know about irionite. Thanks to the Censorate, it has been so scarce in the Duchies that it's considered legendary. The piece I'm wearing around my neck is enough to buy yourself a decent sized barony, if you were to sell it to one of the rich old Imperial families. And not attract the ire of the Censorate."

His eyes lit up. Nothing inspires a poor peasant lad like the idea of wealth. "You should sell it, then!" he exclaimed, enthusiastically.

I laughed and shook my head. "No, I'm going to hang on to it. It is very dangerous, and I just don't know enough about its properties and abilities. No living man does. The last one who did was the Mad Mage of Farise, and he's dead. Before that he was mad, and likely not terribly helpful."

"But the Tree Folk know?" he asked, intrigued that the childhood legends of the little people he'd heard might not only exist, but be talented at his new profession.

"The Tree Folk use it frequently, it is said. Their spellcraft – it's far more subtle and elegant than ours. No human mage has ever successfully found proficiency at it, let alone mastered it, though many have tried. I'm hoping that perhaps – if we ask nicely enough – they will consent to teach us how to use the stone. It would be invaluable in our defense against future raids. Not to mention educational in its own right." I didn't mention *'powerful enough to rouse the military strength of three Duchies against it'*, but I didn't want to complicate the boy's thoughts with political reality.

"I wonder what got them all stirred up like that? The goblins, I mean. My Ma used to see them up in the high meadows, sometimes. Said she would trade meat and leather and eggs for iron tools and sometimes even . . . gems. They make good ironwork, she said. But they never gave us any trouble."

"I don't know," I admitted. "The gurvani I met on the road to Farise were warriors, but they kept to their own territories up in the mountains and rarely bothered the human tribes, not until the Doge's troops started trying to conquer their mountain passes. I can't imagine what would drive them to this. Something pretty powerful, I expect. Or it could be as little as a single shaman with a witchstone trying to prove his worthiness to impress a girl goblin." I fondled the stone in its pouch. "I guess he failed."

That got me thinking, a bad habit of mine when I'm eating. Tyndal knew enough to leave me alone when I lapsed into silence like that. After a while, I turned to back to him with a question. "How *did* this valley come to be settled here, anyway? What's the history?"

"Well, I don't know much – mostly what Ma and her friends told me –

but almost two hundred years ago Sire Koucey's great-great-great-grandsire was given this land for his assistance in the last of the Goblin Wars. The last battle was fought here, near Boval Castle, actually. Sire Koucey's ancestors did something brave in battle and the Duke of Alshar, himself, granted his family the lands of the Vale as a reward, and also gifted him with a harp of gold, twenty cows, among the finest of his herds, and two strong bulls, named—"

"Hold," I said, putting up my hand. "Did you say 'the last of the Goblin Wars'?"

"I believe I did, Master."

"Then I think I may have discovered the reason we were attacked. I knew the gurvani tribes fought against the Alshari when they – we, I mean – pushed beyond the frontier established by the Magocracy to settle. I *didn't* know the last battle was *here*. But it makes sense. The Alshari Wilderlands were the last to be settled, and then only sparsely. We – that is, we humans – were never supposed to go this far into the territory, according to Imperial history."

He shrugged. "Does it make a difference, Master? The Magocracy has been gone for centuries, now."

"It might. I know the Imperials in the East still hold a grudge over the old Imperial Palace, the site of *their* last battle. That's why the eastern Dukes built new ones when they took over, and gave the old Imperial palace at Reymes to the priests of Goma. Where did *your* ancestors come from, Tyndal? Before Boval?"

"Well, on my Mother's side we came with Lord Koucey's company. He gave us the Heights in return." The Heights was the name of the farm that Tyndal's drunken mother owned. She barely held it, now, and she and Tyndal rarely spoke. He often mentioned how nasty she could be, one reason he sought employment elsewhere when he was old enough to leave the farm. Of his father, he spoke even less. Apparently he and his mother had been of very brief acquaintance.

"Ever see any of the gurvani artifacts around? You don't just put those up because you like to decorate."

"Well, there are the forest stones – these carved rocks you can find in the woods – but Ma says the Tree Folk put them there, not the goblins. There are plenty of caves, though. We used to play in them, the small ones near the pastures during the summer. I even saw a few goblins once, hunting. They even waved. There might be a few things of theirs left in them. Ma would never let me go to the ones higher up."

"Very wise of her," I said. I couldn't help teasing him a little. "While the gurvani don't eat human flesh as a rule, it *has* been known to happen, and children are, I imagine, pretty tasty."

"Good to know," Tyndal replied, wide-eyed.

After that, the conversation turned to the usual daily bull session on magic, where Tyndal asked me questions and I tried to answer them without getting frustrated. I was starting to realize that teaching was a lot harder than I'd expected.

When we had sopped up the very last shred of stew and drained our mugs, I paid the shot and had the horses brought around, we got back on the road. I wanted to make as much time as possible before sundown – the gurvani are nocturnal.

We made good time, too. The roads in Boval, where well-traveled, are not bad for a rustic domain. The weather was pleasant, just a slight chill that presaged the coming winter, and the bright autumn sunshine warmed our faces as we rode.

I continued the lesson on warwands from the saddle, as well as I was able, and I was impressed at how quickly Tyndal was picking up the theory. Recent events had spurred his interest in the subject, of course, and he wanted to know everything at once.

We were about two hours north of Hymas on the North Road when we heard screaming in the distance, followed by a particular snarl that I'd heard all too recently.

I glanced at the sun sourly. *They are* supposed *to be nocturnal!* Another scream, another snarl.

Someone was in trouble, and I was the closest thing to a hero within shouting distance. Tyndal was startled, too, his eyes wide at the sound. He was immobilized by the scream.

"*Shit!* Tyndal, arm your wand and *follow me!* Don't worry about attacking, just keep them off my back!" I said as I stood in the stirrups and summoned my defenses. My rouncey steed, Traveler, lurched forward eagerly. I didn't bother looking back to see if my apprentice was following, partly because of the potential embarrassment I would have felt if he hadn't, and partly because I was trying to foresee the situation ahead of us.

Trying to sling spells from the saddle is a very refined art, a specialty of some equestrian warmagi who can get it right most of the time. I'm as good a horseman as a baker's son has any right to be, and had ridden extensively during my professional career, but I still had difficulty concentrating enough to complete the simple reconnaissance spell properly. The fuzzy result gave me only vague awareness of the situation ahead.

It was, of course, more goblins. I could foresee a knot of them clustered around one or two humans. That was adequate enough intelligence to determine my plan of action, but far from ideal. I put spur to flank and drew Slasher with one hand, a warwand with the other and bravely rode into the unknown. In moments I entered the scene of destruction, no doubt cutting a dashing and heroic figure, if anyone had been there to observe carefully.

There was a whole band of them, almost a score. Or at least there *had* been. Two lay still and bleeding, and two more clutched their heads and screamed piteously in the bright sunshine. But the others were surrounding the humans and poking at them playfully with spears and clubs and laughing at their torment.

I was coming upon their band from the rear. They had just started to turn to the sound of Traveler's hoof beats when I was upon them.

Slasher swept the heads off of two as I barreled around the bend. Traveler's hooves trampled a third. He's not a warhorse, but he's quite intelligent, and he knew what to do when I commanded him like this. The momentum of our charge was enough to bowl-over a handful of them in a tangled heap. My wand played across the pile of gurvani as I leapt – or fell, depending on how you looked at it – from the saddle. I was gratified that it chewed holes in their bodies, enough to get their attention.

The goblins had been taken by surprise, but that didn't stop those of them who hadn't fell in my attack from regrouping. Suddenly I was faced with a small and angry mob of hostile little furry buggers.

While I was not thrilled with the prospect, they had turned their attention from their victims to face me, and I hoped that helped. Before my boots had skidded to a halt Slasher was parrying their nasty little clubs and spears while I lined up more targets for my wand in my mind.

I didn't have much in the way of combat spells prepared and hung after the busy night I'd had, so I just fought like hell. A couple of times I even used my wand as a club.

The goblins pressed me aggressively, threatening me from almost every side, but their smaller stature and the potential for hitting allies in the battle made them cautious. I had no such handicap. I poked my sword wherever I felt it would do the most good, slicing arms and legs and eyes indiscriminately.

One by one they fell back, some of them permanently. I used one of the last of my offensive spells to blast a knot of three of them to shreds, and discourage a few more behind them. Traveler, too, was having a grand old time rearing and stomping – he hadn't seen action in almost a year – and I saw at least one crumble from a bolt from Tyndal's new wand.

Their number had suddenly dwindled to five increasingly panicky little warriors who were visibly considering fleeing from my attack . . . when they were hit from the rear by one of their intended victims.

A young farm woman was wielding a stout cowherd's staff with anger and precision about their furry ears. The gurvani squealed in frustration as she brained the first, no doubt disheartened by being attacked from the rear twice in one day.

A sweep of the staff and she knocked another off of his feet, where Tyndal ended his attack and his life with a clumsy dagger blow to the chest. The added distraction of the farm girl's attack made cleaning up the others a lot easier with Slasher and Traveler, and within moments all of the gurvani raiders had been dispatched or fled.

I heaved for breath while my nerves tried to recover from the excitement – it was easier to do this kind of thing when I was augmented, and I made a mental note to re-hang the spell tonight.

I was covered from head to toe in hot blood and black hair. I regarded the woman over the heap of bodies. Indeed, I recognized her.

She was young, perhaps twenty, and her hair was plaited in two long braids over each ear. Her dress was the stout brown plaid wool that was favored in Boval, and it, too, was stained with blood – but so was the end of her staff. Her labored breathing made her breasts swell appreciatively, and I was suddenly reminded of one of my natural reactions to combat. She was quite an attractive woman, I saw, handsome rather than pretty, and she held that staff like she meant it. I was intrigued.

As I said, I recognized her, but in my six months in the Vale I had met a *lot* of people. Even a lot of pretty young women. That didn't produce her name in my mind, unfortunately.

"You! Can you help me with him?" she said, glancing at her companion, who lay in the dirt next to the road, clutching his shoulder and moaning. She didn't drop the staff.

"Uh, yes, of course," I said, confused by her casual reaction to violence. Most women would be squealing and screaming at the carnage and how close they came to death. Hell, I guess I expected her to swoon and shower me with kisses, but she was acting as calmly as if she was selling cheese in the market.

I stabbed Slasher into the ground nearby while I knelt by the fallen. Tyndal came up beside me, eyes wide and darting as he looked for more foes, his short bow now strung and his warwand in hand.

"That was all of them," I said, not as sure as I sounded about the fact. "But keep an eye out for stragglers. While I tend him. This man needs help. Bring my bag from the horse. But keep your eyes sharp!"

He nodded and turned, but that wand never left his white-knuckled fist. He threw a casual wave to the woman, whom he apparently knew, and trotted off.

The injured man was a little older than the woman, maybe twenty-eight, and he had several wounds to boast about. He also had a bloodied harrowing knife in his hand. He stared at me with unreal eyes, and I could tell that there was a problem. The woman knelt beside me and cradled his head in her arms.

"He's going into shock. Tyndal, your cloak! Is he your husband?"

She shook her head. "My brother-in-law, Sagal. We were headed to Hymas for tomorrow's market and they came out of nowhere. How bad is he?"

"I'm not a healer," I warned.

"I *know* who you are," she said, her pretty eyes flashing. "And it's not a healer. But I bet you can do *something*. Or are all you good for is tracking down wandering cows?"

She was right. I'm not a healer, but I had learned plenty of combat aid in the Army, and every spellmonger does a little healing on animals or people, depending on his situation.

"You know, I'm quite good with wandering cows," I said, blushing indignantly. I summoned magesight and pushed my awareness into the muscles and bones of his shoulder.

It was a holy mess. The scapula was cracked and the humerus was crushed, but not beyond repair, and certainly not life-threatening. A stab wound in his gut was more worrying – it wasn't bleeding badly, but it was dangerously close to the intestines. A punctured gut could lead to peritonitis, which would kill him in a few painful days if he wasn't tended to. But that would be in a few days. He needed to be stabilized long before that.

Tyndal brought his cloak and covered the man as I opened the leather satchel that I had carried to Farise and back. My supply of bandages was low, but there was enough there to cover the gut wound. I opened a vial of Memphor's Liquor and poured it onto the bandage before I pushed it into the wound.

The man moaned and his eyelids began to flutter. I took half a dried charro root and crushed it between my palms before sticking it in his mouth and holding my water skin to his lips. It would need a little time to work, but it would likely keep him out of shock if we could get him off the road.

"What's his name again?" I asked the woman while I began to fashion a litter out of Tyndal's cloak. I used my staff for one side, and hers for the other.

"Sagal. He's married to my sister Ela. Their farm is about half a mile back up the road. She's going to go *insane* when she sees him, just to warn you. What was your name again? I just remember that you're the new spellmonger." She didn't seem impressed. So I tried to impress her.

"Master Minalan of Castal, among other places, at your service," I grunted. "Warranted by the Duke to practice general spellcraft and thaumaturgy."

"That's right, I remember you. You set the firewards at Goodman Iarl's place last month. I saw you there that day. My holding is just behind his, up the ridge and north."

"So, now you know me, what about yourself? Do you have a name?" Tyndal and I took the ailing farmer and placed him as gently as we could in the stretcher. He moaned in pain at the movement, but he seemed to be a little more comfortable.

"Of course. Alya, daughter of Roral, of Hawk's Reach. That's our farm."

"I've heard of it. Your dad, too. Well, Alya of Hawk's Reach, I hope you're fond of your brother-in-law. Goddess willing, he will survive. If you are *not* fond of him, there is still time to poison him before he gets home. This is a once-in-a-lifetime opportunity."

She grinned and showed a fetching set of dimples that paled in comparison to her smile. "No, I really am fond of him. He was friends with my late husband."

"A lass as young as you, a widow?" I asked, surprised. I shouldn't have been. A lot of things can kill you in the Wilderlands.

"Yes," she said, her smile fading. "He died in a riding accident a year and a half ago. I gave our farm back to his parents and moved home. I help my father run the creamery, now."

"I'm sorry," I said, and I meant it. Damn it, I wanted that smile back.

"Thank you. Now, can you answer me this: *where the bloody hell did all of these damned goblins come from?*" Her voice broke at the memory of the fight she was just in. "We were headed out to Hymas to see about some shears and some tonic -- Sagal's got a sick calf – when they sprang out from the trees.

"At first I thought they were begging – that happens sometimes," she explained, "and I've traded with the mountain folk food for firewood often enough. But then out came the clubs and suddenly we were fighting for our *lives*. I'm so glad you showed up when you did," she said, gratefully.

Finally. When one does go out of one's way to rescue a damsel in distress, an outpouring of heartfelt thanks and gratitude is to be expected on the part of said damsel. Perhaps some light kissing and hugging. Occasionally the offer of a reward, either monetary or sexual, is added (and usually refused by the noble), but the regulations governing such things are pretty straightforward on the gushes of gratitude, from what I recall of the legends and sagas.

"It was no trouble. My apprentice and I were just passing—"

"Yeah, it would have taken me most of an hour to finish them all off, myself," she said, without a trace of doubt. "Sagal might not have made it by then."

I stared at her just a moment too long, and inspired a blush that showed off every freckle on her face.

"Well, since they were *obviously* interrupting your busy schedule, I'm just happy I could help out."

"They *are* just gurvani," she said, dismissively. "I don't know about this lot, but most of them would scatter at a loud noise."

My face turned serious. "It's *not* just this band. A hundred or more of them attacked Minden's Hall two nights ago. Almost forty people died, buildings burned, it took Sire Koucey and his cavalry to drive them away.

"That's . . . that's terrible! We hadn't heard, yet," she confessed. She glanced back at the bodies of the fallen goblins, some still twitching, while I finished my improvised stretcher. "Not many beggars in that lot, either. Lots of clubs, a few spears, lots of snarling fangs and bloody claws. They did mean to harm us. I just never expected they would do that."

"My lady, I've seen the gurvani fight, deep in the jungles of Farise, and I assure you that they are a *most* capable foe, when properly roused. From what Sire Koucey tells me," I said, on the theory that dropping the name of the local lord might possibly impress her, "they haven't been a problem here since the Goblin Wars."

"That's right," she agreed, thoughtfully. "They've always been very respectful to us. Can we move him back to his hold? It's not far."

"This litter is ready to go. Tyndal, help me get Goodman Sagal home to his wife. Goody Alya, I have no idea what has troubled them so. But now they are troubling *me*, and other good folk, and that is something for which I cannot stand." I tried to sound brave and resolute, and only realized after I said it that it sounded pompous and self-important.

Luckily, I still had some points left from saving her life, and she overlooked it.

Tyndal pulled the litter behind his horse while I let Alya lead Traveler and I cleaned my sword. We walked slowly and warily, but that also allowed me a chance to speak with her at length about all sorts of completely unimportant but vital things. The walk lasted twenty minutes, and by the time we approached the front gateway to her sister's house I was genuinely smitten with the pretty young widow.

Quite odd for a first date, I know. But in fairness, I've been on worse.

*   *   *

Things don't always turn out the way we plan them, as anyone familiar with the gods should know. Trygg knows my life didn't.

"Dad, what can I *do*?" I whined when I was thirteen, seeing my world crumbling around me. I didn't *want* to be a mage – I wanted to be a baker. Like him.

"Do?" he asked, eyebrows raised. "Well, the first thing we'll do is go up to the castle to be seen by the mage," he said, scratching his beard. "It's possible that you have an erratic or weak Talent," he admitted. "This morning's fire could be a unique occurrence, in which case nothing much will change. But the *responsible* thing to do is to get Master Tilo to test you. Or, perhaps you are favored of Briga, the Fire Goddess and patroness of bakers."

While he was a little unsure about the differences between a spell and a miracle, a devotion to the Flame That Burneth Bright *might* lead me to take religious orders in Her name, which would have pleased him immensely, I knew.

"On the other hand, you could possess enough Talent to warrant further training as an apprentice mage. There's plenty of good work for a spellmonger or hedgemage, if they know their craft, and the post of court wizard is a notoriously cushy and lucrative one. Though it's not as stable or as honorable tradition as baking," he said.

When I knew he wasn't mad at me, I felt immensely better, and only partially because of the liquor that warmed me from the inside out. "I suppose we should go ahead and start. Wait here, I'll get Goron to run the shop this morning."

Goron was my oldest sister's husband, and second in line for inheriting the shop and the charter, after me. He'd married my eldest sister the year before, after apprenticing with Dad for two years. I liked Goron. More than I liked my sister. Goron, I knew, would be pleased at the idea of me leaving the baker's trade – he didn't relish the idea of eventually working for a lad half his age.

I nodded and grabbed the jar for another sip while he was gone.

It took us most of the morning to walk up to the castle. It was a strange and happy time for me, walking along the slightly muddy road next to the river at sunrise, my Dad joking and laughing with me, nervous but at-ease at the same time. The liquor had warmed me, and Dad had had the foresight to grab a few sweet rolls for breakfast on his way out. He made me feel a lot better about the whole thing just by being there. By the time we reached the gates of the castle, I knew that I was still his son, and he would always love me, even if I was suddenly "special."

It took us another half-hour to get in to see the vice-castellan, a snooty Remeran who obviously thought that we needed getting rid of. Dad wasn't about to be brushed off like some dirt-farmer, though; he was an artisan of note, he stood his ground, and I was surprised at just how quickly we found ourselves in front of the Baron and Baroness, who were just starting breakfast when we were ushered in by the vice-castellan.

At the time I thought it was because Dad was such an important person in the village – the Baron treated him with respect – though in retrospect the hot, freshly-baked sugar rolls which Dad presented to Baron Lithar, may have had some influence. You could smell those things across the room.

His Excellency listened with great interest to my father's story. Then he asked us to sit with him and the Baroness while we waited for Master Tilo to arrive from his tower, at the other end of the great castle. I was in awe and didn't make a sound. *We were breaking our fast with nobility.*

Master Tilo showed up in good time, just as the Baron was finishing telling us of his son's recent tournament victory. The old mage was resplendent in his decorated robe and richly-embroidered woolen mantle. He arrived in the Hall blowing hot breath thorough his hands (the castle seemed far colder than home, I noticed, and remember feeling sorry for the Baron that he had to live in such a draughty place) and he was just as delighted by the sugar rolls as the Baron and Baroness. He, too, heard my story, and after grabbing the last sugar roll off the table he agreed to test me.

I remember those tests pretty well. He led me back to his tower, through the maze of the castle, and into his mysterious workshop. Master Tilo was thorough at his craft, and wasn't satisfied with the first – or even the twenty-first – arcane test.

He placed stones on the back of my hand and had me tell him about my earliest memories. He had me hold a stick in both hands and spin around clockwise, then counterclockwise. He put a bag over my head and asked me about my favorite colors. He wrapped me in red thread and had me sing.

I felt like an idiot.

When my stomach reminded me that it was closer to noon than dawn, Tilo finally sat down, lit his pipe, and bid me absentmindedly to sit.

"Well, my boy, it looks like you do have a lick of Talent after all," he admitted, kindly

I swallowed hard. "I *do*, Master?"

He nodded, his gray head wreathed in smoke. "Yes. More than we can safely ignore. In fact, in terms of raw Talent, I believe you have more than both my apprentices put together."

My chest swelled with pride even as my heart sank. "So I'm to be a mage, then?"

"Just like that?" he laughed. "*That* remains to be seen. Any idiot can be born with the Talent, Minalan. Talent is just the beginning of magic. If you have not the intelligence, the discipline, the *focus* to master the Talent, the Talent will master *you.* And wisdom. *Always* wisdom. The most powerful mage in the world falters if his wisdom fails him. I *think* you might have the wits to learn, but I detect a tinge of foolishness in you that could prove deadly in a mage," he added warningly.

"I am but thirteen, Master," I said somberly, fibbing my age up a bit. I would be thirteen, come autumn, at least. "I am prone to foolishness."

He laughed, sending thick clouds of smoke billowing out of his nose. "So you are. Can you read?"

"Only a bit, Master. Not well. But I know my letters," I said, proudly.

"Hmmph. We will need to fix that, and soon. Minalan, we have established you have Talent; let us see what we can make of it."

For the next three days I went to the castle at dawn and did not return home until long after dark. My days were spent in lessons on the very basics of recognizing my Talent and learning how to feel its utility and power. And learning how to really read.

Sometimes it was just Master Tilo and I, and sometimes his apprentices helped. The court mage asked me thousands of seemingly simple questions and wrote the answers on a long piece of parchment. I was worried at first that I might get them wrong, but he threw them at me so fast that I didn't have time to worry about one before the next one arrived.

We would take a break every hour or so, then back to the testing and the lessons. I had no idea what the tests were about, but later I realized that my Talent was impressive enough so that Master Tilo was considering sending me elsewhere, where it could be more properly developed.

In the meantime, everyone at home was in a tizzy about my display of Talent. Mama was not happy, of course; I was her *baby*. But my eldest sister was about to make her a grandmother, and that deadened the pain a bit.

My sisters were, in general, loathe to see me develop the Talent, Urah especially. Only two years older than me, most of my chores would fall to her until she found a man stupid enough to marry her. My sisters all began to dote on me even more than usual, as if I were sick and would never get well. All but Urah.

When Dad told the story about how I started a fire because I was so upset with her, she began keeping her distance from me. Mama tried to act like nothing was wrong, and Dad put on his most patient expression when I was around after that. He spent a lot of time in his workroom.

On the fourth day Master Tilo visited the bakery before I could come to the castle. He and my parents sat me down at the kitchen table, where Mama had set a healthy-sized snack and our best glassware, and he unrolled that long piece of parchment. The results were finished, he announced with a stone face. I was not only extremely Talented, but Master Tilo had determined that I had more brains than the average peasant. I could very easily become a spellmonger. Perhaps even more. I was proud, and felt quite the man.

"Minalan, I was lucky enough to be trained at the Inarion Imperial Academy of Magic," Master Tilo finally said. "I didn't serve a normal apprenticeship, like most magi; I was taught in the classical manner, just like the magi of the Magocracy. While I *could* take you to apprentice here in Talry, I already have two apprentices – taking another would be unfair to all of you." My heart fell.

"Now I *could* likely arrange for an apprenticeship with one of my colleagues in Cury or even in Dretsel, but I really believe that you would benefit the most from a more classical education. You have *that* much potential."

"Uh, yes Master," I said, my mind spinning out of control.

"I had a copy of your test results made and sent to Inarion yesterday, with a letter introducing you to the Rector. It will be weeks before we hear back, but you *may* actually have a chance to attend. That is a chance few common-born magi ever have, I hope you understand. A certificate from Inarion will guarantee you a position in a court somewhere."

"L-leave Talry? Leave Mama and Dad?" I squeaked. Suddenly, I didn't feel so manly anymore.

Master Tilo nodded sagely. "It will be a great adventure, lad, long and hard study, and twice as hard as you are not of noble birth. And it will be lonely. But the rewards are worth it, my boy. Pursuing the Art Arcane and learning from such masters is well worth the price."

"But the choice is up to *you*," Mama blurted out.

"There's no guarantee you will even be accepted, son," Dad said. I knew in his heart he didn't want me to be. They were both trying to be brave and think about my future, not their dashed dreams of a baking dynasty.

"Can I think about it?" I said in a small voice.

"Certainly!" Master Tilo said with a kindly laugh. "We have time. But think well and hard on it, and use what little wisdom you have to aid you."

A week before, I would have run away and hidden in the ash heap until he was gone. It had been a busy week, though, and I was no longer the boy I was when I stacked that firewood on that fateful morning. I felt the enormous pressure of abandoning the only life I knew, all of my Dad's plans for leaving me his bakery, for the chance at something almost completely unknown to me. I solemnly agreed to think about it and then went outside to play.

In the days that followed I noticed that the change in attitude went beyond my family, as my mates were starting to treat me differently. Muli, one of my best friends, would hardly even talk to me, and Tiko was scared I would turn him into something unnatural if I got angry.

While I kind of resented their distance, I also reveled in the importance my nascent Talent had granted me. I actually used it to win them back as friends again, by showing them the two or three of the simple cantrips Master Tilo had shown me already. The ability to light a candle with my finger, for instance, made me powerful among the boys of Talry. Soon they were all vying for a position as my best friend, and if I took unreasonable advantage of the situation I can only plead immaturity as my excuse.

One area that did not suffer because of my Talent was my relation with the girls of the village. I had started noticing them a year back, but had not impressed them overmuch with my strength, speed, or prowess at games and races, and therefore hadn't garnered much attention.

Now they showed significant interest. A spellmonger's wife was at least as high an aspiration as a baker's wife, and the thought of being the wife of a court mage with all of its supposed luxury was hard to resist to the village girls thinking about their futures. A few became ardent admirers, though they shyly kept their distance from me.

But one girl, Hedi the Miller's daughter, was so intrigued by my magical reputation that she was willing to overcome her typical village girl shyness. She was two years my senior, and while not the prettiest girl between river and hill, she was handsomely built and had pretty eyes and soft brown hair that smelled *really* good.

She was a curvaceous fourteen-year-old vixen I'd always had a crush on, and she finally took enough interest in me to relieve me of my virginity behind her father's warehouse. I was, if you'll excuse the expression, *enchanted* by girls after that.

By the end of the summer I had convinced four other village girls and two farm girls to "steal" my innocence from me in various ways. And I began to see that there were definitely some benefits to the trade of magic.

Master Tilo continued our daily lessons, which included teaching me to read and figure, as well as schooling me in some of the more basic magical exercises every mage needs to know. But for one solid summer, I was the boy every other boy wanted to be friends with, and the boy every girl wanted to pick flowers for.

As the leaves began to turn color at the end of that glorious summer, a message arrived from downriver. I had, indeed, been accepted to the Academy. I was to report six weeks hence to the Master of Novices in Inarion Academy for introductory training.

I was shocked. I never expected to get in; after all, I was a peasant, or at least a commoner, and the Inarion Academy was built for the magically inclined nobility — Old Imperial nobility at that. Or at least wealthy Coastlords, Sealords, or Riverlords. Ignorant Narasi commoners became hedgemagi or village spellmongers, they just didn't go to one of the finest schools in the Five Duchies to learn the arcane arts.

At the time, I figured that I was just so especially Talented that they couldn't ignore me. What actually happened was more political than magical in nature.

Baron Lithar was a vassal of Count Andro, who in turn swore fealty directly to His Grace, the Duke of Castal. While the coastal Inarion Academy was *technically* within the Duchy of Castal, by tradition and inheritance the local lord of that land had always sworn allegiance to the Duke of Remere.

But since the district would starve without the upriver traffic from the rest of Castal, a sophisticated compromise was reached between the two ducal houses in which the Lord of Inarion (who actually lived seven miles upriver of the town) swore fealty and military allegiance to Remere, with the understanding that Inarion domain would be neutral in any military conflict between the two, and paid a tribute to the Duke of Castal in the name of good relations and low tariffs. Many other feudal obligations and privileges were also split up.

Included in the negotiations was the right of the Duke of Castal to name eighteen qualified appointees to the ancient Inarion Academy of Magic every two years.

That year, sixteen of those appointments had already been made. The Duke wisely deferred the actual selection to his Court Mage, of course, who had found sixteen noble's sons from across Alshar who had at least a lick of Talent in them to fill the quota. My scores were better than most of them, so including me in the applications was not a problem. On *parchment*.

It was politically astute, as well: by admitting me under his auspices Count Andro was able to gain favor from Baron Lithar, an established Riverlord from a distinguished house who had a vote on the County Council (which could elect the count's successor and affect policy on the council) and was respected and influential among the petty nobility of the region.

When Master Tilo explained all of this to me, I was anxious that I somehow owed Count Andro for the boon. But the court mage waved away my objections and gave me my first real lesson in feudal politics. It was all part of the complex exchange of favors, goods, services, rents, rights, and fealties that made up the feudal economy of the Five Duchies, he explained. My appointment was just another line in the ledger, like an estate's revenue or the number of fish taken from a river.

To send a commoner from his baronial village to the great Inarion Academy of Magic brought personal and institutional honor to Baron Lithar, and if he someday wanted a favor in return he might expect me to be well-disposed to him – but there was no outright debt. It was a matter of honor. Baron Lithar was so proud of me, in fact, that he contributed a sizeable purse toward my upkeep while at school, in addition to a little contribution from Master Tilo, and Dad's own generous (though decidedly smaller) gift. I won't say it was a fortune, but it would have set me up nicely on a small farmstead had I spent it that way.

My last few weeks in Talry were bittersweet. Never had the colors seemed so vivid, the smells so potent, the village girls so accommodating. Even my mates were sad to see me go. My family was as restrained as a house full of doting sisters could be. Mama was a sobbing wreck; Dad was grimly encouraging, dispensing a lifetime of fatherly advice with every breath. Me, I was terrified.

My parents threw me a huge party on the eve of my departure, inviting all of my friends and a good number of general well-wishers to the shop to celebrate (it was at this event that girls three and four made the acquaintance of my "magic wand," as I had taken to calling it).

The morning of my departure I was almost glad to be going. I was *exhausted.*

*   *   *

I'm not saying I had been completely celibate during my six months or so in Boval – there were enough maidens and widows and lusty wives eager to reduce their fees by being accommodating – but I had wisely decided against embarking on too many entangling affairs until I had a good handle on the local political situation. No need for a pitchfork wedding or starting a blood feud, if I could help it. That was poor professional practice. I had managed two or three visits a month to a few friendly ladies around the Vale for quite satisfactory (and un-entangling) encounters.

But Alya made me want to stand taller in a way that those casual bauds did not. I wanted to impress her with my strength, enchant her with my wit, and do pretty much anything I could to continue speaking to her. It was an unusual feeling for me, who had been a renowned letch in my previous incarnation as a warmage. And as a student.

But there was something genuinely noble in her bearing, far beyond that of a simple farmer's daughter, which had captivated me. Yet her warmth and wit kept me at odds and excited. It was very disconcerting.

Her sister Ela, a taller, thinner version of Alya, threw a fit when she saw her poor battered husband; luckily the charro root had taken effect by then and he was able to reassure her – had he been unconscious there was no telling what she would have done. Ela had little of her younger sister's composure – quite the opposite. Alya was calm in the face of peril, while Ela seemed to look for every excuse to get excited.

I watched in amazement as the older woman managed to call on nearly every deity I'd ever heard of, and some variations that were new to me, while she simultaneously berated and babied her husband as she led him to their bed. When I was sure he was comfortable I let Alya lead us out of the house and in to the kitchen courtyard and away from her emotional sister.

"Give them a moment," she insisted. "He will need more medical attention soon, if I'm not wrong. I'll run into Hymas and summon the barber. But if you don't let Ela fuss for a while, you won't get the chance to examine him." She sounded frustrated and tired, and I realized what course the barber in Hymas might take with the wounds. Sagal might be looking at an amputation. It was hard running a farm with one arm.

"He's stable for the moment. But don't get the barber, I should be able to help, if you don't mind me using magic."

Alya looked relieved. Then concerned. "Would that *work?*"

"I've set broken arms before," I offered, not mentioning that it hadn't gone well, "and I've tended men with combat wounds. It might take a while, but he's not bleeding profusely any more. But I could use a good wash up before I tend him. Tyn, why don't you grab the kit from the horses, and bring the blue bag, too."

"Use the trough," she said, gesturing towards a wide wooden trough near the well. The water seemed clean enough, and sufficient to remove at least the top layer of grime. I shrugged and stripped off my shirt.

"That was very brave, what you did on the road," she said conversationally as she dug around in a bucket looking for soap. "I expect that from the castle men – strong and stupid is how Koucey likes them. But you're a spellmonger. With a sword, granted, but still just a spellmonger. Why did you do it?"

I told her just enough of my recent military past to earn a few admiring glances – though I think she was more impressed by my giving up the supposedly lucrative and exciting life of an itinerate warmage to become a spellmonger. Or it could have been my shirtless chest. I was kind of hoping it was the former, but I wouldn't turn away interest in the latter.

I could tell she was a no-bullshit kind of girl, so I kept the embellishments of my exploits to a minimum – but I will admit to gratuitously flexing my muscles a little, seeing as how my shirt was off and all. I wasn't as well-built as I'd been in my army days, but I was proud of what I had and didn't mind sharing. As I finished washing up she provided me a rough homespun towel and started to help me struggle back into my clothes . . . when she noticed their condition. She clucked over them, stained with sweat, road dust, black hair and blood.

"Don't you know any *cleaning* spells?" she asked, sarcastically.

"Plenty. They all take two or three days to do." *Except with irionite*, I reminded myself. *Then it's supposed to only take a blink and a wave.* "It's usually easier to wash them by hand. I pay a woman in Minden's Hall once a month to do them."

"I was afraid you would say that," she sighed. "But these are . . . unacceptable. I'll get one of Sagal's shirts for you while I get Ela to wash this one. You won't want her in the room with you while you're healing – or do you?"

"Briga's bright brow, *no!*" I exclaimed, imagining trying to concentrate on spellwork while the older sister clucked in the background. "Give her a task, *any* task, by all means. Have her boil some water, that should keep her busy," I suggested. "I'm going to need a lot of focus to put that shoulder right. I couldn't so much as light a candle with her fussing about!"

"As I figured," she agreed with a smile. "I'll set her to it."

Soon I was kneeling next to Sagal's bed (wearing Sagal's oversized shirt) examining his wounds more circumspectly. I had dosed him with a mild anesthetic to keep him calm during the process. I was sure to inflict a lot of pain while I worked, and I didn't want this big bear of a farmer to come off that table swinging in a panic while I was in a trance.

Tyndal sat on a stool just behind me and to my right. He held a wide, flat, black bowl full of water, with a few drops of Sagal's blood (of which there was an ample supply) splashed into it. It was part of a scrying spell I could use to see the details of his injuries. The spell is a variation on magesight, with the bloody water acting as both a scrying medium to help focus the accuracy of the reading and a connection device to the patient. Once Ela was out of the room and I attained the right state of mind, I was able to use it to see "inside" of Sagal.

And he was a *mess*.

The gut wound was the most serious, so I attended to it first. The small intestine *had* been nicked, and the kidney was bruised by the force of the goblin's blow. Extending my awareness deep into his body, down to the lowest level of those blocks from which all life is built, I was able to understand the extent of the wound and began the subtle spells to repair it.

Such work is time consuming and painstaking, requiring a tremendous amount of focus. As I was racing against sepsis, I did it the easiest, fastest, and sloppiest way possible.

Imagine grabbing two bricks in either hand. Then force them together and apply mortar. With your tongue. While you are in a driving rain.

Yes, it is *that* difficult, and it was not my best skill by far. But the wound was not extensive, just deep, the worst of it also the least of it. Little could be done with the bruised kidney, it would have to heal on its own. But the nick in the bowel that could end his life with infection was mended slowly, but before it could leak much of its contents into his abdominal cavity. As soon as I was sure that there were no leaks in my repair, I withdrew.

At least an hour had passed. I was ravenous and my borrowed shirt was soaked through with sweat. The exertions of the last few days were beginning to remind me of the worst parts of my army days, when we would fight and march for days on end without a real rest. All I wanted to do was collapse next to my patient, but there was far more work to be done.

Tyndal gave me a big draught of cold water and a few sips of wine before I started on the arm and shoulder. I doubled the dosage of painkilling herbs for this. Fixing a gut wound is hardly even painful, compared to resetting bone. I was a little better at this part though. Bones are easier for me. Why, I don't know.

But this wasn't a simple fracture, either. Each individual sliver of bone had to be coaxed back into place. It takes a great deal of patience, and causes a lot of pain. The spell that adheres wounded bone back into place is much harder than the relatively simple "grow!" spell I used on his gut. Each tiny shard had to be aligned and then mortared with a rune, and each took a profound effort and no little expenditure of personal power. I was half way through with the arm when I realized that I was about to collapse.

I had expended far, *far* more energy in the last few days than my body could afford, and healing work requires intense focus and concentration compared to warmagic or spellmongering. It wouldn't have been so hard had I been back at the Academy, or even in the army – but I'd had the vigor of youth to assist, then. The power of Imperial-style magic is the ability for magi to combine their efforts to avoid the perils of just this sort of expenditure. If I'd been working with someone on this, they could keep me going by feeding me power.

But I was effectively on my own, here, no help in sight. Tyndal was years away from the proficiency he would need to actively assist in an arcane power transfer. There was still far too much to heal in that shoulder before the threat of amputation was over. I was about to give up, fall over, and consign myself to oblivion and an amputation when I noticed a pool of power just waiting, asking, *begging* to be used.

The witchstone.

I didn't *want* to do it. I knew the hazards of messing around with strange magics. I didn't have the *slightest* clue about its proper use, or of the dangers involved. Just possessing it made me a criminal under the Bans of Magic, and using it could, theoretically, compel the Censorate to seek me out and put me to death. That was beside the fact that it was an unknown device of immense power from a non-human race which I had no real idea how to use. My reckless behavior to the contrary I am a coward at heart when it comes to thaumaturgy. But I could argue that my judgment was impaired by exhaustion, distraction, and anxiety.

After debating long and hard with myself, I didn't see how I had much choice.

I didn't even take it out of the pouch – I was afraid to touch it with my bare hands. But it *throbbed* with arcane potential, there in the pouch, calling for me to use it, like a crystal glass of purest water in front of a man three days parched. It was just too easy for me to extend my awareness and pull forth the *tiniest* thread of power . . . so I did.

Suddenly I was energized, awake, aware, and *bursting* with vitality.

This, I realized, was what all the fuss was about. The thread turned into a stream, and then I welcomed a torrent of the energy into my system, raw, untamed and unturned. My mind directed it without my consciousness, sending it where it needed to go. Every fiber in my body and soul was washed in the refreshing potency of that torrent.

I took just a moment to revel in the power, and then finished setting the crushed bone in seconds, drawing the fragments together like a lodestone draws metal filings. The spell that had seemed nearly impossible to continue a moment before was suddenly *trivial*.

While I was at it I healed the spider web of fractures in the scapula, too. It fused together under my command without the benefit of an organized spell. Just to be sure – and as an excuse to use the power – I bound the whole thing up with a particularly difficult binding spell, the kind that you usually use to fuse giant blocks of stone together. It's a permanent enchantment, the kind nobles pay large sums for, and it usually takes days or weeks of preparation and execution. Every other bone in Sagal's body could be smashed to a pulp and his left arm and shoulder would remain pristine, I was confident.

I couldn't stop there. If I was to be hunted down and hung by the lads from the Censorate, I wanted to make certain it was worth it. I didn't even need to turn to the bowl for scrying, I could use simple magesight and *see* the damage. I went back and did a more elegant job on the intestine; secured the seal I'd placed on his veins, and then probed his bloodstream for signs of infection as an afterthought. I was almost disappointed when I didn't find any. I was like a kid with a new toy, and I wanted to *use* it.

Finally, I forced myself to let the power go. That was hard. When it withdrew back into the irionite I *remained* energized, like I had slept for a week.

I understood how the Mad Mage must have felt while he was raining magical death down on my squad. It was like the best parts of being drunk and doing magic and having sex and every other wonderful thing in your life, all at the same time. That level of potency was *addictive*, I realized, and I could see the danger in using it. More disturbing was the echo of the spell when I finished. Among the feelings produced by the aftereffects was a tinge of malevolence, perhaps a vestigial vibration left over from its previous owner. I brushed it off. Compared to the great advantage of an endless font of power, a little dark murmuring in my soul was nothing.

I made sure that Sagal was resting comfortably, then went outside with Tyndal and splashed more water on my face to rinse the sheen of sweat away.

I felt *strange*.

My senses were hyper-acute; I could feel the breeze against my face like a whirlwind, and the sounds of the farmstead were amplified to the point where I could hear each individual chicken scratch the earth. Every smell was vital in my nose, from the dung on the great pile to the herbal smell of late summer wildflowers drying in the rafters of the croft. I was breathing hard just to enjoy the feel of air in my lungs. The feeling started to pass almost at once, but already I wanted to delve into the stone's power again.

Coming out of the state was like putting a sack over your head and trying to go about your daily life. That was even harder under my circumstances. I was distracted by the thought – and the intoxicating smell – of Alya as she helped us get cleaned up. She had taken the opportunity to wash up after the unexpected battle herself, and the herbal scent of her hair was nearly enough to drive thoughts of limitless magical power clean out of my head.

"Is there much more?" she asked, worriedly.

"I'm done," I said, marveling at the echo of my voice inside my own voice had. "Sagal will be fine. There should be a few days of weakness while the spells are working, but the bones are healed and the rent in his gut is sealed. A few days of rest and then he can go back to tossing cows around the farm as usual."

She sighed gratefully. "Thank you! What do we owe you, Master Minalan? We aren't wealthy, but we aren't destitute, either." I could tell she was a little anxious about the fee, and I couldn't blame her. That kind of spellmongering was expensive – especially if you were used to Garkesku the Great's usual fee schedule. And it usually isn't much more effective than whatever crappy spells he would have charged a fortune for. With the irionite, I had done month's worth of labor in a few hours.

Even being generous, in an economy that was based on cows I had just rightfully earned a healthy heifer or two, not just a chicken or a jug of cider. That would be hard to keep in my purse, of course. One of the inconveniences of country practice.

"Forget it," I dismissed. Yes, I wanted to impress her with my generosity, but as I had just performed some technically illegal magic, and I had no way to measure how much it was worth on the open market, I felt justified in doing the work for free. "I was just helping out. To be honest, I'm glad I could save him the use of that arm. He's a strong man who doesn't deserve to be maimed for his bravery. If you had summoned the barber . . . well, he'd be Sagal the One-Armed."

"I *insist,* Master Spellmonger," she said proudly – and a little indignantly. "We are *not* charity cases!"

"It wasn't charity," I said, stretching my aching shoulders. The stone had replenished my energy, but my muscles were still not happy. "I usually like to do a few free spells for a potentially lucrative new client. Usually I just make eggs appear out of my ears," I joked.

She didn't laugh. "But this time you saved a life."

"I saved *two,*" I reminded her. "Heroic entrance, remember?"

"I could have handled those goblins just fine on my own, thank you very much!" she said, her eyes flashing. "Thank Trygg you went into magic and not professional jesting. I repeat myself: I insist. *Name your fee."* She didn't seem to be compromising her Stern Farmwife demeanor.

I thought very carefully for a moment, and considered naming such a brazen and lewd act that she would either slap me and stomp off . . . or feel obligated to pay in such a bawdy fashion that we would both be embarrassed afterwards. It would have served her right for not acting the role of a properly rescued maiden.

But in truth I was afraid of the consequences, I discovered – regardless of the outcome. This was no mere lonely farm widow, this was a young, strong, vital woman who was becoming increasingly attractive to me. I decided instead to name a less expensive but just as unmistakable request for payment.

"Fine, then Goody Alya. For my fee I wish to walk with you, alone, into some secluded meadow, with a bottle of wine and a picnic lunch, and spend an afternoon speaking of matters of . . . philosophy."

It was more polite than crude, but my meaning was inescapable. She was well within her rights to refuse for the sake of propriety. Me, I was just trying to get her to forget the idea. She bit her lip, searching my face to gauge how serious I was being . . . and then decided to take the proposal at face value.

But then the wench had the temerity to try to bargain!

"Then how about a walk to a meadow *now,* with no lunch, no wine, and no philosophy? I have something I want to show you," she said, with womanly dignity.

I nodded, remembering that the miller's daughter who stole my virtue had used a similar line of reasoning.

I'd had a rough couple of days. Alya was pretty. She smelled *really* good. And my use of power had created other urges than hunger in me.

"Done. But I reserve the right to come back for wine and lunch at some future date. The philosophy I'll cede. Not my best subject, anyway."

"Done. Now come with me, quickly."

She led me behind the collection of wooden outbuildings every prosperous Bovali cow farm has, through a stone fence separating pastures, and into the stand of woods that bordered a small stream. A path took us up a rise and to a wooden gate, the entrance to another pasture. She hopped the gate rather than untying the thong, which was expedient as well as giving me a healthy glimpse of well-formed leg far up her skirts. I didn't mind. I followed. She could have walked across broken glass and I would have followed that shapely leg.

"This is our smallest pasture," she explained, business-like as we walked. "We use it for calving or sick beasts. In the far corner there is this rock," she explained as she took me by the hand.

"A rock? You want to show me . . . a rock?" I asked, confused.

"A *Goblin Rock*, we call them. You can find them all over the valley. It is said that they were built as shrines by the goblins before we came here. Kids have all sorts of stories about the nasty things they will do if you mess with them, but I'm convinced that they really are just rocks. Nothing strange has ever happened around them, apart from legends, and nothing really magical, as far as I know."

I was a little disappointed. I wasn't interested in seeing a rock. I wanted to see the other leg. But if she wanted to show me a rock, I'd admire a rock. I've heard less-likely stratagems used by maids to get a man alone.

The rock in question came into view and I started to have a sinking feeling that this little walk wasn't going to go the direction I had intended. She wasn't using it as a pretext, she really *did* want me to look at a rock.

I saw that the rock in question was actually a pillar of stone, dark black limestone, I guessed, about twelve feet tall and three across the bottom, one foot across the top. It was smooth, though uneven, fashioned by hand and weathered worn at the edges. No vines or briars grew on it, I noted, though they covered the rocks around it. A perfectly ordinary monolith. The kind many cultures would use as a standard ancestor memorial or phallic shrine as was erected by tribal peoples just about everywhere. Particularly in the Wilderlands, where temples are few and far between. It was just a rock.

Only the air shimmered around it, like it was hot. I could *see* the dance of arcane energy pulsing through it – and I didn't need to use magesight.

"Until an hour ago, while you were healing Sagal," she agreed in a low voice. "I was keeping Ela busy, and went to check on the stock for her. There was a sickly yearling here I knew Sagal wanted to take to market soon. That's when I saw it. It was the humming that drew me to it."

"The cow was humming?"

"The *rock* was humming," she corrected with a roll of her eyes. "The cows won't go near it, now, they've cluttered up on the other side of the other pasture. But it was humming. The humming stopped just before you came back outside. Now why would a rock hum?"

"Because it's content with its lot?" I offered. "I have no idea. But I'll take a look."

Cautiously, I summoned magesight and examined the black pillar. It was pulsing, all right, though it was diminishing in both duration and intensity while I watched. The surface of the thing was covered with wild-seeming spellwork that stood out in magesight like holes in a lantern.

I'd never seen anything quite like it. But I could tell it was an ancient thing, a thing of arcane power, and it had the distinctive spell signature of the gurvani all over it.

I considered using the witchstone around my neck, just to see what would happen, but I had had enough excitement for one day. And this promised to be a very interesting development. Thaumaturgically, I was intrigued, but it paled in comparison to the prospect of exploring the irionite.

Besides, there was something that compelled my attention more than even the allure of thaumaturgy at that moment.

I took Alya by her hand and swung her around, making her scream prettily. "Just guessing, but I'd say it's a *powerful* fertility totem," I told her, confidently. "Clearly designed to incite lust and desire. Ishi's tits! I can't help myself!" and I kissed her in a moment of feigned compulsion. Okay, mostly feigned.

It only took her a few seconds to return the kiss. Reluctantly, at first, but then she surrendered to the moment. I could feel the monolith pulse a little faster, probably due to our proximity, or perhaps that of the witchstone, and I tried to ignore it. This was far more fun than magic.

"Your father doesn't happen to own a flour mill, does he?" I said as I broke that magnificent first kiss.

She looked confused. "No, just a farm and a creamery. Why?"

"Just checking a theory I have," I said, and returned my lips to hers.

Damnedest first date I've ever had.

Chapter Four

Zagor The Hedgemage

"Whilst some adepts despair at the muddled magic of the lower classes of wizards, using, as they do, a murky combination of tribal, Imperial, and wild magic, they are far from charlatans and cheats. Indeed, a goodly number of these lesser magi are possessed of Talent sufficient to place them amongst the greatest of adepts, had they the advantage of proper training. A wise adept will seek out these lower-order wizards and endeavor to discover their secrets, which may reveal hidden truths and powerful advantages to their own practice of the Art."

—   *A Magical Miscellany*

After leaving Sagal and Ela's farmstead Tyndal and I rode north all day and into the night. Just as the waxing crescent moon was at its zenith we finally pulled our horses off the road and into a copse of woods on the outskirts of the hamlet of Malin.

Malin is so small it almost didn't have outskirts. It's even smaller than Minden's Hall, not more than a few hundred people who lived in a score of neatly thatched stone cottages in a rough circle around the road in a picturesque hollow between hills. A tall, thick hedge of evergreens and thorns surrounded the hamlet, more to keep children and chickens in the hamlet than to keep invaders out.

But the lone cottage we sought was not inside the hedge that offered the illusion of protection for the village. It was within what the locals call "pissing distance", up a steep and rocky incline to the north of the hamlet. It took almost an hour to reach it, it was so remote from Malin.

It was a squat, one-room affair of timber, stone, and daubed clay, with a neatly trimmed swath cleared around it. To the south side I could see an herb garden and a spring house, and the intoxicating smell of wood smoke, freshly harvested herbs and goat droppings filled the air.

"Are we there yet?" my smart-mouthed apprentice asked for the tenth time that night. His boredom and exhaustion after the excitement of two battles in as many days had worn through his patience and changed his demeanor. Not for the better.

"Close enough," I said, tiredly. I was tempted to use a spell to refresh myself, but the past few days had drained me to the point where I was loathe to attempt it on my own. The witchstone was calling me to use its power for the spell, but I resisted. There was something *menacing* about it, I felt. And that humming megalithic monument had scared me. Not enough to keep from thoroughly molesting Alya in a pasture in its sight, but enough to keep it in my mind when more important things should be taking that space. I was here to see the Tree Folk, not discuss gurvani iconology, I reminded myself.

While Tyndal was seeing to the horses, I approached the cottage – and almost walked straight into a trap. I could feel it spring up around me like a snare. Cursing, I raised my magesight and studied the ring of wards and glyphs that spun around the simple hut like a golden garland around a pig's neck. They were all homemade, of course; they didn't have the familiar and recognizable shapes and feel of Imperial-style sorcery, but they were effective nonetheless. And because they were made with 'wild magic", cutting through them or disarming them would be difficult and time-consuming.

"Hey, *Zagor!*" I called, cupping my hands around my mouth, hoping I was loud enough to penetrate the tiny windows of the cot. It took a few moments, but soon the little door opened and a large – and I mean *huge* – black dog sprinted out at me. He sniffed me heartily for a moment, unsure about whether or not my intestines needed ripping out, but in the end I guess he recognized me from the last time I had been here. He wagged his tail twice with a heavy thud and allowed his tongue to sprawl out lazily from the side of his mouth.

While I gingerly scratched behind his ears, his master, dressed in a soft fur wrap, came to the door.

"Minalan, if this is another one of your middle-of-the-night drunken visits, I'd just as soon you went and bothered someone else," the hedgewizard coaxed, tiredly. "I've been up all evening trying to cure Goodwife Kasa's baby's colic, and have no time for your foolish revelry! Some of us have to work for our bread."

Zagor was an old man, perhaps in his sixties, but still vital and whole. His beard and hair were still black, and his eyes were merry even as he complained, but the wrinkles around his eyes and mouth showed his age. He was large, as large as Sagal, over six feet tall, and burly, built more like a woodcutter than a mage. Not the kind of man you envision when the term 'wizard' is said.

But the Talent doesn't discriminate about such things. He had it in spades, and had spent a lifetime of learning – mostly on his own, mind you – about how to use it.

Zagor was a native to the Boval Valley, having been born to the parents of trappers in a high-mountain homestead. He once told me that his mama let him chew on *kellisarth* twigs while he was teething and he'd had the Talent since he was six years old. Usually it doesn't emerge until adolescence. Zagor had been "adopted" by the Tree Folk and taught basic magic in their style after his parents died. Then he had been apprenticed briefly to the only mage in the valley, at the time, and when the old man died, Zagor took over his clients and moved to Malin. He had been doing the simple, practical work of a hedgemage ever since.

What's the difference between a hedgemage and a spellmonger? Not much.

Traditionally, a spellmonger has a shop and sells his services to people in the village or town, just as any proper merchant or artisan does. A *hedgemage*, on the other hand, usually lives just outside the village (usually just behind the hedge – hence the name) and sells the same sorts of spells.

More technically, I suppose, you could say that hedgemagi are not trained in the classic Imperial methods, don't rely on texts and books (many are illiterate), and pretty much make it up as they go along.

Technically that's known as "wild magic", practice frowned upon by traditionally-trained wizards. A spellmonger almost always has recourse to at least the most elementary texts for reference and refuge. As hedgewizards are also rarely licensed to practice, they are therefore also technically illegal under the Bans.

The Royal Censorate of Magic spent a good part of its time and resources rounding up such un-warranted magi for punishment in more populated regions. That was one of the reasons I had left more civilized parts and headed for the remote regions of the Duchies. The nearest Censor in the Alshari Wilderlands was probably no closer than Vorone, the summer capital, hundreds of leagues south.

But unlike many of my snobbish Academy-trained colleagues, I don't believe that they have any less power than we do; their biggest difficulty comes in working with other magi. The standardization of Academy training is based, in theory, on using the powers of several magi in concert using standardized spell components and a common lexicon of terminology, while hedgemagi, because of their unique training, techniques and talents, can rarely pool their powers as effectively.

There is also the matter of trade secrets – Zagor and I were on pretty good terms, but I'd seen villages where hedgemagi jealously guarded even the simplest of spells to keep the dragon's share of clients to themselves. I often wondered what kind of magi Zagor would have become if he had had the benefit of my schooling. But I didn't hesitate to consult with him on a difficult case, or just show up with a bottle when the desire to talk shop was strong.

"No, old man," I said, as friendly as I could, "I come on business, and have not a dram of wine about me." That wasn't entirely true – I keep a flask of winter wine for emergencies – but the last time I was here would have been memorable had I not been so drunk I couldn't remember it. "Can we come, my apprentice and I, and beg a fire and a stretch of dry floor? I have a boon to ask of you."

He glanced at Tyndal and me (no doubt using his own version of magesight) and grunted his assent. With a casual toss of his hand a half-dozen of his protective wards came down and his dog (whose name, I suddenly remembered, was Blue) escorted us inside.

The interior of Zagor's hut was crammed to the rafters with herbs and other ingredients. In a hamlet this small he had to be his own herbalist and apothecary, of course. There was none of the mystical crap that adorned Garkesku's shop – or my own, actually – just a few skulls and interesting rocks. Without direct competition there was no need to impress anyone with his mystical powers. Zagor was in the business of making magic, and he did so without fanfare. People knew what he did, and how well, and he didn't need to advertise or impress anyone.

I found that impressive.

He kicked a few stools out from under a table and threw another log on the embers in the fireplace while Blue circled around us and sniffed in awkward places. When we had seated ourselves, the flames from the fire illuminated the room enough to see each other's faces. Zagor took a moment to toss Blue a strip of rawhide before he grabbed an earthenware jug, took a sip, and passed it to me. He might have disliked drunkenness, but he didn't eschew strong drink, and the evening was chilly.

I tipped it up and drank a few swallows of the cold, clear cider that was just beginning to go hard before I passed it to Tyndal. I wiped my mouth with the back of my hand and grunted in approval.

"Now, young man, just what brings you all the way up here to disturb an old man's rest?" he asked, his tone belying his strong words. He was happy to see me, I could tell, but he couldn't let the grumpy old man persona slip. I wished the situation had been less important.

"Nothing good, I'm afraid. The night before last, Minden's Hall was beset by gurvani raiders, almost two hundred of them. We were nearly overtaken, had it not been for the timely arrival of Sire Koucey and his knights. Forty or so were killed."

"'Tis about time for another raid, I suppose," he grunted gloomily. "Though that seems far greater than the Mountain Folk usually muster. There hasn't been a serious attack in almost twenty years. But it is time. The furries are stirring, no doubt. I've seen the signs."

"So I have been told. But this one was no chicken-stealing raid. There was a shaman with them who cut through my wards like a knife through cheese. Because he carried *this*," I said, taking the little bag from around my neck and tossing it to him.

Garkesku I wouldn't trust to even hold the thing, so greedy was the little twit. Zagor wouldn't covet it, though. He had been a wiser mage in his teens than Garkesku would ever be.

"A witchstone," the hedgemage said, without a trace of emotion or surprise. He didn't even take it out of the bag, at first. "Large one, too. Rare it is that they grow to that size." The old man said a few words in a language I didn't know before he unwrapped the tiny bundle and let the bright green stone spill out into his palm. His face contorted with thought. Or something.

"That's why I came here, to seek your advice on it," I agreed. "What do you make of it? Was this an isolated incident or do we have to worry about more such raids?"

Zagor was silent for a while as he probed the gem magically and set it glowing with a soft green light. I waited for sweat to break on his brow, as it had with mine, but he completed the task with no more visible effort than he had made lifting the cider jug.

"We have trouble, I feel," he said, finally, his eyes reflecting his tiredness in the fading glow. "This is not good, Minalan. There will be more raids, more death, more fighting. And more witchstones," he added, almost as an afterthought.

"*More?* How do you know? Did your probe reveal—?"

"Look at it," he said, holding up the stone. "All the surfaces are smooth and clear . . . except *this* one. This flat area *here*," he said, pointing at the stone, "this shows that the witchstone was once part of a larger piece, and was broken off."

"*Larger?*" I asked, amazed.

"Much," Zagor agreed. "The stone that this came from was perhaps the size of my head. Maybe larger."

"How can you tell *that?*" I asked, mystified. Tyndal just stared at the wizened old man, his mouth agape.

"In my probe I saw the bands of the stone. Witchstones build up in layers, usually, like an onion. In this one the layers are very wide, not narrow like they would be if this stone formed on its own."

"But a piece of irionite that big is impossible!"

"Nothing is impossible, lad," Zagor countered, a smile in his voice.

"Zagor, I appreciate your wisdom, but you must realize that a piece of irionite even as big as *that* fragment is rare, almost unheard of. To find one any larger would be the discovery of a century, perhaps the biggest magical discovery since the fall of the Magocracy!"

"The stone does not lie," he said, simply. "And you do not know everything, Spellmonger." With that he set down the witchstone and pulled a similar bag from around his neck. Moving almost reverently, he pulled another piece of irionite out of it.

It was as big as a hen's egg.

I was astonished, and it showed. The few irionite particles that the Censorate held in its custody were miniscule, yet obscenely powerful. The tiny fragment that the Mad Mage had used against us had been overwhelming. The gem I gleaned from the fist of a dead gurvani shaman was likely powerful enough to destroy the valley and everyone in it, should its power be unleashed fully.

But Zagor the Humble Hedgemage of Malin wore around his neck a stone that could have bought him a *Duchy*. Or conquered a few.

"These things are not unknown in the mountains," he said, casually. With a pass of his hand the stone burst into illumination, and suddenly the air in the cabin was thick with magic and our faces were alight with greenish light. I realized just how those tough wards had got there. "My father found this stone in a brook, and set it in my crib when I was a child. He saw it as a gift from Trygg to bless his family. It sings with me, now."

"Zagor, do you realize . . .?"

"Minalan, I *know* what power is here. I am not that old or that foolish. And I know of those who would seek to take it from me and forfeit my life. This stone has been my companion since I was an infant. I know it as well as I know my own mind."

"And you don't *do* anything with it?" Tyndal burst out.

"What great feats of magic could I perform that would make the lives of my people better?" he asked, with a smirk. "I use it when I must, that is all. Not to seek riches or do impressive tricks. That is not what they are for. To do otherwise would betray Trygg's gift."

I sighed, and watched as the glow subsided. Zagor carefully wrapped up his massive stone and put it away before handing the smaller shard to me. I was still stunned. I'd known him six months and never even suspected.

"So is that what you wish to know?"

"Actually Zagor, I came up here on my way to visit the Alka Alon, but you seem to have answered some of my questions for me. If there is more than just this stone – something I would not have believed, had you not told me – then it looks like the gurvani will continue to move against us. I guess we can skip our visit the Tree Folk and head back south. To pack and flee."

"No, Spellmonger, don't do that," he insisted. "The Fair Ones know far, far more about the witchstones than I do. They showed me how to use mine. They have used them since the beginning of time. They will have the answers to the questions you don't even know to ask."

"Such as just how common are these things?" I asked. "Where do they come from? How did they get in gurvani hands? What is the gurvani's purpose in using them? A tithe of those answers would be helpful, don't you think?"

Zagor shrugged. "Tomorrow, you may ask the Tree Folk. Tonight, you must rest. We have a difficult journey ahead, even though the way is not long, and you will need your rest."

*   *   *

The next morning the previous night's revelations felt like a dream. But I knew that the bulge under Zagor's jerkin was real. The old man seemed to have grown mightier than I remembered him. I had a new respect for a wizard who had that kind of power at his command and still had the willpower to not use it casually. I would have been king of all Callidore, had my Dad given me a stone like that.

The old wizard woke us with the sounds and smells of frying bacon, hot cereal, tea, and a warm loaf of dark bread almost as good as what my father made while Blue went from knee to knee begging scraps. When we went to saddle the horses after daybreak, we found a third beast, a shaggy mountain pony, already loaded next to them. I raised an eyebrow in surprise.

"You are going to accompany us, then?"

"Aye," Zagor grunted, pulling on a long bearskin cloak. "This danger threatens the entire valley. The furries have no love for our kind. There will be many more raids. Perhaps the worst ever. The counsel of the

Tree People will be telling."

I shrugged as he made a casual wave of his hand and reset the wards on his house. I had always envied his facility with them and had thought that they were the product of his wild magic. They were so strong, I noticed, that you could feel them and almost see them without magesight. I shuddered involuntarily, now that I knew why.

We went through the tiny village and up a steep trail that climbed the gradient of the mountain to the north at a dangerous clip. It was only a ridgelet, Zagor told us, a final hill before we came to the little valley of the Tree People, but it seemed pretty steep to me. I guess it discouraged casual visitors.

Just over the ridge the forest of the Alka Alon spread out before us, different in nature than the forests to the south. It was a lighter shade of green, I noticed, than the forest that skirted the western mountain spur at the middle of the valley, or the majestic and uncut woods in the sparsely inhabited region at the very southern end.

The trees were a mix of deciduous and evergreen, mostly *natavia* with a few *importasta*, and an intoxicating aroma wafted up from it. Zagor led us down the back side of the ridge, where the trail petered out, and stopped at a lone sharamine tree that stood about fifty yards from the edge of the forest proper.

And then we waited.

"What are we waiting for?" I wanted to know. "Shouldn't we ring the bell, or knock, or . . ."

"Use your wizard eyes," he said, pointing.

I slipped into magesight and studied the edge of the forest. I saw a wild tangle of overlapping wards and spells that would have prevented an army from passing through. They made Zagor's home wards seem like a stick fence. I didn't recognize most of the forms, but I knew a strong defense when I saw it. There was easily enough power in that magical barrier than I had ever seen at the Academy or even guarding the Citadel of Farise. And they were ancient, I could tell, older than many of the trees around it.

It indicated a magical culture that refreshed the wards for such a long period that they had become part of the landscape itself, a hallmark of the enchantments of the Tree Folk. The trees, I noted, were actually *part* of the defense, each tree on the frontier a veritable magical tower against intruders. I whistled in appreciation and tried to explain to Tyndal what I saw. Of course, even with his low level of sophistication it was hard to appreciate it.

"So how do we let them know we are here?" my apprentice asked in a hushed voice.

"They knew the moment we crossed the ridge line," Zagor said. "The Tree People are subtle, lad. They will let us wait here while they prepare a proper welcome, then they will send a guide to take us through the forest. That is the way of the Fair Folk."

Sure enough, less than five minutes later a solitary Alka Alon strode out of the forest to stop at the base of the tree. He was naked, of course, save for a belt upon which hung a tiny pouch and quiver, and one of their diminutive wooden bows was slung across his back.

The Alka Alon stood four feet tall and weighed maybe forty or fifty pounds. His skin was a pale and mottled greenish tint, and his hair was the darkest black where it spilled over his shoulders. He looked up with his big, soulful eyes, and regarded us contemplatively one at a time, and lingered longest on Zagor.

While he was staring, Blue came up and sniffed his butt, and I almost fell off my horse laughing.

Luckily, I didn't offend the little man, who also found it funny. He laughed, a sound like a box of crystal bells falling off a table. The Alka patted the grateful dog on the head and finally spoke.

"We bless you in the name of your Trygg, young Zagor, and welcome you and your friends to our refuge," he said in the Narasi common tongue, his accent perfect and his voice like a silver flute. "What brings you to our eaves?"

"We seek the wisdom of the Aronin, my lord watcher," Zagor answered solemnly. "We have questions we hope he might answer."

The little creature considered thoughtfully for a moment. "It is not our practice to admit strangers to our groves. You, young Zagor, we have met before. Who are your companions?"

It was strange hearing Zagor, who is old enough to be my grandfather, called "young," but the Tree People live a long, *long* time.

"This one is Minalan, a mage from the East, who has come to serve the people of the valley, and this is his apprentice Tyndal, who was born here. They seek the Aronin's wisdom concerning the gurvani. And other matters." The smile faded from the Tree Folk's face.

"I see. I am known as Ardrey, Watcher of the southern eaves. I will guide you into the heart of our land. Stray not from the path, lest you find yourself lost in immortal realms. And perform no magic without permission, lest you upset our own works," he warned, after thought.

That was fair enough. Not only was it common magical courtesy, but after seeing that ward system I didn't want to accidentally spring anything nasty on us. I had a suspicion that the results would become . . . interesting.

Watcher Ardrey unhurriedly led us along a pathway through the outer eaves that I'd swear before Trygg and Briga just wasn't there an instant before. Obfuscation magic, I noted, the kind that the Tree Folk had a reputation for. Crossing into that forest was like entering an entirely different world.

How to describe it? Words don't do it justice. Human words, at any rate, and singing about it in any of our languages would just demean its beauty. The air is richer there than even clean mountain air, with the scents of loams and mosses and hidden flowers. Despite the overhanging boughs there was plenty of light, though it took on a softer, more golden tone. There was little underbrush, unlike more mundane forests, and the little that poked up from the clear forest floor was arranged like little gardens. There was almost no deadwood to be seen, although I saw at least one fallen tree that had been left in the clearing it had made. It seemed more like art than firewood, though.

And the spells. Strange spells, wrought of alien shapes and organic-looking contours, both wild and at the same time utterly ordered, their purposes unknown. That didn't stop me from trying to know. Some of them seemed to be encouraging plants to grow, or water to flow, and some I suspected had been hung where they were purely for art's sake.

The first few hundred yards were almost deserted. I only saw a few

Alka working or meditating or hunting. They seemed to take little notice of us, as if humans and horses dropped by for tea and a chat with their chieftain every day.

Then we came to the first big clearing and I learned the true meaning of the beauty of the Alka Alon.

In my previous encounters with the Tree People, in the jungles of Farise, they had aided us and supplied us, but we never got close to their hidden refuges. Oh, they invited us into the treehouses that they set up at various points in the jungle, small, elegant affairs that looked hardly strong enough to hold one of them but were quite capable of supporting two or three heavy humans – in armor. They used these shelters as lookout posts, hunting cabins, and travelers' huts, they informed us. But we never saw where the Alka Alon *really* lived, or how.

"Behold," Zagor said, motioning to the display in front of us, "The Refuge of Amadia, where the Aronin alone rules all."

I was speechless. I had always considered the Alka Alon to be primitive, yet sophisticated. Amadia convinced me that the Tree Folk only *affected* to be primitive, out of aesthetic choice. Their sophistication was so great that it only appeared as a style of rustic magic. Amadia was gorgeous.

The towers at the edge were made of living *natavia* trees, soaring a hundred feet in the air, with slender bridges running between them at various levels as light as spider webs. The trees near the interior supported large, globe-shaped structures like wasps' nests or beehives, made of a natural-looking material that I couldn't identify. Round windows let in the sun at various points and small graceful balconies jutted out from the bulbs, allowing tree-top gardens in clay pots to add even further to the greenery.

At the very center there was one huge tree, at least a hundred and fifty feet tall and at least fifteen feet thick, upon which was the most massive sphere of all. Obviously a last line of defense and a central civic building, a palace or a temple, this central globe dwarfed the others by many orders of magnitude. Around the edge of the whole urban grove was a swiftly running stream that seemed to flow from one side of the circle to the other without the interference of gravity, a delicate natural moat that seemed more scenic than strategic.

The whole place was so powerfully enchanted that I had to drop my magesight lest I be blinded.

"Come, my friends. I will lead you to the Hall of Welcome," Ardrey said, gently in his beautiful voice. We followed dumbly, awed by the majesty of the place. Even Zagor, who had lived here, so he said, was quietly reverent.

Ardrey led us over the moat, across an elegantly arched bridge and suddenly, as if a door had opened, we heard the singing that some spell kept contained from the outside world.

Calling it "singing" in the human fashion seems insulting. It was glorious, thousands of voices singing hundreds of melodies all at the same time. It was better than a symphony of flutes and harps. It mimicked and improved upon the songs of birds, the tinkle of streams, the laughter of children. Once you hear the songs of the Tree Folk, human music always pales by the comparison.

Ardrey led us to a slender stairway that climbed the trunk of one of the interior trees in a spiral, bidding us to leave the horses to their own devices. I had no problem doing that. There was no way that they could get into trouble here, unless they took a liking to one of the trees that someone was living in, and I doubted that even Traveler was that stupid.

We climbed the mighty stair and entered the underbelly of one of the larger globes, and I was surprised to find it almost as bright inside as it had been in the morning sun outdoors. The walls were translucent, and the windows were more for ventilation than illumination, I found. To add to the light there were luminous teardrops made of magical light – magelights, like human wizards use, if they have the ability – hanging in midair like lamps with a dozen wicks, set every few yards.

We finally came to the Hall of Welcome, which was rather welcoming. There we were attended by several Alka Alon, mostly females (guessed – it was hard to tell, back then), who provided us with sweet water, juices and tasty baked morsels for which my father would have traded one of his children (probably my sister Urah) to get the recipe.

Nor were we unexpected. There were exactly three human-style chairs there made of simple wood, unblemished by tools. Yet they were more comfortable than any chair I could remember. There was a fire in a central stone pit that warmed the place comfortably, providing little light and less smoke, yet made the whole place seem friendly, warm and alive.

"I shall leave you here now to refresh yourselves while I return to my post," Ardrey said in his musical voice. "Worry not— Ameras will be along presently to escort you to the Aronin. Be well and be welcome, my new friends." With an elegant bow, he departed.

"*Damn*," I said, under my breath. "I had *no idea* . . ."

"Few mortals do," agreed Zagor with a rare smile. "The Fair Folk treasure their privacy and go to great lengths to bar any incursions into their realm. Mortals who wander into their forest are rarely seen by again by man."

"But *you* did it," accused Tyndal, in a whisper.

"Aye, lad, and I was but a year or so older than you when I did. But I was desperate, and it was only by the grace of the Fair Folk that I was allowed passage. I lived here for almost a year, though it seemed but a day."

"What was it like?" I asked, intrigued.

"They kept me as a pet to be coddled and played with before they returned me to Malin. They taught me tricks, as you would a favored hound. But even their grace and patience has limits."

"They expelled you?" I asked, surprised.

"Only when they had taught me what I needed," he sighed. "They let me return, at need, but to do so only makes the longing for this place worse. The music, the laughter, the magic of Amadia makes the human places in the world seem dull.

"But that is why they do not tolerate mortals for more than a few months, at most. You can grow addicted to this, need it so badly that you would do anything to get it. Yet if you did live here all the time, you would soon go mad because of your own mortality. No amount of magic can make you into one of them."

"Who is this Aronin that we are going to see? Is he a priest, a mage, or a king?"

"All of these and more," the hedgemage answered. "The Aronin founded this colony countless years ago, away from even his own people. *Aronin* is a title, and not a name. It means 'guardian', in your language. He has nurtured and protected Amadia. All the Tree Folk have one ancient of his sort to look to, though he does not command like a human lord. He is the master of their magic, a living embodiment of the forest and the people together. He is ageless, a great master of wisdom. He sees into the past, the futures, and peers into the realms of darkness and light."

That last bit was straight from one of the Alka Alon epic poems I remembered studying in school. The Realms of Darkness and Light were where the Alkan culture-hero Amioril traveled to gather allies against the demons of legend during one of the fabled wars between ancient Alka Alon wars. I guess Zagor picked that up here – to my knowledge, he was illiterate.

We sat a while in silence, staring at the fire, drinking a strange liquor from wooden cups and nibbling the wonderful confections. I almost felt like going to sleep when a very tall (over five feet) Alkan woman came in.

Unlike the Watcher and the attendants we had seen before, she had long *golden* hair, and a body that seemed more mature, less child-like. In fact, her body so reminded me of a female human that I became suddenly uncomfortable with the naked display of her tiny greenish nipples.

I had never felt arousal associated with a nonhuman. I've heard rumors of those who have, and the legends speak of unlikely romances between human and Alka Alon lovers . . . but I also have heard rumors that Goodman Silao's sons take their pleasure more with their sheep than their wives. You know how rumors go.

"Lady Ameras!" Zagor said, his voiced hushed in reverence. "Trygg's blessing upon you for favoring us with your grace!"

Ameras was achingly beautiful, her long and graceful neck supporting her glorious face like a slender tree trunk. I swallowed hard and realized my heart was pounding as I jumped to my feet.

"Welcome, my friends," she said in a voice like a silver dream. "I trust you have been well treated and refreshed?" We all nodded like dumb animals. Hells, we *were* dumb animals, compared to her graceful beauty. Even Alya wasn't as much a woman as this female Alka was.

"Excellent. I know your errand must be urgent for you to have traveled so far to our realms. The Aronin has foreseen this and is expecting you. Come with me," she quietly commanded, and beckoned us to follow.

She looked pretty human from behind, as well.

The path we took was circuitous, and Ameras explained that it was partially for defense, partially for enjoying the view that the paths between houses were so constructed. What was odd was the fact that we never seemed to climb *up* – no stairs or inclines that I could see – but several times I made the mistake of looking down and, after the vertigo passed, I realized just how *far* up in the trees we were.

We passed what must have been homes and workshops and balls full of happy, squealing Alka Alon children on our way to the central . . . palace? I was not surprised to see the entrance flanked by two serious-looking Alka Alon, carrying bows and stone-tipped spears, who eyed us with suspicion and watchfulness – the first negative emotion I had detected in this beatific place. I was surprised that I didn't see more, to be honest – they were, after all, guarding the embodiment of the forest. Guarding the Guardian. They bowed low before Ameras as we passed. Us, we were just animals to them, animals to be watched.

The interior of the great hollow ball was huge, enough for a great gathering of Tree Folk. I'd almost say that it was empty, except that there were several dozen Alka Alon walking around on errands or conversing quietly, or just singing by themselves or in quiet duets. I looked around for a throne or some other sign or symbol of authority, but I saw none. I guess the Tree Folk didn't do things that way, at least not in Amadia.

"The Aronin will be with you in a moment, my friends. He is in his inner chamber, preparing. Tell me, is it true that our . . . cousins, the gurvani, have attacked again?" she asked, sadly, as if she were hoping that it wasn't true. And as if the last raid had been a few weeks, not twenty years before.

"Aye, my lady Ameras," I said using my best court manners. I felt like a rustic peasant, but I tried to please her with every word. "They raided my village, Minden's Hall, but two nights ago. Nearly forty of our folk were killed. There have been other attacks, too. It is largely about them that we come. But you called them 'your cousins.' What do you mean by that?" I asked, curiously.

She smiled and answered as if indulging a child. I didn't mind; her smile was beautiful enough to forgive a thousand outrageous insults. "It is a pity that your people are so short-lived, Master Spellmonger. Else they would have remembered the truth. Even with your quaint form of writing, your folk seem to lose more than you remember with each generation. But as for the gurvani and the Alka Alon . . . it is a long, sad story."

"I can think of nothing more important than listening to your beautiful voice, my lady. I would dearly love to hear the story of your people."

She smiled at the flattery – some things go beyond species. "A single story of my folk would take years to tell properly to you mortals, and much of import is lost in your brevity. The one you request would take lifetimes to tell properly. But very well. I shall be brief.

"Many, many centuries ago, as it is measured among Men, and long before your folk were spawned by the Void, there were three peoples in the world who were Callidore's Children: the Alon, the *Vundel*, whom you call the Sea Folk, and the *Delioli,* the ones your people sometimes called giants, before they hunted them to the brink of extinction on this continent.

"The Alon were the lords of the land, ruled over by the wisest of Alka. The details are subtle and manifold, but over time our great cities went to war with each other, and the very land was split and divided among us, and divided again, until the very peoples of the Alon were sundered from one another by sect, faction, nation and tribe. Our species itself was divided. Thus parted, their many paths diverted, and across the millennia the Alon became several peoples.

"The Alka Alon, of course, remained the truest to the old Alon in both form and culture. Our lives grew to last thousands of years. But the others strayed far from their roots.

"The far northern mountain tribes of Alon were lesser in stature and in lifespan as they endured many hardships in their seclusion, though their numbers increased. Once known as the *Nara Alon*, they were long sundered from most of the other Alon, and rejected much of their own history as such. Instead they took their name, *gurvani*, from their ancestral spirit, a famous leader of their folk named *Gurvos*, who had led their people out of the devastation of the southern wars and into the safety of the mountains.

"They hid from their enemies in caves, or lived in rude huts, venturing out only at night to escape their enemies. They learned the secrets of working metal from their neighbors, the *Alon Dradrien*, the clans of those you call the Iron Folk," she said, with slight distaste. "That was to prove the Dradrien's undoing, for the gurvani went to war with them eventually, and their cousins the *Karshaki*, and drove them deep under the earth. Only a few clans of them still hide in the roots of the mountains, and they breed slowly, though they are long-lived.

"Then there are those *Alon* who survived the cataclysms by abandoning the old ways entirely, and instead hugged the riverbanks, the *Tal Alon*. The Hoylbimi, in Old Perwynese. You call them the River Folk or the Hill Folk, and they are small, simple creatures who farm and are eager to adopt the ways of Man. They have all but forgotten that they were once part of a great people, and their lives grew even shorter than yours.

"There are the *Hulka Alon*, who roam the Great Valley of the north, the *Firisi Alon* of the northern coasts, and the *Gora Alon* who dwell the deserts. And there are still others, races yet unknown to your people, shards and splinters of our ancient race that have blown across the lands of Callidore like seeds in the wind, and taken root of their own accord. But they were all *Alon*, once. Therefore the gurvani *are* our cousins, though they are poor relations."

All this was news to me, but I nodded my head like I understood what she was saying. Trolls – the *Hulka Alon* – I had thought were mere legend, despite the number of unsavory tales I was told about them as a child. The Sea Folk I had seen myself, for they still swam in great numbers around the coasts and harbors and traded with us between their great voyages. I also knew about the near-mythic Karshaki and Dradrien kingdoms deep in the Kuline Range to the east, only because they supposedly aided my ancestors against the Magocracy before fading back into the obscurity of the impassable mountains. They were the nearest in form to humans, similar enough to be mistaken for stunted men. To my knowledge few had seen a living dwarf in two generations.

But the River Folk were well known to me. The brown-furred Hoylbimi were an agrarian species sometimes derogatorily called "Rat Folk" or "Rabbit Folk," and they had, indeed, clung to the margins of human civilizations. They dwelt on the banks of rivers and hilltops, living underground or in crude little thatched huts, a peaceful folk who lived much like the human peasantry. There was a tiny village of them just a few miles downriver of Talry, I'd heard. Some of them were civilized, and they were quick to adopt the ways of humans, when allowed to. They were great vegetable farmers, though they rarely tried to grow grain.

They would also steal anything that wasn't nailed to a tree. They had a reputation for petty thievery that was only half deserved, and were often found "borrowing" stuff from peasants. Dad used to trade his extra bread and cakes to them occasionally for nuts and berries, which they excelled at collecting. They had a greater tolerance for staleness than his other customers.

And the others? There were rumors, legends and myths. I'd never heard of the Firisi Alon or the Gora Alon, but then my worldly experience was limited to Alshar and Castal, with two years in Farise and six weeks I spent with a classmate (all right, girlfriend) on her spacious estate in Remere.

From anyone else I would have insisted on some kind of proof of their existence, but if Ameras wanted to tell me that she had a cow that gave wine instead of milk, I'd believe her and buy a cup.

"I see," I nodded, more sagely than I should have. "But if the gurvani—"

"Bide, the Aronin arrives," she said, suddenly, her eyes pointing the way. My eyes followed, if for no other reason than to keep hers company.

They lighted on the tallest Alka Alon I'd ever seen, taller than Ameras by five or six inches. He, too, had long golden hair tied into an impressive pony tail, and on his head he wore a garland of tiny white flowers. His face was stern and wise and as handsome as Ameras' was beautiful. The Aronin wore a wide belt around his waist and a dark red cloak of some material I couldn't identify. As most of the other Alka were naked, it's likely he donned it merely to impress us. It worked. He carried an ornate spear like a staff of office, not a weapon. This, I could see, was the epitome of Alka Alon nobility. He could teach the art to a duke.

"My lord!" Zagor said, bowing low. I did the same, as did Tyndal. "I thank you for the grace of seeing us."

"In truth I have been expecting you," said the Aronin. His voice sounded deeper than the others, and a bit gruff, but no less full of grace and beauty. "Young Zagor, you and I shall speak later. Right now my attention needs to be with the Spellmonger." That was it. No further ceremony, no further explanation. I felt like a dog being shown off to a neighbor.

With that he motioned to me to follow him, which I did. Tyndal, thankfully, took the hint and stayed put without protest. In fact, the way he was looking at Ameras told me it was unlikely that he would leave her side for anything less than a dragon attack. Probably not even then.

The Aronin led me up a narrow ramp and into a much smaller chamber. It had the same simplicity of design that the others shared, but there were boxes and bags of leather and cloth scattered about, and there was a large area full of cushions off to one side, which was where he led me. We were seated and he poured two glass goblets full of some potent but soothing liquor that defies easy description. He sat and sipped silently for a long while, regarding me patiently until I felt like I was sinking into his eyes. Finally, he spoke.

"I foresaw your arrival here, Spellmonger," he began, after staring at me for a few moments. "It bodes ill for my people that you have come."

"No less for mine," I replied, quietly. "But the errand is urgent for us. We have been attacked by the gurvani.

He looked troubled. "There is little we can do about our cousins," he admitted. "And no aid that we can lend. But I will give what counsel I may," he conceded.

"How does it bode ill for *your* people, my lord?" I asked, surprised. No one troubled the Tree Folk, history taught us. Or not more than once.

"Our cousins have risen in their might, once again, having discovered their strength. They bear both our people a grudge, in their mind. And this time they will not be easily defeated. The attack on your settlement was no idle blow or casual sortie. It was merely the vanguard. The gurvani will come, and come, Spellmonger, until the valley below is a black sea of their faces."

"But it *was* only a raid," I protested. Even as I said it, I knew it wasn't true. "Not even a real army. We drove them back," I said, weakly.

"The gurvani do not raid so and *never* into this valley. You see, it is sacred to them," he explained.

"Sacred? Sacred how? I've noticed a few artifacts . . ." I said, remembering the Goblin Stone Alya showed me.

"Among the northern gurvani tribes there is *no* more sacred place. It is said Gurvos himself was born here, millennia ago, blessed by their . . . gods. His children learned their style of magic here before they led their people away from the ancient wars. Their short history, such as it is, arises from this place. Being driven from it by the treachery of the *humani* was . . . *blasphemy,* as I understand your term. Recovering it is a holy endeavor. *That* is why they have come in such force."

"Uh, if they wanted it so badly, why haven't they come before now? Man – we humani -- has been here since the end of the Goblin Wars. And not in any great force."

"So it has," he conceded. "They were driven forth a long time ago to you, a very short time to my folk. It has been even longer to the short-lived gurvani. They have waited and prepared for generations for this day. They seek to drive your people from the valley, for they have grievances with you for past wrongs. Then they will remake the valley into a mighty fortress from which they will war on all humani. So I have foreseen. And when they do so, they will likewise war on my people, for they forget our ancient kinship. At the least they will drive my poor folk from this place of quiet refuge and force us to again be subject to the outer world. A pity. We enjoy it here."

That was an appalling notion. Not only did I not want to see this beautiful place destroyed – as well as my adopted home in Boval – but I also didn't want to see the valley turned into a staging area for an invasion of the rest of the Alshari Wilderlands.

With irionite and good organization, they might be able to challenge the Wilderlords of the sparsely-populated regions, but I couldn't see them standing against the combined might of all Five Duchies. But I also knew that it would take months, if not years, to organize a decent resistance with our feudal system before we could bring any kind of military might to play. Wilderlords are tough knights, and the Wilderlands great bow was devastating, which made both top recruits to mercenary units in the south and east. But the population here was sparse and spread out. Defending it would be as difficult as conquering it.

"My lord Aronin, how *can* the gurvani come against us in those kind of numbers? The attack on Minden Hall was nearly two hundred strong, and those were defeated by a bunch of peasants and a handful of Wilderlords. Surely they have neither the numbers nor the organization to do so much damage?"

"So they, like your own folk, turn to magic to make up the difference," he replied, smiling serenely. "And they have planned for an extended engagement. The war-party that attacked your huts was a mere test of their power, not intended as invasion as much a survey of their strengths. Our cousins have been planning this for a long, *long* time by either of your races' reckoning, Spellmonger, since long before you were born. They have hollowed out breeding pits in their warrens, and they have built huge smithies deep underground in the ruins of the Dradrien's old realms to prepare for it. Their numbers are once again high, though crowded, and they are led by a war-leader long dead."

Now *that* took me aback.

He proceeded to tell me a long tale about how my ancestors, after they had conquered the Magocracy, had turned their eyes West. He was lecturing me about my own history, in other words.

Back then, I knew, the present-day Duchies of Castal and Alshar were settled by humans only along the coasts (mostly by Cormeeran pirates-turned-Sealords, Imperial merchants and nobles, and retired veterans from the Magocracy granted their legacies as rich inland farms, who became Coastlords) before King Kamaklavan granted them to his two youngest sons. The Magocracy had even signed a treaty or something with the Alka Alon and the gurvani promising not to cross into those lands north of the Scarred Lands and other natural defenses.

Back then the interior was dominated by the Alon races – notably the gurvani and the River Folk, though the Alka Alon were also present in small numbers in remote cities, refuges, or simply wandering parties on an extended nature walks. The human settlements in the interior were small, at first, expansions of the old Magocracy's coastland outposts on frontier. Mostly the Archmagi kept their promises.

But then my ancestors had to ride down from the northeast and dash all of those plans. Kamaklavan's descendents were content with their rich strips of land and stately plantations for only a generation or so before they tore up the Magocracy's ancient treaty and began claiming whatever lands their barbaric knights could hold against the non-humans.

Once we came north and west of Gilmora, say, they didn't like us much as neighbors, anymore. The gurvani were pushed out. They fled from the fertile lands we sought for ourselves. Year by year we forced them back, taking over their richest lands and hunting the non-humans like animals. By the time of the first of the Goblin Wars, they had only a few organized settlements in the Minden range of mountains – Boval Valley being one. That slow push into Gilmora and beyond brought us humans closer and closer to the gurvani's most sacred lands, eventually struggling against the non-humans in what is often known unofficially bit popularly as the "goblin wars".

This wasn't a real war, more a sustained series of conflicts, skirmishes, raids and battles between the Alshari Wilderlords and the tribal gurvani. What we saw as legitimate expansion into the iron and timber-rich lands beyond Gilmora was to the goblins a tragedy that continuously uprooted the gurvani and pushed them deeper into the mountains.

The Aronin explained that from here that the gurvani's last, desperate counter-attack, a mere hundred and fifty years ago, had been organized under two charismatic gurvani brothers: a mighty war-leader named Grogror and an inspirational shaman named Shereul.

Grogror was a great chieftain who united the disparate gurvani tribes under his kingship, while Sharuel tapped into the forces of irionite with his sect of shamans and unleashed horrible plagues and magical beasts on human kind to stem the tide of advance.

They were successful for a few years (Alshar was suffering an interregnum and dynastic dispute at the time) thanks to our disorganization and their increasing numbers. Then the new duke of Alshar came to power and decided to end the gurvani harassment of his northernmost territories for good.

He wasn't necessarily bloodthirsty – from what I recall, Alshar needed the great forests of the Wilderlands for the timber to construct yet-another great fleet. The Duke sent ten thousand heavy cavalry north beyond Gilmora when the smoldering conflict with Castal finely permitted him to. He rewarded the men with ample holdings taken from their conquest, and it gave him something to distract the great nobles in the rich coastal regions from the wide trail of bodies (some of them family) he'd left behind him on his way to the throne. That much I remembered from history.

The gurvani, the Aronin assured me, were unable to stand against the aggression of armored Narasi cavalry. From then on they lost every major encounter, their tribal infantry and small bows being ineffectual against the new Wilderlords. They gathered their forces for one final push, and about two hundred years ago they came streaming forth from the sacred valley and their other warrens to strike at the few major strongholds of Alshar.

They got their furry little asses handed to them.

It was a nasty, brutal war, with quarter neither asked nor given. The nocturnal gurvani made every night a hell of screams and flames, and every day the gleaming steel and thundering horses of the knights hunted down the goblins and destroyed them utterly when they found them. Shaman and warmage strove for the upper hand in the arcane sphere, and caught many innocents on both sides in the crossfire. Few pitched battles fought, and when they were they were in our favor. Mostly the "wars" were a series of bloody skirmishes against isolated settlements on both sides.

It all came to a head at the Battle of Green River, a hundred miles northwest of Vorone, when the main gurvani army crossed the ford at dusk using magic (gurvani hate water) and ambushed the Duke of Alshar's encampment. If it hadn't been for the timely arrival of fresh Gilmoran cavalry, history might have made a different turn. As it was, Grogror was slain and the surviving remnant of his forces were driven back up into the hills.

In the weeks afterward, the Ducal armies defeated the isolated pockets of gurvani resistance in their mountain strongholds again and again. Eventually, through subterfuge (say the histories) or treachery (implied the Aronin), the Duke of Alshar's men tracked the remnants of the gurvani force to their sacred valley, captured and beheaded the surviving brother, the shaman Shereul, and had him his head publically placed on a pike and paraded around for the prisoners to see in the style of the Alshari Coastlords (who loved to do that sort of thing to their enemies). The gurvani were aggrieved by such a disrespectful display, it was said.

The head was stolen away that night by his disciples who vowed revenge, but the war was effectively over. A few small bands continued to resist the Wilderlords, but most of the gurvani fled the resistance broken. The rest of the conflict was really just mopping up, ushering in an era of relative peace for the wild country. For the humans, that is.

The sacred valley was given in fief to Sire Koucey's family, House Brandmount, on the condition that they keep it clear of all gurvani. The defeated gurvani of the vale put up little resistance and retreated again into the higher mountains of the Minden Range and the lands beyond. The Aronin himself was here to see this, he reported. To him, it was as if it had happened a few years ago.

I could see why they were so pissed at the treatment. Alshari Coastlords have a reputation of playing nasty during war, since most of their ancestors were brutal Cormeeran corsairs who enjoyed such displays over their enemies. The gurvani have pretty typical tribal ideas of respect and honor for your fallen enemies, which they saw as being violated in the treachery and execution of Shereul. *Especially* if their ancestral culture-hero was born here.

"Now the threat is even greater," the Aronin said in his calm, musical voice. "The gurvani have been plotting and preparing for revenge for the last two hundred years, since Shereul was slain. They have been biding their time in their mountain fastness, building up forces, making weaponry, and waiting . . ."

". . .for us to get fat, dumb and happy," I sighed. "The raid on Minden Hall was just a test of our forces and their response."

"Indeed," the wise old Alkan said, gravely. "Nor will they repeat the errors of their ancestors. They would not chance a raid like that unless they could follow it with a more serious threat. The real attack will be orders of magnitude greater . . . and it will come on or before the New Moon."

"Is that prophecy, Aronin?" I asked, not knowing a proper form of address. Imperial magic and the Bans forbid such spells for humans, but the Tree Folk didn't recognize our laws.

"Our cousins are not stupid, though they might be ignorant," the king of the Tree Folk continued, patiently. "They are determined to return to their previous dominion and drive you *humani* as far from the Minden Range as possible. Here, take my hand," he said, suddenly offering his five slender, childlike fingers.

He was doing more than being friendly, as I saw something like an *apis* of curious design form over his palm. I considered trying to create a similar *apis*, then decided that it might be seen as arrogant. The Aronin knew what he was doing. I took his hand.

Flash! We were still seated across from each other, but the room had faded away around us. It was as if we were hovering in the air several miles over the valley, and all of Boval was spread out before us. I realized that we were in the Otherworld, the land of dreams and nightmares where serious magi do their hardest work. It took me several hours to prepare myself for such a trip, but the Aronin had brought us there as casually as I would have opened a bottle.

Spellmonger, look at the numbers of our cousins.

I looked. In the mountains all around me I could see the tiny sparks that indicated, apparently, knots of gurvani. They were gathering on all sides of us, with denser clusters approaching the Mor Tower, Boval Castle, and the fortress of Brandmount. Hundreds. Maybe thousands – such things are difficult to tell, in the Otherworld. But we would be hard pressed to hold out against them, should they all attack at once, I realized. Even with great Boval Castle as a fortification.

Then I saw the hundreds *more* bands still waiting in the western mountains, and yet more on the way, and suddenly I felt great despair come over me. There were enough to easily overwhelm any defense we could put up, and probably enough to mount a credible invasion of Alshar.

See the magics our cousins bring to bear against you.

The scene changed slightly, and I witnessed the number of shaman that accompanied the warrior bands. In most there was a greenish glow that I concluded meant they bore shards of irionite similar to the one I had captured. That made me all the more despairing. There were hundreds. If they had even half the wit to use them, my little speck of witchstone would be of little avail.

Then I noticed a huge green glow in the center of the greatest knot of warriors still left in the mountains. A glow that dwarfed the other sparks below us to near invisibility.

Some titanic force was there to aid them. Not just a mere shaman, even a king among shaman. This was something else, something so powerful that the mighty Aronin was concerned.

I suddenly understood why the single *gurvan* shaman I slew looked so triumphant, even in death. He had that power on *his* side. The gurvani were resurgent, and they were taking no chances.

We are doomed, I moaned.

Perhaps, agreed the Aronin, *Perhaps not*.

Can you not help us? I pleaded.

Nay. We shall not take up arms against our cousins, save in defense, nor shall we do so for them. Yet they pose a threat to my people, as well as yours. That great glow you see is troublesome. A knot of magic that large has not been seen outside our realms since Elder Days. It is controlled by a strange intelligence that rebuffs me every time I try to go near it. I'm afraid that once our cousins are finished with you, they will war with us, out of spite.

Don't count us out yet! I countered, a little irritated at his assumption. *We beat them once; we can do so again.*

Brave words, Spellmonger, he said into my mind. *You shall need such bravery to face the horde that descends upon you. But even at the height of the Magocracy, when the greatest Archmage ruled with the Emerald Staff and the Crown of Souls, the Imperium did not have the might to withstand this power.*

What is it? I asked, mystified.

It is abhorrence, what they have done, an abomination. Our cousins are not evil themselves, but some great force, full of hate and malice has possessed them and promised them glory and power. I know not how they fashioned it so, but the power there, he said, indicating the bright spot on the horizon, *is greater than any since the fall of our greatest cities. It is unlikely that even the remaining realms of the Alka Alon can withstand it.*

Then what can we do? I asked, gloomily. The Aronin seemed to know his stuff, and if he was worried, I felt utterly *doomed*.

This node of malevolence is well protected, now. It lies buried in the heart of the mountains, within a maze of warrens. To strike at it now would be futile. If it can be drawn out, however, then perhaps it can be destroyed. But to do so you must be cunning and stubborn in your defense, so that only the node could break you. It may well cost you your life, and destroy the Valley, but it may ultimately save your people from enslavement and death.

You want me? To stand against that?

With every fiber of your strength, he acknowledged.

I was hoping for a little more in the way of guidance than that, I admitted. *Aronin, I'm just a pretty fair Spellmonger and a mediocre warmage. I have the respect of a few villagers and the friendship of one pipsqueak Wilderlord at my disposal, not armies and professional warmagi. How can I possibly make a stand here?*

You do not give yourself enough credit, Spellmonger. Yes, you are young, even by the count of your own race, but you are vital. *Yes, you have few forces to set against our cousins, but you shall soon have more – this I have foreseen. You are trained in the arts of war and magic, and you have little experience. But you shall strive, Spellmonger, with our help and the help of others.*

Fate puts us where we are needed – even your crude, ignorant race can see that. That is why we help you thus. I cannot foresee if you will be successful, but I know that you will try, *and, if nothing else, lend hope and inspiration to your folk. If you can last long enough to draw out this abomination, then other forces may be brought to bear on it.*

That sounds good in theory, Aronin, but where is this help you are speaking of? Am I just supposed to pull an army out of my ass? Am I going to find the Staff of the Archmage under my bed? Will I be able to pick up Defender-of-Empires at a junk shop?

I was starting to get a little peeved. I came up here looking for advice. What I got was a tale of woe and doom and a lecture on public service and a lot of mystical shit about me saving the Duchies. The Aronin had all but said defending the Valley was pointless, but he was encouraging me to do so in the face of overwhelming odds.

Sure, I'd give it my best shot, if I absolutely had to, but after seeing the forces arrayed against us I would just as soon go become a swineherd on the other side of Upper Vore and leave all this behind me. I said as much.

I braced myself for his fury – *no one* speaks to an Alka Alon that way, much less the King of the local grove. Not without consequences.

Luckily, the Aronin had a sense of humor. He smiled pleasantly, and suddenly we were back in that untidy little room. "The assistance I spoke of is here. First, let me see the stone you took from the shaman."

I handed it over with no witty sarcasm. He took it in his hands, closed his eyes, and began rubbing it back and forth between his palms.

"It is part of much larger piece, a piece that commands it. It was foolish of you to attempt to use it – the one which controls the larger piece instantly knew your thoughts by doing so, had he been paying any attention to it. Here in Amadia it is shielded from even that connection, and I can easily break it."

He sat there, rubbing it for a while, and all around him powerful forces came into play. It was intimidating. It was an awful lot like standing right next to someone who was performing an elegant and graceful dance while you stare down at the hobnailed boots on your two left feet. He was directing titanic forces without breaking a sweat, and it was making me feel pretty inadequate.

Finally, he stopped, and presented the stone back to me, glowing in the center of his palm.

It was no longer rough and uneven, but had become a smooth sphere, a marble of vivid, translucent green almost an inch wide. I reached out my hand to take it when he grasped my hand again, pressing the marble of pure power between our two palms. I felt a surge of energy, like a lightning strike, and suddenly . . .

Suddenly I saw *everything* clearly. I had access to more power now than I ever had. The Archmagi of old couldn't have wielded forces this great, I felt. My every thought was magnified tenfold, a hundredfold, and compared to before, when I had to struggle to build up enough power to fill one measly *kaba*, now I could fill a hundred and not tire.

But I also began to understand just what we were up against. From our cloud-top view I had seen *hundreds* of shaman with these things, and from what the Aronin had said, they were all connected, like some giant *apis* array, to the severely potent central force deep in the heart of the Minden Range.

Trygg and Briga help us all.

"You are now connected with the stone at your very core, at your *shen*," he said, using the old Imperial term for your magical soul, the center of your being, your consciousness. "This stone will now aid you, for not only have I introduced you to its power, but I have left my own mark upon it. Should this stone be placed in contact with one of the lesser stones you face for a time, then at your will the connection to the center will be broken, and the stone will henceforth be yours to command."

"It will?" I asked, dumbfounded.

"Use this gift wisely, Spellmonger, for it is not given lightly. You also may communicate with me through this stone, but at great need only. The rest is up to you."

"Uh . . . my thanks, my lord? It is not an army, but it will be a good place to start." I admit it; I was drunk with power. How could any gurvani shaman stand against me?

"Lastly, you spoke of mighty weapons. While I will not lend you my spear, for that is not our way, should you come the halls of the Karshak Alon, show them this and they will aid you as they might."

"Right. The *Karshak*," I said, dazedly staring at the little globe that shone in my palm.

This, too, seemed to amuse the Aronin. "The feeling you have will pass in a few days, Spellmonger, and you will soon grow used to wielding this kind of power. I have searched your *shen*, and I believe that your body and your spirit are strong enough to bear this burden."

Maybe he was right. It seemed foolish and vain to even contemplate such a thing, but maybe I was just the kind of crazy humani mage who could orchestrate a resistance to this gathering storm.

I finally looked up at the Aronin and feebly tried to grin. "I shall do my best, Aronin. For my people, and for myself. Even should I fall, they *will* remember the name of Minalan the Spellmonger to frighten their pups with at night!"

"Our cousins are nocturnal," Aronin reminded me, gently.

"Oh. Yeah."

Chapter Five

Preparing For Siege

"Beware of entanglements with the aristocracy; for though they seem to promise honor and riches, the nobility rarely holds our profession in esteem, save when it is convenient for them to do so. For they serve their own interests first and oft stand on their honor or cleave to their nobility to rationalize their poor behavior. A wise mage will seek a dozen poor clients rather than one wealthy patron."

- *Master Arcus of Masten*

Three days later found me back in the southern part of the Valley, preparing for another long journey.

We had left the Tree Folk in the evening, after being feted in grand style. Zagor renewed a number of acquaintances among them, and Tyndal's eyes nearly fell out of his head as he witnessed wonders and beauties that he had never imagined in his previous life as a stable boy. I think the lad would have stayed there forever, just to be close to Ameras. I can't say I blame him.

We stopped in Malin only long enough to warn the townsfolk to take whatever they could to the stronghold at Brandmount. There had been sightings of gurvani among the ridges, but no attacks this far north yet. They were wary, but the prospect of raids was enough to spur them into action, particularly with Zagor's respected opinion added to mine. Then we rode back by the old castle – a square, squat tower surrounded by a thick stone wall that seemed woefully inadequate, suddenly – to drop off Zagor and inspect the preparations for siege.

The place was already abuzz with activity, as cows, horses and chickens were loaded into the inner recesses of that moldy pile of rocks and militias drilled inside the barbican. Don't mistake me – Brandmount was a perfectly adequate fortification, and kept in good repair by Sir Remalan, the vigorous younger brother of Sire Koucey, but next to the recently completed Boval Castle it seemed paltry. Hopefully it would be enough to withstand the coming assaults. From what the Aronin had shown me, I had my doubts.

It was designed to protect the peoples of Malin, Brandmount village, the hamlet of Roby, and the outlying farmsteads, and I was pleased to see the castellan in charge of provisions had not been neglectful of stocking up on staples during peacetime, as they often did. I left Zagor in charge of the magical protection, and he promised he would draft the Boliek sisters (two self-taught witches in Roby) to assist.

From Brandmount we rode back through Hymas town and witnessed a similar buzz on a larger scale. Garkesku's shop was closed already, I noticed, as was the Lakeside Inn. Commerce had been suspended and the cheeses normally stored for sale to merchants were being loaded into wains to be taken to the castle, as per Sir Cei's orders.

We stopped in town only long enough to beg supper from a bakery (one of the clients I stole from Garkesku, actually. I used the Secret Handshake of the baker's guild to do it, too. Hooray for artisanal nepotism). They were feverishly turning much of their stored flour into hardtack for the castle, so I didn't bother them much, but with my newfound powers I couldn't resist trying out a small spell that would conserve heat in the ovens, thereby using up much less precious firewood.

We reached Boval Castle by nightfall, and I could see that Sire Koucey was doing his damnedest to prepare. There were sentries crowded into the towers and along the battlements, and the inner bailey was, if anything, more crowded than Brandmount had been, even though it was almost three times as big. Sir Cei was busily directing each new arrival to their designated spot, storehouse, or post. We turned our horses over to the stable boy (a friend of Tyndal's, I found out) and sought out the Sire, himself.

We found him in the donjon, the massive square central tower and place of last defense, in a chamber that served as a combination office and conference room. We could tell where he was without asking – the constant stream of messengers indicated his whereabouts. We waited patiently in line at the door until he saw us. He smiled, waved away the others, and invited us in.

"So, Master Minalan, how fared your quest for knowledge?" he asked, smiling through a tired face.

"As well as I could have expected, lord, and perhaps even better. I now know when the foe will attack, and I know their approximate numbers."

"Then you were a success, indeed! Do we have anything to fear in the next three days? That's the soonest that I'll be able to have the peoples of Minden's Hall and Hymas safely within my walls, and it will take another two days for those in Winakur to join us. I've sent knights to escort them, lest they be attacked on the road."

"You should have no more direct attacks for at least a fortnight, milord, and likely not until the new moon, three weeks hence," I answered confidently. "Alas, that does not stop their skirmishers from harassing our folk as they struggle to bring their worldly goods into safety. Their scouts spy on us even now, concealed among the peaks and ridges. We broke up one such attack on our way north."

"There's nothing to be done about it, I'm afraid," Koucey sighed. "I've increased patrols along the roads and given what escorts I can spare. But three weeks will give us adequate time to lay in a larger supply of stores. As it is," he said, referring to a slate on the table in front of him, "the Castellan reports that we have enough wheat, hardtack, barley, dried fishes, cheeses, beans, salt pork, dried beef and desiccated vegetables to keep everyone in the castle fed at full rations for five months. In addition, the herds that are being brought in could feed us for an additional three months. The cisterns are full and the well is deep. That is where we stand now – with this extra time, we might be able to stretch it for ten months or longer."

"Excellent, sire," I said, knowing we couldn't hope to last that long. I didn't mention that, yet – no need to plunge the man into despair when he was feeling so optimistic. "And how are we disposed for fighting men?"

Sire Koucey sighed more heavily. "Alas, we are not a war-like country, Master Spellmonger. I have eighteen mounted knights, another dozen squires, and maybe two-dozen sergeants and a hundred trained men-at-arms. With the militias called in, we can arm another six or seven hundred, mostly bowmen. Eight hundred fighting men to man the walls, and every one of them precious."

I almost didn't have the heart to tell him about the number of gurvani arrayed against him. I tried to break the news as gently as possible, pointing out that his gentlemen were the match for any three goblins.

But he was no fool. He sagged when I hinted at the numbers he was facing – that *we* were facing. Looking grim and worn, he stood defiantly and declared, "They will take this valley only after standing over my bleached bones and a mighty heap of their own corpses!"

"Well spoken, Sire!" I said with an enthusiasm I didn't feel. "But we are not lost yet. Apart from the intelligence which I gathered from the Tree Folk, they lent me magical aid which might turn the tide of battle." I didn't elaborate because the technical details would be lost on this warrior, as well as raising his hopes falsely. Never tell a client too much information. It makes them uneasy. "But we need more men to man the towers, that much is true. What of aid from Gans and Presan? Or the Count? Has word been sent to Duke Lenguin?"

"Word reached both baronies only yesterday, if our messengers were not taken on the road. I have heard no response, yet, and I fear that both Barons will be more concerned with protecting their own domains than sending assistance to us, a poor mountain relation. That is what I would do, after all. And while I dispatched a messenger to the summer capital, he has already departed from Vorone for the winter. He will not arrive at the southern capital for at least another week. Mayhap a messenger could overtake him on the road, but if Trygg's grace be with us it would be months before any help could be sent."

If then – the Alshari dukes had a history of ignoring the Wilderlands portion of their realm unless they needed more timber and iron for their precious fleets. We could not wait that long. We needed more fighting men, and we needed them now.

"Then we must secure more warriors another way. My lord, as you know I am recently discharged from the Ducal army of Castal. There and after, in my travels as a warmage, I became acquainted with a number of mercenaries. While I realize that you are not a wealthy man, compared to some lords, still there must be enough in the treasuries to hire a few score warriors to buttress your defense. Am I mistaken?"

"Nay, save that you perhaps underestimate the treasury my House has accumulated. When the first Lord Brandmount came to this valley he captured much in the way of treasure from the goblins. It was still substantial, even after we paid our lawful tribute to our liege. Have you not wondered why a land this small could afford a castle fit for a Barony, much less two lesser fortresses? We did not do so by selling Bovali cheese, I assure you. Yes, mercenaries would be most welcome. But the closest city in which you might be able to hire them is Tudry, some five-day's journey by horse. Deploying them would take much longer, unless your magic can speed them along."

"My lord, I propose just that: I shall travel to Tudry and arrange for as many companies as I can to come to our aid, and spread the word that you are hiring more. Many of the Free Companies lack for work since the end of the Farisian Campaign, and they despise ordinary garrison duty. It should not take much to convince them to ride here for the promise of good pay and a worthy foe."

I wouldn't, of course, elaborate on just exactly what odds they faced; many had fought goblins before, and would see the duty as pleasant exercise, not a serious fight for their lives. Fools.

Koucey shrugged. "I have no objection, Spellmonger, provided that you oversee the defensive magic preparations your, ah, *colleague*, Garkesku, has been working on before you leave. You will find him in the West Tower, which I have assigned my magical corps." He said it with a thin smile that let me know what he thought of the other Spellmonger in his realm.

"As you wish, Sire," I said, returning the grin with a slight bow. I took my leave then, as a long line of messengers and soldiers on errands had piled up behind me.

*   *   *

My trip downriver to the Academy was an exciting, grand adventure that took two weeks. In retrospect it was no different than any other river trip I've taken, but when you are thirteen, have never been more than five miles from your birthplace, and journeying on your own such a trip is an adventure by default.

I saw stevedores and polemen, merchants and river pirates, and met strange, exotic people who were not all that different from the folk in Talry. I did see a village of Riverfolk – my first glimpse of non-humans – but we passed by their little settlement without stopping. One of the crew taught me the finer points of dice and another introduced me to

Cormeeran wine. I proved lucky enough at the former to subsidize the latter without dipping overmuch into my purse.

I arrived at the river port near Inarion a much more worldly man, ready to meet my schoolmates and embark on my education. When I first arrived at the Academy (a mix of High Imperial and Post-Conquest Imperial Revival architecture, I learned later), I could see the beautiful spires and hulking mass of the central building over the tops of the townhouses and shops by the gate, and I was suitably awed.

I was much less awed by it a week later. The Academy, pretty from a distance, was a *dump.*

Six hundred years old and poorly maintained, the spires around the top were roped off due to severe structural failure – apparently the spells originally used to allow their graceful slopes to defy gravity were long lost, and not much effort had been put into rediscovering them.

Most of the buildings originated in Imperial times, which means that they were sadly neglected and in need of repair. The main hall on the first floor was built to impress, and its shabby opulence remained stunning despite the years. The classrooms on the second and third floors of the building were less impressive, but completely functional, while the journeyman labs on the fourth floor were almost as dangerous as the decorative spires. The Masters, of course, had much better facilities, usually in outbuildings built more recently.

Inarion Academy was founded almost a thousand years ago as an adjunct campus to the more prestigious Gorrinal Academy in Cormeer. Gorrinal was destroyed in the Mage Wars, before the Late Magocracy was established, so Inarion is technically the second oldest Academy in the Duchies, after Alar, and the most prestigious in the western Duchies.

It sits within its own section of the city wall and has been defended four times in its history. Inarion Academy is a little city within itself, as self-contained as any castle, complete with its own attendant village known as Towertown. The Academy holds about three hundred students at any one time, with another hundred visiting scholars or guest instructors from other Academies or magical firms.

Almost every student there was of noble birth. I don't think I really appreciated that until I showed up at the Registrar's office, barefoot and dirty from the trip, and was told with a scowl that the kitchens were in the rear. I tried to explain myself three times and finally had to produce my letter of acceptance before I was firmly escorted to my quarters by the registrar herself.

I was assigned to the South Tower, where, I found out later, all the low-status students were housed – children of merchants, burghers, country knights, and successful farmers. Plus a few students from the petty nobility, too poor to blend well with the Imperials in the West Tower or the High Lords in the North Tower were housed there. The East Tower was the faculty quarters. We were the social dregs, which made the tyranny of the few noble-born students in South that much harder to bear.

Of course the South Tower was the least maintained. It was rumored that the whole purpose of putting us in such decrepit quarters was to encourage us to learn those spells that contributed to comfort, and I can't say with certainty that the rumors were untrue. I know I studied my ass off to learn how to do heating and anti-vermin spells and the like.

To be fair we weren't treated that much differently than the other students. The instructors didn't really care who your sire was; they cared how well you did in their courses. But our clothes were never as splendid as the Narasi lords or as silken as the Imperial students, and we had no servants of our own. The entire Tower, from First Form to Fifth, depended on the good graces of a few old groundskeepers, three wrinkled maids and a single cook. We ended up doing a lot of the cleaning and chores ourselves.

I was placed in a third floor suite with Dextadot (Dex, to his pals) of Harring, the sandy-haired son of a poor knight, and Timion of Lista, the son of a wheat merchant. For the next four years they would be my best friends and confidants. Both had similar initiatory experiences as I, and both had been sent to the same extra "remedial" tutors as I was. These were mostly lessons in reading, writing, elementary math, natural history, and basic rules of etiquette, i.e. how to behave like nobility and not like peasants. Since the Bans required those with Talent to give up their noble titles and legacies, we were all legally commoners, but that did little to protect us actual commoners.

(A few of the noble boys started to literally lord it over us about these classes, but my mates and I took this guff for only a few weeks before we got fed up with it and staged a "peasant revolt" of sorts, which turned quickly into a spectacular brawl. After that we had their respect, if not their friendship, and were allowed to proceed with our studies in relative peace.)

Magi, at least according to the Academy, were to be accorded the respect of minor nobility regardless of birth status or station. The nobles and the Ducal houses, I have noticed, don't always adhere to this rule. Regardless, as most of our clients would eventually be nobles of one stripe or another, our professional survival depended upon knowing the rules of courts of all sizes.

These extra tutoring sessions were in addition to the regular courses. They started in heavy with Magical Theory and Symbolic Systems, and before I had been there a week my head buzzed nightly with the arcane symbols of my new craft. That didn't leave much time for trouble, much to my dismay.

When I wasn't slogging through some dusty text in my loft, I was in the kitchen, helping the cook with the baking for an extra three coppers a week. All of the boys were required to help with the maintenance, cleaning, and upkeep of the Academy grounds (which provoked much grumbling from the former nobility) but a few of us were good enough at what we did to get paid for it. The first time I made rolls for the cook, she had me put on the pay ledger. Dad was proud of that.

Those first few years at the Academy are a long, pleasant, hazy smear in my life, although at the time they seemed almost hellish. I attacked my lessons with glee, pushing ahead beyond my classmates at every opportunity. I had a strong Talent and a quick mind, and I mastered the basic lessons easily. I also demonstrated a facility for the obtuse subject of Thaumaturgy, the science of magic, and scored top marks in my class. This got me enough attention from the journeymen who instructed us that I was selected for special tutoring that first year.

Most importantly, to my eyes, I was introduced to the magic of the written word, and then turned loose on some of the best libraries in the Duchy. I discovered that I loved reading, after mastering the art, and spent as much time as I could in the Academy's dusty libraries..I learned to master my mind and force the elements of nature to do my bidding. I was guided down the intellectual path trod by generations of students before me, back to Lost Perwyn and the first Archmage. History, poetry, and thaumaturgic texts were havens for me.

I actually went home between my third and fourth years for my youngest sister's wedding. Urah had finally talked a stuttering one of Dad's apprentices into marrying her, and I wanted to surprise everyone. I had made a little money doing spells on the side (completely against Academy rules, but those rules were often overlooked) and I managed to secure transport on a river barge hauling iron ingots up the Burine to Talry and points north.

It was a complete surprise to my family, of course – my Dad didn't even recognize me when I first came into the shop – and my reunion celebration nearly overshadowed my sister's nuptials to the point that I earned several evil stares from her – this was *her* celebration. It was my first time meeting my nieces and nephews, though, and I wasn't about to fade into the woodwork until I had a chance to *ooh* and *ahh* over them.

I saw several of my childhood friends, most of whom were farming or running their fathers' shops. I spent some important time with my very proud parents who wanted to hear about everything I was doing at the mysterious Academy.

After the wedding I caught up with Master Tilo, who looked even more wizened than the last time I saw him. He was almost as proud of me as my parents, and he even allowed me to show him a thing or two in the way of technical advances on some minor spells. He had another apprentice, now, and I was put in the uncomfortable position of being held up as a good example of a good mage. I wasn't used to being a role model (I still am not) but the acknowledgement was good for my ego.

But something troubled me that entire trip. I just didn't fit in Talry anymore.

My sisters' husbands had the shop well in hand, Dad rarely worked at anything but overseeing the most demanding of bakes, and Mama was deeply involved in her grandchildren. I was an exciting curiosity to them, but not much more. Oh, they still loved me, without a doubt. But I was a stranger to them after just a few years. I suppose that after spending all that time being homesick at the Academy that I expected the clouds to part and Trygg and Briga and a host of gods to welcome me back home in triumph.

Instead I stood in the bakery and tried not to get in the way while my family worked.

In an effort to console my self-pity, I went by Hedi's cottage (remember the Miller's daughter?) to visit. Her husband, a prosperous farmer, was in the fields of course, but she introduced me to her two-year-old, and let me pat the tummy in which her second kid was growing.

It was the same old Hedi, though, wild at heart. With a wicked gleam in her eye she pointed out that, as there was no way she could get pregnant at the moment that there was no obstacle to us reliving old times.

I was in a weakened condition and didn't have the courage to turn her down. We did it on her kitchen table while the baby was asleep. While she was just as enthusiastic than I remember (and far more skilled, marriage had been good to her) I knew that this was merely an illicit thrill for her, not a heart-felt homecoming. I left her home feeling even more out of place than when I arrived. I had to face a very depressing reality.

Talry was just not really my home any longer.

*   *   *

Garkesku had, indeed, taken over the second (and most comfortable) level of the West Tower for his own use and that of his apprentices. He had three, all touched by Talent and somewhat knowledgeable in the theories of magic under his tutelage, but none of them the equal of Tyndal. The boy had learned more in six months of study with me than they had learned after years with Garky. Unfortunately, they tended to make up for their lack of skill by parroting their master's arrogant attitudes and mannerisms, which made the whole second floor unbearably unpleasant.

Garkesku had managed to move a fair amount of his equipment and much of his overstuffed furnishings into the quarters from his shop. The West Tower was inside the inner barbican and attached to the main donjon by a series of buttresses and bridges, which made it unnecessary for defense until the outer bailey had been penetrated. It was as draughty and cold as any other place in the castle, but I noticed as I climbed the stairs that Garkesku had an insulation spell going to supplement the brazier burning in the center of the room. That could only mean that my floor, above, which should normally benefit from the heat from his fire, would be ice cold.

The two older apprentices were unpacking crates moved from Hymas Town and looked at me with barely-concealed sneers when I walked in. Garkesku himself was overseeing the third young apprentice, who was unpacking his master's bedding. He still wore that colorful robe and ridiculous looking hat.

"Master Garkesku, it is good to see you settling in," I said, a friendly tone in my voice that belied the expression in my eyes. The bastard was enjoying more comfort in here than the peasants who camped in the outer bailey could dream of.

Garkesku looked up, his eyes growing wide when he saw who it was. Then they narrowed.

"Master Minalan, good of you to join us. I took the liberty of choosing these accommodations in your absence, due to the larger size of my party. I trust you and your apprentice will have no difficulty with the next level up? I figured that a man of action such as yourself would prefer a vantage point where he could oversee the field."

It was a thinly veiled challenge, meaning *I dare you to try to move me out of my quarters!* Had I more time and less patience I might have tried. But he was right: the third level would be better for me and Tyndal, as I would have access to the uppermost battlement and therefore would be able to see farther at my convenience.

It also made for a better position for launching defensive spells. Magic or artillery, high ground is usually more defensible. I still remember how effective such a position had been when Orril Pratt had defended the Citadel of Farise.

"Absolutely correct, Master Garkesku. In fact I will have my apprentice bring my things up tonight. But I wanted to steal a moment of your time to discuss the overall defense strategy."

He gave me a sour look, but motioned me over to a table he had fetched from his reception area. Cleared of the useless clutter it seemed fairly serviceable, and I was surprised to see an accurate map of the castle and the surrounding lands already laid out upon it.

At various places Garkesku had inscribed symbols for spells he was apparently planning. I glanced at them and was mildly impressed. It was by no means complete, but it did have some clever essentials at more or less the right place. Just because I didn't like the man didn't mean he was incompetent.

We went over what he had done, and I suggested a few more – things like preservative spells on the stores and cisterns, strength runes on the gates and portcullis, the sort of thing he could get his apprentices to do without difficulty. We managed to complete the conference without arguing, which I counted as a minor victory, and then I told him about my next trip. He was not happy.

"So you wish *me* to cast all of these spells on my own, then?" he asked, sarcastically.

"None of them seem too difficult, between you and your apprentices. If you aren't up to the task, however, I can always send for Zagor or--"

"I am *quite* capable, thank you," he said, haughtily. "And if it makes the difference between victory and defeat, I will do all I can."

"I'm sure you will," I said, smugly, and went upstairs to inspect our new quarters.

Garkesku had done me no favors in selecting the lower chamber. The third level, a three-story section of tower with wooden floors and lofts, was perforated with arrow slits. While there were wooden shutters on them, the sheer number made the entire chamber as draughty as a bell tower.

Still, it was more than enough room for Tyndal and me to work in, and I knew I could rely on the boy's ingenuity to make it as comfortable as possible in my absence.

I made a few mental notes of items I would want from the shop in Minden's Hall, and others that would have to be purchased in Tudry. Then I went to the roof. Garkesku was correct – from the peak I could see all around the castle, save the spot just beyond the East Tower, which was the same height as the one I was on.

I had no problems with the quality of the fortification – indeed, it was among the better ones I had seen on my travels through the Wilderlands, where rough towers of ashlar and rough stone walls were the rule. Most Baronial castles in the Riverlands were ancient things, whose stones were held together by two-hundred year old mortar; or they were the remains of Imperial buildings that had been added to, not really designed for defense but pressed into service by need and kept because of the expense of building proper defenses.

Boval Castle, though, was almost brand-new, compared to the castles of Castal and Alshar that I was familiar with. Begun by Koucey's father at the start of his reign, the fortress had taken twenty years to complete, and had employed hundreds of local laborers and dozens of imported masons, carpenters, and other craftsmen.

Cut out of native gray basalt from the quarry north of Minden's Hall, the walls and towers of the structure were well designed and resolutely strong. It was also roomy, about three times as large as the population of the Valley warranted. House Brandmount was foresightful enough to know that their lands would prosper. They built large in anticipation of a larger population.

Or a goblin invasion.

The entire castle was surrounded by a twenty-foot wide ditch with a berm of earth ten feet tall on the inside edge. A twelve-foot thick stone barbican, surmounted by an impressive battlement, protected the castle should the ditch be overrun. The outer wall was punctuated with nine small round towers spaced fifty feet apart or so, as well as a large stone gatehouse to the north and a double-sized round tower at the southern point. This last feature was a miniature fortress in its own right, including the siege engines ensconced in the top of the structure and the separate well and stores at its base.

The outer bailey was separated from the inner by a curtain wall six feet thick. This made the outer bailey an ideal killing zone, should the gate be overwhelmed. Until that happened, it was also the main residence of the peasantry who took refuge here -- and their herds. A make-shift corral had been set up near the stables in the outer bailey. It was filled to overflowing with pigs, sheep, and a truly astounding number of cattle.

The roadway between the main gate and the inner bailey had been kept clear, as had a path to the stables, but every other square foot of space was being used for tents, wagons, dogs, cats, livestock, laundry, children, laundry, and the like. The only other clear space was one in the center of the largest grouping of shelters on the larger, eastern side of the bailey, where refugees from Hymas had gathered. The central clearing was being used as a public gathering space and drill field for the militia.

It was interesting; not only had Hymas congregated together, the folk of Minden's Hall had clumped near the main gate on the western side, and the few people who had made the trip from the tiny hamlet of Winakur had created a kind of village-in-exile along the curtain wall near the stables.

The inner bailey was less crowded, as it was reserved for exclusively military personnel. That made it far, far more roomy than I would have preferred. In a siege, wisdom said, one should have one fighting man for every five civilian non-combatants. Despite Sire Koucey's estimates, I could see the numbers for myself, from my tower perch.

With the militias and the few professional soldiers, there were about two hundred men-at-arms (and many that were not that well-armed) available in the inner bailey, another hundred or so in the keep, and yet another hundred camped in the towers around the wall. Around fifty had packed themselves into the gatehouses and other outbuildings. Even if one considered another hundred out on escort duty and errands, that was several hundred shy of the eight hundred Koucey had estimated.

That wasn't good. It took a minimum of forty men to patrol the walls and man the various essential fortifications, but that was far from ideal. Right now the civilians outnumbered the fighters eight to one, not counting the children. There was a recruiting effort going on among the people, and about twenty men a day were pressed into service, but it was clear that there were limits to what these peace-loving farmers could do. We would need several hundred more trained and equipped men if we wanted to hold out for more than a few months.

Our tower was one of two that straddled the wall between the baileys. They were largely empty of people (except for us) and used for storage, but they could accommodate a few hundred more. The first level of each was two stories high, stacked with firewood, cowhides, arrows, bolts of homespun cloth, sack after sack of wheat and barrel upon barrel of salted meat and other consumables.

And cheese. Lots of cheese.

Each was topped by a small wooden observation tower. Perfect for us wizardly types who enjoyed a view. I felt safe here, and it was hard to imagine anyone able to break through that much stone. But the tall stone towers and thick walls were only as strong as the men who defended them, and in that we were sorely lacking.

In the center of the inner bailey was the donjon, a huge five-story square block of stone that was the castle's ultimate defense. Should all else fail, the donjon could hold more than five hundred for quite a while, even against superior forces. Attached to the donjon in the south were two more blocky towers that rose above the rest of the castle and provided an excellent vantage point for directing forces in a siege. That was where Sire Koucey would be, when the time came.

It was secure, for the moment, or the closest thing to security that we could hope for under the circumstances. I liked the vantage point up there. It would do, I decided – I could peg a goblin outside of the walls from here with bow or warstaff.

A real magical corps could have held this castle from nearly any force, indefinitely. But we were poorer in arcane measures than we were in armored knights. Even with my shiny new stone as a reservoir, it was just Garkesku, me and our half-trained apprentices against around *a hundred thousand savage goblins*, as well as potentially hundreds of shamans with their own witchstones.

As sieges went, it was starting to sound like the beginning of a bad joke.

But that problem, at least, I might be able to do something about. I knew people who owed me favors, or wouldn't mind me owing them favors. And I now had a currency beyond mere gold to offer. That evening I decided to try to gain some unexpected allies by magic.

I made myself comfortable in the center of the roof, seated on a cask of arrows, and began a complex spell that I had just had not the strength to attempt before.

It was time to talk to Pentandra.

*   *   *

My fourth and fifth years at the Academy flew by, and every year my techniques and understanding of the magical arts improved. By the time I was ready to produce journeyman-level work, I felt as cocky and adept as any old Archmage. Many of my peers were already opting to take the exams and go into private practice, but I was enjoying the academic environment too much to try to make a living with what I'd learned so far. I submitted to the Board a spell that I had worked on for months, and after rigorous review it was accepted. They allowed me to partake in the Journeyman Trials.

In a way, they prepare you for the Trials from the day you arrive at the Academy. Every scrap of magical lore you have ever learned comes to the fore, as you face one master after another and they direct you to answer questions or perform spells. The Trials last a week, and are held in a specially built building at the very edge of the Academy's grounds.

It was grueling. Only six out of eighteen of us made it through the first time. When my name was called as one of the successful candidates, I was amazed. I'd thought I'd screwed it up royally.

We successful new journeymen (or "senior students", since we weren't technically apprenticed) were given two weeks off to celebrate while our less-adept peers gave it a second go. I spent my two weeks either stalking through the booksellers in town looking for obscure texts or chasing girls around the taverns of Towertown. I also thought a lot about the big decision I had to make.

In the sixth year at the Academy if we elected to continue with our education, instead of seeking work elsewhere, we were asked to choose a particular field of study in which to specialize for the last two years before Grand Practicum and final Master examinations. I chose Magical Theory and Thaumaturgy because I was interested in it and good at it – certainly not because there was a high commercial demand for such specialties. It was pure poverty-laden academics. But it was fascinating.

Master Theronial was an astute instructor with an eye for a good scholar. He took me as one of his assistants and guided my independent studies into the wheels and gears of how magic works. It was through him, then, that I met Lady Pentandra Anna Benurviel, a pretty Imperial girl from Remere.

Now, I had been anything but celibate at the Academy. Towertown was full of young maidens anxious to become the wives of prosperous court magi, and even the ugliest students in the tower could enjoy the favors of young ladies without too much difficulty, as long as the lighting was dim and they could tell a lie with a straight face.

As for myself, my liaisons in Inarion began when the tower's baker sent me with a wagon to the local mill, where I met Misha the miller's daughter (what is it with bakers' sons and millers' daughters, anyway?) and began a long career as a lady's man. Over the years I'd accumulated quite a following among the town girls, never pledging my heart but frequently hinting that I might. Once or twice a girl would try to get me to commit to marriage, but I'd managed to avoid the issue without causing too many broken hearts. As a future professional it just didn't seem wise to give away my commitment – and my heart – to just anyone.

I might have pledged it to Penny.

Pentandra Anna Benurviel was the third daughter of an Imperial family that traced its lineage to several noteworthy Archmagi, and (allegedly) even back to some important people from Lost Perwyn, before the Inundation.

While they were now a shadow of their former glory, House Benurviel still ran several highly prestigious and profitable family magical practices in Remere. Penny had started at Alar Academy, but had come to Inarion to pursue her esoteric studies with Master Theronial.

While she appeared to be the very picture of the demure and reserved Imperial noblewoman, she was, in fact, a kind of demented magical prodigy in an obscure field of thaumaturgy.

In short, Penny studied Sex Magic. *And she was looking for a partner.*

Sex Magic ("eromantics", if you wanted to be technical) was discussed mostly in theoretical terms at the Academy. The faculty wisely broached the subject just often enough to pique the interests of the students, but rarely went into detail until the last few years of study. Even then such a lurid topic was just too much for most of the sage fellows to do more than discuss in the vaguest terms.

Once a popular element in Imperial magic before the Conquest, sex magic has fallen out of favor in the last few hundred years, owing in large part to the prurient attitudes of my barbarian Narasi ancestors.

Imperial families, I've noticed, don't bat an eyelash at things that would make the average Narasi peasant (myself excluded) die of embarrassment. During the height of the Empire the study of the magical aspects of sex (or the sexual aspects of magic, depending upon which school of thought you adhered to) was a highly respected if obscure field of study.

When King Kamaklavan the Great smashed the Magocracy into pieces, sex magic, as it once was practiced, was dealt a profound blow. Under the repressive regimes of the early Dukes, magic was suppressed as an Imperial tool of oppression and decadence. Many of the advanced techniques in eromantics were lost altogether, and the practice went largely underground. Designed to harness the power implicit in the physical practice of sex for arcane purposes, as well as act as a medium for spellwork itself, the simple spells of the Narasi wizards rarely needed that kind of sophisticated approach. And the sexually conservative nature of the Narasi nobility considered the field so scandalous that patronage of eromantics was all but stopped.

Penny was doing her level best to single-handedly revive this lost art.

Quite early in our acquaintance she decided that I had the intelligence, the talent, and the stamina to aid her in her quest. And she didn't often take no for an answer. Our relationship began when I was assigned to her the first day she was there, fetching books from the various libraries she wanted and giving her a tour of our facility.

She seemed unimpressed with Inarion's roughhewn stone, coming as she did from the baked brick splendor of Alar Academy in Wenshar, but she was interested in everything else around her. And everyone. I thought she was just curious – which she was – but the truth was that she was already looking for partners with whom to conduct her research.

She thought I was cute, intelligence, and had stamina. Before I knew what was happening, we were studying and sleeping together (though little actual sleep occurred.) I was already a decent thaumaturge, but with Pentandra's help I accidentally learned more about sex magic than most wizards ever do. That was in large part to Pentandra's native fascination with the art. And her dedication to her craft.

I consider myself lusty, but Penny's capacities were *endless*. Luckily Master Theronial was eager to see the results of Penny's research and was liberal with both resources and time for experimentation.

I never quite knew what to make of Penny. Now, I'm not the handsomest man in the world (or even the barony, if you want to be particular) but neither am I particularly ugly. Puberty had been kind to me, giving me a healthy body which had grown stronger lugging around flour sacks and firewood, a full shock of light brown hair, and two gleaming blue eyes.

Still, that didn't get me much natural credit in Penny's eyes. I was a commoner, I was (relatively) poor, and I possessed only the rudiments of court manners. There were love-hungry former noblemen at the Academy who would have lined up for a chance just to dance with Penny, much less sleep with her but she chose *me*. Trust me, she had other offers aplenty.

Why did she select me? Trygg alone knows. I asked Penny often enough. She usually just said that she really, *really* liked baked goods and left it at that.

I've heard worse rationalizations for a sexual relationship.

We studied together regularly, almost daily, and I quickly learned to respect her intellect and dedication. I appreciated her vast knowledge of magical minutia and thaumaturgy, too. She had cut her teeth on stuff it had taken me years to learn – in her family, the intricacies of spellcraft were bandied about the dinner table the way my family would talk flour and sugar. We could and did talk for hours about obscure topics of mutual interest, or about nothing at all, and count the day well-spent.

She was certainly attractive enough – classical Imperial features, down to the gray eyes and the long straight black hair. She seemed awfully fond of me, I knew, and I of her, but for two years I wrestled with my feelings for her.

In love, in lust, out of love, out of lust, I was never quite certain what our relationship held. Penny seemed to revel in my confusion, claiming that the added emotional tension created a more powerful magical energy field, but she would never commit herself to anything beyond experiment, study, and the occasional good time. Nor would she allow herself to become emotionally entangled with me.

At this point I'm sure you're figuring that I fell *madly* in love with her and followed her to the ends of the earth, with assorted run-ins with her evil relatives and equally desperate suitors dogging my heel. You would be mistaken. Despite our intense level of physical intimacy, we never really became more than just good friends and colleagues – though I would have been hard pressed to say no to such a woman if she'd wanted a more permanent arrangement.

She came from one of the great magical families of Remere, and they do *not* sully their family blood lines with the mongrel barbarians who had conquered them, no matter *how* Talented we might be.

I didn't take it personally; it is hard to argue with their generations of success at producing strong magi. Besides, Mama and Dad would probably not have approved of me marrying a girl "from foreign parts" , even if she was rich (which she was, compared to my family).

I met her "evil" relatives on a two-month trip to her family's estates, and despite her dire warnings they were all really quite decent. Pentandra's father, Orisorio, indicated his respect for any hard-working mage, even to the point of letting me know a friend of Pentandra's could always get a job in Remere . . . but also making it *quite* clear that any more formal relationship between his youngest daughter and a barbarian Narasi commoner was out of the question.

He even knew what we were doing upstairs. *He didn't mind.* I found out later that Penny had been experimenting on the servants since she was fifteen. He respected her work and didn't judge. It took me a week to get over the idea that he wouldn't be bursting into the room with a wand in his hand every time Penny and I tried out a new theory. I had spent the majority of my active sex life consciously avoiding parental scrutiny, after all; the freedom, once realized, was unsettling. We just didn't do things that way in Talry.

It wasn't all sweaty sex and magical nights, though. Penny was a researcher, and by default so was I. Our pillow talk was highly technical in nature, not romantic, and often we ended our bouts with detailed journal entries or a quick jog to the library to look something up. Her passionate brilliance on the subject coupled (no pun intended) with my flair for thaumaturgy produced no less than five short papers in two years, two of them proposing some groundbreaking theories. If it wasn't for the sheer prudish conservatism of magical academics we might have been invited to lecture somewhere.

Eventually Penny completed her studies at Inarion and returned to Remere, where she continued studying on her own. She had proven her place as an Authority on her obscure subject, and that's what she had been after. Her father was terribly proud of her, granted her a small estate, and kept her on retainer with his firm which provided her an income. I felt a great debt to her, as our work together helped establish *my* academic reputation in thaumaturgy in professional academic circles, albeit a bit of a lurid one. Our goodbye was tearful, but inevitable, and we parted great friends.

Truth was, I was relieved. As much as I liked – even loved – Pentandra, and as good as she was at what she did, I was getting a little bored. I was anxious to return to chasing peasant girls and millers' daughters again. They may not have her skill or dedication to the pure erotic . . . but then they never got up in the middle of it to take notes.

*   *   *

The Otherworld is largely unknown to mundane folk, though they travel there nightly in their dreams. It is the realm of imagination, only anchored to our own reality by our thoughts. Some sages argue that it is a byproduct of consciousness; some argue that it is independent of our thoughts; and neither side had been able to prove their case – such is the nature of a subjective reality.

Even among the magi it is poorly understood and much we think we know about the Otherworld is likely wrong. It is peopled by our subconscious minds and a few natural denizens unknown to all but the most learned. The spirits of the Tree Folk and the Sea Folk and even the gurvani travel here, though it is rare to encounter such alien consciousnesses by chance. We are not in the same enneagramatic phase, or something else arcanely significant, which tends to support the by-product school of thought.

It is not the realm of death, exactly, though you can encounter the dead there. Nor is it the realm of life-before-life. But one can become lost and surely die if the utmost caution is not practiced.

The landscape is similar to that of our world, but essentially different. While natural features can often be seen there are other structures, "towers" erected by magi, palaces of court magicians and long-dead Archmagi, floating castles whose builders have retired to the inner confines of their minds, and even stranger "places" congruent with our world but not of it. (I was planning to erect one myself, eventually, once I settled in a single spot long enough to do so.) It is a realm not ruled by any god or demon (though they, too, come here upon occasion). It is a kingless kingdom of shadows, a world turned inside out and upside down.

I mean that last part literally. When a mage is in the Otherworld, there are no stars above him, only an eternal gray. Instead, the sparks of light that can be seen in the distance are the slivers of sleepers' minds that intrude here unknowingly. They collect in the spaces that correspond to towns and villages in the mundane world.

Only magi traverse this place of their own will, and few are brave or powerful enough to do so with any regularity. It is a highly specialized skill, one that few have the courage or need to master. But it is essential to know of it and its rules to perform many different kinds of spells, and there are times when knowing how to get there is important.

We had been introduced to the Otherworld at the Academy, taught its ways and the methods of survival, and then *strongly* cautioned against ever coming here lightly. Those who forsook the advice foolishly ended up dead or mad. It takes tremendous concentration, purpose, and more power than you might think to escape beyond the small regions we visit in our dreams.

But I had purpose, and I now had access to oceans of power, thanks to the little green marble around my neck. Flying through the Otherworld was liberating, I discovered, when you do not have to struggle with every step. I'd taken the drastic measure for no less purpose to summon help, or at least tell someone of my increasingly dire circumstances. Since a letter might take months to cross three duchies, I instead elected to use arcane means. After drinking a calming and utterly revolting herbal draught to encourage the process I went into meditation, invoked the right runes, entrained my subconscious mind to my conscious mind, and then allowed my dreams to become lucid.

As I wasn't technically bound by space and time – not to mention gravity – in the Otherworld, I "flew" to my destination. No need to wear out my imaginary boots or acquire phantom blisters.

I followed the trail of tiny lights across the outer ring of mountains that bordered the valley, and down across the fertile hills of Alshar. The settlements "below" were flickers of sparks, collections of dreamers in hamlets and villages that were sparse where I started. Soon enough I began to encounter larger places. Cities stood out like swarms of lightning bugs, with the sparks from fellow magi producing brilliant fountains in their midst.

I flew across Alshar and then Castal, used the bright lights from the Academies to orient myself, then skimmed along the coast (narrowly missing a pod of Sea People who were collaborating on some errand of their own) and slowed only when I neared the correspondent point I sought in Remere. That's when the real work began among the ancient phantom towers and constructs of magi past and present. Once I had right place I had to find the right light. I was searching for a *particular* spark, a soul-light, if you will, and after only a little fooling around I eventually found it.

Pentandra's light.

She had, of course, erected her own tower, a theoretical construct that resembled a classical Imperial structure, all graceful arches and dainty points. She was working, I saw, as the top of her tower was lit with the magnificence of a mage raising and using power. I took just a moment to firm up my own mental self-image before I intruded. When you have control over your dreams and can look like any representation, it's foolish not to put your best look on. Particularly when you're calling on your ex-girlfriend whom you haven't seen in the flesh in years.

Of course, all of that Otherworldly light indicating magic in action on Penny's estate should have given me a hint of what she was doing, but I managed to be a little startled anyway as I approached her.

Floating in midair was a small, lithe, translucent woman, naked and beautiful in outline, with a wild cascade of gravity-defying hair made of sparks that sputtered and crackled with energy as she moved. She had her thighs spread, and I could tell from the vaguest of outlines that she was mounted upon someone. Around the imaginary bed was a complex magical construction, specialized items akin to kaba and apis but infinitely more delicate, all hooked together in conjunction. Her eyes were closed, but I knew that as soon as her climax hit . . .

I can be patient. It was fascinating to observe the effect that orgasm had on one's Otherworld self.

I didn't have long to wait as she silently threw back her head, arched her back, and thrust her breasts forward. Her eyes snapped open in ecstasy, and I saw the brighter-than-starlight illumination shoot forth. The spell she had carefully constructed sucked in the energy and started moving like a watermill's gears.

Then she noticed me, and it startled her enough so that her creation oscillated out of control and shattered, sending harmless shards of arcane form everywhere.

Son of a bitch! she screamed at me. *Minalan, do you have any* idea *how hard it was to build that?*

I can guess, by the complexity. It was pretty. What were you supposed to be doing?

Penny closed her eyes and groaned in exasperation, though her hips never stopped moving. *It wasn't really important; just a spell I was experimenting with. I was trying to boost the amount of power I can raise through sex magic. So I can try some of the really, really big spells that no one thinks about anymore. It took me a month of research and a week of preparation. You have no idea what you just ruined. But you always did have poor timing.*

My timing is fine, Penny, that's not fair, I argued. *You should have put up some signal, a "do not disturb" sign at the very least.*

I did!

In the Otherworld?

Hmmph. Everyone around here knows not to disturb me when I'm working. I hadn't anticipated a bumbling country spellmonger crashing in on me during my moment.

Ouch. Sorry. I really am. And you know I wouldn't have done it without great need.

She "looked" at me through the Otherworld for a moment. *Yes, I do. It must be pretty damned important, actually, for you to make the journey.*

It is, I admitted. *The little valley in the Mindens I'm working in is about to be over-run with little black-furred goblins. Casadalain. They're very upset about something, there are a lot of them, and we're going to be wiped out if I don't raise some help.*

Gurvani? Interesting, she considered. *But why can't you just zap them? I heard you got pretty good with that sword during the war. And after.*

I sighed. She made it sound so *easy*. Penny never wanted me to go to war or learn warmagic, thinking it a waste of a good thaumaturge, but Duke Rard hadn't really given me much choice.

It would be no problem if there were only a few hundred. Hells, I helped mop up that many just the other night and almost got killed. But there are just too many for easy zapping. And more on the way. There will be thousands, perhaps tens of thousands, in just a few weeks. They plan on making Boval Valley a staging point for invasion into the Duchies.

Boval? Isn't that where the cheese comes from?

Yes, that's where the cheese comes from.

I thought so. It's really good. Goblins, huh? What do you expect a peace-loving young maiden like me to do about that? she asked, batting her magnificently illuminated eyelashes coquettishly at me.

Well, it isn't just gurvani, I said, shaking my head. *And you haven't been a maiden in almost a decade. It's gurvani light infantry backed by powerful shamans.*

So what do you need my help for?

I need for you to hire me a real nasty bunch of mercenaries to get here double quick, before we get cut off, and send these buggers back to their holes. Professional warmagi, preferably, but we'll take anyone. I need you to gather together a powerful magical corps. We need more weapons, too – anything. Arrows, spears, swords, bows, the lot.

Again, Hmmph. Mercenaries are no problem, as long as you can pay for them. Daddy cut my allowance after an . . . incident. But finding qualified warmagi who will be interested in signing on for a defensive, back-woods campaign in the ass-end of nowhere is going to be hard no matter what kind of money you're offering. They're making too much money stinging each other in these silly baronial wars. Like you were doing, until you decided to embrace your peasant roots.

My folks are bakers, not peasants, I reminded her, patiently.

Commoner, then. But that's hardly likely to inspire them more than if you were a peasant.

Time to play my trump. *Tell them that the coin I will pay them in coin they won't find elsewhere. Tell them that participants will have a good chance to get their hands on . . . irionite.*

Irionite? *Are you serious?* Sparks shattered off of her hair as she jerked her head up suddenly.

Very. Here's the proof. I held up my spectral hand and opened it, displaying the ball of raw magic I was holding within. Most un-enchanted objects are not reflected in the Otherworld, but irionite has power even here, and casts a thaumaturgic "shadow". The green marble glowed brightly, vividly, obscuring even the light from her eyes. In the potent glow the faint outline of her supine partner disappeared altogether.

Ishi's titanic titties, Min, where in the six hells did you find that?

A gurvani shaman gave it to me. He wasn't using it anymore. And if the local Tree Folk chieftain is to be believed – and why wouldn't he be?

You do know that they're illegal, right?

Only if I get caught, and there isn't a Censor for hundreds of leagues of here. But there are plenty more. Any warmage who enlists in my cause and fights for the duration has a decent shot at a piece. But it will be a hell of a fight, I guarantee.

Wait, the goblins have irionite? Can they do that?

They don't seem to pay much attention to the Royal Censorate of Magic, I said dryly. *But they've discovered a cache of it, or learned how to make it, and there are dozens of them – if not hundreds – thus armed and headed right for me. This was the piece I took from their scouts, but their main force is still a few weeks out. Do you think that might persuade a warmage or two to come?* I asked, almost pleadingly.

Ishi's tits, Min, if you're offering irionite, I'll come myself. I think I can convince four or five of the locals to join me – I think a few are sweet on me – and I can get more on the way. Once word gets out, you'll be up to your eyebrows in warmagi. My father might even come, for that.

That might not be enough. Nor particularly helpful, in your father's case. It will be a tough fight, Pen. And I don't want you in the middle of it. Hire them, equip them, send them on their way – but stay put!

You mean that? You sound like this is serious, she said, biting her imaginary lip just like she does in the material world.

This is perhaps the greatest threat that the Five Duchies have ever faced, I decided. *Seriously. But don't spread that around too much – I don't want to scare anyone off. But if this assault isn't squashed here and now, while they're still in the mountains, then it will get much, much bloodier once they get past the ridges and out into the Alshari Wilderlands, proper. Alshar will fall, and most of Castal, too. Hell, they might make it as far as Remere.*

You're joking!

Yes, I risked my mind and my life coming to you like this through the Otherworld as a huge practical joke. No, I'm not joking, Penny. I'm desperate. I'm going to need help with this, and I don't know who else I can turn to.

I see, she said, slowing down her gyrations a little. *Min, if you say it's important, I'll trust you. But if you have even a pinch of irionite, it will take more than one little goblin army to keep me away. Do you have any idea what a mage can do with that?*

After keeping one in my pocket for a week, I'd say I have some idea.

So how is it? What is it like to do magic with irionite? she asked, eagerly.

Magnificent, I confessed. *More magnificent than you can imagine. Like having an endless font of power that allows you to skip the crappy parts of spells and get right to the thaumaturgically valid parts.*

Then I'm coming, too. I've been getting bored with city life anyway. Daddy doesn't like it when I travel, but he's also getting tired of me scaring off the suitors Mother keeps lining up for me.

Penny, I'm serious! You stay the hell away! This is a warzone, not an academic conference!

And I'm the scion of a great and powerful family of magi, some of whom were actually warmagi, she countered. *Tell you what: give me a couple of days to get organized, and I'll get to your little bumfuck valley just as soon as I can – whatever help I can hire. Warmagi. Mercenaries. Professionals, too, not like those country bumpkins from Alshar. But you have to save me a piece of irionite, okay? Promise? It would be most valuable in my research.*

Deal, I agreed, reluctantly. *Considering my situation, I didn't have a lot of choice. And thanks, Pen. By the way, who is your victim?* I asked, nodding towards the invisible body that supported her. She looked down and thought for a minute.

Uh . . . Gustaro, I think. One of the new servants. He's not the brightest fellow, but he has the right, uh, equipment for the job.

And stamina, too, I see, I chuckled.

Not really, she objected. *But I dosed him good with a sustaining aphrodisiac I re-discovered. He should stay ready for most of the night. He'll feel like hell in the morning, but . . .*

I'm sure it's worth it, I said, feeling a little wistful. Penny and I had some very good times trying to wear out our bunks back in school. Her experimentation with aphrodisiacs was hit-and-miss, but it had lead to some very memorable times.

I could feel my arcane body start to "fray" with the effort of sustaining it so far from home. *Penny, I've got to go. I've got a lot of stuff to do, including hiring some local talent to shore up our defenses. Sorry for wrecking your experiment. I'll be in touch.*

Good bye, Minalan. And good luck. Remember to duck, she said with a starry grin.

She had said the same thing to me when she had seen me off to the War College, before I'd been deployed to Farise. I smiled back at her, waved, and just to be flashy I had my image explode into a golden shower of sparks as I snapped back into my body.

Showoff! she called after me as her image faded away.

I opened my eyes, and saw that I was still sitting in the chair on the roof where I'd undertaken the spell. I took a few moments to re-orient myself back in mundane space, and two cups of wine before I felt fortified enough to stand on my shaky legs.

Traveling in the Otherworld can inspire a type of vertigo that you never get used to, and if you move too quickly you can acquire a malady known as "reality shock." I've heard of magi who got killed because they lost their bearings and did something stupid. Like accidently falling off of a roof.

Once my head was cleared I went in search of my apprentice. There was, indeed, a lot of work to be done.

* * *

"Remember, get everything you can think of. There's no telling what we might need, and it would be a poor reflection on our abilities if we were one dram of quicksilver shy of a spell," I reminded my apprentice.

Tyndal grinned, but I could see the strain on his face. He was relieved that I'd returned from the scary Otherworld unscathed, after all I'd told him and warned him about the place. But he had been shocked when I told him that he would be responsible for setting up shop by himself while I went trawling for mercenaries for Sire Koucey. He had borrowed a wain from one of the farmers he knew to make a final trip back to Minden Hall, and had recruited two older lads to help move stuff, but he was clearly unused to either the authority or the responsibility.

"Master, what if Garkesku wants to intrude into our—"

"That's *Master* Garkesku, lad, and don't forget it," I reminded him. "I know, he's a pain in our profession's backside, but we must deal with him as best we can, which means paying respect to his position even if you dislike him intensely.

"As far as any intrusions go, stand your ground. That is *my* area, as he and I have already discussed, and I charge you to keep it private. That's a master's order to an apprentice, and he must respect that. If her persists, go to Sire Koucey, if you have to. But use that only as a last resort. Oh. And here," I said, tossing him a purse I had prepared. "Use this to smooth the way if you run into any difficulties. There are about fifteen silver pennies and thrice that in copper in that purse – don't spend it all. And here's a list of items I'd like to have in addition to the stuff at the shop. Don't worry if you can't get it all, it's just a wish-list. We'll make do if you can't find, say, willow bark. No matter what, though, I want you back inside the castle walls within three days. Understood?"

"Yes, Master," he said, humbly.

"Good lad. Kulin's luck be with you," I said, invoking the god of horses and thieves. He grinned at the blessing.

With that I spurred Traveler on his way, and began my long journey towards Tudry. I knew I'd need divine luck myself to make it there, complete my mission, and return in time for the coming invasion. I only hoped that the Bovali could hold out that long without me.

Chapter Six

I Recruit An Army

"The charming town of Tudry is a picturesque example of the best of the Wilderlands; a center of commerce, bedecked in a delightful mixture of Gilmoran, Alshari and native architecture, the hospitality of its folk and the richness of its beautiful surroundings belie the industriousness underlying the town's character. Anyone yearning for the comforts and luxuries associated with the Riverlands or Coastlands may find what they seek in Tudry."

— *Roadbrother Ostus,*

Wandering The Wilderlands Of Alshar

Tudry is a piss-poor excuse for a city, but it's the best that the Alshari Wilderlands has to offer.

It got started as a military camp, a staging area for my ancestors' settlement of the wild areas north and west. It lies at the juncture of the

Moran and the Anfal rivers and is the largest city north of the Ducal summer capital of Vorone, which was both too far away and too political for my purpose. Tudry is the official baronial seat for the Barony of Megelin, and is a major center of trade in this sparsely-peopled part of the world.

It's also ugly as hell.

The original fortress is perched on an artificial motte built up at the river's fork, and the town proper, spreads out behind it like a ragged cloak. The area closest to the castle isn't too bad – local wealthy merchants and petty nobles have constructed townhouses on the three streets closest to the castle, a region known as "Old Tudry," which is technically anything inside the old city wall that cuts from river to river on the north side. It's telling that, in order to enter "Old Tudry" you have to have a pass that lets the guards know that you know someone inside who has money.

Outside the outer wall, though, is a vast slum of poverty-stricken porters and carters, artisans and shopkeepers living in wattle-and-daub homes not far advanced of the countryside peasantry. Most of these people's parents and grandparents were lured into the Wilderlands from other parts of the Duchy with the promise of cheap land and great opportunity. There is plenty of both in the Alshari Wilderlands, as I'd seen, but for some reason these people never made it any farther than here. The iron mines and the sawmills employ them when times are good, but times haven't been good here since before the Farisian Campaign. As it is, there are nearly forty thousand people who call this sludge-pit home.

As a side-effect of the crowded living conditions, there is an over-abundance of unemployed youth with virtually no prospects beyond day laboring or peasantry. For most, the only way to leave the slums is to work at the mines just to the north, become a dirt farmer, or join a private army or bandit troop (or both). Most choose the first, which confused me, considering the life expectancy of the miners was often measured in months. Trying to build the rocky soil into a prosperous farm when produce and grain is already cheap at market is likewise an exercise in heartbreak. That left a career in arms.

But most people aren't cut out for army life. I know I sure as hell wasn't.

Most of the youth available were mere spear-holders, but even a casual mercenary can make a basic living here. Tudry was the only real place in the region where a baron or a baronet or a count could recruit enough hired swords to prosecute a private war against another baron or baronet or count. Then the two hired armies would go at it for a few months, inflict light casualties, take a fortress or successfully defend a fortress, and be discharged back to the slums of Tudry to spend their wages on the hundreds of providers on Whore Street.

Yes, they actually named a street that. That tells you a little about the place.

I made exactly one trip into Old Town upon my arrival and that was to pass a message from Sire Koucey to the local Baron's castellan-on-site informing him of Boval's predicament, and then to a moneylender who took Koucey's letter of credit and issued me a letter of credit in his own name, which the locals would recognize. This was absolutely necessary if I was going to hire any serious warriors.

Next I rented a room at an inn just outside the wall, on the imaginatively titled Wall Street. I had heard that this particular inn catered to officers in private armies and that I could expect to find the men I needed here. It sounded promising, at least, and the rough-looking crowd in the common room was evidence that there were sellswords available.

I was exhausted from the trip, despite liberally using the power of the stone to use warmagic to refresh myself and my horse along the way. I napped for a good six hours before troubling the innkeeper to send up a couple of whores. It had been a while since my last intimate encounter (my tryst with Alya hadn't progressed nearly far enough to be completely satisfying, despite the comfort of the pasture), and the recent events had left me quite . . . *tense.*

I think he sent me his own daughters (I wouldn't put it past him) but I didn't care. They were young (around fifteen and seventeen), clean, and if not up to Penny's standards, they were at least enthusiastic and terribly impressed by my battle scars. I was gratified by the female attention, and more gratified that I could charge the expense to Sire Koucey. Getting laid on someone else's coin is always a luxury.

After a few hours, though, I kicked them out of bed and got down to the business at hand. Hiring an army.

It was about time I was on the other end of that particular job.

*   *   *

After Penny left my final year at the Academy flew by. My advanced standing in thaumaturgy allowed me a certain amount of leisure, but I knew eventually I'd have to do something productive with my life. So I was spending a lot of time contemplating just what I was going to do after graduation.

Theoretically, it is possible for a journeyman to go directly into further study with the Academy to become a Teaching Master. In actuality, they almost never allow this. The Masters want to see a journeyman go out and get his feet wet as a practical mage, either as a court wizard or as a general spellmonger, before you even apply. They also don't particularly like young, talented magi to be sniffing after their comparatively cushy jobs.

Realizing that I had little chance at the former (even baronial courts disliked non-noble magi in that position) I knew I had better find a position in practice as quickly as I could. Otherwise I'd likely become one of the often-despised class of itinerant magi known as *footwizards* – a derogatory term that implied a disreputable and sometimes fraudulent mage who was constantly moving from one domain to another, sometimes just ahead of the Censorate who considers their trade borderline illegal. They are often without the benefit of a horse (hence the descriptive name) and usually strive to avoid the mundane law as much as the arcane law.

That wasn't the bright and glorious future I wanted for myself. I might not know much about the world, but I know I hated walking for a living.

I finished my last few classes, tended to some administrative affairs, and my practicum and fieldwork came and went like pleasant summer breezes. Graduation day approached, then arrived, and suddenly I was standing dressed in full silly wizard regalia, including the four-pointed hat, in front of my parents and hundreds of other spectators accepting my diploma and my professional license from the Rector and Head

Master and bowing before the Magister General and swearing my professional oath before the gods.

For twenty golden, sweet seconds I was a man of destiny, a mage with full legal credentials and the ability to practice my trade anywhere in the Five Duchies. I felt like a god. I shook hands with my instructors as I wandered off the stage, and when I shook the hand of Count Moray, representative of His Grace, the Duke of Castal, he said congratulations with a smug smile and handed me an elegantly calligraphed envelope.

I thanked him and stumbled down the stairs, imagining it to be an invitation to Ducal service, perhaps a post in the magical service, or an appointment to the staff of his Court Mage. I got the damn thing open just as I was taking my seat.

Congratulations! it read,

It is an honor for me to have the pleasure of welcoming you into the ranks of professionally chartered magi.

Under the most sacred Oath you have just sworn, in the eyes of your peers, your lords, and your gods, you are required to render assistance to the Duchy and your people. You are hereby summoned to now render that service, and should consider this notice to be your induction into the Duke's magical corps.

Please report no later than three days after the fullest of the moon (The 4th day of the Harvest Month) to the Commandant of the Ducal War College at Relan Cor for induction and training in the military service of the Duchy. May the blessings of all the gods be upon you and your family!

Duke Rard IV, House of Bimin

Duke of Castal

By Lord Reiman of Lancelawn, Ducal Scribe

I blinked and re-read the letter, twice, to ensure that I had not dreamed it all. As the last of the graduates was accepting his credentials on the stage, I realized that my post-academic life was suddenly in clear focus.

Shit. I was *drafted.*

*   *   *

That night I set up a table in the common room of the inn, had the barmaid bring me a mug of the best ale they had (which was still pretty wretched) and hired a couple of kids to spread the word among the remaining mercenaries that I was looking for people.

Bugger if there wasn't a mercenary shortage.

Apparently, two baronial houses to the east of Tudry had re-invigorated a feud that had been smoldering for almost a hundred years. I forget the names of the principals, but the basic quarrel had to do with a dinky little fief less than two miles wide and half a mile thick (a tiny estate, in Wilderlands terms), which included two tiny villages and a run-down temple to Huin, the agricultural deity that had fallen out of favor a generation ago in more civilized places in the Duchies.

The revenue from the estate was far, *far* less than the cost of either army, but the two lords involved both just *had* to have the domain, and so they squandered a great deal of money on nearly every decent mercenary company in Tudry. Within an hour I realized the dire state of the labor market for mercenaries. There was precious little cavalry left in town, and what infantry there was consisted of escaped serfs from the south, drunks, rogues, idiot spear-holders and over-ripe gallows fruit.

It was a disappointing evening.

The first two "officers" I met with were dead drunk. Now, I don't hold that against them – I didn't drink seriously until I was drafted, and we were in an inn, after all – but before the interview I set up a little truthtell spell, and both "gentlemen" were stretching the truth with how many men and how many horses they had under their command, and in what condition they were in. When I pressed them on it, they got huffy and stumbled away. No great loss.

The next fellow was a blacksmith-turned-mercenary captain, and I could see that he was in it for the money and would shirk his duty the moment he could – including deserting an unfavorable position, preferably with full pay in hand. While I was in desperate straits, I wasn't desperate enough to be cheated. I sent him on his way after the third lie in less than a minute.

The fourth officer I was finally pleased with. His name was Captain Forondo, and he was (he claimed, and the spell didn't disagree) the bastard of a high Remeran noble. Apparently his father had set him up as a captain of a mercenary horse company on the condition that he leave Remere and never return.

Forondo seemed melancholy, but after quizzing him for twenty minutes I decided he knew his business. He had references from several previous employers, and while he did stretch the truth a little concerning the actions he had led his troops in, I chalked it up to a soldier's natural inclination towards embellishment. Forondo accepted my commission for three months, with an option to extend an additional three months.

He would bring just over a hundred well-equipped light cavalry to our cause. The unit was known as the Black Flag (their banner was nothing but a sheet of black cloth) and consisted mostly of Castali and Wenshari horsemen armed with bows, swords and light lances. All had seen combat.

Forondo seemed a little foppish (he oiled his mustache and beard, and he wore a threadbare Remeran silk coat that was utterly out of place among the wool and leather of the Alshari Wilderlords) but blooded and capable, and he was very pleased with the bounty I paid, even if he was uncertain about the foe. Apparently he had never fought nonhumans before.

While cavalry were good, I didn't expect we'd have much need of them during the campaign. Not when we were looking at a siege. Still, every man I could put on the wall counted. We could always eat the horses if things got bad.

I started interviewing infantry after that. That was another mixed lot, mostly armed gangs of thugs who I suspected would desert at the first sign of battle. Them I didn't need either.

There were exceptions, and I took advantage of every one.

A sixty-man light infantry company from the Gilmoran barony of Stillwater, the remnant of a larger auxiliary troop that had been caught raiding their own supply train, was desperate for a posting. Thanks to their larceny they were well-equipped, now, though few local lords wanted to take a chance on a troop with a reputation. They were more than happy to get as far away from Stillwater as possible. I'd have to keep my eye on them, but I knew they'd fight.

Two thirty-man heavy infantry units who were looking for easy garrison duty. I fibbed a little myself, then. They *would* be garrisoning the castle, after all. They didn't have to know against who. They didn't ask, so I didn't mention it.

An impromptu light infantry company formed on the spot when a number of local individuals found out I was hiring, but only hiring full companies. I spoke with four of the elected "officers," and learned only two of whom had had serious previous military experience. Still, that was another fifty bodies to put on the walls. I paid them less, too, since I had to arm more than half of them.

The best finds of all, though, were two groups who came in just as I was about to pack it in for the evening.

First, there was Brother Edund, who commanded the Alshari Wilderlands Chapter of the Militant Order of Gobarba.

The Gobarbs, as they are known, are a fanatical cult of warrior monks dedicated to an old Imperial war-god. The Magocracy had outlawed the cult decades before the Invasion as a threat to Imperial security, but the Order merely went underground or into the hinterlands. After the Invasion no one cared about them – the Imperials had taken to worshipping our gods, for the most part, and Gobarba was a wimp compared to Duin the Destroyer.

In the last four hundred years, they had become a semi-nomadic cult of religious mercenaries that few lords cared to employ as they had a regimen of strict dietary customs and other religious laws that they insisted on following, and they had a nasty habit of torching the temples of rival deities when they got drunk.

If they wanted to torch *gurvani* shrines, I wasn't about to object. The Brothers were stalwart, and they would bring three hundred well-armed, well-trained infantry to Boval. Their specialty was the pike, which was an unusual weapon, but the pike had been Gobarba's ritual weapon.

Besides, they were *cheap.* And enthusiastic. Seven of them could read.

Last, and best of all for my purposes, were the three funny-looking brothers who stumbled in as the Commanding Abbot was leaving. They were short, broadly-built, full-bearded, clad in furs, and had amazingly unkempt hair that they greased with rancid butter. The smell was *vile.*

But the axes in their belts were impressive. The sauntered over to my table and introduced themselves as Furtak, Posnak, and Jordak. They were princes, they said, of Crinroc. I barely contained my laughter.

Crinroc, for those of you unfamiliar with Alshari Wilderlands geography, is an arid, hilly region between two spurs of mountains to the far north of the Duchy, beyond the North March towers. Two different peoples inhabit it, the Crinroc tribes to the west and the Fallad tribes to the east. The Alshari Dukes spent the last few hundred years "pacifying" them (they were the reason that there were North March towers), that is, making them subject to tribute and the Ducal laws. But that hasn't stopped their belligerent ways.

The tribes, clans, and families frequently raid each other with glee, and spend almost as much time raiding the tiny settlements between the Kasari tribes and the Pearwoods. The only real difference between them (besides language, gods, and a few obscure elements of culture) is that the Crinroc are short and thick with shaggy brown hair and the Fallad were short and skinny with straight black hair. They both claimed dominion over the entire region, though neither claim is recognized by the Duchy.

The Crinroc Brothers (as I took to calling them) had been exiled by their clan for some transgression or other, and had taken up the life of the mercenary soldier in "civilized" parts. Since they were short, smelled bad, talked funny, painted their faces in lurid designs, they were generally viewed as poor troops. They fought with axe and mace and shield and sometimes went to battle buck-naked, though most wisely wore waxed leather armor. Not the kind of warrior the Wilderlords liked to represent them even though they were ferocious fighters. I didn't see too much wrong with them, myself. Apart from the Order of Gobarba, they seemed the best-organized company of the lot.

What I didn't realize at the time, though, was the fact that I was not just hiring the brothers and their men (which came to just under five hundred) but also their *wives and children*. Indeed, many of the wives (little roly-poly women with wild brown hair) would fight alongside of their husbands in battle and wouldn't dream of being left behind, their virtue unprotected. Nor did they mind fighting gurvani. They seemed pretty enthusiastic about it, actually, and quickly boasted of all the skirmishes they'd fought in their crappy little land against the Mountain Folk, which I found encouraging when the truthtell spell didn't call them out on it. So I ended up with nearly a thousand short and smelly Crinroc in my little army.

One thing I'll say for them, though. They were very, very loyal. Once they swore my oath and took my coin, they were my fiercest supporters.

The next day I went around to every weaponsmith I could find to buy arms. This was somewhat easier than I expected; for some reason, even with the squabble in the eastern part of the Wilderlands, there was a surplus of weapons on the market. A lot of down-and-out mercenaries sold their swords – literally – when there was no real work to be done. A man has to eat.

I made several quick deals with smiths eager to dump their inventory on me, arranged for their transportation, and inspected lackluster but serviceable samples until I was satisfied that my little army would have at least basic arms. Then I turned my attention to buying supplies to provision it. Mostly I focused on the dried meats and fish, salt pork, beans, hardtack, salt, maize, barley and oats that were readily available in the market.

I even bought a few hundredweight of the local cheese. Everyone thought it was a hoot that I'd be sending cheese to famous Boval, but I bought it anyway. I had only spent about half of the coin Koucey had sent me with, and I'd rather have too much food than too little.

The last stop I made was to the only real warmage in town, Master Cormoran. He was an older gentleman, as much smith as mage, with the bearing of a Wilderlands knight down to his bushy gray mustache. He claimed he was semi-retired, which is the only reason why a man of his skill was languishing in the picturesque but unprofitable pimple on the arse of civilization known as Tudry.

But later that evening in his shop he confided that he liked the low overhead and easy access to high-quality, low-cost iron here, and had settled in Tudry a decade before because of that. Come to find out one of his former apprentices was in service to Castal and had made my army-issued mageblade, Slasher. He even clucked over the technique, though he pronounced it a serviceable-enough blade.

While I was there I took a look at his impressive stock and made several additional, personal purchases, though none of his best work, unfortunately. His high-end mageblades were magnificent, far more elaborate than Slasher – and far out of my price range. Some of the blades on display he'd been working on for *years*. Some were pretty, some were powerful, some were both, and all would have cost me more than I make at spellmongering in a year or more.

Master Cormoran was fascinating to me, and I only wished I'd met him before I'd gone to Boval. I've always had a thaumaturge's interest in enchantment (that's when you imbue an object with a spell, in case you didn't know), and my time in the army had given me a respect and appreciation for quality warmagic enchantments. Cormoran was part of a tiny independent order of enchanting warmagi known as the Order of the Veolicti, specializing in crafting magical weaponry, specifically mageblades. In fact he was the greatest authority on the subject I'd ever met – and I invited him to join me at Boval Castle with the possibility of irionite to lure him.

Master Cormoran wasn't interested in participating in the coming siege, after I'd outlined my situation, but he was intrigued by the news of the gurvani invasion and took my word seriously, particularly once I'd shown him my new witchstone. He was also helpful in that he spread the word to other, younger local warmagi who might be interested in the prospect of irionite. I retired that evening feeling more satisfied and confident than I had in a while. I liked the old guy, and if I did survive the coming war I promised myself to try to acquire one of those beautiful blades.

My last day in Tudry I assembled my forces just outside the City wall. They were certainly not the most uniform or most attractive group of sellswords I'd ever seen. It was a piecemeal rag-tag bunch of mercenaries, mostly afoot, but they were men and they were armed and they were the best I could get. They would have to do. And I was in command, for a change. As soon as the wagons were assembled, the rolls were read, and the rules were read aloud to everyone, we set off on the greatest martial bitch-fest since the Farisian Campaign.

No one can complain like a soldier and no one has more cause. But really, these guys complained bitterly about every rut in the road and every poor meal they cooked. The veterans complained about the leadership and the unblooded rookies complained about the rules. I had to intervene in inter-unit disputes several times, which led me to creating my own little officer corps to control them, demoting two of the elected petty captains in the process. The only ones who didn't bitch were the Crinroc, who treated the job more as a family picnic than a column of war.

I included in my staff the three barbarian "princes," the Commanding Abbot, Captain Forondo, and one Captain Besser, who was the most professional of the officers from one of the smaller mercenary infantry units. I chose Besser because he had also served in the Farisian campaigns and my gut and my spellwork told me he was a good soldier despite his fallen circumstances.

This caused a lot of grumbling among the other mercenary captains, but after an afternoon of listening to their complaints I got fed up and told them to shut up and soldier. That didn't go over real well – a few tried to fight or desert, and there was one abortive attempt to mutiny the first full day on the road. But then my hairy Crinroc Brothers demonstrated their loyalty by threatening to eat anyone who didn't obey an order.

I almost believed them, even though I knew that they weren't cannibals. The mercenaries apparently weren't aware of that, thank Duin.

I won't bore you with the long, slow journey north and west over glorified goat trails and through backwards little villages toward Boval. As I am sure you can guess, it was both long and slow. But not entirely unproductive. I was able to pick up another dozen mounted Wilderlord knights at a hilly domain called Kelso, mostly unlanded "gentlemen warriors" who were bored and greedy, and who saw our little war as a way to pick up some quick cash. They at least had some experience fighting goblins, due to the periodic raids from the Minden tribes. They were well-horsed and their lances were sharp, but the truth is I would have traded the lot of them for a few dozen competent archers with Wilderlands bows. Apparently Huin didn't see fit to provide those, so we settled for the petty nobility.

We arrived at the Mor River ford in western Gans a week and a half after setting out, which I counted as a major victory. I was already sick of being in charge, though in truth the worst of the complaints had settled down the third day when I used warmagic to quell a second rebellion. Mor Tower, which guarded the only traversable pass through the ridges to Boval, was supposed to be a finish line for me, of sorts. I expected to pick up more men there, too, as the pleas from Sire Koucey had gone out to his fellow nobles almost two weeks before, and the three-story Mor Tower had been set as the place for recruits to gather.

Instead I got stopped at a roadblock.

The Lord of Gans had apparently decided that the gurvani threat to Boval Vale was just too serious – there had been an increase in raids even into his lands – and defending his neighbor Sire Koucey's lands instead of his own was unwise.

Instead he was putting up defenses on *this* side of the Mor Pass, and wouldn't let anyone in or out. He sent one of his young Wilderlords to guard the ford, and the hundred men gathered there that I'd expected to include in my army instead drew their bows and swords against me. *No one*, the barely-mustached young Wilderlord snapped imperiously. That included a little mercenary army led by a common spellmonger.

I *really* don't like being snapped at by a man who has never stood in combat, and who further believes that his noble status justifies poor manners. I saw plenty of good men die in Farise because such self-important men commanded them stupidly. This fair-cheeked snot was quite adamant about the Lord of Gans' order, though, proclaiming the Boval Valley was a lost cause, and broadly hinting that my forces would be better spent defending his own realm instead of Koucey's.

I let the rage burn a little in my heart, then called upon a powerful Domination spell. It's actually a pretty easy spell to master, as it has no physical effects – it's a blue magic spell that just makes you seem three times as dangerous as you appear normally to the ones you want to dominate. To the pipsqueak lordling I suddenly became eight feet tall, broad shouldered and fighting mad.

That last part was not intrinsically part of the spell. I was just pissed.

I looked at him, looked at his little roadblock of a hundred or so men, and looked back at my troop column of over a thousand. Then I told my staff to prepare for action.

"My lord," I said as calmly as possible, "we are going through the Mor Pass on our lawful business, in defiance of your lord's wishes. You *may* elect to try to stop us."

"By Huin's axe, we will stop you!" the teenaged knight insisted, haughtily. "And it will be the last fight you ever see!"

"Oh, you misunderstand me," I said, my eyes narrowing. The boy was taken aback, and put his hand on his sword. He was clearly ready to fight us, even against overwhelming odds, in furtherance of his chivalric ideal.

I'm not a knight, though. There are some things the nobility fears even more than glorious death in battle. "If you *do* try to stop me, I will *not* order my men to fight."

"You . . . won't?" he asked, confused.

"No, my lord. I will merely *release* all these men from their contracts. *After* they are released, they will have nowhere to go and no money with which to support themselves. They will doubtless turn to raiding, and inside a week your domain will be stripped so bare the gurvani will have to go around it to find anything worth looting. So what shall I do, my lord?" I said, intensifying the spell.

The Wilderlord considered the matter carefully, a look of confusion on his acne-covered face – for about five seconds. The Crinroc alone made the rest of my mercenaries look respectable, but not by much. Clearly the thought of them all looting the cots and holds of Gans was vivid in his mind. He let us pass, and with just a little more pressure grudgingly promised to petition his lord to send fifty archers to Castle Brandmount as a visible token of his esteem and support for his sister domain in its time of need. After all, he pointed out, nervously, Boval and Gans both served the same baron.

We went past and into the valley without further human disruption. But neither could we expect human intervention. From the time we passed the Mor Tower and its thirty-man garrison, I had everyone prepare to be attacked at any moment from any hillock, wood, or ridge top we crossed.

We began to see signs of gurvani raids along the road, including a few furry black corpses that some lucky archer had got to, but we also saw a few corpses of humans who had been slain and left by the side of the road. More unsettling, a quick scrying told me that there were gurvani sentries and spies hiding about, too, but I was more concerned for getting my troops and their wagons through than hunting them down.

We arrived at Brandmount Castle without incident, and I detailed several wagons of arms and food to be deployed there, as well as assigning the Gobarban Order and about half the independent mercenaries to Sire Koucey's younger brother, who looked like he would break into tears of gratitude. They needed the infantry badly – Brandmount was an older fortress, not designed to be defended by cavalry, nor had it accommodations for that many horses. The Order's pikes would mean more there than at Boval Castle, and splitting the mercenaries kept them from fighting amongst each other. The rest I took south toward Hymas to reinforce Sire Koucey.

The landscape was eerily quiet as we rode south, passing Hymas Lake and the isolated farmsteads and pastures that surrounded it. The cottages were empty. I saw few farm animals and even less people the closer we came to the castle. But there were signs of struggle here and there, not just abandonment. Occasionally I saw the head of a gurvan or two stuck on a sharpened stick next to the road. It was a uselessly defiant, overly gory gesture, but one that was good for human morale.

At least security near to the fortress was good. As we approached Boval Castle, we were stopped no less than four times by sentries – the first three were jumpy peasant militiamen in leather jacks and wielding spears, axes and pitchforks, while the fourth were real men-at-arms spared from the Castle for the duty. Each time my long train passed a checkpoint the Bovali broke into cheers.

As we lumbered up the last stretch of road approaching the Castle, proper, peasants lined the roadway to cheer us on, throwing flowers in our path (a first for my Crinroc barbarians, who were more used to less-savory objects being thrown at them by Narasi peasants). Sire Koucey himself was waiting at the main gate of the castle in full armor and mounted on his warhorse, his tired face split into a toothy grin, as I rode ahead of the long column spread out behind me. He stood in the saddle to shout a greeting.

"Hail, Master Spellmonger, well met!" he bellowed to me over the cheers of the crowd. "I see you have hired us an army!"

"Of sorts, if you aren't too picky about the term," I said, glad the men were mostly out of earshot. "I left just under half of my forces at Brandmount Castle with your brother to shore up defenses there. But I have over five hundred with me . . . plus friends and relatives. And arms and ammunition, as well."

"They are graciously welcomed. I had no idea that you would be able to secure so many so quickly, but I applaud your efforts. Feeding them might be difficult in the days to come, but every man on the battlements is one more who can slay goblins."

"As to feeding them, I took the liberty of buying several wagonloads of provisions while in Tudry. Enough to cover the mercenaries, and then some. They are at the rear of the column, along with a fair number of additional arms."

Sire Koucey looked impressed and relieved – he hadn't discussed that before I'd gone. He nodded toward the mercenary cavalry and the Wilderlands knights who were in the vanguard of the march. "You are a wizard, indeed, to have chosen so well and with such foresight"

I grimaced uncomfortably. I felt more like I was leading a circus, not an army. But after leading them, I was more than ready to turn them over to their new master. "I'd like to think so. Your neighbors in Gans gave me trouble about crossing their lands, but I convinced them to let us pass. They may yet send some archers to Brandmount, though I wouldn't put them on the rolls until they arrive in earnest."

The old knight looked wearily at the eastern ridge and sighed. "I know all about that. I've had three messages in your absence. My fellow Wilderlords were not pleased with the developments in Boval of late, despite the increase in goblin raids on their own lands. Things have been busy here. You may have seen the severed heads along the road. Yet Gans and Presan have not had a tithe of the action we've seen, and cluck in alarm like frightened fowl, not brave knights. They have yet to send us anything but their tepid good wishes. They fear for their own lands, and I suppose I cannot blame them.

"But come inside – much has happened since you left, and there is much to discuss. Join me at luncheon and I will brief you."

Far be it for me to pass up a free meal, especially after eating trail rations for the last week. I nodded and rode in, Koucey himself leading Traveler to the stables as a sign of honor while the castellan came forward and started organizing the arriving mercenaries, arranging for their camps to be pitched inside the inner bailey, away from the villagers.

A good move – the locals would object to foreign warriors sharing their rations and ravishing their daughters, and the Crinroc, in particular, might take offense at some of the Bovali peasants' harsh jibes at their tribal ways. Best to keep a good strong wall between them.

After seeing to my horse, I followed Koucey into the great donjon and up into his private chamber, where we found lunch was already set. It was quieter than the last time I had been here; we were only interrupted thrice between our first bite and our last.

"So," the old knight said as he wiped honey away from his moustache with his finger, "Exactly what have you brought me and how much did it cost, Master Minalan?"

I took out the manifest I had prepared and slid it across to him. He read over it and nodded. "Excellent work, my boy. Not what I hoped for, exactly, but well under the budget I gave you. A few more knights would have been helpful," he muttered. No matter where they're from, the chivalry think that heavy cavalry is the epitome of the warrior's art. "Well done nonetheless. Now let me fill you in on what has passed since your departure . . ."

For the next hour he told me about the steady increase in gurvani raids across the valley interfering with his folk coming to the Castle. Most were mere skirmishes at dusk and dawn, the time when both races were awake. Some had been full-on nocturnal attacks, picking off isolated crofts or caravans on the road. Small squads of five or six gurvani would set upon whatever isolated peasants they found, but avoided our warriors like the sunshine, and never attacked at all unless the odds were distinctively in their favor.

That didn't always help – Koucey's brother and two of his men were ambushed riding towards Boval Castle a few days ago, though they had been driven off. Apparently the gurvani weren't used to attacking cavalry, or well-armed humans, and the younger Brandmount had left a pile of seven heads next to the road as testament to their foolishness. Koucey was quite proud of that.

More often the resistance was weaker and the goblins got the better of the bargain. Mutilated human bodies had been found in the fields and ditches of Boval every morning since the first attack on Minden Hall. They were usually stripped and despoiled, and occasionally positioned obscenely in ways designed to terrorize the human population. The gurvani struck without regard to gender or age, and that had raised the ire of Koucey's already frightened subjects. But it also speeded their preparations for a siege.

No one wants to wake up and realize that Grandma is lying outside the chicken coop, stripped and eviscerated, or that Junior had wandered off to meet a girl by moonlight and had his testicles cut off and stuffed – well, no need to go into that.

The attacks had had one important benefit: everyone was taking the goblin threat seriously, now, and wasted no more time in getting their families and livestock relocated behind stout fortress walls.

When I inquired after our laughable magical corps, Koucey nodded approvingly in a way that made me automatically nervous. He told me how Garkesku had led his apprentices on a three-day whirlwind tour of the castle grounds, laying wards, using strengthening runes on the walls, gates, and towers, making suggestions about fire-fighting barrels scattered throughout the area, and generally being far more useful than Koucey (or myself) had expected.

Was this a new side to Garkesku? I really couldn't say. To be honest I barely knew him, even in a professional capacity. While I found his business practices questionable and his skills overrated, perhaps there was something more to the other spellmonger than bluff and blunder. It bore some investigation, at least.

After I traded news with Koucey over the wisdom of spreading the word of the impending crisis, I bowed out of his office and let the man work. It was time I checked on my own preparations. I passed through Garkesku's empty quarters on my way and went up the wooden stair to my new chambers.

It was my turn to be impressed. Tyndal had done a masterful job arranging the barren tower into a genuine workspace. He had found ample private space for my professional items in those cramped quarters. I still wasn't completely happy with the situation, as I saw the plain straw tick where it sat on the floor. The castle was infested with rodents and bugs, and that just didn't look particularly inviting – not after enjoying a fluffy wool-stuffed tick back at the shop. But it was the possibility of rats that got to me more.

I've disliked rats intensely ever since Farise. They grew as large as dogs in that tropical climate (especially in an occupied city, with plenty of corpses to feed upon) and they were all over every ship that took port there. I remember seeing them strut across the decks in broad daylight like they owned the ship, and the best efforts of the ship's cats and my own magical rat-traps barely put a dent in the population.

Then I remembered the sailor's trick for evading the pests at night, and I decided to have Tyndal secure a bolt of cloth wide enough to construct two hammocks we could sling from the stone walls. I've liked hammocks ever since I saw them in use at sea. They seemed especially helpful in the tight quarters of a castle under siege. And that would also free up more space for our work.

Essentially satisfied, I went back down to the grounds of the inner bailey to make certain the mercenaries were settling in well. While their contract was technically with the Lord of Boval Vale, since I was the one who recruited them I felt obligated to see to their comfort.

The Crinroc brothers were actually settling into their camp on the eastern side fairly well, though in a circular arrangement that reminded me of a nomad camp and was difficult to integrate into the rest of the encampments. The regular mercenaries encamped on the western side of the donjon, and while their tents were lined up in a reasonably orderly fashion, the illusion of organization stopped there.

I almost felt ashamed. The Crinroc were barbarians, outsiders, tribal savages. The other mercenaries were my people, Narasi, and they were botching up just about everything they touched and arguing over every point they could. I tried to gently intercede in one of the dozen or so conflicts between factions that had formed in the unit, but quickly became entangled in the opinions and supposed rights each unit claimed to have. I finally got pissed enough to discharge a particularly loud cantrip to get their attention.

(Interesting note: even simple magic was much easier to do with the irionite. Before, it had taken at least minimal concentration to perform even a candle-lighting, but now I tossed out my hand and a flash-bang-smoke cantrip materialized with almost no effort on my part.)

"May I please have your attention, you *misbegotten sons of poxy whores!*" I began, politely, as I stepped on top of a pile of crates just to be heard in the silence after the cantrip burst but before the smoke cleared. It was a flashy effect, but it worked admirably to get their attention and remind them just who the nine hells they were dealing with.

"Since you *obviously* don't have the sense to pour piss out of a boot, I'm going to have to restore some order, or the locals will start confusing you with the Crinroc! If anybody takes offense to that, they can bring it to my attention, right here, right now!" I said, patting Slasher in its sheath over my shoulder. "We will be glad to discuss whatever petty concern you have, and settle it quickly – one way or another!"

There were grumbles and chuckles, but more of the latter than the former. They had spent almost two weeks on the road with me and knew my stern face well. Dozens of their own faces looked up at me with a mixture of surprise, regret, and anger. But they quieted down. They took me true to my word.

Most of the trip I spent concentrating on the march and hadn't worried much with the quality of troops I was leading. That had to change now, and for the entire afternoon I dived into the task of integrating them with the rest of the besieged army with a vengeance.

It was actually pretty simple, it turned out that apart from the Crinroc I had a few hundred infantry of various sorts and a few dozen cavalry troopers. Most were the Black Flag, and therefore under Captain Forondo, who was pretty good about keeping discipline. My infantry, however, was rotten.

They weren't bad, man by man, but they were definitely not a unit, and some were questionable even as arrow fodder. I re-organized them into two fifty-man companies, dissolving previous "units" to create them, and told off seven as officers.

I put Captain Besser in charge of the whole thing – there were some older and presumably wiser heads there, but I *liked* Besser. For one thing, he listened to me. He reminded me more of the professionals I had met in Farise, and he didn't take any shit. Nor was he very heavy-handed, which sounds like a contradiction, but isn't.

Of the other six, I made two Lieutenants, each in charge of a company, and four Ancients, each in charge of a twenty-five man platoon. I had the Ancients wear a yellow sash, the Lieutenants a blue one, and I made Besser wear a bright red plume in his helmet, much like Forondo's. In any regular war situation I would have worried that the insignia would be confusing during pitched battle (colored sashes are commonly used to distinguish sides in regular "civilized" warfare) but I figured that when the enemy is uniformly short, dark and hairy the color of a man's sash wouldn't matter.

Then came the hard part: arming them.

Almost all of them had swords of one sort or another, because in Alshar you weren't a fighting man unless you carried one. These were personal items, not usually supplied by the client, but after inspecting

264

some of those rusty sticks I had over a dozen sent back to the smithy for repair or replacement. I had purchased a few score short infantry swords – the type useful for defending a narrow passageway or the top of a battlement – and I distributed them among the mercenaries who needed them.

The rest were more difficult. I had a pretty fair-sized armory at my disposal, so I had good choices to make. In a siege, though, which weapons are going to be most useful? Long sharp pointy ones, or heavy, blunt short ones? How about archery?

In Castal, and in the coastal regions of Alshar far to the south I knew the siege weapon of choice was the crossbow. They are ideal for keeping besiegers at bay or, conversely, clearing battlements of defenders. You can teach a peasant how to use one in a few days and they are both relatively accurate and extremely powerful. But they also took a skilled artisan to create and maintain, and the Wilderlands was short of quality arbalests.

But nearly every peasant in the Wilderlands hunts for game or has to contend with predators after their herds and livestock. That made them somewhat skilled at basic archery. Much of the peasant militia were armed with the great hickory-and-yew laminate bows known elsewhere as the Wilderlands bow, as tall as a man and ideal for sniping at wolves and bandits, but arrows were something that, I knew, we would be perpetually short of. Wilderlands bows fire arrows up to three feet long. Ideally they are also laminates, the shafts made of hard hickory on the front and lightweight cedar in the rear. They used iron or steel points and were fletched, usually, with goose feathers. Every archer tended to make his own arrows, and though Koucey had a goodly supply stashed in his store rooms it wouldn't take long to empty them during a busy siege.

But shooting at wolves and shooting during war are two different things. Archers are most deadly when firing in volleys, something most of my men had only a vague idea of how to do. The Wilderlands bow takes up a lot of room when it's employed, too, not an ideal for battlements where men frequently stood elbow-to-elbow. They're also constructed to fit the man who will fire it. Though there were a few score of them in storage they aren't like crossbows. You can't just hand them out and expect folks to be proficient with them.

I finally told off one platoon (which seemed to have an abundance of bows already) to serious archery practice, while I made the other platoon in that company sword-and-shield men. To the other company I issued spears – perhaps not as long as the pikes of the Gobarban Order, but several campfire conversations with the Commanding Abbot had given me ideas about just how they could useful in a siege.

Once the troops were well ordered I set their new Ancients to drilling them in basic maneuvers while I dealt with the unit where egos where more important to success than arms: the horsemen.

*   *   *

I showed up for my induction into military service on time. I was hung over, whored-out and ready to piss myself in fear and anxiety, but, Duin and Trygg help me, *I showed up.*

It was partly out of fear of the Censorate's famed hunters, who would pursue a mage as an oathbreaker if he did not, but I also showed up partly out of a sense of relief that I didn't have to decide what to do with my life just yet. Even with my credentials it would be hard to get a position, I knew. Despite my academic success, few professional firms want to invest in a mage right out of school, untested and untried, unless there was nepotism or family ties involved. I was looking at a year's worth of wandering around, starving to death and trying to establish a name for myself, had I not been drafted for the campaign. At least His Grace's summons gave me a steady – if paltry – income, meals, a billet, and some direction.

The same held true for about a third of my class of new warmagi: everyone who was not related to someone powerful enough to buy their way out or pull strings was present at the ancient hulking fortress of Relan Cor that rainy autumn day, not out seeking a position. Not coincidently, many of the guys from my Tower were there. But we weren't all born commoners. Some of the North Tower lordlings, sons of knights and lords, were eager for the combat experience. There were also a few gutsy Remerans who weren't ready to settle down with the family firm just yet. The Magical Corps seemed like a decent proposal for all of us at the time . . . which just goes to show you how woefully ignorant we were of the political situation at the time.

While we were in school the renegade province of Farise had been systematically raiding the trading fleets that regularly made the lucrative trip from Shutek, Unstara and the southern archipelagoes to various parts of the Duchies. They'd also raided the important shipping between the rich port cities of southern Alshar and the eastern duchies, disrupting the cotton, tobacco, and wool trade (not to mention taking high-born passengers for ransom).

This was nothing new; the Farisians had caused trouble for the Powers-That-Be since before the Inundation of Perwyn.

Farise isn't even really a country. It's a kind of city-state. It was founded about the middle of the First Magocracy as a pirate haven for Cormeeran corsairs who used it as a base to raid Imperial shipping between Alshar (which had been settled by fellow Cormeeran corsairs who had retired with their riches to become wealthy landowners) and the rest of the Magocracy, and it remains a port city to rival any in the Duchies to this day. Its location at the cape of the Farisian peninsula gave it a perfect position for raiding. The city grew up around the port and extended north to foothills. It was a good place to spend pirated loot or retire to after a life of trading and raiding.

When the pirates got too bad, the Archmage (I forget which one) sent a fleet to reason with (read: *conquer*) the miscreants and establish order. In their place he installed one of his distant relatives he feared was conspiring for the throne. The new Imperial regent took the title Doge, and from that point on Farise was an outpost of Imperial civilization and an important trading port. The Doge ruled the province in the name of the Archmagi and things settled down.

Then a few hundred years later my ancestors, a bunch of horse-riding, illiterate barbarians from the great northern steppes had gotten tired of being pushed around by the Archmage decided that enough was enough. With some assistance from some treacherous rebels and disaffected magi, the Narasi clans invaded the valley of Vore, swept away the lackluster Imperial military resistance, and conquered all of the old Magocracy within two lifetimes.

Except for Farise. My people are not very good sailors under the best conditions, and we were apparently so involved with looting the pristine civilization of the mainland that we overlooked that remote little outpost. The Doge continued Imperial traditions and took in plenty of expatriates fleeing the barbarians. A few even tried to form a Magocracy-in-Exile in response to my ancestors' heavy-handed approach to magical regulation, but the Doge would not surrender political power and most of those pretenders fell as quickly as they rose.

Farise, both the city and the narrow strip of cultivated land around it, is at the end of a long southward-jutting peninsula that is almost impassable. Jagged mountains form a spine for the land, and savage jungles on both coasts cut off any decent access from the mainland. It was far easier and cheaper for merchants to sail around it between Castal and Alshar than to contend with the wild tribes of human, gurvani, and Alka Alon who range these areas. The local wildlife is especially vicious. Strange diseases often infect those who venture into the jungles, and the near-constant rain makes travel all but impossible. So if you want to attack Farise, you'd better have a strong navy. Stronger than the Farisi.

The Doge and his cronies had been left alone by the Duchies for the most part during the last four hundred years. But that didn't mean they didn't stop raiding. The Farisi seemed to think that just because they controlled the strategically placed Farisian peninsula and had a powerful native fleet that they had a right to tribute from any Ducal ships passing by.

This had happened before, of course. Usually it was an excuse to shake down the Coronet Council for protection money, and usually the council paid with only a little grumbling.

But there had been an incident involving the family of one of the Dukes, the Doge's pet magi had started using dangerous spells (and irionite, as we discovered later) and one thing led to another toward war. By the time I left the academy the Coronet Council had decided that an independent Farise was a luxury they could not tolerate. In a rare show of solidarity the three western-most of them – Alshar, Remere, and Castal – had authorized a joint mission to secure the rebellious old Imperials. They pooled their military assets and went to war with the Imperial remnant, intending to invade.

This was actually the second time an invasion had been ordered. The previous year the Coronet Council had authorized a punitive fleet to trim back the "pirates" in a show of naval force. It had, after all, worked for the Magocracy) it was commanded by a mariner friend to the Castali Ducal Court. He proceeded to ruin the fleet in a series of vicious battles in the Farisian Straight, narrowly losing or destroying every one of his forty great warships (and hundreds of ships carrying occupation troops) because the Doge employed his court wizard, Orril Pratt, to destroy and confuse them with magic. The designated admiral at least had the good grace to die in battle at sea and avoid the shame of his failure.

But like their horselord ancestors had done with the Magocracy, the Dukes of Remere, Castal and Alshar (with the tacit support of the other two) finally had enough of the situation. The added insult of losing two score warships to the Farisi was too much for the honor of the five Narasi Dukes. Invasion plans began afresh, and a fully staffed Magical Corps was called for to combat the Mad Mage of Farise.

As it was easier and cheaper to draft magi fresh out of school than to hire well-established mercenaries, the Warlord had *us* pressed into service before we could find real jobs. The Campaign Warlord figured he could take the pesky little city-state within the year with a few hundred well-trained, well-armed warmagi at his disposal,.

Only it hadn't quite worked out that way. The Doge 's ally, Orril Pratt, might have been unstable, but he had also acquired a chip of near-mythical *irionite* from somewhere and wasn't afraid of the Censorate or the dangers of using it. No great fleet could approach Farise by sea while he was on watch. By the time I arrived at Relan Cor he was wreaking havoc on even the light patrol boats the Dukes used to regularly probed the Farisi coastal defenses.

Large squadrons were broken up by mage-wrought storms, or sunk when their hulls began leaking uncontrollably, or burst into magical flames. The might of the Mad Mage was such that even the most powerful magi in the eastern Duchies were unwilling to face him. Defeating the combination of his magic, Farise's unassailable geography, and the sailors who expertly handled the shallow-draughted, yellow-sailed penances of Farise was *not* going to be easy.

But it had to be done. The Dukes said so.

Which is how three weeks after graduating from Inarion Academy and *finally* getting my credentials to practice magic, I found myself instead standing in a soaking cloak in a continuous drizzle, drops of icy rain running down my nose, while a strange man with a jaw like an anvil screamed into my face and questioned the legitimacy of my conception and birth.

I found my time at the War College . . . *constructive*. For the first nine weeks we were shoved in a barracks with the young nobles who were training for officer status in the infantry. Indeed, most of our training was identical to theirs: swordsmanship, horsemanship, archery, unarmed combat, small unit tactics, logistics and supply, scouting and reconnaissance, command-of-battle, siege craft and field fortifications, war rites and battle rituals, leadership, first aid, and all the other crap they feel every officer should know. We weren't technically field officers, but the Magical Corps traditionally billeted with them, so we learned what they learned.

Like marching. We marched *a lot* – too much, I thought at the time; not nearly enough, I know now. We marched in armor and out, with packs and without, and even without shoes for two unbearable days.

We were outfitted in the standard Magical Corps armor, a kind of waxed leather vest with steel plates sewn over the vital areas, and taught how to give them basic enchantments to augment their protection. Despite their ugliness they did have a one-size-fits-all kind of security about them. The basic pattern left plenty of room for movement, wasn't too heavy, and didn't keep you from casting spells in combat. Mostly.

We also got our mageblades. Those are the specialized weapons of warmagi, somewhere between the length of an infantry sword and a cavalry sword, with a point, a double-sided blade, and spaces cut within to lighten them and allow room for custom (and theoretically devastating) enchantments. The style had been around since the Magocracy, and they are traditionally worn on the back, attached to a leather harness and drawn over your shoulder. They, too, were standardized and unadorned, but nearly every student eventually paid to have theirs customized to fit them better. A few even learned enough blacksmithing to do it themselves.

We were required to give them names to aid in spellcasting. I named mine Slasher, because that's what it seemed best at.

After we were reasonably trained in the standard ways of war and were given the opportunity to participate in the Mysteries of Duin (I declined –

the only goddess I really worshipped was Briga, who has little to do with warfare) the weather began making it more practical to study indoors. We were separated from the rest of the officers to learn the ancient and potent craft of warmagic.

Even with my years of study at Inarion, I was still amazed by the things I learned at War College. Inarion gave me a theoretical basis for understanding spells. At Relan Cor I took my precious knowledge of the human body and learned how to destroy it a thousand different ways.

I learned things about the forces of light and shadow (photomantics), fire and ice (pyromantics) and toxic, corrosive and explosive chemicals (battlefield alchemy) that I never would have *dreamed* were possible at Inarion.

I learned how to build a warstaff, warwands and a hundred nasty magical traps and weapons. I learned the art of illusion, concealment and misdirecting an enemy's gaze to where I wanted it. I learned to strike without hesitation or remorse, just kill, kill, *kill* . . . until my objective was complete.

Our head instructor was the legendary one-eyed Master Durgan Jole, a warmaster and warmagi famous a dozen-times over. The scrappy old man gave us the benefit of his forty years as a magical mercenary, working with each and every one of us until we could all hold our own in duels both magical and mundane.

Support magic was a big part of the training. Warmagi are rarely front line troops, we're specialists, and usually we specialized in keeping frontline troops safe, comfortable, and informed. We learned spells to inspire our friends and drive our foes to despair. We learned to clear fear from our minds and focus utterly on the task at hand.

Late in our courses they taught us advanced warmagic techniques: how to supplement our own bodies' energy with magical energy to restore ourselves from fatigue, how to speed up reflexes and hone my perceptions with magic until I was more than a match for a regular infantryman. Warmagic allowing us to move three times as fast as the fastest mortal, and twice as far in the same time.

We learned his seemingly endless bag of battle cantrips – small spells not inherently dangerous, but useful in the faster-than-a-blink world of the warmage. Camouflage, stealth, armor spells, clairvoyance spells designed to gather enemy intelligence, counterintelligence spells to avoid enemy intelligence, and a special three-day tutorial on healing battlefield traumas that was as useful as it was morbid. It came complete with fresh corpses.

We practiced war games all winter, and I adapted myself to the soldier's life. Very different from the life of an academic, but just as rewarding, in its way. When spring finally came we were deemed ready to face the Doge and the Mad Mage. They split us into three groups, depending upon our overall performance.

Group A was comprised of those whose physical performance was not considered strong enough to make the trip. Group A would be in charge of Strategic Magical Support, keeping the weather in line for the amphibious assault and scrying enemy positions.

Group B was made up of those who excelled at one particular type of warmagic: the sneaky type, the brutal type, or the healing type. Group

B was taken aside for advanced training in their field of excellence and destined for special missions.

Group C was anyone who was left. I was in Group C -- it seems Thaumaturgy and Magical Theory were not considered highly useful battlefield skills. I didn't mind; I was ready to go and wreak havoc on the enemies of the Duchies, thanks to the miracle workers of the War College. Master Durgan Jole and his fellows had taken two hundred bookish students and turned them into a pack of vicious and highly efficient killers adept at the craft of warmagic.

A pity he never made it back from Farise. But then neither did many of his students.

*   *   *

The Black Flag mercenary company were about as professional a cavalry unit as I could have hoped for in the Wilderlands, setting up their camp and seeing to their horses without too much acrimony.

The Kelso knights, however, were a haughty bunch of aristocrats who had been born with silver candlesticks up their arses. They didn't want to bed down next to common troops. They didn't like the food. They objected to the wine. They complained about the pay. They didn't like the duties they were assigned. They didn't like the entertainment possibilities. I almost put them with the Crinroc out of spite, after one particularly nasty debate, when Sire Koucey arrived and saved the day by hosting his noble Wilderlord peers in the keep.

The Kelso knights profoundly irritated me. They were just as much mercenaries as the rest of them, but for some reason a *noble* mercenary feels he has the right to bitch that the sky is the wrong shade of blue and water is too wet. They tend to think that regular military rules don't apply to them. The chivalrous mercenaries were warriors, but they weren't really *soldiers*, used to taking and executing simple orders. Everything was open to discussion, debate, and everyone felt entitled to advance his stupid opinion before any course of action was carried out.

Sire Koucey offered them a large chamber (which they complained about) and seats in his hall, instead of making them eat with the common men, to which they reluctantly (and vocally) agreed. I was just as glad to get rid of them, as they were causing trouble in the Black Flag. Forondo may have been a nobleman, or at least raised as one, but the mercenary captain knew how to soldier and the Wilderlords just didn't. It took a whole day of arguing to finally sort out where they would live and what they would do. I let Koucey deal with the matter of their pay. I was just too tired.

As dusk approached, and I was reasonably certain my men were well provided for, I stumbled back up to the tower. Garkesku still wasn't in, but I found Tyndal unpacking the gear I'd purchased in Tudry like a good apprentice. I spied one package in particular and decided that it was as good a time as any to present it to him.

The last few weeks had taught me how much I appreciated the lad's thoughtful consideration and his genuine desire to please. Sure, he was an uneducated commoner, but I had a newfound appreciation of his pragmatic earnestness after dealing with the knights of Kelso. After a brief inspection of our quarters I sat the boy down on my own stool, poured him a glass of mediocre local wine and toasted him like an adult, if not an equal. Though he was bordering on embarrassment, he awkwardly returned the toast before he downed it with a satisfied sigh. I'd have to watch that – he was starting to drink like me.

"Tyndal, you know perhaps better than anyone else in the castle what we are up against, here. We may not – hells, we will probably *not* survive, but we at least we will go down fighting like men instead of being murdered in our beds or ambushed along the road.

"But that means each of us will have to do some fighting. And if we are to be fighting men, then we should be adorned as such." With that I pulled out the oilcloth wrapped bundle that he (thankfully) had yet to put away and undid the coarse string that bound it.

Within were the weapons for which I had paid a high premium to the Tudry warmage, Master Cormoran. First was a mageblade, similar to my own Slasher, only built to Tyndal's height and arm-length. The scabbard was plain black unadorned leather, and the hilt was brass, but the blade was superior to that of a mere infantryman, worthy of any golden hilt and bejeweled scabbard.

It was by far the least of Cormoran's stock. The Veolicti Order were fine weaponsmiths, and produced superb steel mageblades that were flexible enough not to snap yet strong enough to cut through all but the stoutest armor. The edge of the sword was keen and flawless, and the flat was brightly polished. Most importantly, it was made to bear offensive spells, like a warwand. Cormoran had thrown in a small warmage's harness for just a few pennies more. Tyndal was in awe as I belted it around him and slung the blade over his right shoulder.

Next I gave him the bow I had picked out, a little too short for open battle but well-suited to the siege I was expecting. There was nothing especially magical about the bow, but it was well-built and strong, and the two score of professionally-made arrows I purchased were well fletched with gorgeous gray goose feathers. Every boy in Boval knows his way around a bow – House Brandmount had not seen any reason to limit hunting rights for its yeomen and freemen – and I suspected that with practice he would learn to shoot exceptionally well. The goblins should give him plenty of practice.

Lastly, I gave him the professional-strength warwand I had bought for him. It was a multipurpose weapon, as it could use the regular magical blast, or convert that power into either flame or steam. There weren't that many charges on it, but he could always add some more, once I taught him precisely how.

"Master, I have been busy while you've been gone," he said smugly, after accepting my gifts gratefully and graciously. "I've been practicing what you showed me." He handed me the warwand that he had started on the road, his first. One I never expected to work particularly well. It was all but covered with runes now, and I could feel the vibrant power in it.

I raised an eyebrow – I was impressed. "That is superior work, my boy. But don't add any more, now."

He looked disturbed. "Why not?"

"Because that's not the best wood for the use. You've loaded the thing up tight with arcane power. Add any more and it will break. When a warwand breaks, it will usually kill the wielder and destroy everything around it in a sudden and unpredictable explosion or wave."

He paled when I said that. I chuckled. "I wouldn't worry about it, lad – it's a stout enough wand. Keep it close at hand. But in battle you should work on the larger one I bought you for now. It's more efficient and can handle a lot more energy."

Pacified, he poured us each another glass, unbidden.

"To the life of a spellmonger under dire circumstances!" I toasted, and poured it down.

I suddenly realized that I was very, *very* tired as the wine hit my belly. I sought out my mattress and sprawled out, pausing only long enough to take off my boots and my harness. The hammock idea would have to wait. If I saw any rats, I decided as I drifted off, I'd just change them into something a little less interesting.

*   *   *

The next morning I was up with the dawn, on the roof of the tower, overseeing the magical situation. Garkesku and his oldest apprentice were with me, still a little skeptical of my abilities and my judgment, but unwilling to argue with me openly anymore. I *had* produced an army, after all. That wasn't something Garky was able to do.

I was surveying the hills with magesight, looking for scouts or skirmishers in the forests. I wasn't having much luck, but magesight, even with the benefit of irionite, doesn't work nearly as well in daylight.

While I was up there, however, my attention was distracted by a lovely young girl, who looked about seventeen or so, bathing in the outer bailey. The curtains that were suspended from poles protected her modesty from passers-by were long and opaque, but from my vantage point I could see everything that Trygg had graced her with. She had dark blonde hair and a shapely figure, and I could tell she had a pretty face, too. I'd been so involved in war preparations that I had almost forgotten that there were women aplenty in the castle. Indeed, the outer bailey had almost every woman in the valley within its walls. This one was quite lovely, well-formed and delightfully female.

I made a mental note to make her acquaintance . . . then suddenly realized that I already had. I increased the focus on my magesight and confirmed that yes, indeed, it was the farm widow Alya who was bathing so enticingly. She was kept from further lechery-at-a-distance by my irritating colleague.

"Master Minalan, is that a rider?" Garkesku pointed to the road in front of the gate. I swore under my breath and turned away from that lovely sight to the realities of war. It was indeed a rider, I saw, and one on a very lathered horse. I magnified my magesight with a whispered command. The man was an armored Wilderlord who bore the banner of Brandmount Castle from the point of his lance.

"He must be bearing news," I said, forming a spell to allow me to hear his words. Clairaudience – the "long ears" spell they taught me at Relan Cor – has never been a strength of mine, but *everything* was easier now that I had my witchstone. As the spell activated it was as if I'd had a plug of wax removed from my ears, and I could hear the man's breathing and the panting of his horse as he rode past the guards into the stables as if I was riding next to him. One of Koucey's senior staff, Sir Norlian, was there and demanded the message.

The goblins have attacked Mor Tower, cutting off the Mor pass! the messenger said between labored breaths. *And a large band of the bastards has the temerity to raid Hymas itself! I saw as I came past!*

"Guess what, Master Garkesku?" I said, a lump in my throat.

"We are at war," the older mage replied. I was surprised – I didn't think he'd had time to hang the same spell I had. Nor the power. Hells, I doubted that he even knew of the Long Ears. "We are at war, and Hymas is burning."

"Yes, you're right," I admitted. "How did you know?" I asked, turning to face him. He and his oldest apprentice were staring at the distant town, where a long, black plume of smoke rose up over the trees and hills.

"I saw the portents in the sky," he snorted, dryly. "So the rider agreed with my assessment?"

"With one addition. Mor Tower is under attack, and escape out of the vale is cut off."

He hung his head sadly, and looked depressed. "Then we are at war, and we are all going to die," he said. I didn't say anything in reply, although it was the perfect time for some optimistic chatter.

When I heard the rider talk of Mor Tower, I suddenly felt as if an iron door had slammed shut. The reality of our situation came bear. There were thousands of gurvani creeping down the mountains, angry and determined, led by shamans armed with irionite. There was a malevolent force that was urging them on. There really *was* no other way to get in and out of Boval unless you wanted to try the gurvani-infested mountain ridges. I suddenly didn't know what in the nine hells I had done to get trapped in such a situation. A quip, or at least a hopeful phrase, might have cheered the other spellmonger. I couldn't think of one off-hand that might serve.

But mostly I didn't say anything because I had to agree. We *were* all going to die.

Chapter Seven

The Last Charge Of The Bovali Knights

"When engaging an enemy, honor and victory demand that lesser troops stand aside and allow the chivalry the privilege of practicing their trade on the battlefield; for rarely has a battle been seen as won until the clash of lances and shields takes place. Indeed, there can be little other purpose in the affair of war if the knights who are the backbone of the military are not given the chance to prove their worth in heated battle."

- *Count Ascor of Faranal*

-

Castles *stink*.

They look so lofty, strong, and imposing from a distance. The peasantry often considers them palaces – but they aren't. They're oversized military fortifications with a fairly small resident staff. In peacetime the number of residents is small enough not to notice the many odors involved. Most people who have been fortunate enough never to have to depend on one to save their lives will not appreciate this, but castles in wartime smell worse than a pigsty.

First there was the barnyard stench of the tightly-packed livestock which fades into the background pretty quickly, especially if you are accustomed to it as most of us are. Personally, horseshit smells pretty good to me, almost symbolic of the majesty of the beasts. Usually it was saved up to be spread on the fields as valuable fertilizer, but in a siege it just got piled up outside of the castle wall until better times. Add to that the aroma of pig, chicken, the ubiquitous cow and miscellaneous small critters, and it can get pretty ripe. Especially around the slaughtering pit. Most of the offal was fed back to the pigs or mixed in with the manure.

But in addition to the aroma of the animals is the mass of infrequently washed agricultural humanity crowded into the outer bailey under tarpaulins. A few thousand men, women and children, none of who bathed all that regularly in the best of times, were suddenly crammed ass-to-elbow into a confined space, along with enough privies to (theoretically) service them all. Hastily dug latrines dotted the outer bailey, but that's a *lot* of poop. It all went into the moat, the protective ditch that surrounded the castle, as a deterrent to invaders (but also because, frankly, there wasn't a better place to put it) where it festered and fermented and stank like, well, poop.

It gets worse. Mixed in with the natural sweat of men and women working diligently on any number of labors was an almost palpable stench of fear, I noted. These ordinary people were confronted with the possibility of violent death from an inhuman enemy, and that produced a particular smell distinct from the ordinary sweat of daily living and honest toil.

The barbers and physicians had set up shop and contributed the odor of vomit and diarrhea to the air. They hung evergreen boughs from their tents to try to mask the smell of sickness, but it was laughably ineffective unless you held it directly under your nose.

Odors of wood smoke from cooking fires and the moldy smell emanating from barrels of stagnant water placed strategically around the castle in the event of fire added to the stink. The work sheds that lined the castle walls and housed all of the artisans necessary to keeping a siege running contributed to it. Blacksmiths, with the associated acrid tang of coke fires, chandlers rendering tallow into candles, tanners with the ungodly stink of purification and powerful tannins, all added to the revolting stench until it was almost overwhelming.

The combination of this riot of smells forced me to use a cantrip that deadened my nose just to get through the day. While I couldn't taste my food properly with the spell, I wasn't missing much (castle rations are poor even for officers), but it was a small price to pay for the luxury of not gagging every time I inhaled. Thankfully it was potent enough to combat the worst of the odors and let me do my job. The only smell that was powerful enough to make it through the spell was the sickening scent of fear. That smell permeated every nook and cranny of Boval Castle. And with good reason.

The smoke over Hymas on the horizon caused quite a commotion in the Castle the day before. The peasants and townsfolk camped in the outer bailey saw it just a few moments after we did and quickly gathered to peer over the walls in dismay. A frightened moan ran through the crowded campground as the grumblers and whiners who had been *certain* that the rumors of gurvani attacks had been exaggerated or fabricated entirely by the nobility suddenly realized, as their shops and homes burned in the distance, that their lives really *were* in danger.

The black cloud made them anxious and restless. Some spread the rumor that a massive goblin army had already arrived. If a stout little town like Hymas could fall so quickly, the reasoning ran, then an attack on Boval Castle surely couldn't be far behind.

I couldn't argue with that, especially after witnessing the pillage that the gurvani vanguard put to Hymas town by means of magesight. They stole everything they could and burned the rest. Any civilian stragglers were captured and slaughtered, and the remaining men-at-arms patrolling the town were driven back to the castle.

That many anxious folks inside the castle, witnessing their life going up in smoke on the horizon, made the smell even worse. They didn't know what was happening to their homes, though they could imagine well-enough.

So when Sire Koucey ordered a cavalry force organized to investigate and, if possible, drive off the goblins, I volunteered just to get away from the stench. While I knew it was probably a futile effort, it was psychologically very important for us to at least appear to strike at the goblins so that the Wilderland peasants would cling to some hope of better days and brighter futures.

Besides, I figured we might as well use the cavalry we had available while we could. In a matter of days, if not sooner, I fully expected us to be locked up in this pile of stones where horses were more of a liability than an asset until the meat ran out. For now I wanted to escape from the smell of fear of terrified men more than I feared the smell of goblins.

Sire Koucey decided to lead the horsemen himself, as was his chivalrous prerogative. He sent a messenger to me that afternoon ordering me to prepare the mercenary cavalry for a patrol with his gentlemen and to meet him at the gatehouse. I honestly wasn't yet trusting of their loyalty, so riding with Sire Koucey, Sir Stancil, and his other sworn Wilderlords seemed a fair idea. So I strapped on my weapons harness and found Captain Forondo, who had anticipated the order and had the men already preparing their mounts.

The Black Flag moved with more military efficiency, if not quite precision, than the Wilderlords. While the knights' horses were being saddled and their armor was being strapped on their bodies by squires or other attendants, I sat with Sir Forondo and briefed him on the geography of Hymas. The Kelso knights rode out of the stables almost merrily and seemed eager to get out of the castle and into glory. I ignored them while I discussed the situation with Forondo.

Sire Koucey joined us presently, and I made formal introductions between the mercenary captain and the Lord of Boval Vale whom they served – purposefully slighting the Kelsoi. I'm just that way.

The two men were a study in contrasts. Koucey was, of course, far older than the mercenary captain, and shorter in stature. His longish gray-white hair and beard spilled out of his helmet onto his shoulders giving him a stately mantle that seemed to embody what he was: a Wilderlord knight trained from birth to fight with sword and lance in the defense of his lands. He wore a shimmering coat of well-blued chainmail augmented by steel pauldrons, and he wore an ornately decorated longsword on his hip. His surcoat was emblazoned with the simple device of his House, a white cow on a green field. He had a look of grim determination that barely masked the fear and anxiety I knew was in him – fear not for his own life, but for the lives of the people entrusted to his care.

Forondo, on the other hand, had the weary look of the professional campaigner about him, as well as the cautious air of a mercenary. Tall and lanky, he wore his long dark hair in a serviceable ponytail under his unadorned steel cavalry helmet. His well-scuffed leather and steel armor seemed a little too large for him in places, though he seemed to be able to move with alacrity in it. He wore no surcoat or device, only a black headband around the brow of his helm and a black wool mantle to identify him as captain of the Black Flag.

His sword was a plain, serviceable cavalryman's longsword with the triple spiral of Trygg on its brass pommel. He had a short handled mace dangling from his belt by a lanyard as well as a long dagger tucked behind the small of his back. Neither was decorated, that I could see. Though he bore a serviceable lance, it was a tool in his hands, not a scepter of office, and it lacked a pennant.

Forondo ordered his subordinates about without recourse to vile profanity – though he used the ordinary sort as liberally as any military commander does when dealing with mounted troops. His mood was melancholy but practical, and while he had some fear in him, it was no more and no less than the fear that any professional soldier has before going into battle and uncertainty. He was just doing the job he'd been hired to do.

The two men got along famously.

Koucey outlined the plan quickly and succinctly: this was not a punitive expedition, this was an attempt to locate the enemy, engage them, if numbers were favorable, gauge their defense, and retreat safely back to the castle. Forondo agreed wholeheartedly – a mercenary captain doesn't like to risk his men unnecessarily if he can help it, and a captain of horse is more protective of his beasts than of his daughter's virtue. The two commanders traded war stories and advice until messengers arrived reporting on the readiness of both the Black Flag and the much smaller Kelsoi heavy cavalry unit.

"My lord," I said as Koucey strode purposefully towards the step that led up to his mount, "I beg leave to come with you. Most probably the gurvani have shamans of their own with them, and I am loath to leave you undefended against magical attack."

Koucey looked concerned. "I had expected you to stay here, in case this is a ruse designed to lead us away from our strong points."

"My lord, this castle will not fall on the absence of one man, even a warmage. The wards are as tight as they can be made – I inspected them myself. And Sir Cei is firmly in charge of the defense. But if I might say so, as *you* are one of our strong points, milord; should we risk your death? That news would be devastating to your people. Yet I know that you want to see the foe with your own eyes. Therefore I think it would be best if you were accompanied by a warmage, and there is no one more suited to the task than I."

Koucey scowled, but nodded. "Have your rouncey brought around, Spellmonger. Today you shall see how the knights of Boval comport themselves in battle, Huin willing!" There was a fire in his eyes that was part pride and part frustration, like a boy being made to wait overlong for his name day presents. I bowed and went to see about Traveler.

Much to my surprise, he was already saddled, and Tyndal was grooming him in the stable when I entered. He grinned when I arrived and told me he had guessed that I would want to accompany the troops. Traveler looked magnificent – the boy had a keen eye for horses, and I could tell that he'd also used a few subtle cantrips to make his coat look even glossier than it would have anyway. For a rouncey gelding he was almost as handsome as a destrier.

Tyndal also brought down my warstaff and my blue riding mantle, and another one of the warwands I'd purchased in Tudry. I thanked him and gave him a few instructions about the tower before I trotted Traveler out to where the other horsemen were assembling.

I was actually looking forward to the expedition as much as Koucey. If nothing else it would get me away from that smell.

*   *   *

The battle plan for the Farisian Campaign was simple – not as simple as the first, disastrous marine assault on the sea fortress, but not much more complicated. Another great fleet would head out with troops from the Remere and Castal (and nearly a thousand mercenary crossbowmen auxiliaries, Merwyn's contribution to the fight) aboard, including an entire elite Magical Corps assembled specifically to try to combat the storms the Mad Mage wrought with his witchstone – and eventually storm his palace.

Meanwhile, under cover of deceptive spells and departing in darkness, a second force would land three hundred miles north of Farise on the eastern side of the narrow, mountainous isthmus that connected Farise with the rest of the world. Its mission would be to hack its way through the jungle, up the mountains, down the mountains, to eventually come up through the swamps north of the city-state and attack Farise in its unprotected rear.

Brilliant strategy. Unless you happened to be in that group. I was.

The invasion force set out a full two months ahead of the planned naval assault. Five thousand Alshari infantrymen, two hundred combat engineers, a medical corps, and about fifty of us new War College graduates landed on the western side of the peninsula, at the only possible landing point between the mainland and Farise. Six thousand men set out on the Long March.

Count Odo, a Castali lord with considerable experience in the arts of war, was given command of the overland expedition that hit the beach in the nameless eastern cove that was our staging ground. Cavalry was all but useless, there, where the paths through the jungles were too narrow and soft for real horsemanship and the vegetation so thick and wild that horses could not properly forage. We did have two score wagons loaded with supplies, but they were drawn by oxen or mules, not horses.

Most of the infantry were horribly overdressed. The Narasi ducal troops were used to the much cooler temperatures in the north, not the subtropical climate of Farise. As a result they left much of their heavy armor and woolen gear behind them on the trail south. Within days the entire column was dehydrated and ill. Disease was rampant, as were injuries due to heat exhaustion. Desertions would have been common had there been any convenient place to desert *to.*

It took more than sixty days to negotiate our way through the passes and woodlands of the Farisian mountains. Wild human tribes and gurvani clans held much of the territory, and to make matters worse we heard the tantalizing sounds of the Tree Folk reveling through the jungle on our tortuous trip. We even met with their representatives a few times to try to gain their support. They were polite, and steered us clear of dangers they knew of, but they would not aid us directly.

Farise had done better than we at gaining friends in the mountains, but then they had more practice. Seven times human tribes friendly to the Doge ambushed us. Only twice were we able to camp peacefully, in the territories of gurvani who hated the Farisi and their human tribal allies. As helpful as they were they could not stop the bodies piling up from skirmishes and disease. Nor could they feed our large army successfully. We ran short of food, water, medicine, bandages and other amenities before our march was half over.

That endless march through the jungle remains one of my most intense recurring nightmares. The days were a long, hot and humid exercises in endurance. As a warmage it was my duty to protect my company from magical attack, but even magic has its limits. It is difficult to concentrate on something as complex as a warding spell when you are dehydrated, physically exhausted and sleepless.

The nights were just as hot, perhaps, but filled with the noise of thousands of creatures our tired minds could only imagine. Snakebite (and bites by other things that weren't snakes) took their toll. If it weren't for the anti-insect cantrips we had to renew thrice daily, we would have been eaten alive by bugs.

Nor were we unopposed as we marched. Despite our attempt at "surprise", you just can't disguise the movements of an army that large, no matter what spells you cast. The Farisi had centuries of history defending those passes, and while they never brought a real army against us they sent plenty of warriors to slow us down. There were periodic raids and ambushes, snipers and kidnappings by the Farisi bad guys. I killed my first man on one of those, almost accidentally, and I lost several good friends to the brutal raids. The dusky Farisi warriors were good soldiers fighting for their homeland, and many of the human tribes in the area were allies of Farise.

I'd like to say we gave as good as we got, but that wouldn't be true. Most of the time the feather-clad warriors faded into the jungle before we could get our defenses ready. We didn't feel like an army expedition; we felt like a bunch of scared and tired little boys lost in the woods after dark.

And that was just the jungles. Once we were in the mountains, it got *worse*. The heat let up because of the altitude, but the cold became worse with every step we took. Massive thunderstorms swept in from the sea almost every night. Four times we got lost as we tried to navigate the maze of ridges and passes of that wild place. The Farisi resistance was even more pronounced.

Every morning, it seemed, we would lose another man or two to something nasty in the night. If it weren't for the timely assistance of the Alka Alon steering us away from a hidden Farisi fortress ready to slaughter us, we wouldn't have made it at all. We were three weeks late when we finally spotted the towers of Farise in the distance from the mountain passes. When we drew up to our planned camp only thirty-three hundred men remained in fighting shape. Only our sheer numbers and a few good commanders got an army to Farise, proper, at all.

It was on the Long March that I met Sire Koucey and his men. A Wilderlands mountain lord from the farthest west of the Duchies, he had volunteered to serve with a hundred of his folk. He had a quaint accent and an engaging smile, and led his troops well. I was assigned to support his unit a few times, and I found him a pleasant companion and a doughty warrior – one of the few knights who kept his armor despite the heat, and rarely complained about the lack of horses. Sire Koucey was always encouraging his men to do their best and do their duty with honor under the most trying of circumstances. When Count Odo died of a fever, he was part of the noble council that met to elect his successor.

Even at the end of the march, with a third of his men dead or lost to the jungle, he persevered in his duty and kept up the morale of his troops as we prepared to attack Farise from the rear. I respected that, as well as the way he could drink. He was a leader worth following.

*　　　*　　　*

The damage to Hymas Town wasn't as bad as what we anticipated, though I knew the townsfolk would be devastated by the sight.

The gurvani had torn through the town throwing torches at anything that would burn. They had written what I assumed were obscenities in ash and blood on every conceivable surface, and the blood of whatever farm animals were unfortunate enough to be caught by the goblins was splattered all over the place. Only about a dozen homes had actually burned completely, thanks to the rainy weather and damp thatch, but there was plenty of damage to the others for the sheer hell of it. Doors were bashed in, furniture was hacked with axes, feces were used to pollute household shrines. The streets were strewn with all sorts of cast-off goods rejected as loot, then destroyed for the pleasure of its destruction.

A few gurvani lingered there, likely as rear guards or picket troops. I scryed to scout the town as best I could and discovered a dozen or so camped out in one of the shops. When I told Koucey about it, the old knight angrily dispatched a dozen troopers to torch the place and kill any who tried to escape. While they sought retribution I rode Traveler to a quiet spot and tried a more potent location spell. I wished that I had time to construct a proper magemap, like I had for Minden's Hall, but Hymas was not my town, so I had to make do with ordinary battlefield scrying. I knew that the gurvani were still around – the fires and the mess in Hymas was too widespread and thorough to be the work of only a few.

The irionite sphere made it easier to find them by far – I wished I had it in Farise. As I took a mental walk around Hymas I did, indeed, discover a few more outposts and scouts, but the troops I figured had to be massed someplace were not within the town limits.

Then I found an area just outside of town that seemed to belie magical scrutiny. Obviously, someone was trying to mask their location, which ironically revealed it to me. While I am not terribly familiar with the town, I did remember a copse of trees to the south of town, known as Reza's Howe, where some of the local devotees of Yinka, (a minor fertility and nature goddess originally from one of the wild human tribes that the Narasi settlers had adopted) performed their rites. It took a little arcane pressure, but I was able to warp the defending wards and discover the approximate size and nature of the foe. There were a few hundred goblins encamped in a hollow near the center of the grove.

That made sense. The gurvani are not an urban folk; most of their settlements are small, and a town like Hymas would seem a strange and foreign place to them. They would not try to occupy it as a human army would. The grove gave them a better defensive posture, and one they were more familiar with. The trees would protect the goblins' sensitive eyes from the daytime sun, keep them in comfortably familiar surroundings as they rested, as well as make a cavalry charge dangerous for the cavalry. Once I told Sire Koucey about it I knew he'd try anyway, and count on the armor of his men and their ferocity to carry the day.

That wasn't a particularly bad plan – I didn't relish the thought of fighting tree to tree – but I had a better one.

Of all the elemental magics there are, fire is the easiest to summon and the hardest to control. The candle-lighting cantrip is usually among the first spells a student ever learns. It's quite easy: focus a stream of magical power on one spot, convert magical energy into a directed burst exciting the atoms of the tinder to incandescence, feed it oxygen and then heating it up to the point where it bursts into flame. I've seen some magi who were so good at this that they could cause a block of granite to burn like coal.

What I had in mind was, by comparison, *much* easier. While the magical wardings protected the gurvani from any direct arcane attack – you can't really hit what you can't see – we human warmagi are subtle. In this case I wanted to smoke them out.

In ten minutes I started a dozen tiny fires at different points in Reza's Howe by employing the substantial resources of the witchstone. While it had been almost a week since the last strong rain here, the topmost leaves in the Howe were dry enough to burn better than the thatched roofs of the town. The cloud cover that the gurvani shaman had summoned was dark, but not rainy. Most of the woodlands around here could be counted upon to hold a fair amount of underbrush, and the Howe was no exception.

With a little magical encouragement I found some dry spots that could be ignited at a distance. And once a fire like that is started, it quickly dries the water out of the surrounding vegetation enough to burn it. I placed my tiny blazes well enough to know that their smoke, if not their flames, would become a problem for our gurvani visitors before long.

Then I set my own wards, to keep us from being as easily detected as they were. It's not that their wards were poorly cast – it's that they were unsophisticated. Experience had taught me how to go about it properly for situations such as this.

I trotted back to where Sire Koucey and Captain Forondo were milling around on their horses, overseeing patrols and the like. Forondo was smoking a longish pipe of pungent sokel root shavings (a nasty Remeran habit left over from Imperial times – my people smoke *vobiril*, a pleasant and sweet smelling herb. Sokel root smells like a used pair of infantry boots when it burns, but the Remerans love the stuff) and Sire Koucey was consulting a small parchment map of the area he brought from the castle. The Lord of Boval Vale looked stricken upon seeing his lovely town and revenue center damaged so callously, but his chin was set with determination to take the destruction to his enemy.

"My lords, I've scryed the area," I began, not bothering to bow (which is hard to do from a horse, anyway, and while I still have a sensible commoner's respect for nobility, I learned in Farise that a count and a peasant are virtually indistinguishable when they've been disemboweled).

"Your report, Spellmonger? Have you found them?" Sire Koucey asked, worriedly. "The devastation they have wrought . . ."

"I have detected a large troop of goblins in the little wood known as Reza's Howe, just to the south." I used my regular wand to point out the spot on Koucey's map. "Their numbers were hidden from me by magic, which means that they have at least one shaman with them, probably using a witchstone. From the size of the shield and the other signs I would say that there are at least five hundred goblins in those woods."

Koucey paled a bit, but nodded. Forondo looked grim and even more depressed. We had less than two-score men with us.

"Our horses would be cut to pieces if we got among those trees," the Lord of Boval Vale said, shaking his head discouragingly. "While I know goblins prefer holes and caves, I can quite imagine that they would take advantage of the trees, and drop on our cavalry should we try to drive them from the wood. It's what I would do in their place." Captain Forondo nodded in agreement.

"I concur, lord, which is why I took the liberty of igniting a number of small fires in the wood by my Art. In a quarter candle's time there should be enough smoke and even some fire to drive them into a clearer space nearby – where we can attack them while they are in disarray."

"Where is this place?" Forondo asked, curiously. "Will we have room for a proper charge? Or must we send for archers from the castle?"

I tapped on the map at a spot just to the west of the Howe. "If memory serves, this adjacent pasture here, Goodman Ishav's, will be a natural place for them to regroup from the Howe . . . and a suitable battlefield for us. It is low, at the base of the rise that presages the town, and clear of stumps, if memory and magic serve. We can hide our advance from their scouts behind the dome of this hill to the north and still manage enough room for a cavalry charge, Huin willing. And they aren't expecting us," I reminded them. "They think we're all still holed up in the castle. I doubt their scouts have reported back, if your men were thorough in their attack."

"What of magical intelligence?" Forondo asked, thoughtfully. "Will their shamans not see us coming?"

"I have placed a shield over the entire town to protect against that, and it is more cleverly designed than their wards. While the goblin witchdoctors are canny enough to cover their troops, they did so very selectively— selectively enough that the very absence of return on that one particular spot in essence revealed their position. That is a mistake I will not repeat. Everything from the lake shore to the southern road is blanketed by my cloak now."

I had done that almost as an afterthought, easy to do with irionite. While my wards might reveal the presence of magi to our foe, it would also hide our movements enough to attack. The witchstone made them stronger than I could manage on my own, too. It wouldn't hold up to concentrated scrying, but it would make a casual glance at our troop formations difficult and screen us from a direct arcane attack.

"Well done, Master Spellmonger!" Sire Koucey said, a gleam returning to his eye. "Captain, if you will tell of a score of your more lightly armored riders, we can send them around the back side of the Howe through this field, here, and hit them in their flank just before our knights charge."

"Let's make it two score," the Remeran said. "My light troopers are not as well-equipped to make a direct charge, unlike your knights, my lord." That was true enough. More than half of the mercenaries used javelins and bows, not the heavy lances favored by the Wilderlords. "By doubling their number thus we present a more credible distraction. I'll put them under Ancient Iric – he is the most experienced skirmisher in the Black Flag, and has the wisdom to know when to break off."

"Quite right, Captain! *Herald!*" Sire Koucey called out for his messenger to relay the orders.

"That's a good plan," I agreed, rubbing the growing hint of beard on my chin. "I think I shall accompany the skirmishers, if you have no objections, Captain. I've no lance, and Traveler is a rouncey, not a charger, and I'd be almost useless in the full assault. But a spell or two might just convince the goblins that the force they face is the real threat, or at least confuse them, which will give the knights ample time to build up speed for a charge."

The orders were dispatched quickly, and before too long I was riding with Ancient Iric and around forty other horsemen south and west, around the back of Rexa's Howe.

Iric was typical of the mercenary soldier I'd seen, deadly serious about his craft and full of black humor. He was perhaps the shortest cavalry trooper I'd ever seen, just a hair over five feet, but he rode like he was a growth on his horse's back. We chatted while we rode, but I kept a constant eye on the growing trails of smoke that were coming from the grove. A little more power from the witchstone to feed the flames oxygen kept the smoldering fires lively, and the damp leaves only added to the smoke. I could hear the alarm calls and harsh coughs of the gurvani even without a spell.

By the time we had made it to the southern end of the Howe and crossed the streamlet (more like a ditch, actually) that bordered it to the west, the woods were actually ablaze enough to see flame, not just smoke. Twice we came across individual gurvani who had escaped from the smoke by fording the stream, only to be cut down by our arrows with the sun in their eyes. It almost didn't seem fair, and for a the briefest moment I regretted the odds.

But then I remembered the bodies of my helpless neighbors in Minden's Hall, hacked apart by night, and that steeled my heart for the slaughter to come.

I felt a wave of magical energy pass just as we crossed the stream, and I readied a defense, but it was not directed at us, I thought. It took me a while to puzzle out the radically different style of magic used by my gurvani colleagues, but I sensed that the spell was more a hastily-built fire-dampening casting than combat magic. No doubt the shamans concluded that some idiot on watch had let the cookfires get out of control, or something similar. That happened often enough when I was in the army. There are such idiots in every unit, I think.

I was tempted to throw something nasty at them, but knew that might spoil the surprise of our attack when we were counting on it. Instead I chuckled and countered with a slow, steady breeze from the west, which fanned the flames even higher and covered the pasture to the east with a thick blanket of smoke. That would make a dampening spell more difficult. Gurvani were already pouring out of the wood as it began to burn in earnest as the pine trees, thick with sap, started to catch fire. Reza's Howe would be no more than a well-fertilized field when we were done. I hoped the goddess would understand.

A quick check by scrying also told me that whomever had been holding that warding spell was distracted enough by the unexpected fire to let it slip away. My spell showed a large knot of little black figures spilling out into the eastern pasture in no particular order. I waited until at least three quarters of them were safely out before I began to hang a few more useful combat spells. When I was done, I signaled to Iric, and he quickly formed up his men for the charge.

Being part of a cavalry charge is one of the most exhilarating and terrifying experiences you can have. On the one hand, your heart races as the artificial thunder of horses' hooves overwhelms every other sound and the sensation of pure speed overtakes you.

On the other hand, there is the very realistic possibility that your horse will mistakenly run into the point of a spear or a pike, or that he will simply step into a hole and send you flying. Traveler was a pretty smart beast, compared to most horses, but even he got carried away in the charge. Horses love to run fast in a herd, and even a rouncey like Traveler must have fantasies of being a destrier or charger. As we approached the thick cloud of smoke and the thicker crowd of unorganized, choking and coughing gurvani, he did not slow or break stride.

The foe ahead, a group of more than a hundred, finally realized they were actually under attack and not just the subject of misfortune. They were clearly dismayed at our approach, an emotion enhanced by the three useful war spells I cast to aid us: one an illusion to make our numbers seem twice as large as they were, one to amplify the noise we made, and one targeted directly at their fear. With the witchstone, I was spending energy like a soldier on leave spends his pay.

We closed in fast. Arrows twanged from bows, and javelins were hurled at the black mass of goblins before our men shifted to weapons suited to hand-to-hand fighting. They might not have carried lances, but their swords, maces, axes and hammers were more than a match for the goblins' comparatively puny weapons. As Iric's men ploughed into the mass of shrieking goblins, swords waving and spears thrusting, the confusion of the collision was sufficient to allow me to slow Traveler down to a trot and start slinging even more deadly spells.

My first use of irionite in combat was even more exhilarating than the cavalry charge. I had already cast more spells today than I would have in a week as a spellmonger – or as a professional warmage, for that matter – and I wasn't even winded. The screening spell alone would have made me tired, before irionite, not to mention the wind spell, the scryings, and the illusions.

But with the little irionite sphere in the bag around my neck it was as if I had access to an endless well of magical energy, and I used it lavishly. Bolts of death flew from my hands as I struck down each gurvan who crossed my path. Slasher flew from its sheath and hacked at their heads and necks at triple speed, as if it had a mind of its own. I fought using my magesight, which allowed me to see through the thick smoke as if it were a light mist. I slew several gurvani who never even saw me. Traveler's hooves merrily stomped the shrieking survivors to pulp.

We had maybe four minutes of pure violent mayhem before the goblins got themselves organized enough to put up any effective resistance. Most, I noticed, were using crude but effective iron infantry swords instead of their traditional maces and wooden clubs, and many had little round wooden shields bossed with iron. Not that they did much good against trained warhorses and determined mercenaries. Especially not when their unit was as organized as an overturned beehive and half-blinded by smoke.

A few spears and a few arrows flew at us and one or two of Iric's troopers went down, but at that close range I think the goblins did more damage to each other than to us as they flailed about. I was surprised at the number of bowmen (bowgurvani?) among them. From what I understood the gurvani prefer slings and javelins to bows, but they had picked up the craft. Archers can turn the tide in a battle, of course, but only when their fire is massed and well disciplined, and this was neither.

The greatest advantage to a cavalry charge, on the other hand, is momentum. When you get a man on a horse moving fast enough it takes an awful lot to stop him. But after our four minutes, that momentum was spent. Individual troopers were attacking knots of gurvani, but the gurvani were starting to come together in larger masses, groups big enough to pull a man from his horse if they worked together and had enough leverage – and once on the ground the advantage was definitely theirs.

Iric knew his craft. When he saw a rough defensive line start to form through the smoke, it was time to go. He blew a horn that signaled a strategic withdrawal to his men – which is different from a retreat, as they explained to us in War College. When you are *winning* it is a *withdrawal*; when you are *losing*, it is a *retreat*. The horsemen obediently finished off the opponents in front of them and then started back the way they came to regroup.

I stayed, which sounds like suicide or bravery, depending on your point of view, but the truth was I could do more damage here covering their retreat (sorry, their withdrawal) than I could regrouping for another valiant charge. Koucey and his men would be hitting them shortly, and while our attack got their attention and hurt them some, there was still plenty of fight left in the goblin troops. I could at least do my best to distract them.

Besides, it gave me a chance to try out a few of the more exotic war spells that we were taught, but that I never had a chance to use properly. Usually they take hours or even days to raise enough energy to hang. With this newfound power at my call I couldn't resist playing around with them a little any more than a brewer can resist sampling a new pint of ale.

I wasn't that concerned for my personal safety, and perhaps I should have been. I was mounted only a few dozen yards away from the center of their unit, with enough little black hairy bodies piled around me to make me a daunting target. My personal defenses discouraged the few arrows they lobbed from hitting me – though they were becoming more numerous as the goblins gathered strength and organized.

A few brave souls tried to rally their mates by charging directly at me, swinging their swords and growling. But as I burned them down (sometimes literally – their hair burns quickly and I favor incendiary spells in combat) as soon as they approached more than twenty feet, the number of volunteers to kill me diminished as the pile of bodies around my horse grew. For a long while I just stared at them menacingly as I decided upon which hoary old war spell to throw at the next one to attack.

Goblins frustrate easily, and these poor idiots were already half-choked with smoke and half-blind in the sun. So they screamed at me and threw rocks and occasionally feces, but it was clear they were not at their best. They were pretty spooked by first the fire and then the attack. They huddled together on one edge of the pasture, trying to put their shields together in some kind of rough defensive formation, while their shaman tried to counter every sorcery I was hurling at them. I had just decided upon a really complicated but satisfying spell to try out (a nasty one from Imperial times that turned blood into a kind of congealed jelly; it usually took at least four magi to do it) when the shaman finally stepped out to challenge me.

I could tell what he was instantly by the sudden glow in my magesight (using arcane power lights you up like a chandler's shop) but his costume would have given him away if my spellcraft hadn't. He wore a shaggy mountain goat cloak and a headdress made of feathers and bone and leather, and he bore a staff in his hand. That staff almost stopped me.

It was a four foot long section of very straight weirwood about an inch and a half in diameter. The heel of the staff was shod with a sharp iron spike, which made it a dangerous mundane weapon, as well as a magical one. The head of the staff was a cage of iron enclosing . . .

Another chunk of irionite.

Shit.

I should have suspected it – and, in fact, I did – but being faced with another witchstone in the middle of a battle was daunting. At least this time I had some parity.

I abandoned my previous spell and concentrated on dumping power into a hastily-created theoretical construction. After my last encounter with a gurvani shaman, I wasn't willing to pull any punches. Whatever he was going to try, I wanted to be ready to counter.

I didn't expect him to try to *argue* with me.

The shaman lumbered forward, his staff held in one hand, unthreatening but undoubtedly at the ready. He came to the line of bodies I'd piled up, looked down at them, and then back up at me, his lip curled in a snarl.

"*Mage-man!*" he said in Narasi, the language of the men of the Five Duchies. I was surprised. I shouldn't have been. I knew that the gurvani were capable of learning human speech, and I'd even seen one or two who had been taught to read.

"Mage-man!" he repeated. "Leave this Valley now! The *haku*gurvani come to eat your brains if you don't! Many, *many* gurvani! Many *kanga* stones! If you love your life, you run away, run away!"

During this charming soliloquy the shaman had begun a kind of dance, rhythmically hopping from one foot to the other. "Mage-man, *run!* Your bones will be gnawed by our young! We will eat your flesh! Run, run, the Great Ghost comes for your soul, little man! He comes for revenge! He comes to take back what is *ours!*"

He ended his speech with a blood-curdling scream, which was echoed enthusiastically by the several hundred goblins at his back. Many were still coughing in the choking smoke, but many more were dancing on their own, brandishing their swords and clubs or thumping them on their shields in an effort to be intimidating.

I'm not ashamed to say that it almost worked. Here I was, alone (for the moment) against at least a couple of hundred screaming gurvani warriors. An impulse to kick Traveler into a gallop in the other direction seemed awfully tempting. I'd be a liar if I said otherwise.

But I stood fast, pride or honor or just plain cockiness kept me from flight. Or maybe I was just eager to practice more warmagic. I stood fast and raised my own warstaff.

With magesight I could see the symbols of the shaman's magic awhirl around him, and across his troops – which explained why more of them weren't choking to death in the thick smoke from the grove. The spells he had up were very basic defenses, from what I could tell – simple, but extremely strong. Any arrow or rock aimed for him would miss, any sword or mace would never land on his body. Nor was he vulnerable to regular warmagic. A casually tossed bolt would dissipate harmlessly around him, or, possibly, be reflected back on the caster.

Which really was a shame, as the spell I had been planning on using would have been *very* impressive.

"Gurvani!" I screamed back. "*You* will die if you stay here. There are armies coming, armies that will drive you back into your dens in the high mountains! This valley will be filled with gurvani skulls, and there will be no more young to gnaw my bones. You have attacked us, and we will strike back hard. Lay down your arms and return to your homes! Remember the great war, gurvani! Remember the fates of Grogror, gurvani, and the mighty shaman Shereul who died at our hands!" I was hoping that invoking their historic heroes and their failures might remind them of how outmatched they were.

Much to my surprise they started *laughing,* instead. That wasn't *quite* the effect I was hoping for.

I was even more confused now, but I was buying time, both for Sire Koucey to charge his heavy cavalry and Forondo to get set up for the second charge and for a brilliant idea to come to me if they failed to do so. I was getting nervous; I would have felt better with more horsemen to back me up, and the sight of a small army of hairy little bastards laughing at my most vicious threats wasn't helping my nerves one bit. I tried to keep that from showing on my face. I don't think I was successful.

The shaman stepped forward again and grinned unpleasantly. His canines had been filed into vicious fangs and his voice was loud and harsh as he challenged me, waving that wand around.

"I am Ri-ken, Mage-man. I am shaman of the Arinka tribe, the Red Hand tribe. My ancestors fought yours in the Great War. Then they fought for their homes and the sacred cavern, and you slaughtered them like pigs! Now many years have passed. It is time for *you* to fight for *yours*. We will recover what was stolen from us! We will dine on your flesh! It is the will of the Old God! He will bring justice to your people, justice and death! But Ri-ken will have the honor of bringing death unto you!"

He seemed pretty sure of himself. I could understand why. There's nothing like a huge chunk of irionite to give a mage confidence. By that time I thought Koucey was *never* going to come riding over the hill, and I wondered what was keeping him. Did he stop somewhere for a pint? Did he have to take a piss? Prior social engagement?

My brain was all out of subtle magics that might quickly take down his defenses. So I improvised.

I gestured with my finger and the ground beneath Ri-ken was suddenly as soft as cotton under his bare feet. It's a spell that alters density, mostly in granulated materials, although I think it could work on solids if you powered it enough. I'd never done it on anything larger than a salt cellar, because it requires a lot of power to enhance the field. But then I had a lot of power, and the area affected was vast – about three feet wide. He sank calf-deep into the suddenly-loose ground, shrieking with surprise. In an instant he was about a foot shorter, and too surprised about the sudden change in density of the soil, not to mention his immobility, to do anything practical about it. Another gesture ended the spell and he was mortared to the spot just below his knees.

His arcane defenses were still up, but his attention had wavered enough to allow me to attack – holding a magical shielding spell takes concentration. He was too good to just let it expire, though, and while I weakened his defense I had not dropped it. Just to be certain I sent a magical bolt in his direction – and it missed him completely. Instead it caught a goblin behind him for full effect, sending him reeling backwards among his fellows, much to the dismay of the other troops. The shaman began frantically waving his arms and drawing power from his witchstone in an effort to counter my spell, which allowed me a moment to knee Traveler forward and moved Slasher into an attack position. If the others weren't going to do it, I could charge them all by myself.

That's me. A one-mage cavalry unit.

They teach you that at War College: when the conventional fight gets hard, rely on your spells; when the arcane forces you face are too strong, hit something with your blade, hard. Or, in this case, a horse. Traveler was a rouncey, not a warhorse, but neither Ri-ken or Traveler apparently knew that. We were going at a quick trot In seconds, and the panicked look on Ri-ken's face was priceless as he realized that I was about to run over his hairy little ass.

But I wasn't – really. One does not waste a good horse (and your only mount) unless the situation was dire, and it wasn't . . . yet. I just needed to make him think I was.

As I bore down on him, he did about the only sensible thing that he could: he reversed the staff so that the sharp pointy end was aimed at me, and he braced himself. It was bravely done – had I really been trying to run him down, I would have probably impaled my horse on it just before my horse would have collapsed on top of Ri-ken. But that wasn't what I was after.

As I neared the struggling little bastard, Slasher was in my hand weaving through the air flashing in the sun. With a war-cry I perfected in the jungles of Farise, I aimed a blow at his head, which made Ri-ken flinch – then I brought it up sharply against the body of the staff in an underhanded motion, the angle of the blow slapping the flat of the mageblade against the shaft. Ri-ken had expected to die, not become disarmed.

The magical weapon leapt from the surprised gurvan's hands and flew through the air, where my free hand caught it neatly with the help of some warmagic. Responding admirably to the reigns, Traveler executed a neat turn around the left side of the flabbergasted witchdoctor, stomped on some furry black toes that were too slow in moving out of the way, and trotted me safely back to where we started. The whole episode took about sixty seconds. And now I had his witchstone, and the stick he carried it around on.

Ri-ken was irate, screaming for my blood in his own language. He didn't have to translate – I knew what he was saying by the way his troopers suddenly grabbed their swords and started toward me. I held up the staff triumphantly and pointed at them, ready to blast the first one that crossed an imaginary line about thirty feet in front of me. It was a total feint, but they didn't know I didn't know how to use gurvani magic.

"Tell them that I'll bake the first six that come any closer, Ri-ken! And after that I'll get nasty! Do it! *Do it!*" I commanded, trying to keep my words simple enough to be translated.

I guess the disarmed shaman tried, but his angry troops didn't respond. They swept forward like a black, hairy tide. I realized that I would need a far more potent demonstration than a few bolts could generate if I wanted them to be in a position to take a charge. Tucking Ri-ken's toy into a saddlebag I pointed my new warstaff and fired off an impressive ball of fire toward the group. That made them pause -- at least those who weren't hit by the blast. Hair catches fire quickly, and a few goblins got serious burns from the spell. I raised my staff at them again, and they watched it like a conductor's baton.

"You who have wrecked Hymas, I call vengeance down on *you!*" I said, or something like that. I could already feel the rumbling. "You have all died for *nothing!* You failed your gods long ago, and now you will fail them again! *Here come the horse demons!*"

Koucey had finally arrived. My sphincter unclenched the tiniest bit.

Barreling down the hill like a shiny spear, the hundred or so horsemen I had been anticipating had finally arrived. The goblins noticed them, too, and halted their advance to turn and gawk at them as they barreled toward their disorganized flank in a V-formation, their lances couched..

I had to admit, it was almost as impressive to witness a cavalry charge as it was to take part in one. Sire Koucey, flanked by Sirs Roncil and

Stancil and followed by the other Wilderlord knights, plowed into the gurvani flank with a mighty clash and a chorus of war cries, and began sowing mayhem with sword and lance

Then the Black Flag's squadron, freshly re-formed, attacked them from the other side, with Ancient Iric leading his men into the thick of their band. There were less warcries and flourishes in their fighting but the men knew their business. It really was beautiful, in a violent and gory sort of way.

The slaughter took about ten minutes to complete. Though the gurvani outnumbered the horsemen three or four to one, they were demoralized and confused after being hit from behind twice in one day, and their short stature and shorter weaponry were designed for killing each other, not mounted, armored knights. They went down under the spears, swords, and hooves of the Black Flag and the Wilderlords like ripe grain under a scythe.

I didn't participate in any important way, although I helped reserve squadron keep any survivors from escaping to regroup or warn others. I would have helped the wounded, too, if there had been any. It's not as if I was lazy or a coward. This was more massacre than battle, and there were men better equipped to deal with it than I. Ishi's tits, they lived for this sort of thing.

I watched Ri-ken, still buried up to his knees, get wounded in the shoulder with a spear, unable to dodge or do anything else productive but bleed. He looked at me with a terrible anger and shouted. Not a curse, as I expected, but a warning.

"*He* comes, Mage-Man! The Great Ghost comes to damn you all! *He is coming He will—!*"

Before he could utter another word some trooper lopped off his head with a cavalry axe, then trampled his bleeding body until the legs broke off.

When no more hairy foes moved in the bloody pasture, I rode through the carnage to meet a widely grinning Sire Koucey. Captain Forondo was having a hard time finding anything to be depressed about. It was a victory. Cavalry charges are what knights are made for. We had but three casualties, and only one fatality (a broken saddle strap and a chance impalement); a remarkable result of what could have been a nasty encounter.

"Have you espied any more, Spellmonger?" Sire Koucey asked, not wasting any words on battlefield reflections. I shook my head, but looked up at the mountains.

"These goblins were easy to spot, my lord. They were clumsy, unsophisticated, and mere raiders. But the day is failing, and come nightfall I have no doubt that Hymas will crawl with their kin. We have struck a blow here today, but we will not save the town, I'm afraid. Nor the castle. This band was over twice as big as the one that hit Minden's Hall, and I'm afraid the next lot will be thrice this size. A mere vanguard, and little else. I would recommend that we police the area and return to the castle with all haste."

"Very well," nodded the Lord of Boval. "There is little left in town that cannot be replaced, though the cost will be dear. And I must say that these mercenaries of yours performed admirably, for sell-swords! My own men did a poorer job of attack than the Black Flag," he admitted – the one fatality had been a young squire. "You have a good eye for fighting men."

Captain Forondo blushed and stared at his saddle horn, and I have to admit that I felt the weight of Sire Koucey's praise, myself. You have to understand that the professional mercenary is not often commended for his work, particularly by the nobility who employs him. His employers often hope that he will be killed before he is paid, and the civilians he comes into contact with are usually annoyed that their hard-earned taxes have gone to support a fighting man with no loyalty but to his purse.

Captain Forondo did sit up a little straighter in his saddle, "Well, my lord, I can only hope that the barbarian infantry in your employ will fare as well." Forondo nodded towards the rod I held in my hand. "I see you have picked up a souvenir."

"I thought it would look nice in my new quarters," I shrugged. "But if nothing else it was an instructive duel. We were damned lucky the thing didn't blow us all away, had something gone awry. These goblins play with powerful toys, Sire. But they have little idea how to use them to fullest effect. Mayhap next time we will not be so lucky."

With a nod and an uncomfortable sigh, Sire Koucey nodded, and then ordered Sir Roncil to oversee the policing of the battlefield while I did my best to suppress the fire I'd started in the first place.

Most of the "loot" the goblins gathered from the town we left there to burn, but the troopers wisely took every iron mace, sword and axe they found. They could be reformed in the smithies of Boval for things we needed – like arming the peasant militia, making arrow heads, or even nails.

Ancient Iric's troops were detailed to collect goblin heads for display, and when we set off for the castle there were over two hundred and fifty of the stinking things in sacks. By dusk they were all impaled on posts at the crossroads near Hymas. I doubt that they did any good as warnings, but I know that the sight of a victory, however small, encouraged the morale of the peasants who saw them from the battlements.

Nightfall was fast approaching when we rode through the gatehouse and into the outer bailey. I wanted beer and I wanted to bathe, after the day's exertions, and I wanted to deconstruct the gurvani wand and remove its witchstone. As the last horse came through the iron portcullis and huge wooden doors were swung shut and bolted.

The faces we passed were anxious, but relieved to see us. Sire Koucey made a point of calling out by name to those of his folk that he recognized and engaging in spirited banter. My new liege was well-liked. That's an important consideration at the beginning of a long siege and a harsh winter.

After handing Traveler over to the grooms I made my way back to my tower quarters, more tired than I thought I'd be. I shouldn't have been surprised. While the magical power at my disposal was orders of magnitude above what I was used to, and came to bear as easily as breathing, my brain was still the same old brain. The intellectual exhaustion that comes from indulging in too many spells in too short of time can have devastating effects, so I vowed to myself to watch it after I stumbled twice on the stairs.

Garkesku, I noticed was enjoying a roast chicken dinner that made a waterfall out of my mouth. It wasn't standard castle rations, but I suppose he had a right to trade for extra food – that was inevitable in a siege. He even offered me some, but I could feel his apprentices glaring at the back of my neck, so I politely declined, knowing that they would split the leftovers from their Master's table.

I briefed him on the little cavalry raid and relayed the bare bones of Riken's speech, and then excused myself, pleading exhaustion. I had taken the precaution of wrapping the gurvani warstaff in my saddle blanket before I came up to avoid his questions about it. If he had known I now possessed two pieces of irionite, things might have gotten tense, not cordial.

When I finally got my tired feet to drag me up yet-another flight of stairs to my chamber, I dropped the wrapped staff on my workbench, grabbed a loaf of hard bread and a sausage from the larder, and washed it down with a jack of ale instead of wine. I needed my wits about me for this next bit. While the thought of a big cup of sweet red reward was tempting, I didn't want to fall asleep while working with such powerful magics. That might be awkward.

I cleaned myself up a little, took off my weapons harness, noted with pleasure that Tyndal had erected two large hammocks out of broadcloth and suspended them, and generally puttered around the lab avoiding the thing on the workbench. When I couldn't think of anything else that needed doing, I finally sat down, removed the blanket, and began my examination of the first gurvani magical weapon I'd ever seen.

For the record, the thing was exactly four feet, five and a half inches long from sharp pointy spike to elaborately-carved weirwood head. The wood of the shaft appeared to be some type of hardwood (Fokewood, probably – pretty common in the mountains, and very thaumaturgically conductive) and had been carefully polished and sanded. The spike was just an ordinary hunk of iron. The decorations on the staff head were made of bone and leather, and copper wire bound the stone tightly into it. The stone itself was around three quarters of an inch in diameter, although only a portion protruded from its housing. I made notes and a quick sketch of the thing on parchment before I started tearing it down. The spells on the thing were powerful, of course, and almost completely unfamiliar to me.

That didn't stop me. I was trained in Imperial style thaumaturgy, which is a well organized and systematic approach to the subject of the science of magic that has been refined constantly since the first Archmage began writing it down. My own ancestors had used a more individualistic, shamanic approach, not unlike what Zagor used. There were other schools, too, either derivative of the Imperial schools (which were, in turn, derived from the Alka Alon, so it was said) or crafted by individual traditions like the Cormeeran seamagi, or the Wenshari witches.

The Order of Avital, for instance, which is a Vorean clerical order devoted to the God of Magic (whom no one pays any attention to anymore, even in Merwyn, except the Avitalines), has a wacky but effective system that bears only a passing relation to the Imperial school. Then there are the Seamagi, the home-grown magi of the coasts who have taken a cultic interest in the Sea Folk and use a derivative of their magics as their own. The witches of the Wenshari countryside use a hybrid of Imperial styles and elements borrowed from tribes in the Kuline Mountains.

And then there are also the thousands of self-trained or apprenticed hedgewizards, footwizards and village witches throughout the Duchies who have improvised personal "systems" that are loaded with superstition, expediency, and mixed with folk religion. My teachers at the Academy used to sneer at them, good naturedly, condemning their beliefs while mining them for useful information. The Royal Censors hunted them like dogs for their temerity and lack of credentials.

The gurvani system of shamanic magic was, I assumed, a lot like my ancestors' original practice out on the steppes, much of which has been lost. Most tribal people's magic is similar in function, if not in form, after all. The symbols are different, of course, but one thing we learned in Thaumaturgy was that *all* magical systems are inherently similar. As I scanned the thing with magesight I could see at least four major spells whirling around the length of the stick, unfamiliar but not unknowable.

I dug out my own sphere and began disassembling them with care, shunting the excess power I drained from them into *kabas* which I could use later if I needed to. I was especially careful – I had a classmate who blew two of his fingers off when he was carelessly disassembling an old wand he found in the research library at the Academy. He was kind of a tool, so it served him right, but the event had made me cautious.

The enchanting spells were typical for a warwand, though cruder than I was used to. There were binding, holding, directing and projecting spells to channel the powerful forces available through the witchstone at the head. When I had safely disarmed them, the physical object was no more dangerous than a walking stick. I was amazed that there weren't any anti-tampering spells on it, but guessed that no ordinary gurvan would touch a shaman's staff.

I pried the head apart with the blade of my dagger and held my breath as the irionite tumbled to the bench just like any old rock. It was, indeed, about three quarters of an inch thick, irregular, and had one fairly flat surface that lent credence to Zagor's assertion that these stones were cut from a larger piece. I still didn't know how that was significant, but I did know that it scared me. There was a taint to it, I recalled the Aronin instructing me. I didn't dare touch it barehanded, yet.

Using a pair of wooden tongs I picked it up and gingerly set it into a wooden bowl. Then I set my sphere beside it and went and poured the cup of the strong wine I'd promised myself. The link banishing process should have taken around an hour, according to Aronin. Just to be sure, I waited two hours before I went back and checked it.

In the meantime I wandered down through the crowded great hall and out onto the grounds of the inner bailey and watched the Black Flag and the Crinroc tribesmen drilling for night battle. I was pleasantly surprised to see my young apprentice sparring with wooden practice swords with one of Forondo's troopers. Tyndal saw me and grinned, which was a mistake. His sparring partner took advantage of the break in his concentration and whacked him in the shins, then proceeded to lecture him about focus.

I chuckled to myself and left, not wanting to be responsible for more bruises. The lesson reminded me of my first three weeks at War College, when Ancient Zym was daily screaming in our faces about how we held our blades like broomsticks. Night had fallen, and soon it would be too dark for them to practice anymore even by torchlight. I didn't have the strength at that point to summon a real magelight, so I let them practice until they couldn't I just wanted to watch.

The Crinroc didn't have the polish that the Black Flag had, of course, but those dumpy, shaggy little men made up for it with enthusiasm.

Their "drills" looked an awful lot like a game between children, right up to the point where one of them was knocked unconscious. Furtak and Jordak were the leaders of the opposing sides, while their brother Posnak watched from the back of a wagon and gave advice in their guttural barbarian tongue. I climbed up the wagon and joined him.

"I heard the horse-boys wiped out a company of goblins today, Minalan," he grunted out in thickly accented Narasi.

"Yes, we took almost three hundred heads," I remarked.

"*Solak!* Keep your shield higher or – *ouch*, that must have hurt. Good work, Minalan. Plenty more goblins are coming," he said matter-of-factly. "Plenty more heads to take."

"You are right," I agreed. "How are the men here treating your people?"

Posnak shrugged. "Well enough, for horse-boys. They call us names, thinking we don't understand, but they are happy to see us. We call them names, too. Food is good. Walls are thick. Just waiting for goblins."

I couldn't argue with that.

I took my leave of the barbarians and wandered to the outer bailey, using the excuse of checking on my horse to hide my true intentions: finding Alya, the freshly-bathed widow I'd spotted this morning.

The outer bailey had gotten a little more organized, but the stench of the crowded encampment was still just as overpowering, and promised to get worse. Militia men bearing white baldrics and armed with cudgels patrolled the interior and did their best to break up fights, settle disputes, and make certain that the tiny cook fires allowed were being burned safely – a fire could wipe out most of the population of the southern Boval Valley just as easily as the goblins could, and probably quicker, too. Fire protection spells only work so well in such a situation. Vigilance is the best ward against them.

I skulked around the bailey anonymously after checking the stables. I said hello to old clients and cast a few useful minor spells where needed. Along the way I made a few subtle inquiries about Alya's whereabouts, trying not to elicit too much interest. I didn't see her, so I finally gave up when it got too dark to see and I was too tired to continue, and went back to the lab. It had been over two hours.

Tyndal was back, too, toweling off the significant amount of sweat that he had built up during his swordplay lesson. He shot me an excited grin before regaling me with tales of his prowess at his newfound art. I listened patiently while I removed the now-purified lump of green amber from the bowl and put it in a small silk bag. I wish I knew the trick that Aronin had used for re-shaping it, but the shape and form didn't matter much when it came to arcane power.

Or maybe it did; I just didn't know.

When my apprentice had wound down a bit, he started asking me about the raid he'd heard the men talking about. I told him as much as I could, sparing him the details like the groans of the mortally wounded gurvani that sounded almost exactly like the moans of mortally wounded men, and the look of terror on the faces of our foes as they realized that they were the objective of a cavalry charge. I almost felt bad for that. Battle isn't glorious on its face, particularly. But I wanted him to keep his enthusiasm, as he would need it sorely in the coming days.

"What did Ri-ken mean by the *Great Ghost?* Is it one of their gods?"

I shook my head. "I don't know. And I have no idea. The mythology of the gurvani hasn't been studied much, and the culture of this band seems to depart in many ways from the common, run-of-the-mill Mountain Folk."

"How so?"

"Their weapons, for instance; they have far too many swords and shields and bows – those are man-tools. And this pure hatred they have of us, that is unusual. The gurvani I saw in the jungles of Farise were not overly fond of men, but they didn't go out of their way to give us problems, either. The Great Ghost could be an avenging god, a lot like Reme was for the East Islanders. Or Briga is for us." Yes, Briga is a fire goddess, and the patron of bakers, smiths, and chandlers. But she's also a goddess of vengeance. We get a lot of use out of our minor divinities.

Then I had to stop and explain how the inhabitants of the three small islands to the East of Vore, descendents of Merwyni shipwreck victims who had become pirates, had fought against the Empire for decades at sea under the theocracy of Reme, after their uncooperative priest-king had been assassinated by Imperial spies back in the Middle Magocracy period. The Reme cult still practices today, I'm told, though without the fervor or bloodlust for vengeance shown in centuries past.

"So this Great Ghost, who probably *is* a god of vengeance, has some sort of physical form or an avatar who is leading this war," he suggested, thinking. I had to admit, I was impressed. I had seen plenty of far more experienced warmagi take a while to come to the same sort of reasonable conclusion.

"So it appears. The avatar is more likely. He's probably a great general or tribal chieftain who is also a shaman who lucked into a hoard of irionite. That isn't unknown – in fact, that's sort of how the Magocracy was founded, by some accounts."

"Too bad we don't have a priestess of Trygg here. It is said they can keep any evil at bay."

Again I shook my head and smiled at the naiveté of youth. "Not to dispute the teachings of Trygg, Tyndal, but a priest has no more or less power than any other man. Even of the Great Mother. Perhaps spiritual power – there are some temples who have magical orders in them. But a priest is just a man. A priestess is just a woman. Without rajira, or the presence of a divinity, their power is cultural. Besides, who is to say the goblins *are* evil?"

The question shocked him, and rocked him to the core. "But they attack us for *no reason*, they slaughter our people and burn our towns! How can they *not* be evil?" he asked, astonished at my intellectual temerity.

"To *you*, perhaps they are. But by those standards your ancestors were just as evil. When the Alshari warriors you are descended from came to this valley they burned gurvani villages, slaughtered gurvani warriors, and drove the few survivors into the mountains where they had to fight the elements and each other to survive. In their minds they are just taking back what is theirs – from us evil *humani*."

"That's *different*," Tyndal snapped. "The Duke of Alshar *granted* us this land. It was ours, not theirs."

"And who gave it to him? Not the poor gurvani who lived here. They'd never heard of Alshar, or the Duke. They lived here for thousands of years, and one day they get invaded by a bunch of men with swords and horses who have been told that they own their land. *Of course* they fought tooth and nail, just like we're doing, to try to keep it out of the hands of 'evil.' "

"I don't care," Tyndal said, defiantly. "I'm *not* going to leave my home for a bunch of stinking, stupid goblins to take over! We showed 'em today, and we'll show them again!"

"Tyndal," I said softly, "*Don't* underestimate them. I learned as a warmage that you must respect your enemy in order to defeat them. To not give your foe the respect that he is due gives him an opening in your defenses that he can exploit. These gurvani are not only worthy of your respect, they will *demand it*. When I fought Ri-ken today the only advantage that I had over him was better training and quicker wits – and a few score of cavalry. It could just as easily have gone the other way.

"So far, we've been lucky. The Great Ghost, or whoever is leading them, has just sent in scouting and raiding parties so far. The mere vanguard of his invasion. The real armies will come all too soon, and when they do you'll see why bravado and courage are two entirely different things."

I don't think I really convinced him, but I hoped I'd given him something to think about. I wasn't defending the gurvani, exactly, but I was empathetic to their history. I'm certain humanity would have done the same in their situation. Or at least some of it. Punishing them with moral judgments for what we, ourselves, would do seemed like the height of hypocrisy.

That night I sat straight up (not recommended in a hammock), my heart pounding and a vicious sweat breaking out on my face and body. My tunic was soaked through. I had a dream about Ri-ken, back on the battlefield, his bloody face turned to me in defiant anger, his voice echoing in my head: *He is coming!*

I didn't know who *he* was, but I was suddenly so afraid of *him* that I had wet myself.

Also not recommended in a hammock.

Chapter Eight

Boval Castle Under Siege

"It is the lord's duty to his domain to provide adequate defense for his folk during a time of war or crisis. Like a ship at sea, the lord is captain of all within the walls, for only by his command can a proper defense be provided against the foe. Let all who seek refuge within give the lord their obedience, lest the folk perish due to discord and acrimony."

\- *The Book of Duin the Destroyer*
\-

The brief thrill of our minor victory was completely gone three days later, when the siege began in earnest.

It started when a cavalry patrol was ambushed not a mile from the castle doors, killing ten men, eight horses, and our jubilant mood. The survivors beat a hasty retreat back to Boval Castle, where our archers turned the gurvani pursuing them back with volleys of arrows. That was the last time we were able to freely send our horsemen out. From that point on, we were really under siege, not just preparing for one.

The weather was not helping, of course. It was being magically manipulated by the goblins, keeping a thick cloud cover over the entire Valley, which made it seem like twilight even at noon. This was for their benefit, as it allowed them to put many, many more warriors on the field when the bright light of day was held in abeyance. It occasionally rained from the clouds, but mostly it was just dark and dreary all the time. It depressed our warriors and frightened our civilians. Night was almost a relief, except for the fact that it was at night when the gurvani were most likely to try to scale our walls.

In an effort to counter this dreariness, I started casting magelights in strategic locations.

This is easier than it sounds. Magelights are arcanely-powered spheres of light that produce no heat and no smoke. Nothing actually gets burnt, you see.

Most people don't realize that light is just a form of energy that can be produced from just about any matter. There is a whole host of technical terms in Imperial for the subject (called *photomancy*), but the upshot is if a mage causes a piece of matter to be charged with magical energy in *just* the right way, it will emit light. Hence, *magelight*.

The more energy, the more light. If you alter the spell slightly and use a rune or two, you can pump an object full of energy and have it released slowly, over time. Useful stuff, but usually beyond the capabilities of the average spellmonger. Me, I plastered magelights all over the entire castle, gleeful at how easy it was with irionite. Plus it kept our spirits up and kept stray goblins from hiding in the shadows.

At first the bands that attacked us were the usual screaming, jabbering horde that would rush forward to the edge of the moat, hurl a few javelins and rocks over the walls before retreating a safe distance – usually carrying some wounded, as our little archer company was getting better with practice. Gradually, though, the black knot of gurvani who hovered just out of bowshot grew. By Day Four of the siege there were almost a thousand of them, and their sorties on the castle became more organized.

So we prepared to repel them.

For most that meant drilling and practicing with our weapons. Our peasant militia had been so augmented by volunteers that we did not have enough trained warriors to lead them. Thanks to my shopping trip, however, they were all adequately armed, if not armored. Many also had their own bows, and the butts got plenty of use as they thudded practice arrows against straw effigies. But mostly they worked with the plain spears and short infantry swords from the castle arsenal.

They drilled constantly in the inner bailey, working on small unit tactics with the Black Flag and our mercenary infantry. This basically consisted of rushing forward in a mob and killing everything in sight – which sounds like poor military tactics, except that this was a siege and anything less than that level of viciousness could kill us all.

For me, preparing involved casting complicated spells in anticipation of the inevitable arrival of more powerful gurvani shamans.

Magical warfare comes down to various levels of attack and defense spells; it is quite straightforward in that way. If your offensive bolt is stronger than your enemy's shields, he goes down. If it's weaker, he gets the chance to chew you up.

But there are thousands of subtle variations on this theme that make magewar a tricky and lethal business, and warmagic a powerful help to it. Like any other style of warfare, to win you must assess your own strengths and weakness as well as your enemy's, and then concentrate on their weak spots while protecting your own.

Our weak spot: little hope for reinforcements and too few magi to begin with. Their weak spot: unsophisticated magic that concentrated a great deal of power in the hands of the individual shaman.

To help our case I had spent much of my waking time (and Tyndal's) when we were not lighting up the place building a scale model of the castle and the surrounding countryside. This model was as accurate as I could make it, including elevations, types of material, and scale. While the effigy looked like a child's toy more than a sophisticated magical tool, it was a very good model for our situation, and it provided an excellent metaphor for the castle. It also took up a great deal of space in my workroom.

But by using it as a kind of altar, a magical staging area, I was able to prepare a lot more damage to our besiegers than I would otherwise. Mostly, I used it in gathering intelligence. By marking out the area where the gurvani were setting up their camps around the castle, I was able to see exactly how many and what kind of troops they were assembling without leaving my quarters. The relative comfort of scrying and spying like that didn't make up for the result.

It wasn't a pretty picture. On average more than five hundred gurvani were arriving outside the castle every day. By the third full day of the siege I saw that they weren't just the scouts and vanguard troops that we'd seen up to now.

Very large, almost man-sized gurvani warriors, complete with leather armor and swords and vicious attitudes, began marching into their camps chanting aggressive-sounding war songs to the cheers of their fellows. Using magesight and inference, as well as scrying, I learned that they were given the best rations, the best accommodations, and seemed in charge of the military situation.

On Day Four, some sort of general showed up, flanked by two shamans and accompanied by two-wheeled wagons pulled by a strange variety of draught animals and protected by an entourage of big ugly goblin bodyguards. It was the first time I had seen the gurvani employ oxen or other domesticated beasts, some clearly looted from some human farmstead, others raised themselves. The wagons were filled with supplies, mostly dried roots and salted meat, weapons and tools.

Tools with which they could make siege engines. That was *not* good news. To my knowledge the gurvani didn't utilize fortifications the way we did, and therefore would not know how to break through them. But I suppose after two hundred years of studying the situation, you pick up a few things.

After bringing this information to the attention of Sire Koucey, he doubled the fire watch and ordered *me* to do something about it. Well, ordered is a strong term. He *requested* that I make certain that as few siege engines as possible be deployed against his fortress, seeing as how it costs a literal fortune to build and it was the only thing between us and certain slaughter.

So I did.

Their weakness was that they hadn't actually started to build any siege engines, yet. That didn't mean that they were unprotected. The shamans who accompanied that column had learned from their predecessors' mistakes, or perhaps they were just a better class of witchdoctor, but those encampments had powerful wards on them, wards I couldn't lightly break.

Either way, my first few attempts to burn their wagons at a distance failed miserably.

Luckily, I'm not a one-trick footwizard. As most of the tools involved were metal, I decided to alter my tactics and use *water* and not *fire* against them. That was a more subtle and harder-to-defend-against type of warmagic.

I told Tyndal of my plan, explained the magical principals behind it, and together we cast a spell that caused the rapid oxidation of everything in those wagons.

When I mean *rapid*, I mean that by the next morning nearly every axe head, adze, pick and shovel in that convoy was rusted to near uselessness. Iron blades had hidden flaws that made them snap when used. Shovels broke in two when any amount of pressure was put on them. Adzes had their edges rusted to the point where they were useless for serious work.

In the meantime, Sir Cei, the dour castellan ostensibly in charge of the castle's defense, had assigned Garkesku the duty of making life as uncomfortable as possible for the goblins.

You might think I was irked at this plum assignment being handed off to the competition, but I had to admit when it came to being a professional pain in the ass Garkesku was the obvious choice. Even Sir Cei could see that. On the more practical side, Garkesku did have years of experience with the everyday types of spells a spellmonger sold, while I was a relative newcomer to the business.

His work gave him an advantage. After all, if you can cast a spell to keep insects away, can it be that hard to cast a spell to draw them closer? He did, and the gurvani camp was infested with irritating pests and stinging bugs for weeks afterward. He threw spells to make their foods moldy and sour the bitter type of beer they drink for breakfast, lunch, and dinner. He had spells that sent the odor of putrescence waft through their camp and spells that produced blood-curdling sounds during the day, making it difficult for them to sleep. I found he was especially good at diseases – as any good village spellmonger should be – and by Day Six of the siege one out of three gurvani was stricken with nasty diarrhea.

Between the bad food, the rusted tools, the insects, the sleep deprivation, the stinks and the shits, those would-be invaders were getting further and further behind schedule for their mission, i.e., slaughtering all of us. I admit, I was impressed, and said so in front of Sire Koucey, which helped my immediate relations with Garkesku tremendously.

Sire Koucey was not idle during this slow-down. Twice he sent cavalry sorties out to harass the teams of gurvani engineers who were trying to put together a catapult or some such just out of bowshot. Our people were repelled each time, but we delayed their start for at least another week and took only light casualties.

The fateful day came, however, when they were able to get one lonely trebuchet kind of working, and we could see them with magesight having a really good time flinging rotten pumpkins over our walls. The trouble was, the machine couldn't handle a missile heavier than that without falling apart. The peasants began making jokes about "pumpkin raids," and a few of the more far-sighted among them dutifully cleaned up the exploded mess and planted the seeds in pots and barrels around the castle.

Before another week passed, the goblin army outside had tripled in size, with no end of reinforcements in sight. Someone high up in the hairy hierarchy decided that they were being made fools of by our subtle magic and big ugly horsemen.

That night (Day Ten of the siege, if my records are accurate) the goblins started making a mad dash for the moat, throwing in bundles of faggots, and then dashing away again. Our archers pegged plenty of them and added their corpses to the refuse in the moat, but plenty more made it without injury.

After a few hours of this there was a swampy "bridge" of sticks that allowed a few of the little buggers to cross the moat – only to be shot at the base of the wall by our snipers. That didn't deter them. They continued trying to back-fill the moat, and they continued dying.

We could not let that stand and expect to survive. After I thoroughly scanned the area for hidden traps, we lowered a dozen men down from the walls on ropes and they undid much of the filling. The bundles of sticks we hauled up to be dried and used for firewood. The bodies of the goblins were looted for iron and decapitated, their heads used for the traditional morale purpose. We even got back most of the arrows we expended.

It went like that for another week. At night the gurvani would try to chew through our defenses, both military and magical, and during the day we would undo most of the work that they had done. We were holding our own and trying to defend against the inevitable *ennui*.

But their army kept growing.

As we observed, the new troops were even better trained than their earlier brethren, marching in columns like a human army and using superior man-weapons.

Among the new units was a full company of archers, which made our defenses a little more costly to man. While the gurvani bows were shorter, they also seemed to be stronger in weight for their size than ours, so that their average bowshot was just a few score feet under ours. They also used a shorter, lighter arrow. Of course, we had a height advantage that they didn't, but they were figuring things out a *lot* quicker than I expected, and that had me worried. Clearing the moat became a little more dangerous for us, but the supplies of soggy firewood continued to be gathered every morning.

Scrying their encampments was becoming more difficult even with the model. Their shamans had started putting up shields that obstructed the view of a meadow just beyond the regular gurvani camps, so I figured the likelihood of there being something nasty brewing was high. The gurvani shields were too tough for me to remove by brute force – directly contesting a spell with any mage who has a chunk of irionite is hard, even if you have your own chunk. After they lost a few camps to raids it seemed that the two were taking it in turns maintaining the shields of every camp. They also began taking stronger countermeasures against Garkesku's inspired annoyance spells, which meant that their troops were in a much better mood.

As far as getting any more messages out, that was just unlikely to happen. I don't know how they did it, but I could no longer access the Otherworld. That disturbed me.

The lack of strategic intelligence was also bothering me. In our daily Council of War at the castle, his staff (myself included) kicked around ideas about how to cure it in Koucey's study. Most of the conventional military leaders were quite content just to sit back and wait for the gurvani to try to break the siege and then die gallantly defending the castle. But I wasn't. Sire Koucey, who was aging a year for every day that passed, agreed with me, and authorized a reconnaissance action.

So on Day Fifteen I led a small raiding party over the walls at noon – while the goblins were able to fight under the overcast skies, they still disliked the brightness of the noon sun peeking through. I chose twenty Crinroc for my band, led by Furtak, and we conducted a raid of our own.

The barbarian mercenaries were eager for war. They painted themselves various mottled shades of green, blue and gray with mud and herbal preparations, and added some green leafy foliage to help disguise themselves. I added a Glyph of Un-noticeability to each one, just in case.

You often hear in old stories about how the spies of the Magocracy used "invisibility" spells to slip by enemy lines, but at the Academy they insisted that this was crap and ancient politics. Invisibility is a terribly complicated photomantic spell – it involves bending light, which means harnessing truly titanic forces – and doesn't protect against any sounds you might make.

Un-noticeability, on the other hand, is fairly straightforward. The key to sneakiness is not to not be seen, it is to not be *noticed* – a small but important distinction. The Glyph I used was a War College standard and, therefore, probably unknown to the gurvani. It's a Blue Magic spell that works on the minds of your foes and simply causes them not to pay attention to the enemy sneaking through the shrubbery behind them. To that end it actually worked better than any invisibility spell I'd heard – just not for the gurvani. Whether you lived to see them or not, you could still *smell* them. The gurvani are not overly fond of baths.

I snuck through the outer defenses of the camp with my merry little band of homegrown raiders and into the edges of their busy encampments for a few nights. Security was lax even by sloppy gurvani standards, with few pickets or patrols this close to the castle. You didn't need to be an adept to find your way around them. I was surprised how adept the Crinroc were at this type of operation; the warriors made nary a sound as they moved. Furtak explained that the Crinroc are good hunters used to stealthy movement. As long as you didn't worry about the smell of rancid butter, they were able to move about without much notice.

Despite the darkness the ground was littered with thousands of goblins sleeping with their hairy cloaks thrown over their faces – the 'day shift'. There were tents here and there made of crudely woven mountain hemp, but they seemed to be to be designed more for protecting equipment and supplies than housing troops. Several times I had to step over a snoring goblin to keep going, and on two hair-raising occasions my boot slipped and I accidentally kicked one. Each time the *gurvan* in question snorted and rolled over, oblivious to our presence.

Why didn't we just slit some throats and retreat? We weren't there to start trouble. We were there to *gather information*.

I had my barbarian band hide in the brush while I crept into the center of their camp, to the slightly more ornate tent that I guessed (correctly) was the headquarters of the besieging general and his staff. I found a comfortable spot behind a barrel of that nasty bitter beer and started taking notes about the size and nature of the army that faced us.

About an hour later I crept back to my barbarians. I was *shaking*.

We made it back to Boval Castle without incident, and I had three glasses of wine before reporting to Sire Koucey's War Council.

"I had a hard time understanding them," I admitted, "but of this there is no doubt: there are no less than *sixteen* shamans, now, all of whom are armed with witchstones." I reported, quietly. "There are thousands, perhaps tens of thousands more goblins coming, and each wave seems better armed for war than the last. They have foraged or made tools, so they are building a new collection of siege engines."

"Of what sort?" Sir Cei asked, curious.

"Catapults thrice as large as the Pumpkin Thrower they started with, battering rams, protective frameworks, and at least four great siege towers tall enough to surmount the wall and cross the moat. We may have as long as four days, probably three, before they make a serious advance on our position."

Sir Olve, one of Koucey's pet knights and likely a distant relative, stood up and made an impassioned speech about dying valiantly in defense of the land and the people – very poetic, but unproductive. Ideas about how not to die valiantly were tossed around, but there didn't seem to be any clear answer. I certainly didn't have one that could contend with all of those forces arrayed against us. I went to bed and tried to catch some sleep before the inevitable nocturnal skirmish.

*   *   *

The attacks became more intense each night. We repelled them easily enough, at first, but we started to lose men, men who couldn't be replaced. I did my part by illuminating the areas under attack with bright magelights so that our archers could see their targets, and occasionally took a turn on the battlements with my warstaff – as did the rest of the "magical corps." But it still did not dissuade them. Or drive them from the field.

Four nights after I had made my first daring foray, the first real siege engines started inching their way toward the walls, surrounded by a sea of black furry faces. Stones were flung at our walls at far greater velocities than the "pumpkin thrower" had been capable of. They did little against the strong walls of the keep, but occasionally they would land in the outer bailey and hurt some of the peasants. The civilians soon learned which areas of the bailey were dangerous and which were effectively shielded by the walls.

The catapults and ballistae didn't worry me . . . much. Every now and then they would lob a pumpkin full of flaming oil into the castle, but our anti-arson spells and vigorous fire prevention program made this more of a bother than a threat.

What worried me were the five siege towers that loomed like newly-made mountains in the distance – mountains pulled by oxen that were approaching at the rate of twenty yards an hour.

The major advantage of a castle in a siege is the fact that the defenders have this *whopping* big wall to throw stuff down from. It gets pretty discouraging to the attackers if they get a rain of rocks and arrows on their heads every time they charge the gates. Ladders can be employed to climb the walls, but seeing as how easy it is for one or two burly infantrymen to push the top of the ladders over with the poles that were scattered across the battlements for just such a purpose, the gurvani had stopped that foolishness quickly enough.

Siege towers are made for getting around that problem. Basically, they are large wooden towers on wheels or rollers that can be pushed up against the wall of a castle, or as close as the attackers can get it. Once in position, they drop a plank or bridge over the battlements, and over the moat, effectively eliminating the height advantage of the defenders.

These were worse than normal towers though, I saw, as each one had at least one or two shamans in their peak to direct and magically aid the attack. I could see them by magesight, and could feel their witchstones approaching in my bones. It was easy enough to see their plan. Once their shock troops took a section of battlement they would be free to lay about them with bolt after bolt of destructive magic. Those towers *had* to be stopped, somehow.

We tried shooting fire arrows at them, to no avail. The goblins had been smart enough to cover the exteriors with wet hides and blankets and the same sort of anti-arson spells we were using. We tried shooting them with rocks from our own ballistae, but the mass of the stones just wasn't enough to do much damage to the thick oak, hickory, and redwood structures. Our archers concentrated their fire on the oxen that pulled the towers into place, and their drovers. While fun, it was futile, as they had plenty of other drovers to replace the fallen, and ate the dead oxen.

The towers were well-protected magically, as I found out after wasting several standard shock bolts and fire bolts and such on them.

All of our attempts to smash the menacing structures were in vain. They just kept coming. Like a dagger being slowly drawn across our collective throats, they inched forward. We prepared as good a defense as possible, but we all knew what our chances were if even one of those towers made it. One breach in our defenses would be all it would take to let the growing horde of goblins inside.

I paced the top of my tower, staring out at the glacial progress of our foes, and tried to think of a plan while the civilians prepared for the assault below me.

The possibility of dropping really heavy rocks on them had occurred to me. With the two witchstones I had, I could probably lift a boulder magically for a while. The problem was that it would take most of my power and all my concentration, leaving me wide open for a counterattack. I couldn't take that chance, not when I wasn't sure of the outcome.

I could also summon a nasty storm – weather magic is fairly easy, but very dangerous and harmful to Nature – but that would only delay them, and make life for our folk miserable as well. Besides, the dark clouds that hid the sun from us for so many days were clearly under their control.

The answer came to me while I was showing Tyndal how to strap on his new mageblade over his shoulder, fixing each knot with a cantrip to keep it from slipping – which could prove annoying and deadly in battle. That's when the answer to our problem suddenly hit me.

*　　　*　　　*

Things were better after we arrived at the outer defenses of Farise, proper. After the jungle and the mountains we would have fought with our lives just for a clean bath and a hot meal. That's almost what happened, at first. More of a mob than an army, we attacked the Doge's storehouses, great brick fortresses full of food on the other side of the city from the port where the main attack was expected. We slew the Farisi like vengeful spirits and gorged ourselves on their rich, strange-tasting rations.

After three days of rest and pillage on the outskirts of the city, we marshaled our resources and struck at the inner city in a highly coordinated attack with the fleet. The Farisi had not seriously considered that our little army of three thousand might be a serious threat. As we never attacked a garrison until the odds were heavily in our favor, their losses were light – but strategically significant.

When the final assault to capture the city was launched, the fleets of the Five Duchies pushed their way into the harbor and fought the Farisi squadrons to a standstill. Meanwhile we used the leverage of our earlier raids to push behind the great encircling wall of the town and force the Doge to re-position is troops away from the harbor, which they desperately needed to defend.

Caught between the two forces, even the Mad Mage's witchstone wasn't enough to keep us outside of the city walls and out of the docks.

There were the usual lucky turns of events which contribute to a successful assault – enemy stupidity (happens in every military organization), random factors falling in our favor – it helped our cause tremendously when their heavily-bribed port commander led his marines against their former employers for the promise of a palace and a post in the new regime. The Mad Mage and his patron could only look on impotently while one half of their army attacked the other half. The battle and subsequent looting of the city was ugly, perhaps legendarily so.

Then the veterans of the Long March pushed into the center of the city, and it was bloody. The Doge's best troops were mostly pirate marines, infantry-on-boats, and they were tough. The city watch was likewise tough, and toward the end of the three-day battle for the city even civilians were picking up arms to defend themselves as the battle de-evolved into house-to-house fighting.

I don't like making war on civilians, but if a man has a spear in his hand, to me it looks like he just joined the army, and I didn't hesitate to cut him down or blast him into bits. I was too tired to pay attention to the bronze warriors' loyalties. For three solid days we fought them without rest or quarter. The landward army, including a few crack Kasari rangers, was responsible for capturing a good third of the city before the naval forces were able to overcome, with heavy losses, the port fortifications and take another third.

By the end of the third day of fighting we controlled the waterfront, the town, and the farms and plantations around the city. But we weren't done until Orril Pratt and his sponsor, the Doge, was defeated. We rested (and systematically sacked the city) while our fearless leaders argued about strategy and tactics and politics. The only thing we didn't control was the Doge's palace, where the Mad Mage had his tower and a thousand loyal crack troops. Our surprise attack turned into a siege. While this concerned the War Marshal and his staff greatly, we grunts didn't care. We were *pillaging*.

A city with the size, age, and wealth of Farise has a lot of accumulated treasure to steal. I know I got my share. The looting was *amazing*. We took everything of value, and there was plenty. Antiques from Imperial times, gold, silver, brass, silks, fine wines, tapestries, *everything*.

Farise was a stronghold of pirates and merchant princes, and the only poor people were the slaves (many of whom turned on their masters and welcomed us as liberators . . . then joined us in looting. They knew were the best of it was, after all.) I did my share of looting myself, and even acquired a stylish residence when the previous occupant got himself killed defending it. When things settled down, about a week after the attack, three other warmagi and I moved into the pleasant townhouse and caught up on our sleep while the generals tried to figure out how to smoke the Doge out of his fortified palace.

But Orril Pratt wasn't going to go quietly. Every few days the Mad Mage would unleash some new horror on us from his tower, we would defeat it, and then everyone would rest for a few days. Then we would try an attack and he would beat it off with that damned witchstone of his. Then everyone would rest for a few days.

One night I woke up to find the streets crawling with soldiers who had already been killed once. The Mad Mage had sullied himself with necromancy by animating the recently dead, of which there was an abundance, and throwing them at us to keep us occupied.

Necromancy is one of those darker areas of magic that most nice wizards just don't talk about. But it isn't particularly hard, if you have enough power. It was horrifying to fight the living dead, especially if you encountered someone you once knew and for whom you had grieved. The surprise zombie attack took us another three days to put down, and a special meeting of the entire ducal Magical Corps was called to prevent similar spells in the future.

Three days after *that*, a mysterious plague broke out among the portside infantry. That took us another week to cure, and we lost almost a thousand men to the fever – almost as many as we had in the invasion proper, or the Long March.

The week after that nothing wooden could come within bowshot of the Doge's Citadel without bursting into flame. We lost several siege engines that way, and not a few engineers, and even fire-retardant spells were useless against that kind of power.

We figured the palace would be easy, after the city, but the Mad Mage kept not dying, which was irritating. This went on for a month and a half. When a black mist that seemed alive crept out of the Citadel to suffocate all who encountered it, the War Marshal had had enough. He was losing men without gaining anything in battle against the Mad Mage. He called upon his own magi to do something about it.

Finally, the famous Wenshari warmage, Master Loiko Venaren, worked out a way to assault the palace and the Citadel without slaughtering a thousand of our men in the process – just a few magi.

I won't go into detail about the attack here – perhaps later – but the Magical Corps played a large role in the battle. That final battle was the greatest assembled collection of warmagi since the fall of the

Magocracy. Some of the finest magical warriors of my generation fought the Battle of the Doge's Tower.

A special force from Group B assassinated the Doge once they broke into the palace, and the combined might of close to two dozen warmagi finally contained the death-dealing Mad Mage. Master Loiko himself dueled the man, and ended up destroying the focus of a powerful spell at a crucial moment. The Mad Mage's head essentially exploded. We got the doors of the Citadel open and a flood of infantry came through to mop up the survivors.

The next morning, to the cheers of his troops, the War Marshal made his triumphant entrance into the castle on a white horse borrowed for the occasion. The banner of Farise was struck and the ensigns of Alshar and Castal were raised. The last vestige of the Imperial Magocracy was conquered. Yay.

Oh, sure, we had a minor guerilla war to contend with (at least five thousand Farisian troops had escaped into the jungle to form a resistance) but *we held the city*. Only two-thirds of us survived, but at the end of the battle it was the Mad Mage's head that was stuck on a pike, the Doge's palace a smoking ruin behind it. In the end it was a crack squad of nearly invincible veteran warmagi who penetrated his defenses and defeated him after a lengthy and deadly combat.

The Battle of the Doge's Tower revealed what a witchstone could do up close, in the heat of battle, and it was terrifying. The Mad Mage flung power around like a child throws a new ball, converting it into a hundred deadly forces that struck our men.

The spells he worked that night were potent enough to have burned out the brains of any normal mage foolish enough to try them. There was little pattern to the way he did it – they called him the Mad Mage for a reason, after all – so finding adequate defensive spells was more a matter of luck than skill. By contrast, he batted away our attacks as though we were flies until Master Loiko Venaren found a way.

The stuff of legends . . .

*   *   *

The best battle magics, my instructors at the War College used to say, are the little, subtle ones that your enemy doesn't see coming. My plan for the siege towers at Boval Castle was along those lines.

I talked it over with my apprentice for a while, ran it past Garkesku, and ran a simulation on the model in my quarters. Once I had come up with a fully developed plan, I presented it to the War Council and Sire Koucey. They loved it and, despite some misgivings about their role in it, they agreed.

The next morning two of the towers were within bowshot of the castle, and the other three were not. The bulk of the gurvani infantry had retired to their shady hollows to rest up for the big battle the next evening, leaving only a skeleton force to guard the towers, catapults, and ballistae that were still being moved by the day shift. By skeleton force, I meant about eight or nine *thousand* gurvani warriors – far more than we could handle – but it also meant ten thousand or so less than we would face on the battlefield that night. Yes, the goblins had been arriving in that kind of strength.

I called my Magical Corps to the top battlement of the main gate, which looked like the most centralized position facing the foe. I had the archers keep up some harassing fire, and they were doing pretty well, considering that most of them had only been shooting seriously for the last few weeks. Garkesku, his three apprentices and Tyndal gathered around me on the battlements as I explained the spell, explaining their roles to each in turn.

When I was done, Tyndal looked out doubtfully at the swarm of goblins beyond the wall.

"Master are you certain this will work?"

I shrugged. "I have no idea. But I'm hopeful."

He shook his head. "Maybe we should have evacuated. That seems more sensible than this."

"While I dislike your apprentice's impertinence," Garkesku said, solemnly, "I cannot fault his reasoning. If I knew that this was what we would be facing in this siege . . ."

"This is your home," I said, evenly. "If you love it, it deserves to be defended. Don't worry – this spell should have an effect. Hopefully a dramatic one."

"Enough to break this damnable siege?" Garky asked, skeptically. "Or are you expecting an army of relief from Duke Lenguin for this forgotten little domain?"

"Perhaps he likes cheese," Rondal, his second apprentice offered. "A lot."

"Regardless of what help may or may not arrive, the defense of this castle rests with us," I said, firmly. "If we all play our part and manage to make this work, we can set back the goblins' plans for weeks.

Perhaps long enough for help to arrive before winter sets in. But that won't happen if we run away. Now, do you all remember your roles? Each one is vital, in its way."

To Garkesku I gave responsibility for our defense. He would do his best to deflect or absorb incoming magics, which shouldn't be too much of a problem until we were well into the spell. Once the shamans realized we were gathering a great working they would throw everything but my Aunt Bebe's butter churn at us to stop us.

This was something else Garkesku was pretty good at; once I'd taught him a few simple defensive spells he'd become very proficient in their use. He didn't even challenge my authority on the matter. I guess he was as scared as anyone else in the castle and hoped I could pull off a victory.

To Tyndal I gave the responsibility for masking what we were up to. He would play with the elemental chords, disguising our true spell behind a tapestry of interesting but misleading arcane signals. Nothing elaborate – just enough "hints" of spell elements to make them think we were hiding something big and powerful behind our wards.

To two of Garky's the three apprentices I gave the task of helping me extend the range of the spell. A spell usually needs to be directed by a conscious mind if it is going to work properly, and while I'm pretty good at that sort of thing, we weren't talking about curing a bunion here. We had to affect more than *eight thousand* gurvani all at once. By using the minds of Garkesku's two senior apprentices to extend the range of the spell it was likely I could (I hoped) cover the entire force. The third, youngest – Urik – was in charge of general support.

Me? I directed the whole thing.

This is what Imperially trained magi are best at, working in a group. It gives us an important edge over our shamanic or solitary colleagues. By working together in concert we can not only raise and channel more power, we can individually concentrate on specific aspects of a spell, content in knowing that the others in the circle will handle their part without us.

There is always the potential for failure, of course, as a hidden doubt in the mind of one person in the circle can cause a chain reaction that destroys the whole spell – sometimes explosively. But when it works, it works well.

I had my own doubts, but not in the circle. I had carefully selected each of the roles the others would play, and no one was assigned something that they couldn't handle.

I set all of them to begin their meditations while I spoke briefly with one of Koucey's officers, coordinating their mission with the result of our spell. This is more important than it sounds. Most warmagi act as if regular warriors are only good for spellfodder, but I had learned better in Farise. If the magical corps and the infantry aren't properly coordinated, then the whole damn mission can blow up in your face and kill both divisions. When the Wilderlord in the bailey signaled that he and his men were ready, I went back to the battlements and began the working.

With a nod from me, my men each formed an *apis*, so that we could share power. More accurately, I would give *them* power – with a piece of irionite in each fist, power wasn't going to be an issue here for a change, sharing it was. Instead of a standard *apis* I formed a *stelapis*, a magical form that allows a single source to shunt power to many others. It was unusual in standard Imperial magic – after all, the reason that the *apis* is so important is that it is rare for a single mage to be able to raise enough power for a really big spell – but we had learned the technique as part of our training all the same.

Slowly I drew power from the stones and sent it to be distributed, causing the *stelapis* to glow in my magesight. It began to flow out to the apis of the others, and I relaxed and focused on keeping it moving.

Garkesku began his portion of the spell, laying a thick sphere of defensive magic about our circle. When it was complete, he nodded once.

Tyndal then began his spell. When I was convinced that there were sufficient signs to mislead any self-respecting gurvani shaman of our true purpose and counter it, I took a deep breath and started the major part of the work.

I watched with detached interest through magesight as the five towers crept closer, the gurvani catapults were towed into place, and thousands of goblins scurried across the field like ants on honey bread.

This is where it would get tricky. I began to form in my mind the glyph *tera*, the unbinding. It was the polar opposite of *kere*, the binding glyph that I'd used that morning on Tyndal's sword belt.

Glyphs and runes have no innate power of their own. They are symbolic representations, visual and mental metaphors of abstract concepts. True, their shape usually has some relation to the concept – *tera* looks kind of like two pieces of rope the moment they become untied, if you look at it right, for example.

The concept behind *tera* is just that, unbinding, loosing. Used in conjunction with other glyphs it can be used to express quite a range of ideas. For example, *tera*, drawn below the runes for *rock* and *head* will help a spellmonger remove a rotten tooth from someone's head – although a barber's pliers help. Drawn above the runes for *iron* and *secret* and most unhexed locks will fall open as if you had used a key. It's a very useful basic cantrip that most magi know.

What I was doing in this spell wasn't technically any more complicated than using it to unlace the bodice on an unsuspecting peasant lass (one of my favorite tricks at the Academy). I was simply boosting the power by orders of magnitude.

The glyph glowed in my magesight, safely hidden behind Tyndal's obscuring shield. I let power flow like life's blood from the irionite stones in my fists and directed it into the glyph, empowering it into activity, and soon it blazed in my mind like a righteous star.

Still I poured power into it, far past my unaugmented limits, far past the point where any spell so simple had been powered before, to my knowledge. I could soon feel the residual power crackle the very air, making the hair on my scalp stand at attention. Hells, my very *bones* vibrated with the power.

With one tiny part of my mind that wasn't busy maintaining the glyph or directing power, I saw that the three apprentices had done their parts. The field ahead of me was scattered with tiny blue pinpoints, like candle flames, visible only to us. That was Rondal, the middle apprentice, doing the casting.

This was a control spell known to the Imperials as *Urandra's Net*. Every *one* of those thousands of points was essentially the same as the blue flame that Rondal had cast on the edge of the merlon in front of us. Every *one* of those points reflected every *other* one, like a fisherman's net with mirrors at the juncture of each set of cords.

That was all. It wasn't more complicated than that.

When I saw all was prepared, I waited for the moment of *pavad*, the Time of Timelessness. That's a more difficult concept to explain to folks who don't use magic. Someday, if I ever understand it completely, maybe I'll try to come up with a perfect metaphor for it.

What it boils down to is that at some point during the casting of a spell of this nature there is a *single instant* that is the perfect time to release the power and activate the spell, like a professional archer loosing his arrow between heartbeats. Old magi know the time by experience. Every mage tries to release the spell at the time of *pavad*, but essentially we're all guessing. I know I was.

I did it anyway, moving the huge glowing glyph into the blue flame by force of will, releasing my breath, and discharging the spell.

By the principal of *Urandra's Net*, the glyph reflected itself to the tens of thousands of *other* blue flames. For all practical purposes, I had just cast the *tera* glyph a thousand times over the host of gurvani at our door.

The effect was sudden and explosive, and far exceeded my hopes. Everywhere among the gurvani army, wherever there was a tied knot or a fastened belt, it came undone.

The knots that held mace heads to handles were unraveled, the knots that held on their cloaks and rough armor became untied. Bowstrings snapped, and arrowheads and spear points fell off of their shafts. Shields fell away from their handles. Harnesses unbuckled and ropes frayed. In an instant, thousands of weapons and armor became completely useless.

Most importantly, the siege towers that they had spent so many days building fell apart as the bindings that held them together ceased to function. Gurvani warriors – and shamans proudly overseeing the battle -- fell from the towers to their deaths, while others were crushed under the tons of lumber suddenly raining down on them. At other points the massive pressure that was contained in the yards of sinew that formed the springs of the catapults were released explosively, killing dozens in their vicinities. Never have you imagined an army going to hell that quickly.

It was a scene of utter chaos, and *I had caused it.* I took a lot of professional pride in that. But I wasn't done.

At my signal the gates below us were thrown open, the iron portcullis was raised, and the drawbridge was lowered, all in an instant. Every one of our horsemen charged into the suddenly unarmed, suddenly confused goblins, their lance heads, spear points and swords flashing in the dim sunlight that managed to penetrate the clouds above. Behind them were most of our infantry, including five hundred butter-stinking barbarians who looked as fierce as any gurvani warrior.

I was drained buy the massive spell, but even drained I still had plenty of power at my command with two shards of irionite to draw from. I knew I would pay dearly, later, but we *had* to press this momentary advantage as far as we could, or we risked all of our lives. I signaled Tyndal to begin the second phase of the spell. The easy part.

The Net was still active, and Garkesku still looked to our defense, but Tyndal no longer had to fool any shamans. He started casting another simple rune, the light rune *eos*, into the blue flame. It's the one you use to activate a magelight, only this time we weren't merely trying to illuminate. I fed power to him, as I was unable to concentrate on anything more complicated than that at the moment, and let him cast the spell.

Below us the dim battlefield suddenly flared with brilliance, as a light as bright as a dozen torches suddenly blazed across it. It was a spectacular effect, and not without an impact on the battlefield: the nocturnal gurvani detested bright lights, and our men could suddenly see as clearly as under a clear noonday sun. The Battle of the Thousand Lights, as survivors called it later, had begun.

I wish I could say that it was a total slaughter, a rout, but that simply wasn't the case. Our men fought hard and well, but the gurvani did not turn tail and flee in a mass as we'd hoped. Oh, plenty of them did, but plenty more stayed to fight against our warriors with whatever scraps of weapons they could salvage from the pile of litter at their feet. They fought with savage bravery and vicious desperation, and many of our warriors died because of gurvani bravery.

But enough of the enemy died, too, and their siege breaking plans were damaged. Within a half an hour our Wilderlord cavalry were at the far edge of the field establishing pickets and running down stragglers while the mercenaries and the Crinroc mopped up the chaotic center around the five massive piles of firewood.

I watched tiredly as our hairy warriors hewed goblins with their axes like so much kindling. The Crinroc fought with great spirit, and a surprising amount of precision, and they provided a stable center in the battle for our more civilized warriors to depend upon for support and reinforcement.

I just watched. As I said, I had done *my* part. What work was to be done had to be done quickly. I estimated we had an hour, maybe two, before the surviving generals would be able to gather a strong enough force of his sleeping warriors to re-take the field.

Garkesku was toning down his defenses – nothing had challenged them yet – when Tyndal and I hurried down the stairs to join the fray. There a couple of stable boys were holding our horses already. In seconds we were galloping across the field after the mercenary cavalry, the thousand lights casting our shadows a thousand times. It was daunting. I felt dizzy and giddy and elated and exhausted, but Traveler is an excellent mount. He passed corpses without reaction and leapt piles of debris in our way, the heaps of wood and skins that had once been a frightening offense.

I could see our targets by the glows of their witchstones, which were blazing brightly in my magesight. There were seven of them scattered about the battlefield, and I aimed to gather every one like a child gathers flowers in the spring.

I'll spare you most of the gory details, the moans of the wounded and the cries of the dying, the gruesome sight of a young man in shock, vainly trying to stuff his intestines back into his body, the smell of a thousand bowels loosed in death. Battlefields are all much the same, and best to be avoided, if possible. I had been in them before and didn't want to be in one now.

I had a mission. I tried not to think about the countless horrors that were happening all around me as I busied myself harvesting fistfuls of arcane power from the dead and dying shamans.

Here and there we came to knots of real fighting, where a few goblins had taken defensive positions and were managing to not get slaughtered quite as quickly. We helped the conventional fighters when we could, blasting the goblins with our wands at propitious moments before they could regroup, but we primarily focused on racing to find the green amber nuggets we sought. The only time we stopped more than a dozen heartbeats was to witness a duel between a gurvani warrior and one of the Crinroc princes – Posnak, I believe.

The gurvani had taken a longsword from the hand of one of our slain warriors and was using it quite efficiently to keep the hulking, bearded mass of Posnak away. In his other hand he held a stick of wood that may have been a section of spear once, and this he used to knock the great iron axe away. They stood toe to toe, surrounded by soldiers who were unwilling to take a victory away from their chieftain but also unwilling to allow him to fight un-reinforced.

I reined Traveler to a stop as Posnak was executing an intricate series of passes with his blade – if you have ever seen a Crinroc axe-man in action, you know it is as graceful as an Imperial silk dancer and as bloody as a butcher.

The gurvan he faced was doing a passable job blocking, but he was falling back slowly. The goblin returned the blows as well as he could, but the human-sized word was too long for him to balance properly, and Posnak had the advantage.

Still, the gurvan fought with amazing coolness, and when he exploded into a furious attack on the Crinroc prince I was almost unsurprised to see his unwieldy blade suddenly hovering a half an inch above the furry throat of Posnak. We were about to be short a Crinroc Prince.

The muscular gurvan paused and looked around at the humani warriors surrounding him, warriors who were preparing to strike on their own. The gurvan glanced up to me, and then looked Posnak dead in the eye and did the last thing I expected him to do. He threw down his blade and dropped to his knees in front of the Crinroc chieftain, chin held up proudly, black eyes squinting in the glow of the magelights.

"Kill me quickly, *humani*," he said in passable if accented Narasi. Crinroc shrugged, hefted his axe and was preparing to strike.

Something tugged on me, though, and I commanded him to stop, emphasizing the point by magically holding the axe in the air.

"Wait," I said, pointing. "Do not kill him."

"He fought well!," Posnak objected, scowling. "He deserves to die honorably!"

"We need him alive. *He speaks Narasi!* Bind him and have him taken to the castle dungeon. I will interrogate him tonight."

"At once, Master!" Posnak said, motioning to two of his men. They took the goblin and bound his hands behind his back.

After this victory, the Crinroc treated me with the respect usually reserved for their own "princes." Posnak himself patted the goblin on his shoulder in a comradely manner before returning to the mopping-up operations. It had been a good fight, and the Crinroc relish a good fight like they enjoy rancid butter. But in a good way.

I returned to my own task. We made our way to the site of the nearest ruined tower, where a group of our men were already hitching their horses to great timbers to be hauled back to the castle. Most were bloodstained and covered with black hair, but it was useful materials. There was a soldier stationed nearby with a spear, dispatching the wounded goblins entangled in the mess and watching for surprises.

"Sergeant, over here!" I shouted to the militiaman in charge of the salvage operation. "I need two more horses, and a half-dozen men. Shift this beam *here* –" I pointed, and for the next ten minutes we disassembled one edge of the pile, searching by sight and by magic.

At last I came to the shattered wand of a dead shaman, on which was a single green stone. Placing it into a specially prepared pouch, we thanked the men and rode on to the next one.

We recovered six of the seven witchstones but we took some losses, too – the last shaman had speared one of the Black Flag and escaped with his life and his stone on the man's horse. The others were dead or soon to be, and this pretty harvest made it all worthwhile.

By the time we had finished finding the seventh stone, it was growing darker (our magelights had long since died out), and the screen of horsemen was beginning a measured retreat back to the castle.

The defiant and outraged screams of the goblins could be heard just beyond the forest line where they prepared a counter charge. We had no intention of being there when that happened. We grabbed what we could off of the field and headed back behind stone walls for the evening.

By the time the sun fell behind the western horizon the great gates of the castle were closed. The inner bailey was heaped with unsorted loot, lumber, iron, even leather and cloth and some of the more edible foodstuffs we'd recovered. The civilians were climbing over the piles and cheering, save those who were tending the wounded in the field hospital Sire Koucey had erected near the front gate in preparation.

Of those there were many. They cheered me and Tyndal and my magical corps – even Garkesku – when we entered the Bailey.

I wish I felt like cheering. As I came through a messenger headed for Sire Koucey's study told me the score of the battle. We lost nearly a hundred and twenty men in the attack outright, and almost twice that number had been wounded. That was light compared to the blood of no less than five thousand goblins that stained the field. But the towers had fallen, and we had bought ourselves a little more time.

When I finally climbed the stairs to my quarters I noticed Tyndal saying he wanted to continue celebrating in the bailey. I should have suspected something was afoot then, as he said this through a yawn, but I was so tired myself that I nodded blearily and continued my stumble.

As I shed my clothes by candlelight (I was too tired to use a magelight) I noticed a dark shape in my hammock. It leaned forward, and as a cascade of honey blonde hair fell away from her face and spilled over her bare breasts, I recognized the face of the pretty widow. Alya.

"Your apprentice said you had an eye for me," she said in a sultry voice. "I feel it is my duty to show you how appreciative we are for your efforts." I studied the curve of her throat and the shadows that the candle cast in the valley between her magnificent breasts.

Despite my sorely used body, I had the usual reaction. Suddenly I felt superhuman.

"Well," I said slowly, "I guess it would be rude for me to refuse an earnest demonstration of appreciation."

Damn Tyndal!

Chapter Nine

Urik's Rebellion

"The responsible use of magical power must be properly conveyed through accepted and acceptable instruction by qualified masters. Entrusting the details of the powerful magics to those who lack the maturity and insight to use them properly is therefore forbidden, and those magi who are found guilty of such a breach shall be held accountable."

- *The Royal Bans On Magic*

I didn't leave my room for two days. Tyndal kept us fed – at least I think it was Tyndal. Every six hours or so, someone would leave a basket full of food in front of the door. But it could have been the damned gurvani, for all I knew. I didn't see the boy once for two straight sunsets. The respite with Alya was that enjoyable, and the cold autumn rains encouraged me to stay indoors.

I just couldn't think of any place else I'd rather be than in that hammock, in her arms. Alya was the tonic my tired soul needed. She wasn't complicated, like Pentandra, and she wasn't opportunistic, like . . . well, like most of the other girls I'd bedded. She seemed genuinely happy to be with me, and I found that intensely flattering.

On the morning of the third day I rolled over in the hammock (a feat which takes practice) and noticed that Alya was gone, and I tensed. Then I smelled frying bacon, and I relaxed. Soon the scents of fresh brewed tea and toasting bread joined it, and I allowed my eyelids to gradually lift themselves. I was rewarded with the sight of a naked Alya tending the small brazier Tyndal and I used to cook upon. Well, mostly Tyndal. That's the whole point of having an apprentice. Cheap labor.

The light from the arrow slits told me it was midmorning and not raining for a change. Then it did double duty by bathing her in one of those golden glows that you tend to associate with otherworldly creatures. She didn't realize I was awake, and I admit that I watched her with great interest as she went about the business of cooking breakfast. Naked.

Alya was a real find. She was utterly beautiful, in a distinctive, peasant-y sort of way. Her facial features were bold and pronounced, her eyes were the brightest shade of blue-gray I'd ever seen, her hair was a field of ripe wild grains. She had the bearing of a queen and the body of a healthy, lusty peasant maiden. Her feet were a little big, which I had noted to our mutual amusement the previous evening. I didn't mind. They matched.

We had talked incessantly when we weren't otherwise occupied, and I had learned a lot more about her than I had at our earlier encounter. The middle daughter of Goodman Roral, a prosperous freeholding farmer and herder of some repute at the hillside farm known as Hawk's Reach.

She had taken charge in the cheese sheds for the last year, after returning home to try to forget her grief, and while the memory of her young husband still burned in her heart she at last had started to entertain the idea of love again . . . when the gurvani invasion interrupted her courting prospects.

I had made quite an impression on her apparently, though she didn't think I was interested in a serious relationship or expected anything more than a quick tumble. I didn't admit that I was, but then I didn't say that I wasn't. I was still getting to know her. I was glad that she had made it to the fortress before the gates had shut. Her sister and brother-in-law Sagal were also here, out in the bailey. But it was her I wanted to see.

Alya had seen me around the castle several times since she and her family had arrived, but didn't want to disturb me. She still thought I was handsome and charismatic, and she knew I was brave and resourceful – her brother-in-law was doing very well, now. But she didn't want to intrude, or presume an affection that might not be returned. She told me that I was comely enough that she expected a long line of lusty maidens awaited me at my door every night.

I found *that* hard to believe – while I am not as ugly as Furtak, I'm no handsome prince. After our fourth or fifth bout she admitted coyly that she had been drawn to me since we first met, and even admitted feeling eyes on her that day when I saw her from the tower, though she could have been exaggerating.

But my apprentice was aware of my interest. Tyndal had approached her in that lanky, too-shy way of his and asked if she was spoken for, yet. He then mentioned that "his lord" had expressed an interest in her, and asked if she would be willing to meet with me again to pass the time and fight the boredom implicit in castle life. She was agreeable. And my tower room was dry and heated, compared to her small allotment of space in the bailey.

I enjoyed just being with her. Alya was smart, as well as beautiful – she had increased profits at her father's farm while she had been in charge of the cheese shed. She could read, at least some, which is rare in a woman in Boval Vale (or a man, for that matter). Indeed she had actually read five or six books, which made her a scholar by local standards. She had an abiding curiosity about the world and a quick and sharp wit.

Best yet, she had over a year of repressed tensions to work out. All in all, a wonderful companion during this time of stress and crisis.

In my mind her wholesome, noble image crumbled a bit when a strip of bacon popped over the coals, sending a drop of hot grease to splatter on her left breast. She shrieked and dropped the bread she was buttering (butter side down, of course) and rubbed her burned breast while she made a face.

"Ishi's tits!" she yelped, as she rubbed at the burn. The bacon grease instantly transformed her from the well-behaved woman back into a fussy peasant housewife. I couldn't help but chuckle, which startled her again.

"You're awake!"

"Never fry bacon naked," I admonished her. "Or didn't your mother ever teach you that?"

"It was never an issue at our house, but I'll keep it in mind. It's about time you woke up." I swung my feet over the side of the hammock and stood, realizing that I was naked too --- then smiled when I recalled why.

I quickly crossed the cold stone floor and bent to kiss her bacon-flavored wound. Reaching out with my mind I repaired the tiny burn without even tapping into the power of the witchstones. At least the blemish was gone, and wouldn't chafe against her clothes. If she ever wore any again. The effect tingles, and it had a predictable effect on her nipple.

"Boo-boo is all better now," I said, grinning.

"Damn! It really is! That's great. You know, you're a handy one to have around."

"Let me show you just how handy –"

"*After* breakfast, you tireless letch. I'm *starved!*" She handed me a toasted trencher with bacon, fried eggs, and a thick wedge of cheese on it. I paid her a kiss in return and sat down at the small table, which I noticed she had cleared of all the debris that two bachelors can accumulate in a few weeks.

That was the first unmistakable sign, I realized, that I suddenly had a *girlfriend.*

Surprisingly, even with the prospect of death and doom just outside the castle wall, the thought pleased me.

Alya joined me a moment later with her own trencher – still naked – and handed me a mug of strong country tea as she sat. Breakfast was excellent, as good or better as I could have done on my own, and the company was certainly engaging – we chatted lightly about nothing in particular for a long while.

As I finished the meal, however, the way her tussled dark blonde tresses spilled over her chest, just managing to cover her nipples, started to get to me. I approached her with all the subtlety of a randy dragon and pulled her into my lap. Only by a knock at the door spared her from a thorough post-breakfast ravishing.

I groaned and let her free. She giggled guiltily and tried to throw her shapeless chemise over her head in a token of modesty, while I reluctantly pulled on a more-or-less clean tunic from a press. After being naked for two days, wearing clothes was suddenly a novelty.

It was Tyndal at the door. My apprentice stumbled into the room looking like a refugee and smelling like a beer barrel. The look in his slitted eyes was all too familiar – I had seen it in a mirror on many occasions.

"Good morning, Master," he mumbled as he sloughed over to the stove and poured himself a scalding mug of tea. "Sleep well?"

I glanced at Alya, who had found a comb and was tugging her hair into shape. "Well enough. I'll have to find some way to thank you for such excellent service." Tyndal glanced up at Alya and smiled.

"I just thought that, you being so busy with the defense of the castle and all, that you would neglect to reintroduce yourself."

"Tyndal, I hope that we didn't throw you out of your quarters," Alya asked, concerned.

The boy shook his head – which he immediately regretted – and shot her a shy grin. "You aren't the only lady of the castle who is 'grateful' to the Magical Corps after the last battle. I did not lack for a comfortable bed. I just wish that I had declined that last mug of beer."

"Let me fix it," I said, grabbing the pouch with my sphere off of the table. In seconds I had transformed the alcohol in his blood, although I could do little with the soured contents of his stomach, or the pain in his head. Some things you should just have to suffer through. Besides, if they bothered him enough he could manage the simple spell. Still, his eyes got wider and brighter, and became a less malevolent shade of red.

"Many thanks, Master," he gasped gratefully as the spell subsided. "I actually came here on an errand. Sire Koucey has summoned you and Master Garkesku to the Council Room. All the officers shall be there. It is to be held at noon which," he said, glancing out of an open arrow slit at the sun, "will be in about half an hour."

I grunted, disappointed that my lust would go un-sated for a while longer. If the meeting was in the Council Room, instead of his study, that meant that this would be one of those huge councils that accomplished little. It would be long and boring and wouldn't be over with until every junior assistant captain of the trash disposal committee had had their say. At the least, it would kill the afternoon. I sighed and grabbed another piece of bread. I had better ideas for how to kill an afternoon.

But duty calls.

"Very well, then, I guess I'll have to go. Tyndal, if you would be so kind as to fill the copper tub with water and then heat it – with magic, mind, no fires – I will have a quick bath before I go."

"I heartily agree!" Alya spoke up. "You were starting to smell."

I gave her an indignant glance, reminding her silently of why I had worked up a sweat. "Just for that wisecrack, you have to help bathe me!"

That would teach her.

*   *   *

For six months after the last, climactic Battle of the Doge's Tower, I had the pleasure of being part of a conquering occupation force, with all the duties and privileges associated therewith.

Mostly that meant loot, girls, guard duty, girls, drunken stupors, girls, reprisals against rebels, girls, indulgence in unimaginable luxury, girls, interrogation of prisoners, girls, bargain shopping, and girls. I even got a little sight-seeing in.

Farise was a very pretty city (even after we got through with it) and the people were nice (even after what we did to them). I liked the tropical climate and the exotic foods. I perfected my command of the Imperial language of Lost Perwyn (which the Farisi spoke in a debased form, with plenty of Cormeeran influence). That was helped by liaisons with a number of local girls, whose dusky and exotic Imperial appearance reminded me pleasantly of Penny.

The Coronet Council installed Master Venaren as the military commander of the city, a rare token of respect for the Ducal Magical

Corps. That raised a lot of objections from the regular nobility who'd had their eyes on that position, but the Council was clear – and Master Venaren was mostly above the politics that infected the occupation forces.

In return for our service in the battle he made the quartering and boarding of the magical corps a top priority. After we won the war there was a bumper crop of widows and maidens around, not to mention slaves whose masters had been killed in defense of the town, and apart from some initial resistance the victory was not marred by strife. The Farisi seemed content to be ruled from afar, again, after the mess the Doge had made of the city. It helped that Master Venaren was not a punitive man, compared to the barons and counts in the occupying army. He kept order in the streets, making Farise a comparatively civilized occupation. But he didn't discourage fraternization, and I took full advantage of it. Had I not been careful to do the proper spells, likely I'd have a dozen half-dusky bastards crawling in that exotic port city by now.

But after six months, even cushy garrison duty gets old, and without significant opposition to our rule there was little reason to keep a fully-staffed magical corps on hand. About the time we started growing restless we began receiving orders to return to the Duchies and be discharged from service. I was a little shocked. I had grown used to the soldier's life. Mustering out seemed to panic me. I would need a job, after all. My return to civilian life put me right back where I had been on graduation day.

Well, not *quite*. I had a pile of loot and a generous payoff in specie for my service, more than my father made in profit at his bakery in ten years. One of the reasons the Magical Corps was the first unit to be discharged, I've heard, is that we were comparatively expensive to keep. Infantry are cheap, cavalry (apart from knights acting as officers) of little use to the occupation, so my fellows and I were taking up a large part of the budget. Once the overt magical threat was gone, regular infantry could be used to pacify rebels instead of us. So we were paid off and shipped out as fast as the clerks could write the orders. After that, I had enough treasure for a real stake, capital I could use to pursue just about anything I wanted to do. I just needed to figure out what to do.

On the stormy, rat-infested trip back to the Duchies I thought long and hard about my future. I had made up my mind to return to Talry, visit my folks, and maybe look around for a court job, when a baron from the Giram Hills who was also heading back offered me a handsome sum to help him attack his neighbor's castle, seeing as how the man was still on duty in Farise. He was willing to pay a premium price for veterans in the surprise campaign. Giram was on my way, so a small digression was not troubling. While I questioned his ethics, I welcomed his gold.

When he stood triumphant on the donjon of his hereditary enemy's stronghold four weeks later, I decided to go back to Talry and visit my folks. On my way out of the keep, a mule bearing my treasure at my side, a fellow warmage mentioned a knight banneret who was involved in a boundary dispute with his cousin in the coastlands and was looking for military help resolving the issue. After that it was a knight who wanted assistance settling an inheritance dispute. And after that . . .

A year and a half later I had four mules to tote my treasure, an account with the Temple of Ifnia, and a growing reputation as a reliable mercenary warmage. Oh, I tried my hand at regular magic between military gigs; I worked with a few spellmongers, studied a few weeks with this court mage or that, but the lure of quick gold for doing a simple, if dirty, job was just too potent to ignore. My reputation was growing. My financial reserves were growing. My skills at warmagic were growing.

I also felt a growing dissatisfaction with my lifestyle. The problem was simple: *I didn't like violence.*

But I was *very* good at it.

*   *   *

I was right about the war council meeting on all accounts. It was an obvious opportunity for propaganda, designed to congratulate ourselves for the accomplishment of still being alive. I couldn't argue with Koucey's logic – we needed all the morale we could muster.

First the old knight, sitting on a chair that was one point away from being a throne, gave a long, solemn speech about his brave ancestors first coming to this land, their cunning defeat of the gurvani, their effort to build a peaceful and prosperous domain in this fertile valley, etc. etc. Having wetted his lance outside of the castle walls Koucey looked a little less like a condemned man today, and a little more like the leader he was. He was hopeful.

Someone had found a clean surcoat for him, and someone else had shaved his cheeks and brushed his hair. His sword was laying across his knees, and in one hand he held his mace-of-office (a little ceremonial club given to him by his baronial liege as a symbol of his dominion in the domain). He seemed upbeat and positive, which was a welcomed change from the gloomy melancholia he'd started to sink into.

The other member of the council assembled around him included the castle's officers, the leaders of his fighting men , and the elected representatives of the peasants of the outer bailey. Sire Koucey singled me and my "magical corps" out for special praise, thanks to our creative spellcasting. But the cavalry still got the most glory, as befitted their station. We all cheered at the appropriate times during the speech, and I tapped into the power of the irionite to make the cheers seem louder than they actually were. It amused me.

When Sire Koucey was finished with his speech, he turned the meeting over to a succession of officers for reports – quartermaster, stores, physicians, and pretty much anyone who had a title and wanted to brag about how well they were doing. Then the war leaders had their turn recounting the recent battle in glowing, if not legendary terms.

When they were done Sire Koucey finally asked for a report from the Magical Corps, and Garkesku and I stood up at the same time. I gave him a glance – I didn't mean for it to be threatening – and he sat down again.

"My lords and goodmen, the Magical Corps can report that the counterattack three days ago was an utter and absolute success. Due to proper planning and execution the enemy's means of breaching our defenses were taken from the field, significant casualties were inflicted, and the Corps captured several items which will greatly aid in our future defense."

"Sire Koucey, my lords, if I may," Garkesku interrupted, standing again. I felt like glaring at him, that time, but I was kind of curious as to what he would say. Reluctantly I bowed and let him take the floor.

"My good lord, while I have every confidence in Master Minalan's ability to direct our magical defense – he is a trained warmage, after all, and we are all damned lucky to have him here – I feel bound to inquire as to the disposition of the magical items he mentioned in his report. I would not endeavor to bore a layman with the specifics of it, but while I do not question Minalan's ability or genius at the arts of war, I do wonder if he has disposed of the booty of the counterattack to exploit its maximum effectiveness. Older and wiser heads, with more experience in such matters, may be better suited to use them better."

I blinked. *He wanted the witchstones*

"I think it would be more appropriate," he continued, "to distribute this new bounty of arcane artifacts. Trygg forbid that anything dire happen to our leader, but it seems foolish to conserve such power in one pair of hands in such a dire situation. He was trying (without using spellcraft, just the practiced voice he used on clients in his shop) to sound both apologetic for questioning my command and righteously indignant about not getting the stones. He made my decision a matter of castle security. "I feel it is in the domain's best interests that Master Minalan should consider how best to distribute these powerful assets among our Corps, and not keep them tucked away for protracted 'study'." He looked at me with raised eyebrows, as innocent as a child. I think the bastard had limed his beard again, too.

While he was droning on I thought about the matter for a moment . . . and was forced to concede that Garkesku had a point.

I had eight stones in my possession, after the battle, and now that they had been in contact with my sphere they were safe from gurvani influence.

I was still getting accustomed to the power available from one stone. It was a heady feeling to use such forces, and it was getting easier, but I was far from plumbing the limits of its power. But I did know that trying to use all of them at once would likely burn out my brain. Nor was there any good reason to keep the others from using their vast potential in our defense, after being carefully instructed in their use. I could fall off a battlement any time, after all, and in my absence the rest of the magical corps – and likely the entire castle – would be screwed if no one else knew how to use them.

I shrugged and did something Garky clearly hadn't expected. I agreed with him.

"I don't see why not. Have the, uh, magical corps convene on the roof of the tower two hours before dusk, and I will distribute a witchstone to each of you."

He bowed to me graciously, and the meeting continued without further acrimony . . . even though I was upset about the demand.. I sat back down and endured another dozen reports on how successful the fire prevention effort has been, the anti-vermin program, and the distribution of rations while I brooded over Garky's sense of entitlement.

It didn't get interesting until it was time for acting Petty Captain Goodman Loas to report.

Loas was a big man, barrel-chested and broad shouldered, a well-respected farmer in the Hymas district. He was kind of an aberration in Boval Vale in that he raised mostly sheep, as opposed to cows . . . but no one argued with his knowledge of husbandry for either beast. He was regularly consulted for his expertise by everyone in the Vale.

374

He had a prosperous holding, a large family, and brothers and brothers-in-law who would follow him in peace or war. In a more prosperous, more civilized domain he would have been named a yeoman.

His military career was less practiced. He had been elected captain of a few dozen men who made up the militia companies from Winakur, and had led his men bravely in their limited capacity. I had heard that he had kept a band of gurvani from hitting the cavalry's flanks on the battlefield, so even the gentlemen knights listened when he spoke.

"Sire Koucey, gentlemen, my fellow goodmen. My company performed as well as can be expected. We attacked the foe as ordered and lost only one man, old Barner, who had his neck broken by one of those foul beasties. My son Werin lost a little finger that he'll miss. There were no more serious casualties, thanks to Trygg's grace.

"But that's neither here nor there. What I want to ask you, Sire Koucey, is . . . *just what are we doing?*"

The old knight was startled, and cleared his throat before he spoke. "Can you be clearer, Goodman? We are defending ourselves against a vicious invader. I would think that that would be obvious. Or perhaps I have misunderstood your question?"

Loas leaned on the spear he carried like it was his more-accustomed shepherd's staff and spoke like he was talking about the weather with a neighbor at market, instead of an *official* military officer contending with his liege during a time of emergency.

In a more civilized domain he might have been dragged away and hanged for his insolence and temerity to his sworn lord in a time of war. Things are a bit looser in Boval Vale, however. Arbitrary punishments were frowned upon, and the lack of serfs or bondsmen permits plain language that is frowned upon in larger domains. As he glanced around the hall the crowd looked back at him like he and Koucey were debating in a pub, not as if a commoner had been insolent to his lord.

"Sire, I know what we're doing, I'm no simpleton. A month ago, I was worried about how many sheep the wolves would get this winter. Now I'm a soldier in a castle surrounded by enemies, with no help in sight. My poor friend Rollo has lost his entire family in a raid, my fields are in ruins, my home abandoned, and my sheep are destined for slaughter, not the clipping sheds."

"Yet you yet live," reminded Sir Cei, sternly, from Sire Koucey's side. "Thanks to your liege's foresight and preparation."

"Not that I'm ungrateful, Sire. I *do* yet live, and my family has lost a finger, is all. And we struck 'em a good one, we did. I killed seven, myself, me who never struck a blow in anger in my life.

"But for what? We struck them hard, but they are still there, and more arrive every day – we can see that from the walls, my lord. Are we to be rescued? Will the baron send troops? Will Duke Lenguin? Enough to stop that *whopping* big army of goblins out there? And what if he does? He can drive those monsters back up into the mountains, but what's to stop them from returning? I can't tend to my stock when I'm worried the likes of them are lurking about, just waiting to brain me with one of their clubs. I love my lands, but my life is worth more to me."

"Aye!" shouted one of the other farmers-turned-militia. "You sent word to Vorone *weeks* ago. What of it? And what of the Spellmonger? Can't he send for help with magic? When will it come?"

A raucous murmur built up around the far end of the hall, where the peasants congregated. I watched Sire Koucey struggle to answer the uncomfortable questions, and I could see he was not up to it. He glanced at Sir Cei several times, but the castellan had no answer.

The problem was that Loas, like Garkesku, had a very good and very valid point that made Sire Koucey as uncomfortable as I had been about the witchstones. He could count, as all shepherds can, and he knew roughly how many of the foe faced us. We were already badly outnumbered and the goblins kept arriving at our doorstep like leaves in autumn.

Even if every man in the Alshari Wilderlands took up arms and rode to Boval's defense, it would be hard to drive back a tide that great. The aftermath of such a battle would leave the valley a scorched wasteland, and the prospect of eternal guerilla raids on the farmsteads and crofts was all too real to Loas and the men he spoke for.

So why were we holding out here, instead of making a dash for the passes and living to fight another day?

I had been thinking the same thing, lately. Currently Boval Castle was a lifeboat against the storm, a place of refuge against the onslaught of the gurvani horde. We could wait here safely for some time, thanks to our preparations.

But what were we waiting *for*? Duke Lenguin would see the loss of Boval a minor concession to the gurvani that could be won back at a later date, after he properly prepared. But in a feudal society that might take years, decades, *lifetimes*. Particularly in the sparsely-people Wilderlands. The cavalry would not ride over the hill, swords flashing, any time that I could foresee. We could hold out for a good long time, but for what? The inevitable result would be the same. We'd just be starving when the end came, the longer we held out.

That great green glow I had glimpsed in the west was coming toward us, a concentration of irionite so large that the Tree Folk had warned of its potential to warp reality itself. A handful of knights, a castle full of peasants and a couple of spellmongers would not keep it at bay, much less defeat it – that much was clear. It was becoming increasingly obvious that it wouldn't be a question of *if* we would be overwhelmed, but *when*. With winter approaching as well, the battlefield victory we'd managed would be a hollow memory in a few short weeks as the gurvani increased their strength enough to overwhelm us entirely.

I watched Sire Koucey try to respond, his face twisted up in a mixture of anger and frustration. I knew an explosion of emotion would be bad for morale, so I intervened.

"My lord, I would like to answer Petty Captain Loas, if I may," I said, bowing toward Sire Koucey. The old man looked relieved and anxious at the same time, but nodded permission for me to continue. "You are correct, Petty Captain. But you have confused the subjects of tactics and strategy.

"Our primary goal has been to persist in this place, which affords us good protection, and defend ourselves against the foe. That is a *tactical* problem. Where we go from here is a *strategic* question, and one that has been on all of our minds – Sire Koucey's most of all. But the tactical situation must be settled before we even know what our strategic options are."

"What about you, Spellmonger? Have you no spells to send for help?"

I nodded, solemnly. "Aye, and I have. And help may be on the way –
or it may *not*. I have not been able to penetrate the magical cloak that
the gurvani shamans have placed around the castle to find out. I say to
you again: worry about keeping the goblins from our walls, and your lord
will worry about our ultimate course."

Loas took a long moment before he sighed and nodded his head in
agreement. Sire Koucey looked to me gratefully, and asked for the next
report.

It was a temporary fix to a serious problem, though, and we all knew it.
Every day we were here our odds at survival grew less, that was clear
to us all. It would be against human nature to surrender to the
inevitable, and rescue seemed a dim hope at best. Flight, at this stage,
was nigh impossible with the Mor Pass occupied, as well as most of the
vale beyond our walls. The more I thought about it, the more I was
coming to the realization that we'd made a mistake by deciding to stay
and fight against the goblins, instead of fleeing. That would have at
least preserved the lives of the people.

Damn it, Koucey, I thought to myself as we left the hall, *just what the
hell* are *we doing here?*

*   *   *

"Gentlemen," I began, later that evening on the top of the tower, as
darkness began to fall, "I want to remind you just what titanic forces you
are about to encounter. In one moment you will be as powerful as any
mage since the fall of the Imperial Magocracy. You will be exposed to
power you would otherwise never wield. I don't pretend to understand
it, how it works, or what eventual dangers lay in its use. But I will give
you this caution: *be careful with everything you do!* A misstep could

burn your brain to a cinder, or make you a hazard to everyone around you."

The faces of Garkesku's apprentices were pale and even their master looked shaken. Tyndal, standing at the end of the line, was trying to decide if he was more scared or more eager. Eager won out, as I knew it would. It's hard to describe to an outsider, but to a mage this kind of power is more addictive than breathing. The desire to wield the power was palpable. I'd noticed it in myself, and made a point to keep an eye on it.

I had the irionite nuggets in a basket, each wrapped in an insulating layer of cloth. They had spent two full days in contact with my sphere, more than long enough to neutralize any hold the shamans might have had over them, but I hadn't wanted to take chances.

I had struggled over which stone to give to which mage all afternoon, but I think I finally had decided. Each stone had a particular feel about it that is difficult to describe. I honestly didn't know if that feel made any difference or not, but my instinct told me to match the stone with the person.

I haven't spoken much of Garkesku's apprentices up to now. For the longest time I had lumped them all together in my mind as mere appendages of their sleazy master. They weren't, of course. They had very separate and individual characteristics that I had just started to get to know.

Eldest was Fenar, who was becoming a competent spellmonger in his own right. He was about nineteen, and he could have set up shop on his own had his master allowed it. Fenar didn't excel at any particular thing, unless you counted the snotty attitude his master had taught him – he was *really* good at that.

Fenar was a bit of a bully, I guess, but in every craft the senior apprentices have that kind of overbearing attitude toward their juniors. He was the son of a Hymas fisherman, and he had the same flat-headed view of the world that his father had. He could have made a decent warmage, with his temperament. I had selected a centimeter-wide, irregular shard for him that hummed with quiet but thickly available power. Fenar didn't need sophistication to complicate things for him.

Garkesku's middle apprentice was around fifteen, a studious young lad named Rondal. He had been the product of a union between a castle servant and any one of a number of knights, men-at-arms, or passing travelers. He bore no stigma of his bastardy – the people of Boval had pretty relaxed social standards about such things – and I know he held out the hope of the possibility of noble parentage in his mind.

Rondal was a bright kid, a little nearsighted, and he excelled in alchemy, for which I envied him. I'd never done very well at the subject myself. He was smart and Talented enough that I had toyed with the idea of sponsoring Rondal at the Academy to fully develop his abilities, but I hadn't wanted to piss in Garkesku's front yard. He was still growing into his full adult shape, but he had a lot of promise. I had selected a largish chunk that was flat on one side for Rondal. It seethed with power, but had more focus than the other pieces.

Lastly was Urik, a twelve-year-old, whiney little snot who was chubby, bordering on fat, and a little more excitable than the others. He had an intermittent Talent that seemed to favor telekinetic abilities. It might develop into something pretty impressive, someday, but at twelve, when your Talent is first manifesting itself, it often appears sporadically. Some days it's almost overwhelming and others it won't appear at all.

That can be pretty frustrating for a mageling, and between that and the constant abuse from the two older apprentices – and their pompous master – I couldn't really blame him for whining as much as he did. I had reserved the smallest piece for him. As I handed it to him I stumbled, briefly, realizing that I had just given a child a weapon more powerful than the Mad Mage had used against an army of magi. He accepted it eagerly.

I hoped I knew what I was doing.

For Garkesku I had selected the largest piece. It was almost as big as my sphere, and I had picked it for him not only because its size, but also because of its relatively low power. I don't know if there were impurities in the nugget, or if it had somehow lost a little of its magical efficacy, but I hoped that by limiting his access a bit I might reign in his ego. He had a solemn look on his face, but there was a gleam in those eyes that made me uncomfortable. I tried to quell the doubt I felt about giving it to him. Desperate measures for desperate times, I suppose.

Tyndal had earned a special reward, I had decided, and so I had given him what was, to my mind, the most potent of the remaining stones. A cautious and good-hearted boy, while he was headstrong and impulsive, I still trusted him not to abuse the power I was giving him. He took the green amber as eagerly as the others.

For a good ten minutes they stood around and just stared at the irionite, exploring the arcane details of their stones with their minds. As they became acclimatized to them with my encouragement and direction they started experimenting with drawing forth power.

We went through a number of basic drills to practice, and for an hour the tower top was filled with flames and lights and hovering stones and fanciful illusions. I'm sure it looked eerily spectacular from downstairs. Hopefully the arcane display would boost the castle's morale and lower that of the gurvani, whose large nocturnal patrols also witnessed the feats.

It was on the gurvani that we next turned our attentions before retiring for the evening. I had each mage prepare and fire a magical bolt at the foe, who were easy to spot in magesight. The patrols knew enough to keep out of bowshot, but the stones allowed magical attacks at a much greater range than even the great Wilderlands bows the archers employed. Once my magical corps saw how easy such a thing was, now that their natural talents were augmented, they spent several minutes gleefully showering magical death and mayhem on the patrols outside of the walls, until they sought cover. I doubt they killed more than a score of gurvani during the exercise, but I know it was both instructive and satisfying after the weeks of siege.

Even Urik had no trouble conjuring an impressively potent blast – indeed, he seemed better at it than the scholarly Rondal, which pleased the younger apprentice immensely. Eventually the harried patrols summoned a shaman, who put up decent enough defenses to make the impromptu assaults too difficult to be easy fun. Then the gurvani shamans sent a bolt back toward us. I easily blocked it, but it signaled an end to play-time.

"You all have been exposed to the power of irionite, now. Keep your stones in their protective wrappings at night, and do not let *anyone* else handle them. Have a bite to eat and get some rest – these things will wear at you if you're not careful. Tomorrow we will use them to further strengthen our defenses. That's all," I said, and watched as the excited magical corps filed down the steps. Tyndal lingered, a fire in his eyes.

"Master," he began, "I had no idea how . . . *powerful* the irionite makes you! I feel like I could kill every gurvani from here to the other side of the mountains, or fly through the air, or . . . *anything!*"

"Easy there, lad," I cautioned, patiently. "It will take you months, if not years, to learn how to use it properly. Hells, I don't even know very much about them yet. Let's take it as slow, and explore their potency as the situation warrants."

"Master, I have a question," he asked, thoughtfully. "With access to this kind of power, why *haven't* the gurvani leveled this castle by now? How could they *not?* If they have dozens of shamans using them, then what is preventing our fall – other than your defense, that is," he added smoothly. Every apprentice learns how to suck up to his master, I suppose. I shrugged.

"Actually, Tyndal, I've wondered about that myself, of late. You're right; they should have overwhelmed us long ago. They waste their warriors on their attacks when it would be easy enough to blast their way in here, and it isn't *my* efforts that have stopped them. Oh, our defensive spells are adequate for most of the more subtle forms of attack, but they would do little against a dozen shamans making an all-out attack on us with their stones. The truth is I have no idea. I sense that their siege is part of some larger plan."

"Something to do with the – whatever-it-is – that approaches us daily?" he whispered.

"Yes," I sighed, "I'm afraid so. Our time is running out, and while tonight was fun I honestly can't see any good way out of our situation. I'm beginning to regret that we stayed to fight."

"I'm not," Tyndal declared, holding up his stone to admire it. "I wouldn't have this beauty, if that was the case. But I do hope we survive long enough for me to figure out how to use it properly."

"If the exposure doesn't send you mad," I cautioned.

Tyndal couldn't think of anything to say to that, and neither could I. As powerful as they were, we both knew that power was also very dangerous. We went downstairs and went to bed. Tomorrow would be a long day. And we had yet to realize just how right we were.

*   *   *

Sometime long past midnight I sat bolt upright in shock. If you every try doing this in a hammock, you will discover that sitting bolt upright is not only difficult, but potentially disastrous. Having someone sharing your hammock while you do so is even less recommended. Alya looked at me angrily, having been rudely woken from a sound sleep and almost dumped on the floor.

"Bad dream? Or are you feeling randy again?" she asked, irritated, as she struggled to hang on to the sides of the hammock.

I ignored her. There was trouble afoot.

I could feel the vibrations throb through the tower like a low bass note – someone was using a lot of magical power around us. It *had* to be an attack. The shamans had finally found a way passed our defenses and gotten a strike force inside the castle itself, I reasoned. But the wards were still in place, I saw when I checked. That was even more confusing.

I called to Tyndal, who was awake for the same reason I was. That reverberation of power couldn't be ignored by someone with even the smallest Talent. He knew there was a problem, too, but he didn't panic, as he had the first night of the invasion. With a nod he flipped me my mageblade from where it had been hanging while drawing his own. I started for the stairs to the top of the tower.

"Minalan!" Alya complained, worriedly, "where are you *going?*"

"We're under attack!" I called back. "Stay there until I come back for you!" Her pretty eyes went wide and she shivered under the blanket.

Tyndal was already starting up the ladder to the fighting deck at the top of the tower when we both realized that the emanations were coming from *below*, not above. Reversing course immediately, we spilled down the stairs into Garkesku's chambers.

And into a scene out of one of the nine hells.

Garkesku was smashed flat against a wall, struggling to move. There didn't seem to be anything holding him up, until you used magesight. Rondal was floating ineffectually through the air, waving his arms in a manner that would have been hilarious under other circumstances. Fenar was writhing around on the floor, engulfed in bright blue flames, silently screaming, as my mageblade quivered in my fist.

There weren't any goblins here, that I could see. That just left . . .

Urik.

He was near the arrow slit of the tower, facing the others. The boy was lit with an insane glow that crackled the air around him, so potent were the forces he had unleashed. He had a maniacal expression on his face, a leer of insane satisfaction that I had last seen on the Mad Mage of Farise while he was hurling bolts of death at my squad.

Urik was taller – he had levitated himself about four feet off the ground, and had four witchstones whirling around his head above his brow, adding to the angry green glow on his face. I stopped dead in the doorway for a second and just stared at the scene.

"Ah! Master Minalan!" the boy said, with relish, his grin broadening in an unpleasant manner. "How nice of you to join us! I was just telling *Master* Garkesku and *Senior Apprentice* Fenar how *shitty* it was being a junior apprentice." He glanced at the burning figure of Fenar. "Let's see, I had just finished talking about how *educational* it was doing all of their fucking laundry. I guess I can talk about how *fulfilling* it was getting beat up and teased all of the time, just 'cause I am youngest. I guess the bloody shoe is on the other bloody foot, now, isn't it?"

He laughed giddily as Fenar writhed in agony. Still no screams came out of his mouth, but it wasn't for lack of trying. The flames burned at his flesh, making it smoke and blacken.

"Urik, *don't!*" I yelled, as Tyndal slipped into the room behind me, taking in the situation. He held his sword down at his side, doing his best to conceal it. He had a wand in the other hand. Smart boy.

But Urik wasn't watching him – he was focused on me and my blade. "*Fuck you*, master mage! You thought you were so godsdamned superior to us! All you had that we didn't was the witchstones, and I've got *four* of the things, now! Do you know how long I've waited for this chance? I waited until they were all asleep, before I took them. I always *knew* I was better than all of them, and they *hated* me for it! I was better than Fenar, I was better than Rondal, I was better than our vaunted master, and I was even better than *you*! And you *all* hated me for it!"

"No one *hates* you, Urik. We know how good you are, but you don't know everything you need to, yet," I said, soothingly. I was struggling to find a spell that might calm the situation, but nothing was springing to mind. The boy clearly did have Talent, perhaps more than I'd realized – I'd had a hard enough time wielding the power of two stones, and he had four of them, now.

"*No one* hates me?" he scoffed in disbelief at me, his eyes full of rage. "Then why did they make me do all of the shit-work around the lab? Why did they make me do dishes and sweep, night after night? Why did they call me names? Why did they yell at me, and beat me up? Why did our master call me stupid and useless when he couldn't wipe his own arse without our help? *Why does Fenar bugger me every other night, master mage? Huh?*"

"Urik, just put the stones away!" I urged, blanching at the revelation. "We can talk about all of this, but not until—"

"I don't *need* to talk, any more! I told Garky, and he didn't do anything about it! The 'Senior Apprentices' Prerogative' he calls it! Says it's part of the price we pay for our magic! Why does Fenar do that, huh?

Because he *loves* me? *Oh, Urik*," he said, in the mocking voice twelve-year-old boys everywhere know instinctively, rolling his eyes and fluttering his eyelashes. "I love you *so* much that I want to shove my—"

Tyndal chose this moment of distraction to fire a volley of magical bolts at the kid with his wand. The attack took Urik by surprise, but he easily blocked it with the sheer power of the stones.

I rolled across the room and sent another bolt at him from Slasher's arcane arsenal, summoned on the spur of the moment, and knocked him back a-ways.

Urik recovered quickly, though, and it took every ounce of my power to keep from falling to the bolt he returned at me. The expression of magical power is a function of the mage's emotion; put enough behind it, and it increases, particularly for warspells. Such rage, such emotion filtered through the power of four stones was daunting. It was like trying to stand up straight in a windstorm. I'm lucky he didn't blow a hole in my head.

Thankfully, Tyndal didn't let up on his attack, searing the air with his just-learned magical strikes. The part of my mind that wasn't preoccupied with staying alive took a moment to appreciate the ease with which he summoned the spells and their apparent elegance, and I felt proud of my apprentice. He fought bravely and cleverly. Every bolt was different, in an attempt to foil the boy's defense, and a few did actually get through. I threw a couple of low-strength attacks at him myself while I thought furiously, mostly stunning and blinding spells I had hung on Slasher against future need.

There was no way that Tyndal and I, even combined, could match the raw power of Urik's irionite halo. Like the gurvani shamans we had faced, I realized in a split second, we would have to finesse an attack. Overpowering the overpowered apprentice was just not a possibility. Hell, it should have been easier than taking out a shaman, as Urik wasn't nearly as well-trained – Garkesku was pretty stingy with passing on spellwork.

The problem was the reckless way that the boy was drawing power from the stones, flinging it around without a thought to the consequences, and the random manner in which he fought. It was a wild assault on anything and everything, raw power driven by madness and anger, with little control. How do you fight a bolt of lightning?

Twice I tried a frontal assault and I'm lucky that I wasn't killed in the attempts. The first time he flung me back against the wall (just missing an arrow slit) where I slid to the wooden floor in a daze. I had to dodge a wildly writhing Fenar as I recovered while Urik dealt with Tyndal's latest attack.

The second time put me flat on my back, staring up at Rondal floating lazily by. The frightened apprentice tried to say something to me, but the roar of the fight between Tyndal and Urik made his words meaningless. I had to stop this now, I realized, or the boy would tear apart the tower itself. I prepared myself for a third direct attack when I saw what Rondal had been excited about.

The shields around Urik were solid, almost impenetrable. With the power he had at his disposal and the will borne of adolescent rebellion he had enveloped his body with a swirling globe of radiance, the thickest defenses I'd ever seen. I couldn't have blasted him with anything significant.

But Rondal had noticed that Urik hadn't thought to extend the protection to the actual *stones* that powered it. All four were orbiting above his head, *outside* of his robust defenses. Perhaps he thought that they would protect themselves. More likely, he had probably overlooked the weakness entirely, the sort of oversight any apprentice can make.

That gave me a modicum of an idea. As potent as they were, the witchstones were still only pieces of amber, no harder or more resilient than any other rock. Indeed, much less so than most rocks. With them hovering outside of the defenses they powered, they were vulnerable. *They* could be attacked, even if Urik could not.

Gathering myself up for the attempt, I nodded to my apprentice and indicated that he should keep the boy busy. Tyndal redoubled his flurry of assaults, sailing bolt after magical bolt at the glowing spherical shield around the boy while dodging the raw power Urik volleyed back at him. He wasn't entirely successful, but he kept moving.

I took a deep breath and cast some warmagic, the spell that increased my speed and my agility measurably, and could, perhaps, let me get away with the damnfool stunt I was planning.

I waved my sword menacingly as a distraction and sprung at Urik, who was laughing madly at Tyndal's wild dance. The boy gave me a glance, a sneer, tossed a stray bolt in my direction, and returned his attention to my apprentice – I guess it was just more fun to beat up on an older kid than an adult.

My enhanced reflexes allowed me to anticipate and deftly dodge the attack, while simultaneously dropping my blade to the floor – if I had tried to do this un-enhanced, I probably would have disemboweled myself. I sped toward the defensive globe of the twelve-year-old tyrant, my hands free.

That last part is important, because instead of crashing into the boy (which would have been unlikely, if not impossible, considering the potency of his defenses) I crouched at the last second and vaulted over his head, the augmentations of the warmagic allowing me to clear the top of the defensive globe by mere inches.

I swung my legs up over my head, gave myself a little telekinetic push to ensure I'd make it, and in less than a second I had two of the witchstones in my palms. They burnt my hands with the power that was flowing through them, but they came away from the boy's control as easy as pulling a nail out of wood.

When I had landed behind him, I had shifted the balance of power in our favor. Urik's shield weakened considerably, and Tyndal's bolts were starting to have an effect. I had three stones in my possession, now, and I knew I had to end this thing quickly – the duel was having a profound impact on the integrity of the tower around us.

I didn't really think about it. I raised both stones, accessed the one around my neck, and with the combined might of all three I unloosed a massive shock bolt directly at one of Urik's remaining stones.

It shattered, or more accurately *pulverized*, into dust-like shards and smoke. In doing so it released a thunderclap of pure magical power that overtook everyone in the room. Tyndal fell to the floor at the psychic shock, while I was knocked backward by the pure force of the response. Garkesku fell from his uncomfortable perch on the wall, and poor Rondal plummeted a good fifteen feet to the hard floor. He took it in the shoulder, which was painful but spared him any more serious trauma.

Fenar was perhaps the least affected, as he was already on the floor and already unconscious, his skin a mass of nasty red welts from the magical blue fire. I saw he was having a hard time breathing, and his limbs spasmed uncontrollably as the blue flame died around him, snuffed out by the wave of power. We were, for the moment, safe.

Me? I lost consciousness. It seemed like the right thing to do.

Ten minutes later I came to, cradled in Alya's lap and surrounded by Sire Koucey's confused men. Tyndal was still out cold, but Garkesku and Rondal were awake, if shaken. Fenar looked like someone had run him over with a wagon and a team of four wild horses – and then backed up.

Alya held a cup to my lips and I tasted wine, coughed, and tasted it again. There was a little blood from my lip mixed in with it.

"Take it slow, Love," Alya cooed, worriedly. "Just go slowly . . ."

Tyndal awoke soon after Sir Cei helped me to my unsteady feet. My hands stung from the raw power of the stones that had passed through them.

We all finally gathered around little Urik's body. It was a mess.

His head was charred into an unrecognizable mass by the arcane blast, leaving only his blankly staring eyes to show that it once had been a face. All trace of boyishness was gone – he was a corpse, a dead man whose features had been aged by magic and flame. The air was filled with the aroma of ozone and cooked flesh – and something else. I didn't think about it at the time, but the smell would eventually come back to haunt me, later in life. In those nightmares you don't want to mention, lest they come true.

Sire Koucey wanted answers, of course, and between Garkesku and myself we tried to inform him about what exactly went wrong.

He tried to be understanding, but it was obvious that the duel had deflated his hopes that a creative magical corps could overcome the vast army that besieged us. With Urik dead and Fenar in the infirmary, unlikely to survive the night, our resources had been cut by almost a third. He started to demand someone take responsibility for the disturbance, but I politely stopped him.

Recriminations could wait. I didn't have the capacity to argue, right then, and told him so. He instead had Urik's body removed by a couple of drudges, and sent the monkish physician to examine the two surviving magi. They would have other quarters to finish up the night, he promised, well away from the traumatic scene.

I dragged Tyndal upstairs with Alya's help, drank a draught of spirits, and went back to bed, where horrible nightmares tortured my helpless soul. Urik's dead eyes stared at me, pleading, all night long. I awoke several times, screaming, feeling guilty about sleeping after such a disaster.

But, hells, what else was I *supposed* to do?

Chapter Ten

The Prisoner Speaks

"The native casadalain of the Wilderlands are a peaceful tribal people who rarely cause strife within the Wilderlands, despite their reputation. They are as slow as most peasants and even more unsophisticated, lacking the ability to organize or even speak our language except in the rarest of circumstances. As they rarely venture forth from their dens during daytime, there is little to fear from these comical nocturnes. The much-discussed 'goblin wars', commonly seen as important to the establishment of Narasi rule over the Alshari Wilderlands, were clearly more based on persuading the casadalain to peacefully leave lands that the gods had clearly granted to the Wilderlords for hunting and farming."

— *Roadbrother Ostus,*

Wandering The Wilderlands Of Alshar

The incident in Garkesku's chambers was later known as "Urik's Rebellion" and grew with the telling, as such things do. While most of the particulars of the story – as it is popularly known – are wrong, the one accurate part of the magical folk tale is that it marked the point where I started taking personal responsibility for the disposition of the witchstones. I didn't even realize it myself, at the time. All I felt was a deep sense of loss, despair and personal failure over the tragic death of a poor little boy.

Needless to say, I didn't sleep very well for a while, though I was mentally and emotionally exhausted from the unexpected duel. Alya did her maternal best to comfort me, but the dreams were just too vivid. And that was a problem.

When a mage's mind becomes that disturbed, bad things can happen. My proximity to the irionite stones – and, I realized later, even the dust motes of the stone that I had blasted – interacted with my subconscious mind in strange and unexpected ways. Alya woke me twice when objects began flinging themselves around the room, and once when the temperature dropped to below freezing. I considered taking a powerful relaxant from my herbal inventory, but settled for another mug of strong wine.

I insisted on examining Urik's body the next morning, over Alya's protests. She felt I had been through enough, and while I didn't really want to argue with her, I felt obligated to the poor lad. Sire Koucey, Sir Cei and Garkesku came with me. It didn't take long to establish cause of death – Urik had died due to a massive arcane power surge to his brain. Kind of like being struck by lightning, only from the inside.

Such a thing isn't necessarily fatal, but his only chance of survival from such a surge would have been to channel it, much as I had to my "fire demon" during that first raid in Minden's Hall. But he had neither the skill nor the sophistication to realize that, or the time to do it properly.

As I magically probed what was left of his skull, it became clear to me that I couldn't have saved him even I had managed to get the rest of his stones away from him. On the contrary, it was likely the theft of the first two stones started the cascade that killed him, not the destruction of the third. By the time I blew it into dust, his brain was already burning out from the inside.

It was sad. I didn't have the time, energy or inclination to school Garkesku on how he ran his teaching program, but I think he found a valuable lesson in the experience anyway. He was down to one apprentice now, as Fenar was completely incapacitated; while he yet lived, there was an even chance that he would not live to see sunset. Whatever primal forces Urik used against his abuser had irreparably damaged his brain as well as his body. While we took a look at him, too, and did our best to make him comfortable and heal his more superficial wounds, his mind was gone. The senior apprentice was dead in all but name. While I can't say whether or not he deserved it, I knew we could ill-afford to lose him.

Tyndal and Rondal appeared to both be recovering, as was Garkesku. Urik had spared them for later, I guessed, after he had tormented his tormenter.

I pondered the grim situation after looking in on the boys. There *had* to be a way to control the stones . . . or their users. Otherwise they were just too deadly in any hands, mine included. Irionite had turned Orril Pratt into a maniacal killing machine, and transformed a bratty little boy into a potent weapon of vengeance. The witchstones were too powerful, even in hands theoretically trained to use them.

I started to see why the Magocracy was so paranoid about them, and why they had been banned altogether by the Censorate. Yet I had not gone mad, yet. I thought.

A better way *had* to be found. How did the Tree Folk deal with the issue, I wondered? I got the feeling that the Aronin had absolute authority in such things among his people, but then again the abuse of magic was not a serious issue in that wise and ancient culture.

I was pretty sure that I knew how the gurvani dealt with it: that looming Presence that was even now skulking its way towards us controlled the shamans with an iron grip. If one went mad, the consequences would likely be swift and dire for the transgressor.

I discussed the problem some with Tyndal, who was good at bouncing things off, and even a little with Alya, once I got back to my quarters and assured them that I was all right.

It was a surprisingly fruitful discussion between the apprentice, the farm-girl, and the spellmonger. We discussed the ethics and responsibility of the magi in general, and the important ramifications of the stones, and the place of magic in society, and a whole host of things that three commoners were not supposed to know much about. As it was mostly common-sense we were discussing, it really wasn't that hard. But I'm sure we would have scandalized the nobility, had there been any about to overhear us.

What came about I will discuss in more detail later, but at the time our discussions were interrupted by Sire Koucey, who was still in shock at seeing the full force of the stones unleashed in his castle. He seemed far, far more respectful of me than before, as if I could turn him into a toad or something.

"Master Minalan, I know you have grave matters to consider, and I would not keep you from them," he said, after entering my quarters with a page. "However, for the last several days the keeper of my dungeon has asked about the disposition of the prisoner you took. Shall we execute him now, or did you want to interrogate him first?"

It took me a few moments to realize just who he was talking about. Events had been too intense and severe for me to remember quickly. Then it all came back: the aftermath of the Battle of Lights, the fight with the Crinroc, the surrender. It seemed like years ago, not a few days. I blinked.

"Well, yes, I *would* like a word with him. He's the only non-shaman *gurvan* I've met who speaks our language with any fluency."

I didn't add that he might even be able to offer insight about the *thing* that was leading our enemies here so efficiently. He wasn't a shaman, he was a warrior, but he had to have at least a little intelligence information about his army we could use.

The hideous events of the previous night had almost made me forget what dire straits we were in. Our days here were numbered, one way or another, and I had to face that fact before I could get around to restructuring the entire magical hierarchy and regulations of the Five Duchies, dealing with the invasion, and other minor issues. But those facts also demonstrated how precious little time we might have left.

"In fact, I'll see him right now."

*　　　*　　　*

The dungeons of Sire Koucey were small and, thankfully, mostly unused. In Boval, after all, punishment for offenses was usually meted out by fines, or, if unaffordable, as work detail, not imprisonment,. And was a rare occurrence among the prosperous peasantry.

But following custom the knight had built a series of cells and a small "persuasion" room underneath the main donjon, just in case. Currently the cells were filled with food and supplies, but there were a few empty cells available. My gurvan occupied one of these.

Koucey insisted on sending a couple of arms men down with me "for my safety" – which was ludicrous. They had the gurvan chained to a wall in heavy iron manacles, and if I hadn't proven I could take care of myself by now, I don't know what would convince him. I made the guards wait outside the cell and entered with the jailer, a small and polite man named Leron. He started to bring in a torch, but I knew the light that would make the gurvan uncomfortable. I could use magesight easily enough, and he would be happier and more cooperative in the dark than under the light – and threat – of flame.

The gurvan raised his head when I came in, and to his credit he didn't flinch. He sniffed the air a few times then relaxed to his fate. I bid Leron to bring me a stool, which he did in short order, and then I began my interrogation.

"My name," I said, slowly, "is Minalan. I am a spellmonger for the castle. I am the reason your head does not now adorn the castle wall."

The shaggy head looked up at me. Sighing (at least I think it was a sigh) the gurvan straightened a bit.

"My name is Gurkarl. I am Second Claw of the Bloody Fist band. I thank you for not executing me. I take it you plan on starving me to death?"

I realized that it had been at least *four days* since his capture, and Leron, for all his politeness, had neglected to feed the prisoner or provide him much water. I summoned the jailer again and asked him to bring a goodly selection from the supplies we had captured. He slinked off to do so, clearly thinking that feeding one of our foes while we were under rationing was a fundamentally bad idea, while I continued my interrogation. Which ran more like a conversation.

"I am sorry. I had no intention of starving you. The jailer thought you would be executed in quick order, and did not think to feed you. I would have come sooner, but I was . . . preoccupied with other duties."

Gurkarl grunted. "It is good to know that you have not totally given up the famed human kindness in the middle of this war. Among my people, if you are going to kill someone, then we at least let him die with a full belly so that his spirit does not come back to haunt us."

I managed a grin, despite myself. "That's very wise of you. You earned at least that much by sparing my friend's life. Perhaps you can earn more. I seek information."

He nodded slowly. "I thought as much. Shall we begin here, or do we proceed directly to torture?"

"Let's start here," I said. "I'm not a torturer. And let's start with how you know my language so well."

"That is not of any military importance, so I'll answer freely. I am originally from a clan of miners in the southern part of the Shularkava range – you call them the Mindens. My father and uncles traded ore from our mine to a human village in a valley south of here, near the Land of Scars. I spent a lot of time in their village, and even worked as a blacksmith apprentice to the smith who bought our ore for a year. I learned the Narasi language from him and his family," he explained, reasonably.

"I see. So why did you take up arms against my people if you knew how harmless they are?"

He laughed bitterly. "*Harmless?* Perhaps in your eyes." We were interrupted by Leron, who delivered a basket of provisions taken from the gurvani camp. He had included an earthenware jug of that nasty bitter beer they like so much, as well as a slab of freshly cooked bacon, black bread, and a bunch of the dried roots. Gurkarl started for the basket as soon as he saw it, but was caught up by the chains. He sighed with resignation and sat back down.

"Release him," I commanded. Leron looked at me like I was crazy, but he slowly unlocked the manacles. "I will ensure he does not escape. And there are guards right outside." The little jailer skeptically finished unshackling Gurkarl and then left the cell in haste.

"My thanks, Spellmonger," the gurvan said, rubbing his wrists. "In return for your kindness and generosity, I shall tell you everything I know. No need for torture, although I'm sure you'll get around to it eventually. You won't find it very helpful, I'm afraid. I was a minor officer in a unit of shock-troops. I know nothing of grand strategy."

He dug into the food with the greed of one who has not eaten in days. I can't say that his table manners were impeccable – considering there was no table in sight – but they were no worse than the Crinroc. Perhaps better. While he sated the aching in his belly he started to speak his story in that gravelly voice of his, continuing to eat during pauses.

"I come from a clan of miners. My clan had operated our iron mine for almost a hundred years, Spellmonger. What we did before then I do not know. Our histories do not go back to a time when we did not mine that vein. I remember picking up stray chunks of ore even as a pup.

"My clan lived in the tunnels we had mined before, and after a hundred years we had a spacious and comfortable place to live. A clear spring gave us clean water, and the little hollows of soil nearby provided us with roots and vegetables.

"I was one of four pups born to my mother that year. My brother and sisters and I had a good life. Our clan's trade with the *humani* made us wealthy, by the standards of my people. Our shaman was a wise old gurvan who taught us the important lessons: how to read and write our language, how to dance our dances, and how to sing our songs. He told us the stories of our people. Of histories and prophesies. And of our gods.

"My clan was held in high esteem by the other clans, and my uncle, the chief, Karza, was seen as a figure of great importance. No disease or misfortune befell us. We warred with neighboring clans from time to time, mostly over territory, food, fuel, and mates, but the battles were not fierce, and rarely did anyone die in them. Our warrior society was skilled, but they never fought another gurvani clan with iron. We used wooden clubs, and spared the victims as our slaves.

"When I was ten years grown, which is the age of adulthood among my people, I accompanied my father and uncles on their thrice-yearly trips to the *humani* village of Yescot, in a valley to the east of our mine. My clan sold their ore to a *humani* smith there, a huge fellow named Bolo.

"Bolo had a big family, many pups, and a good wife. He traded us cloth and grain and such trinkets as my people enjoy in exchange for the ore. When I was old enough, my uncle asked Bolo to let me work with him for a few summers to learn his trade. He made me sleep in the barn, but other than that he treated me well, better than his *humani* apprentices.

"When I had learned all that I could from Bolo I returned to the mines, where I built a forge and made tools for the clan. It was an honorable life – smiths are highly regarded, under only shaman, in gurvani society – and I prospered. For six years that was my life. I took a mate. We had a litter, and I built a good home for us.

"But then things changed.

"Among my people, Spellmonger, there are three types of shaman. There are the *golonosti*, those who tend to the needs of the tribe, much the same way you probably do your *humani*. The *golonosti* are our teachers, our healers, our priests, our history keepers. Then there are the *ragonasti*, the wanderers. They are clanless, moving from settlement to settlement and trading news and songs and spells for food and lodging. There are *ragonasti* who have great status among my people, but most of them are simple singers and tricksters whose magic is in their tales. Every clan likes a new *ragonasti* to come.

"And then there are the *urgulnosti*, the Great Shamans. They are the gurvani who speak for all clans, whose magic is their wisdom. It is said that they speak to the gods and see spirits constantly. It is a great honor for a clan to produce an *urgulnosti*. It is rare that more than a dozen such live at one time, so uncommon is the talent necessary to triumph in the mysteries.

"One spring, almost a dozen summers ago, my clan was visited by one such *urgulnosti*. He was an old gurvan, with long, gray ears and a rheumy eye. He said his name was Horgu, and he preached about a new day.

"Our tales were full of the olden times, when we were the masters of all of Callidore, not simple mountain people. We sang of the times when legions of our folk fought the furless, the *humani*, for the right to live in our own lands. They were sad songs, wistful and vengeful, which made. But we knew them only as songs. When he sang them, they moved many of us.

"Horgu vowed that a leader would arise like those of old, like Gurvos the Great, Grogror the Warmaster and Shereul the Great Shaman, and lead us to victory over the *humani* devils."

"Devils?"

"Oh, I knew your folk were no more demonic than my own, but the wars between our people have made you legendary figures of oppression. They are just songs to entertain us around the dawn fires, designed to scare our cubs and make them brave.

"But Horgu insisted that they were not just songs. He said that the *urgulnosti* had worked a mighty magic, and that Shereul, who had been cruelly betrayed by the *humani* and slain in the last great war, would soon live again. He said that Shereul would bring back the golden ages of the past, when daylight could pass over our sleeping heads without fear of *humani* hunters taking them before dusk. He promised us wealth and prosperity for all gurvani, and high honor for all those who served in Shereul's army – Shereul the Great Ghost, he called him. He told us to watch for the symbol of the black skull in the future, for that would be the symbol of the new army – the Horde of the Great Ghost.

"I thought old Horgu a fool – our shaman are skilled healers and proficient magicians, but they did not have power over Death. They surely did not have the power to bring Shereul back from the dead after two hundred years. I thought him a fool, but I kept it to myself out of respect for his age and rank. It was a good story, and it gave my clan hope. He left the next night to spread his tales to other clans.

"Horgu was not the last shaman to visit our clan. Over the next two years number of shamans came, dressed like *ragonasti* but with the powers of the *urgulnosti*. They performed mighty feats of skill with their magic, far beyond what our *golonosti* were capable of. Warriors who bore the standard of the Black Skull accompanied them.

"You must understand that in gurvani civilization there are many warrior societies. When a young gurvan comes of age, he must pass a series of tests and trials, and he is bid upon by the various societies. I was a member of the Bloody Claw, but there were also members of the Notched Tooth, the Impaled Heart, and the Iron Fist societies represented in my clan.

"They hadn't been more than social gatherings for generations – when we did battle with other clans, we fought as a clan, not by Society. I had never heard of the Black Skulls, but I assumed that they were merely members of a society from a far-off clan. They came in ones or twos, at first, then in larger groups. They were all mighty warriors who always wore their armor – real iron *humani*-style armor – and they always slept with their weapons ready. Even I was impressed.

"Every time they came they encouraged our young warriors to enlist in the Great Army, away at Black Mountain, *Korgol Vural*, the largest of our ancient fortresses to survive the great wars. It is very remote, deep in the spine of Callidore. It is said that Korgol Vural was the last fortress Gurvos commanded to be built before he ascended among the gods, but I think it is older than even that great one. So it is a place of great meaning and myth among my people. The Black Skulls and the shamans were insistent. They encouraged all warriors to join the cause.

"A few did, each time they visited. I resisted. I had a family and a good profession, and some moderate wealth. Indeed, since the rise of the Black Skulls, the other clans were buying more iron than ever, and I worked at my forge from dusk until dawn for weeks. Demand was so high that we didn't even need to sell our surplus to the *humani* towns – probably a good thing, in light of the evil stories the Black Skulls told of your folk, and what they did with the iron.

"Every year more and more of our young folk left to join the Great Army. Even females enlisted, which was against custom. But the power and the majesty of the Skulls was difficult to ignore. Every year the stories grew more and more fantastic. To hear it, one of the ancient generals had come back to life – or maybe it was a god. Speculation was rampant. Those who scoffed against them were punished. I was wise. I kept my mouth shut and kept working my forge.

"Finally, about five years ago, a troop of the Black Skulls came by with the Mace of Garl, one of our holiest relics. It was said to have been the weapon of the Garl, the Old God, before He was cut up in battle and made into the other gods. The Skulls said that the Old God had been reborn in the Great Ghost, and it was time to take back the sacred valley which had been so evilly taken from us. We would use it to see the Great Ghost to the Cavern of Karumala, our lost, most sacred shrine.

"It was a token that could not be denied, and when they summoned all of our warriors under its shadow I had no choice but to leave with them. I bid my mate good-bye, put on my armor and weapons, and marched with the other members of my society towards Korgol Vural.

"The next few years I drilled endlessly in the massive caverns of the fortress, with thousands of warriors from every clan drilling with me."

"Tell me about this great cavern," I prompted.

Gurkarl grunted thoughtfully. "It is a massive underground fortress deep in the mountains, the greatest of our works of old. Nearly a hundred levels, it is said, a place where you could wander from chamber to room and die of old age before you could set eyes on all of them. The upper levels were our barracks, our training ground. The lower levels were the realm of the shamans. We were not allowed there.

"We practiced under the eyes of the great Warmasters and the *urgulnosti*. They ruled our bands like tyrants, always making them stronger. When we weren't drilling, the shamans preached to us, preached of the coming new age, when we would once again take our birthright. They showed us their stones, the stones of power, and did great magic with them to show us why we would be victorious this time.

"They taught us the *humani* art of war, the war of machines and swords and armor, not claws, clubs, and bravery. They spoke of the Arisen One, of Garl the Old God Reborn, Shereul the Great Ghost who would restore us to our destiny. I went to the sermons and tried to stay awake. I thought the Great Ghost a mere myth. Unbelievers and deniers were tortured to death for all of us to see. I kept my mouth shut about my doubts. But then I learned that there might be something to the legend.

"Our generals and our priests ruled over us, but they were not the true powers of Korgal Varul. There was someone else there that not even the officers were allowed to approach, someone who was always surrounded by a dozen Black Skull bodyguards. A large figure draped with black cloth, round at the top, like he was wearing a helmet of great size.

"Once a gurvan from another unit approached it unbidden and was cut down before he had advanced two paces. *That* is our leader, I think. It *might* have been Garl the Old God. Perhaps it was Shereul the Great Shaman. It might have been my Aunt Durga, too, under all that cloth.

"A year ago, after I had long become accustomed to life in Korgol Vural, the orders came: We were to march. Lots were drawn, and the Bloody Fist band was chosen to lead the Second Thrust against the valley. I was a good warrior, and had made Second Claw in the band.

"We marched for months through the darkness under the mountains. It was a strange and exciting trip. As part of the Second Thrust, we were supposed to provide support for the vanguard troops who were supposed to have wiped the *humani* out of the way by the time we arrived. We were to garrison this castle until the next Thrust came, then move on the mouth of the valley. If it pleases you to hear it, Spellmonger, we were supposed to hold every inch of this valley by the last full moon. Your resistance here has thrown off the shamans' timetable. They are quite irritated with you, so I heard."

"Glad to hear my efforts are being appreciated," I said, finally. The images I had picked up from his mind, through a little interrogation spell I had quietly cast, whirled around my head. The massive armies yet to come, the hundreds of thousands of warclubs prepared for human heads, the grim determination of the generals, the fanatical gleam in the eyes of the shamans, the glow from a hundred or more witchstones, all of it pummeled my mind.

But in the back of it all was the black-draped figure with the round head, the Old God Garl, as Gurkarl had called him: the Great Ghost. That was the focus of the magic. It was he – it? – that held the reigns to the rest. It was he who was making his way toward the valley.

"So what will you do with me, now that I have told you all I know?" the *gurvan* asked, licking the last of the foamy beer away from his lips with a sharply pointed tongue. "Torture? Execution?"

"Maybe later," I said absently. "Right now you are my only link to the gurvani. I can't throw you away so lightly. How far will the invasion go, do you think? Assuming, for the moment, that I cannot stop it somehow?"

Gurkarl laughed harshly. "You *cannot* stop it, Spellmonger. This is only one Thrust, and not the best armed. Several more will come to this valley. There are more troops to the north and to the south, already making their way deep into human lands. Eventually we will burst forth and take the battle to you, wherever you might live. You may slow us here, but that is a temporary matter. The Great Ghost, the Old God comes, and so powerful he is that he can wipe this pile of rocks from the land with a thought. The shamans and the Black Skulls will not be satisfied until every last *humani* is dead."

"But *why*? And why now? And why this place?"

That gave him pause for thought. "How much do you know of the last war between our races?"

I shrugged. "Some, not much. The usual. Your folk invaded our lands, and we drove you back into the mountains."

"We were not *invading* your lands, Spellmonger. We were defending ours from *humani* encroachment. My people had an agreement with your Empire about where our lands met with theirs. When your tribes conquered them, they ignored the agreement. For years we struggled against their new settlements, fighting tooth and claw to keep our lands intact. Your people didn't fight fairly, though. Not honorably. You betrayed us time and again.

"In the last war, you not only betrayed us and executed our leaders under a flag of truce, but you took for your own our holiest of places – after you said you would respect our gods! Bah! Have you no idea what this war is about?" he asked incredulously.

"What holy places? I've seen the huts the gurvani use as temples, and the stones in the fields, but—"

"The shamans' huts? No, not those. I am speaking of the lands given to us by our gods, places of great reverence. Like the Lake of Nara, where the Mother Goddess was inseminated by the Mountain God.

411

And the Grove of Gilor where the Old God was born. There are shrines to our gods throughout this valley.

"But holiest of all is the Cavern of Karumala, where Garl slew the Five Demons, and later married the goddess Bireka. A cavern filled with silver and gold -- Bireka's dowry -- and holy relics," he said, eyeing me intently in the darkness. "A cavern that now has a monstrous, blasphemous . . . *castle* built over it."

It took a moment for that to sink in.

The gurvani were assaulting this worthless province with unbridled ferocity – and this explained why. They wanted their lands back, of course, but there were better lands to be had within their grasp. Their attack made more sense if we were sitting on something else they wanted – some*place* else. Someplace *holy*.

It also explained how Sire Koucey's family, House Brandmount, the lords of a valley with more cows than people, could afford to build a fortress like Boval Castle, easily as stout a fortification as owned by any great baron of the Wilderlands.

They didn't get it by selling cheese. They got it by stealing the accumulated wealth of the gurvani, which just happened to be stored in the cavern located, say, under the most defensible place in the valley.

That explained why Sire Koucey had been so nervous about the prospect of invasion, why he was so adamant that the castle be defended, and why he had built the mighty castle here in the first place.

He knew it was coming.

"That *bastard!*" I swore. "Let me guess: the leaders of the *humani* back then promised that your holy sites in this valley would be honored if you laid down your weapons. Then, while they negotiated with your leaders, a troop of men raided the valley and took control of those sites, and your treasury."

"The gold matters not," Gurkarl countered, nodding. "The Cavern held *holy* relics, relics of our past greatness, when we were lords of the world and the *humani* had yet to fall from the sky. It was the place where our most sacred mysteries were conducted. Your warriors slew an entire generation of shamans, and then looted our sacred places like the blasphemous bandits they were. If only we had been stronger, smarter, if the Two Brothers had not fallen by your treachery and might, then we would have avenged ourselves, back then.

"But your people slew our warriors in their sleep and butchered our cubs in front of their mothers. Aye, I bear your race no ill myself, Spellmonger, but my people owe yours no less than the blood we've spilt in revenge for those wrongs. It is why I am prepared to die, now, Spellmonger: because I am the first gurvan in my lifetime to come so close to the Holy Cavern of Karumala!"

"I'll not argue against your cause for vengeance," I admitted, suddenly feeling dirty. House Brandmount, Sire Koucey, this out-of-place castle all made sense, now. I could easily see why the gurvani were angry enough to raise the dead and build an army to retake the place.

My indulgence lasted only moments, though, when it was interrupted by an explosion so loud I could feel it even in the depths of the dungeon. It reminded me of the wave of power that Urik had unleashed, but I felt no magic around me. I whirled, thoughts of the horrible previous night filling my head.

What have those idiots done now? I asked myself. "What was that?" I asked the guards.

"That," Gurkarl said sanguinely, "was probably the outer wall falling. We have been building tunnels for weeks, now, to drop that wall. We are a people of the mountains. Above all, we know how to dig. Perhaps you should go attend to it. Oh, and thanks for the meal. It *really* hit the spot," he said, with a sigh of satisfaction.

Chapter Eleven

The Mine And The Breach

"The Wilderlords understand that erecting even a rudimentary defense, such as a simple wall or tower, is more than adequate defense against the dangers they are likely to face. Their neighbors are unlikely to war with them, outside of personal feuds, due to the ample availability of land, and while there are, indeed, occasional raids by non-humans such as the casadalain or their cousins, the brown-furred Hoylbimi, the idea that they could overcome the stout fortifications of the meanest Wilderlord is laughable."

— *Roadbrother Ostus,*

Wandering The Wilderlands Of Alshar

I cursed myself for my own shortsightedness as I raced up the stairs, the guards just behind me. I could already hear the screams of the victims, the alarmed cries, and the tumult of war through the thick stone walls, and I couldn't help but feel guilty. People were hurt and dying all because I forgot that goblins live *underground.*

I had made an effort to erect a spellwork that was proof against sappers – there are all sorts of nasty things that you can do to someone when they're underground to break their concentration on their digging. But I hadn't emphasized those kind of spells, as I believed that the ground of the valley was too rocky – an eternal complaint of the farmers – to dig through easily.

But this was war, and the gurvani were familiar with these rocks – they were the rocks their ancestors prayed on. Tunneling might be a challenge but not impossible. Especially using magic.

When I reached the surface I realized that things were not *quite* as bad as I had feared – but not by much.

True, the outer bailey wall had been breached, but it had not fallen. In the northwest corner of the wall a hole had opened the size of two wagons, taking a generous chunk of the wall out in the process. Gurvani warriors were streaming through, plying their clubs and swords against the peasants gathered there.

It wasn't a slaughter – there were several dozen peasants, now part of the militia, who had grabbed their spears and knives and pitchforks and were staunchly defending the stalls and tents that had become their homes in the last few fortnights. The sentries at the top of the wall were dropping stones and arrows on the invaders with some effect. But the defense wasn't organized enough to be effective at anything but slowing the advance. With a glance I could see that it soon would be.

Already the warriors from the inner bailey were starting to stream out of the gate in full armor, swords, shields, and spears, fighting the dirt-covered goblins wherever they met them – and winning most engagements. Civilians and militia gratefully got behind the quickly-forming line and by the time I got to somewhere I could do some good there was a kind of rough shield wall protecting most of the residents of the outer bailey. The tide was by no means stemmed, but it had the staunched the flow of goblins into a stream, not a flood. That being said, they controlled a significant and growing portion of the courtyard, almost a quarter.

I had made a practice of wearing Slasher if I left my private quarters at all, and before I realized it the blade was in my right hand and my sphere was in my left, and I was looking for the best place to use them. The swords of the armsmen who had accompanied me were drawn as well, and with a wordless battle cry we ran toward the breach. There was no time for organizing an ordered defense against the unexpected attack. More soldiers from the walls and towers fell in behind me as we met the first of our attackers. By the time I got to the edges of the breach, a place where the gurvani were still moving forward, I had about two squadrons of defenders with me. Our strategy was simple: the foe had come in, and had to be driven out.

I activated the warmagic spells I had hung to be more effective in that endeavor. The power of the sphere allowed me to increase my speed with a thought, and in seconds I was in the thick of the fray, Slasher slashing and lightning growing thick from my fist. The next several minutes found me facing fanatical furry face after furry face. The attackers were determined and deadly, as I passed a dozen human corpses along the route. I strove to be more so. My hands seemed to move of their own volition, as they do when my warmagic takes effect.

For me, time slowed to a leisurely crawl, allowing my sword and my spells to strike with unerring accuracy. There were plenty of targets for both. I didn't even bother with a rational defense – I avoided their clubs and blades, true, but I never parried. It was easier to just *not be* where their blows were landing. There was no conscious thought in the fight – just duck, slash, leap, stab, dodge, blast, spin, kick, turn, smash, swerve, strike, and press forward, ever forward, toward the breach.

I slew a score of goblins in ones and twos before I had made my way half across the courtyard, a dozen more after I reached the first row of tents and stalls being demolished in the fight. Slasher was dripping with blood and fur, and when I had an instant where I wasn't killing someone, I sent a superheated blast of magical fire to burn the blade clean of the gore. Believe it or not, the weight of blood on your blade has an effect. It slowed me down. Removing it by magic, instead of just wiping it down, had the additional effect of blinding – and terrifying – a few of those goblins who faced us.

It was interesting to note that they had chosen midmorning to attack. I suppose that made some kind of strategic sense, catching us off-guard, but it did seem to waste their warriors in a rather appalling manner. Of course in a war of attrition they had us outnumbered handily. The gurvani I faced literally threw themselves savagely at every human they came across, armed and unarmed alike. Their fervor and dedication made more sense now that I knew that they were being led by a revived god and were on a genocidal holy war. I helped a few more die for their cause.

By the time that I had made it to the outer edge of the tent city, reinforcements had arrived in force from the inner bailey – notably the Crinroc infantry with their grim axes. They matched the gurvani in ferocity, attacking wildly and with a casual regard for property damage or bystanders. They grunted savagely as their axes bit flesh, their warcries in their strange tongue at odds with shouts of "Boval Vale!" and

"Koucey and Boval!". The Crinroc stuck together, though, guarding each other's backs and pushing toward the breach valiantly. Their sudden appearance allowed those few women and children who had not been taken by surprise in the first attack to slip past their lines, and for that I was grateful.

But that line kept getting pushed back.

I glanced behind me to see that the Black Flag, minus their horses, were forming a more organized defensive line in a rough circle around the incursion, and a glance at the walls told me that more archers, led by the regular castle garrison, were filling the walls and turrets of the castle to snipe at the invaders. This made it more expensive for the goblins to advance, but whoever was in charge didn't seem to mind paying the butcher's bill.

Tents obstructed my direct view of the breach but I could feel the metaphysical tug of magic being hurled around at the base of the wall, bumping against our wards. I ran to the top of a parked wagon to see where I could lead the men following me effectively; my vantage point showed me that our foe had established a firm bridgehead inside the walls, someplace that could be defended against counterattack. There were at least three shamans with witchstones, acting under the direction of a huge, nearly man-sized gurvan in black iron-studded leather armor, and surrounded by a platoon of viscous little devils with spears longer than they were tall.

Not all of them were fighting us. Others were moving dirt, stone, and bodies of the slain into a rough defense around the opening of the tunnel. But as I watched more and more poured through the breach, fresh and ready to fight. The overcast sky made it easier for them, I suppose, and the gurvan general seemed to know his business. He directed the new shock troops with an expert hand to where they would do us the most harm while the shamans cast warmagic spells, mostly in support and defense, on behalf of the raiders. I tossed a bolt toward the general to test his defenses. It was neatly deflected.

For ten hour-long minutes the action was furious as we humans fought desperately against the goblin shock troops. The screams of the dying, the wounded and the merely terrified made it difficult for our valiant defenders to stay organized, but the arrival of the Crinroc and the Black Flag managed to stabilize the situation, if not contain it. After ten minutes the fighting had settled down into a rough battle zone comprising about half of the outer bailey. Any civilians that hadn't been able to escape were dead or dying, and many of the tents that had been their temporary homes were broken or burning.

The advance had finally been halted. A semicircle of our men prevented any gurvani from pushing any further without paying a price, and our archers were using their shafts liberally from the walls and towers around them. Any goblins who made the attempt to push past the line the Crinroc were gleefully slicing up. While our pet barbarians were making little real progress toward the breach, around which an increasingly tough defensive line was being erected, they kept it from hemorrhaging further.

The knights from the inner bailey finally showed up, armed and armored, and took charge of the situation. Sire Koucey stalked up and down behind the lines, shouting orders and encouragement through the thick wall of smoke that was building up around the breach. Sir Cei was in a tower, directing the archers to focus their fire at specific targets. Sir Roncil was holding the strategically important section of wall between the breach and the main gate – if that fell, and the gates were flung open, the rest of the battle would have been over in a few hours.

Despite the courageous rally and spirited defense of the bailey, my heart was sinking. I felt like a sailor on a boat with a hole in the hull.

I took a few moments to breathe and let my senses fade back to normal while I assessed the whole situation. Things were finally stable enough for me to try to decide what to do – but what the hells was I *supposed* to do? How do you patch a hole when the water keeps rushing in?

I was saved from the thought by a runner from Sire Koucey, who had spotted me through the chaos and sought me out. All Counselors, he said, breathlessly, were to report to the stables, which the Lord of Boval had made into his command post. He particularly wanted to speak to me. No surprise.

I nodded and stumbled in that direction. Along the way I talked a scared little girl of maybe ten out of a cup from the jug she was carrying. I thought it was water or wine or beer, but it turned out to be this morning's milk, still warm from the udder. Finer milk I have never tasted. I did my best to comfort her, and actually pointed her towards the southeastern wall of the inner bailey where the survivors of the attack were being treated. I also laid a small calming spell on her, almost as an afterthought, as she couldn't find her parents. They had been living under a tarpaulin within a stone's throw of the breach.

I told her they were probably waiting for her in the opposite corner, and to not be afraid. They were probably dead, of course, but no need to disturb her with the thought.

I wished someone could tell *me* not to be afraid. My bowels had turned to water, and my breath kept catching in my throat.

Sire Koucey and his knights were huddled around a sketch of the situation laid out on a bale of hay with the help of a pile of rocks, horse shoes, tack, harnesses, and other equine paraphernalia. I nodded and leaned into the discussion about the defense. Sire Koucey looked up at me, finished his orders to an Ancient, and then spoke to me harshly, fire in his eyes.

"Spellmonger! It was *your* job to prevent something like this!" he said, his mustached lip curling in disdain. "What in the name of Huin's Axe *happened?*"

"The enemy mined the wall and breached it," I reported, lamely.

The old knight shook his head in disgust. "First last night's debacle, and now *this?* I thought I had a warmage who could prevent this kind of tragedy! I thought I had a worthy wizard protecting my domain! Is that peasant wench of yours draining your wits as well as your sap?" he asked disdainfully.

I let him live.

To say I was taken aback is an understatement. I was shocked. His tone was imperious and ungrateful and entirely unwarranted, under the circumstances, and it raised my ire. Had I not done the impossible by wrecking five massive siege towers? Had I not built a magical corps for his pissant little domain out of nothing? Where was the respect I'd come to expect from the knight?

Suddenly Koucey wasn't the noble figure I'd built him up to be in my mind. He was a bully in armor with a title and a sense of entitlement.

This little lordling and his miserable excuse for a homeland would have been *carrion* right now if it had not been for me. He had no right, nobility or not, to adopt such a manner with me – especially in light of Gurkarl's revelation about his ancestors' role in the conquest of the valley.

This son of a son of a treacherous bandit was deigning to be sharp with me, Minalan the Warmage, who held now more power in his hands than any living mage.

The crack about Alya was particularly unwarranted, and ignoble of him. I might not love every woman I've bedded, but my budding relationship with one of his subjects was a sensitive subject, one a gentleman should have known to avoid. I could have burned him down where he stood just for that.

I started to seethe, and my mood was evident by the crackle of green lightning that cascaded through my hair. I checked my ire – one effect, I'd found, of a mage maintaining close proximity with a stone for any extended period of time was his unconscious thoughts and emotions were occasionally expressed magically. Tyndal displayed it a little, too, and he's a lot less level-headed than I. While this is impressive while you're having sex or laughing at a jest, I could see already that there were going to be some drawbacks to using irionite regularly.

It is easy – all too easy – to let arcane power obey the whims of your subconscious thoughts and let your feelings become reality. Had I been raised as he was, that's just what would have happened in that heated moment. I suppose what the only thing that saved Sire Koucey from being roasted to a cinder was my own upbringing as a commoner.

All through the Five Duchies, the common folk treated the nobility with respect. They were richer, more cultured and presumably better than us in all ways, after all – and to do otherwise could find you dangling from a tree. That ingrained deference alone allowed me to overlook this son of scoundrels and thieves while he insulted my woman and, *damn it,* just didn't appreciate me after what I'd done for him. Another peasant myth shattered: that good and loyal service is rewarded handsomely by nobles who are actually noble.

The knowledge that a thousand other human beings beyond Sire Koucey were also in jeopardy intruded into my mind, and that gave me the strength to recognize the importance of not killing him in a fit of rage.

I've often wondered since if I made the wrong decision.

I chose my words very carefully, as the middle of a battle was not the best time to argue personal matters with one's liege.

My eyes narrowed as I stared at him and said, in a slow and deliberate voice, "My Lord, it matters little how they did it. The fact is, they did do it, and we must drive them out. I think they are contained, for the moment, but come nightfall I'd guess they will try to break out in strength. We *must* be prepared. I suggest we firm our defensive perimeter around them, move as many civilians as we can into the inner bailey, and prepare to receive their charge." Venom dripped softly from every syllable.

Sire Koucey held my eye for a moment, startled at my tone and realizing the impolitic way he had approached the subject. He grunted a sigh, then, as if I had stated the obvious – which I had – and turned back to his makeshift map.

"Agreed. Let's double the number of archers we have on the walls –
use the best of the peasant militia for that. I'll have Sir Roncil gather a
work corveé to begin building a field fortification around the outside of
our current lines, and include a small redoubt every twenty paces, if we
can. Sir Cei can shift the tower ballistae from here and here to *here* and
here, so that they can cover the courtyard. When enough of the
fortifications are done we can retreat our infantry behind them. I'll have
the Black Flag break out more pikes, as well, and ready torches and
watch fires."

"A . . . *suggestion*, Sire?" I ventured, acting as if it didn't really matter
whether or not he heard it. The men around him looked from me to
their lord and back again, seeing the stress between us for themselves
– not a good sign, in terms of morale, but I was past caring. Sire
Koucey turned back to me, sighed again, and nodded.

"As to the disposition of the troops: Let's put the garrison soldiers and
the Black Flag on the fortifications, and withdraw the Crinroc to behind
the front lines until they are needed. The mercenaries and your own
troops will be more disciplined in holding the line than the barbarians or
the militia, particularly if they are using pikes. If pressed, the militia can
reinforce the regulars; but if some gurvan really, *really* wants to get
through badly enough, *let* them . . . then close the line back up. The
Crinroc will handle them."

"And how about our magical corps?" he asked, a hint of a sneer in his
voice at the term.

"My men will do our best to neutralize the three shamans providing
magical support. Doubtless there will be more of them there by
nightfall, but we can do what we can. We can also provide defenses for

our own troops. Indeed, I shall convene my staff immediately in my quarters and prepare contingencies. Then, my Lord," I said, meaningfully, "I will report back to you as to our preparedness, and inquire about our strategic situation. As well as speak of less pressing matters," I added, my mouth tight.

Sire Koucey raised his bushy eyebrows, and with a toss of his gray head dismissed me without another word.

I didn't bother to bow when I left.

*   *   *

I was finally headed back to Talry to see my folks when I ran across Sire Koucey, from the Long March, in an inn in Innisby. I'd lost track of most of my old comrades from Farise, after the occupation, and it was a pleasure to encounter the old gentleman again. He was looking to buy copper and rye, sell cheese and garnets, and hire blacksmiths, masons, and carpenters to come to his enchanting little mountain land and improve his holdings. He had a big castle, he boasted, and needed the labor to finish it. He was also investigating the prospects for a second marriage, his first wife having died with a fever, and perhaps one for his younger brother.

We sat up late into the night (he was buying the wine) reminiscing, and after telling the usual number of war stories and acquaintances from the campaign or the regretful loss of comrades in battle, he told me, in glowing detail, about the Valley of Boval, where the women and the cows were renowned for their udders.

The majestic views, the beautiful vale pastures, Hymas lake steaming fog in the morning's light – he painted a beautiful picture. Sire Koucey told me about his plans to finish his great castle, take another wife, have children (he was still virile at his age, he assured me) and live happily ever after. He told me of the enclave of Tree Folk and the idyllic existence his subjects enjoyed.

He made it sound like a mountainous paradise, and sometime after midnight – and after way too many glasses of wine – I enthusiastically agreed to follow him back to his beautiful land and take a look around. Perhaps become a spellmonger, I mentioned. I was pretty sick of warmagic, at that point, and even more disgusted with my clientele. I longed for something simpler, more stable, and with better prospects of seeing my next nameday. While he already had one in his domain, Koucey assured me that there was a need for another, and plenty of business available for an opportunistic young man.

I was sick of warfare. I was tired of excitement. I wanted to find a quiet little place leagues away from the nearest battlefield and pull my crappy career in warmagic far behind me.

Even by morning's light the next day I stuck to my resolve. After three years of war I was entitled to a little rest, a little peace. And idyllic Boval Vale in the glorious Mindens was the perfect place to find it.

It seemed like such a good idea at the time.

*   *   *

I was studying the magical diorama – far more comprehensive than the hay bale map Koucey was using – when the rest of the magic corps joined me to plot how to seal the breach. Instead of just sitting in a corner and looking pretty, Alya stared out the arrow-slit to the courtyard below, calling out corrections to the map as the situation changed slightly. She was as shocked over the suddenness of the attack as anyone, particularly since she'd lived in the outer bailey and knew everyone there, and the job gave her something useful to focus on.

She had narrowly escaped the battle herself, having gone to visit her sister while I was in the dungeon with Gurkarl, and had just made it back to our quarters (yes, I guess they were "ours," by now, I realized with a start; the thought was no displeasing) when the gurvani breached the wall.

In a panic she had grabbed my bow and had lobbed a few arrows at them before realizing that she was no more an archer than she was a mage. By the time I had arrived she was curled up in a corner, crying as she watched the chaos unfold. Her cheeks were still stained with tears as she called out corrections to our map.

The others were almost as despondent, and it wasn't all due to the gurvani. Garkesku's face was ashen, and his hair had suddenly developed bright white streaks in it since Urik's Rebellion. The scrawny spellmonger paced around the tower chamber like a caged animal about to be sacrificed. His remaining apprentice, bookish Rondal, was sullen, silent, and could scarce drag his eyes from the floor as he sat like a sack in a chair by the diorama.

Tyndal, ever faithful, was the most enthusiastic of my men. He knew the gravity of the situation, and had even helped in the counter-attack (he had been practicing swordplay with the mercenaries again and had fought beside the Black Flag, though only with a wooden sword). With two of our number gone I'd have to improvise something within our power to do.

That I had little idea of what that was troubled me, but I tried not to let it show on my face. I looked around at all of them and prayed to whoever was listening that the luck that had kept us safe from the goblins and our own shortcomings would continue for a little while longer.

"Gentlemen," I began, clearing my throat from the smoke that was still thick in the air. "It has been a very rough few days, and I know we are all tired and afraid. I know I am. But there is no time for wallowing in self-pity. We have a situation that needs to be dealt with, by magic, and very little time. Come nightfall, we might well all be dead."

Nods and stares. Alya started crying again, and then choked it off. She still hadn't heard from her family after the attack.

"This is the situation as it stands: gurvani have breached here, under the northwest wall, and have built field fortifications to cover a few hundred paces around that breach to prepare it for an extended stay. There might be five hundred of the foes now within our walls, behind that line, and they will be reinforced steadily come dusk.

"Our goal is to stop the flow of gurvani before it gets that far and assist in mopping up the ones who have invaded us. Arrayed against us are at least three shamans, perhaps many more on the way. They are well-protected against direct attack, and our previous tricks are likewise warded against. I am open to suggestions, because I'm fresh out of ideas."

Garkesku snorted disdainfully, and then looked away. But he gathered around the model like everyone else.

"My specialties do not include repelling invaders," he said, flatly. "This is my first siege. I'm not fond of it," he added, lightly.

"If only we had a giant dog," Tyndal said, idly, as he studied the representation of the breach I'd added to the model. "It's like a gopher hole. Our dog used to dig them up all the time."

"More like an ant-hill," Rondal managed. "We've no way to know where their tunnel even originated."

"Ants are stupid, though, and these beastly goblins are not. There is no honey that will lure them," Garkesku added.

But there was.

I thought about the cavern that was hidden somewhere under Boval Castle and tried to think of a way to use it to our advantage. Perhaps if we had more time we could bargain possession of it for our lives . . . or attempt something daring.

But we didn't have that time, and approaching Sire Koucey with the matter would be difficult in the best of times. The old coot wasn't about to give up his beautiful castle, to anyone. Even if I had my way, using the cavern as a bargaining point called for a lot more finesse than I could manage after the hellish time of the last few days.

"How about a counter-tunnel?" Rondal asked hesitantly.

"What do you mean?"

"Dig a tunnel under theirs, and then come up from beneath them. An undermine."

I considered for a moment. It wasn't a bad plan, but too time-consuming and manpower-intensive, even with magical assistance Gurvani were natural diggers; even aided by magic there was no way that a counter-tunnel could be dug through the rocky ground in time to do any good. I said as much, but congratulated the boy on his thinking, which earned a sneer from his master.

Another three or four suggestions were bandied about, none of them practical for the situation at hand. We stared at the map and moved pieces representing our forces and the gurvani from place to place, but the plans kept getting too elaborate to put into action, or failed for the lack of resources.

We did have some useful insights while we worked, though. We took turns scrying the tunnel and the goblins within, updating our model as we did so. We discovered that it came in from under a nearby hill, where they could dig without much notice (we had noticed it earlier, actually, but to our inexperienced eyes it looked like a bunker against our missiles or a quarry for the field fortifications they were constructing). The entrance had been disguised from our scrying by magic and activity. Its true purpose was kept hidden from our scrying by a group of privacy-minded shamans, I guessed.

But what we did discover was important. And impressive. The tunnel was roughly two hundred and eighty yards long, six to ten feet wide, with pockets every forty feet or so where gear could be stored and goblins could rest. It was deepest just under our wall, plunging down almost a hundred feet below the surface before sloping back up at a steep angle.

The gurvani engineers had taken great pains, it seemed, to avoid hurting the castle's physical defenses overmuch. The shamans, likewise, had cast spells to keep us from collapsing the tunnel by magic. Especially under the moat, which would have conveniently flooded the tunnel. I wasn't sure why they were being so delicate with the mine. Perhaps they planned on making it their summer home next year.

The problem was that even if we succeeded in fighting them back into the tunnel, they could easily out-flank us by digging around us. Indeed the tunnel branched out in a few other, incomplete forks, prepared as a contingency or as miscalculation, I guessed. But many of them could be continued to penetrate the walls again. Stop one breach only to be confronted by another in your rear. No, this serpent needed to be cut in half, and quickly, before it grew more heads.

I just couldn't think of an easy way to do that without killing a lot more people than I wanted.

I was getting frustrated, as it was starting to get dark outside. People were going to start dying soon if we didn't hit upon anything workable. The heaps of rock and wood that were our next make-shift line of defense were manned and ready, but they wouldn't hold out long against a prolonged assault buoyed by attrition.

"If we bring the rocks of the wall down on them, they'll have to retreat," Tyndal offered, eagerly.

"And we'll have an even bigger hole for the next lot to worm through," Garkesku pointed out, disdainfully.

"Perhaps we could just persuade them to go away?" suggested Rondal, nervously.

"Not with those shamans fighting us," Tyndal pointed out. "Just scrying that breach was hard enough."

We needed a plan. I looked at the map and scowled. There just wasn't a particularly elegant way to go about this. I came to a conclusion.

"Okay, we need to quit trying to finesse this thing, and just hit it in the head."

"Won't that just force them to try another approach?" Garkesku asked, sourly.

"Let's just focus on the magic and forget about grand strategy for a while," I cautioned, evenly. "First, we need to protect our people behind the barricades. The shamans are working defensive and support magic at the moment, but they'll soon move on to offensive magic, unless I miss my guess. Without us there is nothing that will stop them, and our defenders will be down before they strike another blow. Tyndal, Garkesku, I'm putting you in charge of that. Divide the line in two, starting from the mid-point between these two towers, and start planning magical defenses."

"What kind of defenses?" Tyndal asked, doubtfully.

"So far the shamans have only thrown basic combat magic at us, but you should plan for fire and cold, and lightning, too. I am wagering that they will rely more on the raw power of the stones than subtler spells.

"Rondal, I want you to go on the offensive. Throw everything at them that you can against that redoubt, and vary it quickly, before they can adapt. Try not to hurt the wall, but if that's what it takes, then so be it. Cover any weaknesses in the center, between Tyndal and your master, but mostly stay on their furry black asses like an obsessed flea. And try not to get in the way of the infantry, will you? The longer they stay alive, the more effective a shield for your attack.

"If the tide seems to be turning your way, do not be fooled: do not, under any circumstances, follow the gurvani back into their tunnels. Even an enhanced warmage would have a hard time fighting clear." Rondal nodded, squinting thoughtfully at the map.

"And what about you, Master?" Tyndal asked, expectantly. I stared back at him and sighed. He expected some intricately plotted spell that I would pull out of my ass and save the day with, like I had with the unfastening spell. There was no reason why he shouldn't – so far, that's exactly what had happened. The fact that inspiration wasn't exactly lighting up my mind meant that perhaps today he would be disappointed.

I'd hate to disappoint a doting apprentice.

"Tunnels have two ends. I'm going to sneak over the wall tonight and see if I can't stop the flow of enemies from the other end," I said, confidently.

Dear gods, don't ask me how, I prayed as the other magi nodded in appreciation, *because I don't have the faintest idea.*

Thankfully, they didn't. Instead they all looked at me if I had the perfect plan in mind, parts of which were just too complicated to reveal. I wasn't about to discourage the notion, especially not before a battle in which their confidence would play a crucial role. If they fought like demons because they thought I was out there valiantly slaying goblins by the horde then I wasn't going to tell them otherwise.

"All right then. We have our basic assignments; let's talk tactics."

*   *   *

For my part of the mission I chose an escort of ten fast Black Flag troopers, the best that Captain Forondo could loan me. I had to admire the man; he was way out of his element, which was normally charging gallantly into battle on the field of combat. Instead he was plotting instead the intricacies of a siege, with which he had little experience.

Yet he had not once lost command of his wits or his morale. He was approaching the situation as a problem to be solved, not a certain fight to the last man, which I could appreciate. The ten men he loaned me were veterans unafraid of the dangers of goblins at night. At least that's what he told me. We would go on horse, to try to cover the relatively unguarded stretch of land between the wall and the

Before I left I checked in with my magic corps in their designated positions and made certain they knew what they were supposed to do. I gave Alya a kiss and a long embrace at the gatehouse before I departed, wondering if I'd ever see her again.

Finally I hung a dozen of my own spells, checked the warwands in my harness, loosed Slasher in its scabbard on my back and sped off on Traveler out the front gate like a real gentleman, the Black Flag troopers following behind me.

The sun was already setting and I could hear the disturbing sound of gurvani war drums from their great encampments ringing the castle. They played those drums every night, for some reason. It's a spooky sound when you first hear it, but over the course of the last weeks it had become a familiar part of the background noise, until everyone in the castle had grown used to it. We even started to criticize the various drummers' performances with the peculiar sort of gallows humor that the besieged quickly develop. Tonight was one of their better, more dramatic percussionists, I noted. Quite fitting for one likely riding off to his death.

I called the men into a gallop, maintaining a tight formation, and cast some simple wards around us that would discourage any gurvani from noticing us as out-of-the-ordinary. We galloped to a point about half way between the castle and the small hill that concealed their digging, encountering few pickets.

The field was fairly clear of gurvani patrols, which I thought odd but welcomed all the same. I had loaded up on additional and more complex concealment spells before we departed, but I was unsure of their effectiveness – and overuse of such spells can attract as much attention as carrying torches as we rode. Even with the remnants of spells and counterspells overhanging the land around the castle like smoke from fires, providing some residual interference against casual scrying, I didn't want to take any chances. Stray magics can have a subtle impact on even the most potent and well-directed of spells. Calling attention to ourselves by casting spells to not call attention to ourselves is one of those subtle points good warmagi learn early on.

Poor warmagi usually don't live long enough to develop that subtle sophistication.

I led the troops quickly and directly to our business, portraying an outward confidence that I now wore like a favorite hat. Truthfully, I had only the barest hint of an idea for a plan. I barely understood what I was going to do, much less knew how I was to do it. I was kind of hoping something would occur to me before I got to the spot I had picked.

It didn't. At least not immediately.

We slowed to a trot, dismounted, and then a walked the horses until I was over the spot I'd chosen. There was a weakness here that we'd theorized might be exploited. Perhaps not, but that's what I was here to figure out. I muttered in the Black Flag officer's ear as the first of the stars came out.

"Keep on guard, petty-captain, and keep your men quiet. See that I am undisturbed for a few moments, would you?" The man nodded, and then ordered the men into a casual defensive position around me while I prepared my spell.

Scrying from a distance we had noticed (actually, Rondal had noticed) something interesting about one particular bend in the tunnel. It veered left (as I faced the castle) for about thirty five feet, then back again for about twenty. There was no obvious reason for it – ideally, a mining shaft should travel in as straight a line as possible. A fifty-foot spur broke off to the right and then stopped. I had thought it a contingency tunnel, until Rondal pointed out that it was probably a simple jog around a rock too big to move. Apart from cows and lusty peasant girls, such rocks are one of the things Boval grows in abundance.

Upon further examination closer to the site (directly over it, actually) the small scrying glass I carried showed that the obstacle the gurvani had avoided was not merely a rock, but a seam of low-grade coal – not uncommon in this area, though rarely exploited. That gave me an idea.

While I know coal is mined in the south, in the Wilderlands, where wood is so plentiful for fuel, mining coal for the purpose of heating and cooking was rare. It's used by smithies and occasionally by doctors and barbers, but the Wilderlands has plenty of trees to get through before the common folk relied upon it for heat.

I paced it off as the spell showed me what I wanted to see in the glass. The seam carried on for about ninety feet, roughly parallel to the wall of the castle, then petered out to the northeast and southwest. The gurvani were smart sappers – going around the seam was easier and safer than going through it. But their excavations around it had exposed a considerable portion of the seam inside the tunnel as they sought its end.

And coal *burns* if you can heat it up enough, I reminded myself.

That was pretty much the gist of my plan. The tunnel itself was protected against casual scrying, but I was right over it and powered through that spell. It had a few other enchantments here and there that I guessed were safety-related, such as anti-cave-in spells, spells against water pooling, that sort of thing – mining magic isn't really a specialty of mine.

I could tell that one kept fresh air flowing from the tunnel head, allowing the sappers to work without having to open ventilation shafts which would have given their position away to our observers. The spells they were using were pretty powerful, too, from what I could understand of them. Too powerful to break them up lightly without them noticing almost immediately.

But I wasn't going to try to dispel it. Indeed, I hoped to use it – and that seam of coal – to make things *very uncomfortable* in that tunnel before long. It took me a few moments to piece together what needed to be done before I did it, but it was a basic alchemy/thaumaturgic magic. Something I could have done in my third year at the Academy, if they had taught such useful applications for spells. And I had access to almost limitless energy.

Concentrating very hard, I brought into being a spell component that did nothing but *dig . . . sort of.* It was a variation of the grinding spells warmagi use to keep their mageblades razor sharp, wherein tiny swirls of magical energy abrade the steel the same way a good whetstone does – only a lot more thoroughly and completely. It was also something the gurvan had not protected against. After all, who would want to make their ugly tunnel more polished?

Casting it was easy. Nothing interfered in the area under my feet. Expanding it to a massive area was harder, and harder still was linking it alchemically just to the coal. But with enough power and enough desperation you'd be surprised what unlikely things you can accomplish.

Like a rough rock across soft wood I sent the spell past their basic subterranean defenses and started it working on the exposed face of the vein. It was completely invisible to those who weren't gifted, soundless, and should not cause any particular notice even upon close inspection. I wasn't worried about more invasive scrutiny from magical professionals, either. From the locations of the sparks of their stones all the shaman were clustered at either end of the tunnel.

The busy little souls who toiled under our feet like so many ants were sappers and shock troops preparing for an invasion, and they had better things to do than to notice a little more dust in the air than normal. Hey, it was a tunnel. Tunnels are supposed to be dirty and dusty. That's what I was counting on.

I set up an independent guidance component to the spell so that it would continue without my direct supervision, and then turned my focus toward a second spell. This was something that I hadn't done since the

Academy, in a lab, in broad daylight, with a qualified master overseeing me. I was doing it now in the dark, surrounded by enemies, under immense pressure. My only advantage was the power I could throw at the spell.

It was basic Alchemy. If one takes certain rocks or natural mineral-based oils and applies various forces of nature to them, they behave in interesting ways according to their alchemical nature. Most people are almost entirely ignorant of these things, except when a craft has a need for them and learns to exploit the alchemy of nature. For example, among its other properties, coal has within its dark exterior certain gasses which, when released and properly mixed with air, are flammable. Even explosive.

Indeed, I was fairly certain that the gurvani air circulation spell was designed as much to keep such gasses from pooling up dangerously as it was to allow the sappers to breathe fresh air. Coal normally outgasses fairly slowly. I needed to improvise something to make it do so rapidly. Applying pressure to it arcanely and increasing the surface area affected should, theoretically, increase the rate of outgassing.

Call it inspiration or intuition or genius – or pure rutting luck – but I came up with a perfect spell. It was semi-autonomous, like a leak-seeking spell I used for thatched roofs, and hurried along the outgassing by very rapid vibration. It mimicked the actions of a bug, eating its way through the coal seam like a termite in moist wood and leaving behind tiny invisible wisps of volatile gasses in its wake. If I could wait long enough for the *right* amount of gasses to build up . . .

My spellwork had taken awhile, and the men in my escort were getting nervous. Goblin patrols had come within fifty feet of our party without discovering us, but they made the horses skittish. The sun was already behind the mountains and twilight was upon us. Before very long it would be dark enough for the gurvani assault to begin in earnest, and if the traffic below our feet was any indication, it would be an impressive one. But there are some things you just can't hurry. I checked on the progress of my spell, scryed the tunnel, and generally killed time.

I was almost getting bored when our horses neighed and two of the beasts went down with black-fletched arrows jutting out of them.

A gurvani patrol, complete with a witchstone-wielding shaman, had eluded my "please don't notice us saboteurs" spell and had successfully snuck up on us. If the horses hadn't caught their scent, (the goblins are generally unfamiliar with horses, and horses react poorly to the dank odor of goblins), we might have been completely surprised.

The attack gave me something with which to occupy my time while my spells were working. It certainly broke up the boredom. I almost smiled behind my snarl as I drew Slasher, wrapped my fist around my sphere, and guided Traveler into battle against the goblins with my knees. I could spot the entire patrol with magesight, without using a light of any sort, and it wasn't that large. I had worked up a fair bit of anger and frustration the last couple of days and I almost welcomed the simple clash of steel on steel as an opportunity to vent.

Besides, I carried a fair bit of guilt knowing that I had left my apprentice and the other odds-and-sods of Boval Valley's magical corps the fairly hopeless task of stopping a concentrated assault through the breach. By all rights I should have been the one facing down the coming attack. Perhaps I could expunge my soul by dying valiantly in battle, I reasoned. Then, at least, the responsibility would be someone else's.

Garky's for instance. That brought a genuine smile to my lips as I charged into battle.

The contest was fairly one-sided, at first. Our mounted troopers were in relatively open country and able to maneuver. The score of goblin light infantry we faced was outnumbered and out-powered, and their first few ranks fell before our lances and swords before they could be reinforced. I had a grand time letting fly with bolt and flame and blast in those heated moments. I was far more used to the flow of power from the sphere, now, and I felt more comfortable using it, particularly with the warmagic spells I'd been using so frequently.

But the Black Flag troopers were stumbling around, not always able to defend themselves in the dusky twilight against naturally darkened foes. Not everyone has the benefit of magesight in battle. Almost as an afterthought I hung a big flare spell over the skirmish so that the troopers could see their targets, a magelight designed to glow fiercely and then fade. It provided light for my bodyguard and temporarily blinded the patrol.

But I was not the only wizard on the battlefield. The opposing shaman held back at first, too, to see where he'd be of the most use. Apparently he was taking my measure, seeing just how adept I was using the irionite, observing what kind of mage was messing with his tunnel. I didn't even spot him among his fellows until I was about two ranks into their flank, chewing up their left side while my men did similarly to their right.

But then he revealed himself, throwing back a dark mantle he'd taken from some poor human victim, and revealing his power. Suddenly I had a bad feeling about the battle. Kind of like when your mother catches you playing in the mud in your festival clothes.

The other shamans I had faced had been provincial rubes, compared to this fellow. He was large – he stood almost five and a half feet tall, and was visibly well-muscled, even under all of that hair.

And what hair it was! Unlike his fellows, it wasn't as black as midnight. He had taken lye or some other strong chemical and bleached his pelt a ghastly shade of dirty white, much like Garky did with his beard – all except for a skull-like patch around his face, which he left black. When compared to the writhing mass of black fur that opposed us, he stood out like a beacon.

Perhaps that made him more of a target, but he never seemed concerned about the possibility that he might be slain because his coat was more reflective. Nor was he naked and unarmed, as many of the other shamans had been; he was wearing a boiled leather cuirass, dyed jet black and heavily tooled with snaky patterns of gurvani fashion that seemed to writhe in the flare-light. He held a black iron mace, all forged of one piece of metal, and around his neck was a smooth bead of irionite, glowing eerily as he worked his spells. He wore on his head not the animal skulls of his low-rent colleagues, but a well-wrought helm of black iron, fashioned in the stylized likeness of a darkened skull.

A shaman of the *Black Skulls*. The gurvani elite warrior society driving the invasion, of whom Gurkarl spoke. This would be *fun*.

I didn't say a word, nor uttered any war-cry, as I prepared myself for the coming fight – the time for soliloquy and psyching myself up was past. By my rough calculations I had another four or five minutes before the gas levels in the tunnel would demand for further action. I should have plenty of time to finish him off and still complete the spell . . . and if I didn't, that meant I was dead and this mission would not be my concern any more.

So I bore down on the shaman with everything I had. I sent a hail of magical bolts at him from the spells on Slasher . . . and he shrugged them off like annoying mayflies. In return he lashed me with a whip of blue lightning, which my own personal defenses were hard pressed to handle.

I countered with both a shower of black fire from Slasher and a bolt of searing heat, from my left hand, and we were *off!*

A straight-forward magical duel is a thing of beauty for the participants, a little less aesthetic (and potentially more dangerous) for any bystanders. Both human cavalry trooper and goblin light infantry hurried away from the space between us, and none on either side would dare interrupt, for fear of getting caught in the magical mayhem sure to ensue. While a few continued to engage each other, here and there, most contented themselves with watching the fight between magi. That left us plenty of room to try to take each other apart while our forces fought their separate battle.

This guy was *good*, too, compared to his fellows. He was calm and unemotional, and acted with a preternatural sense of what I was going to do next that unnerved me. He was intently focused, his black beady little eyes staring beyond me as he cast attack after determined attack.

I was hard pressed to defend them all, and only by relying on brute force and lavish amounts of energy from my stone was I able to counter at all. Unaugmented by irionite I would have fallen in the first minute. I was in full battle-mode, of course, my sense of time slowed to the utmost limit of my control, but there was no disguising how close to getting me he got, moment to moment. When I actually had a half a second to throw an attack, it was as if he had already figured out what I was doing and had a counterspell in the works.

Frustrated, I began concentrating on avoiding his attacks rather than beating them back. That gave me a little more time to plan my own attack on the Black Skull shaman.

Imagine a ten-year-old armed with rotten eggs, all throwing them at you at once. Then imagine that you have a pot lid no bigger than your head to protect yourself. Sure, you can stop most of the eggs with your shield, but sooner or later someone will get lucky and get to go home smelling like putrid sulfur. It was like that.

I found myself slipping into a deep warmagic trance like I hadn't really been in since the Farisian Campaign, not really recommended while on horseback. But it was necessary, if I was going to unseat the goblin mage. I tried to look beyond his attacks, beyond his patterns of defense, and discover exactly *why* this furry little witchdoctor was dueling like an accomplished adept. There was something off about him, I noticed, and between volleys I tried to realize what it was.

Then I realized the problem. *This shaman wasn't the only one riding around in his skull.* He was being possessed – I guessed – by the Old God, The Great Ghost, the Dead God, that super-shaman that started this whole invasion. I was up against a serious Power, and I knew from that moment on that I would lose this fight.

Oh, I tried even harder, but I realized that I could try as hard as I wanted and never get any closer to destroying the Black Skull shaman than I was when I first saw him. The Old God was feeding him direction and power in a way that none of my tricks could match, even with irionite.

About the only way I could possibly counter was with the help of another god, a human god. And there didn't seem to be one handy.

The Black Flag riders had been forced to retreat further back in the field as gurvani reinforcements started to arrive. I didn't blame the men. Had I the time and the strength I would have screamed at them to ride, ride as far and as fast as possible, fly, you fools, back to the illusory safety of Boval Castle. But they wouldn't abandon me, curse their stupid little warrior's hearts. A few of them died as a result.

As the duel got more desperate, I closed with the Black Skull until I could try to strike directly with Slasher. But he was as ready for a physical attack as a metaphysical one. The iron mace met my steel in a soul-rending crash of sound, and then we were dueling in earnest.

It's hard to cast spells while you're fencing, even with a mageblade (that's why we hang them before battle, not try casting them in the middle of one), but I was inspired by desperation and the potential for failure.

I kept up the power of the magical assault as much as I could while I tried to cut his heart out with my blade. He defended admirably, occasionally taking a hit, more often dishing one out . . . but nothing lamentably ensued. We danced to the ring of steel and iron for endless minutes. Our duel was a complicated series of strikes and spells met almost perfectly by a complementary series of parries and counterspells. Even with warmagic augmenting my strength and stamina, I soon tired. His mace landed, albeit glancing, on my shins, my ribs, my shoulder, but I kept it away from my face and head and spine.

I tried for every advantage, resorting to cheap cantrips to distract him when more potent spells were useless. I even tried to step on his toes. The result was inevitable.

Exhausted, wounded in a dozen places, my chest beating like a bellows, I on Traveler, looking down on the white goblin as he looked up at me, thoughtfully. Had I the moisture to do so, I would have spit at him.

But then that ghostly, horrific voice sounded out of the gurvan's mouth and that put aside my personal feelings. Traveler was already lathered – he was a rouncey, not a warhorse. The shaman wanted to take a moment to gloat. It was hard to not let him.

"So *you* are the mortal mage who impedes me," the shaman said in my own language. His voice was the low, gravely tone of his people, but it was augmented somehow. And in perfect Narasi. I felt it in my bones.

"Minalan the Spellmonger, at your service," I gasped, affecting the brogue of the Wilderland country folk. Poorly. I don't think he got the joke.

"Spell . . . monger?" the voice asked while the Black Skull's lips moved and someone else's words came out. Don't ask me how I knew, I just knew it wasn't his.

"Licensed by the Censorate for general practical magic," I boasted. "Master Minalan of Minden's Hall. Do you need magical help? Perhaps you're lost and need help finding your way? Have a missing chicken or other livestock? A wife with a straying eye? Warts? Unsightly blemishes? Need a charm against fire, flood, or mange? Something to get that wooly white pecker up, perhaps? I'm your man. Reasonable rates, negotiable terms. Payments in kind gladly accepted." I don't often run my mouth in the middle of battle, but I needed a chance to catch my breath . . . and if this clown was stupid enough to offer me one, I was going to take it.

But then the thing had the nerve to laugh at my joke . . . sort of. "You are no country mage, are you, Master Minalan? You have access to powers far beyond your colleagues. And the stink of the Alka Alon about you. A warmage, I would guess, or a Court Wizard on holiday."

"No, I really am a spellmonger. I can show you my credentials, if you'd like. Still, I was enough to bury Ri-ken and his fellows handily."

"A simpleton with no real potency, save what I granted him and his brothers. Nor does your own power make you his better. Your title makes no difference. *A hundred* human adepts would be no match for me," he boasted.

"You really don't look like much, from up here," I pointed out, finally catching my breath.

"No, not this shell, as you have guessed. I am still far from this sacred valley . . . but I am coming. Soon. If you survive this contest then you and I shall become very well acquainted, Master Minalan. I shall delight in taking you apart like a child's toy, and putting you back together in a way more to my liking."

"Well – wait, I don't think we have been properly introduced," I called back, weakly. I had bruises starting to blossom everywhere. "I didn't catch your name."

"My people call me the Great Ghost," he said, that iron-headed mace slung defiantly over his shoulder. "The Old God. Shereul the

Deathless, among other names. That shall be sufficient, for now."

"But you're not just old, you're also dead – or didn't you realize that? Yes, I know all about the cave," I said, desperately grasping at straws.

"The cavern is sacred," the shaman insisted.

"I know, I understand. I *know* that's what you're after, and it's not grazing rights for your goat herds. Sire Koucey's ancestors betrayed you and your people and you want your holy cave back. I can even understand that. I'd be pretty pissed off, too. Look, you can have it. You can have the whole damn valley. Just let my people go forth from here in peace!"

"In *peace?*" said the terrible voice with a mocking laugh, a sound so painful I would have torn off my ears if I could have moved my hands to do so. But the voice commanded your attention, if not your obedience. "I will leave you alive, Minalan, and as many of the others in that pitiful pile of rocks as can survive the assault."

"That's incredibly generous of you, but—"

"I will need you all as sacrifice to re-consecrate our holy sites," he finished. "But even that is not why I am here, Minalan. I am here for revenge. I do not care if your people stay or go. I will find them eventually. Every *humani* will be found, every last whimpering child of yours, and they shall all be sacrificed upon my altar! Their blood shall sanctify our gods, and their flesh shall feed my troops."

"You're making a terrible mistake," I gasped, trying to figure out a way I could kill him without moving too much. "We taste *awful!*"

He ignored my feeble jibes. "As for Koucey and his kin, I have special plans for them. They will repay us for their line's treachery, and the price will be more than they can bear."

"Take him. Just let the rest of us go!"

"Let you go? You do not amuse me. Do not arouse my ire. My ancestors may have been foolish enough to treat with your kind, but I will show none of their weaknesses. The sacred valley is only the beginning, mageling. All of the lands of Callidore will one day be my dominion.

"You have fought well, I grant you that. You have bested several of my chosen priests. I will make your death a quick and merciful one on the sacrificial stone. After you have witnessed all the other humani deaths, of course. Such is your reward for your temerity and your success."

"Isn't that selling the colt before the mare has been brought to stud?" I said, trying to regain even a shadow of strength. Slasher lay on the ground at my feet, and my sphere was dark in my palm, its power nearly spent from the lavish way I'd fought the duel. The power was still there, but it took a lot more time to access. Who was I kidding? I was running on sheer bluff, now.

"Hardly. Your folk lie at the beginning of ruin. You will soon capitulate."

"Really? Because you still haven't taken the castle, after months of trying, and we only have a pitiful few Wilderlords guarding it. You have raised mighty armies . . . and they have broken against it like waves on the shore And you know what has been stopping your incredible war machine? Me! Me, a village spellmonger, a few other bumpkins, a handful of cheap mercenaries, and sheer human determination. We *can* drive you back. We can hold out. *Help is coming.*"

"Help? *What* help? Your fellow *humani* have sealed the mouth of the valley against us, and cower in fear at our mention. They prepare for our onslaught, though it will do them little good. We have already outflanked their defenses."

"Any man is worth any three gurvani," I sneered. "And a human spellmonger can trounce any gurvani shaman." That was pure bullshit, but the longer I kept him talking, the longer I had to recover. Warmagic takes it out of you. So does getting beat with an iron club.

The Black Skull showed his teeth, and it wasn't a pleasant smile. "You have seen less than a tithe of my forces, Minalan the Spellmonger, and yet but little of my magic. The power stones you seek so greedily on the battlefield? The ones you pull from the corpses of the least of my followers? Stones like these I have by the hundred! Mere shavings and gravel, doled out to my lesser minions. You crave their insignificant power and think yourself mighty, but you are a fool chasing a fool's power. Even the charm borne by this loyal gurvan is meek, compared to what I have at my disposal. And that is only the beginning. You shall see, Minalan; when I arrive, should you yet breathe, at last you shall—"

I never found out what he had planned for me. His gloating speech was cut off by the crackle of arcane lightning that surprised us both. A powerful magical bolt came out of nowhere and neatly severed the Black Skull's spine about half-way down his back, leaving a smoking black hole in his dirty white chest. It killed him instantly, I'm certain, but his jaw kept speaking long after his lungs could no longer fill his mouth with air.

A side-effect of this welcome development was the ending of the spell that had held me so securely in my saddle, as I lost consciousness for a split-second. I plummeted onto the rocky ground, spraining a wrist as I landed and adding abundantly to my growing collection of bruises. I considered not getting up again. After being faced with another round with that powerful shaman and near-certain death, however, I welcomed the stimulation.

It also gave me the opportunity that I was looking for to launch my attack on the tunnel. I wasted no time. I summoned every last bit of power I could muster from my depleted stone and blasted a bolt of white-hot heat straight down through the earth into the heart of the coal vein. The gasses I had been releasing into the tunnel started to burn instantly, which ignited the large volume of coal dust I had created. Like a flour mill bursting with dust, the air in the tunnel was thick with gas and raw flammable surface area. The resulting explosion stole my hearing away for a few moments and sent me sprawling to the shaking earth.

I dug my face out of the dirt to greet my rescuers, sure that my apprentice had somehow managed to cut his way through the entire army of goblins to come to my aid. I was moderately surprised that it wasn't Tyndal.

Instead it was a tall, lanky man with dark hair, a cheesy mustache, holding a staff that was taller than he was. Over his shoulder was the hilt of a mageblade that looked nearly enough like Slasher to be its twin. I had trouble placing the man's face, familiar though it was – I hadn't seen it every day for the last few months, and I had almost forgotten I'd had a life before the Siege. His name was Terleman, and he was a warmage I'd fought beside and bunked with in Farise.

The mustache was new.

Standing behind him was Pentandra, dressed in black riding leathers and carrying a short sword and a smoking warwand. Others milled behind her in the darkness, making the Black Flag mercenaries a little nervous at the unexpected rescue. I didn't feel very rescued. I didn't even have the strength to summon magesight. Penny looked concerned and kneeled by my head.

"Aren't you happy to see me, lover?" she said in that too-happy tone of voice that people use in the presence of the dying.

I examined her face. "Penny. About fucking time you showed up," I growled, and threw up in her lap. After that I passed out. Again.

Chapter Twelve

The Warmagi

"Of all of the divisions in an army, among the most useless is the so-called Magical Corps. Though their magic can occasionally be relied upon for intelligence or support of general troops, individually they are poor fighters, bookish charlatans whose claims of 'power' are rooted in their tricks and deceits. For the expense I would rather hire camp-followers and harlots, for they possess more fighting spirit than the toughest warmagi."

— *Duke Lenguin II of Alshar*

We were saved. Only not really.

Around noon the next day I stalked from one end of my tower to the other, looking alternatively at the work parties trying doggedly to fill the vacant hole under the wall in the outer bailey, and the seething mass of short black hairy troops just out of bowshot beyond the castle wall. I thought back on the last few days' events and was torn between giddy excitement and hopeless despair.

Funny story, that. While I was out trying to get myself gallantly killed, my little magical corps – two traumatized children and a hopelessly scheming poseur – had scored surprisingly well against the foe.

I think part of it was that they didn't know how difficult the task should have been. Assaulting a bridgehead is a daunting prospect for the veteran warmagi. The three had come up with a simple strategy of varying the types of spells they threw at the invading force within their limited capacity – and likewise limited how much force they put behind each new casting.

Never throw the same spell twice, was the idea, and don't focus overmuch on power as much as speed. With that kind of nuisance harassment, the gurvani shamans had to summon a different defense each volley, which is time consuming and drains power. It kept them busy and didn't leave them much time to support their troops effectively with scouting and scrying. When their infantry advance too carelessly into the area between their field fortifications and ours, hilarity ensued.

When the vanguard of their troops had crossed into that area, Tyndal threw an activation spell that detonated his warwand, placed there for that purpose. Not the one I bought for him. Remember the first warwand he built, that rough-hewn, over-stuffed twig I cautioned him about? All those spells, packed as tight as a cork in a bottle, were bound up into that little unstable piece of wood.

Well, my smartass apprentice decided to experiment with dangerous mystical forces while my back was turned. He *continued* to power the thing, enchanting it as frequently as he increased the bindings to the straining point, and then cast an almost elegant meta-spell to allow the wand to discharge all at once in a loud, devastating discharge. The shamans' defensive spells, toned down to deal with the various low-power bolts harassing them, were neither prepared nor positioned properly to avoid the blast.

Over a hundred gurvani were slain in the outer bailey at one instant, and thrice that many were wounded. At least one of the shamans was standing in close proximity to the blast and was killed. While the defenses built up around his witchstone absorbed a portion of the force, it wasn't enough to save him – though thankfully his irionite was not destroyed.

The whole thing was as dangerous and stupid a stunt as you could ask for, and would have made Tyndal subject to military justice in a real army. But it did have the twin saving graces of both working as planned and saving the day.

Immediately after the blast, while the smoke and dust was still billowing, the castle's archers discharged a volley just over the rough stone redoubt that encircled the breach, at near point-blank range. My irregular magical corps increased the ferocity of their attacks, augmenting it with blinding and deafening effects in the air over the confused and demoralized goblins, while the mercenary pikemen pushed forward all around the circle, interspersed with shieldmen braced on the redoubt. The Crinroc were chanting a hauntingly discordant hymn – or dirge – or jolly drinking song – in their native tongue and waiting for anything uglier than they were to get through the pikes.

The sudden, ferocious attack was enough to begin a general retreat around the mouth of the tunnel. The congestion between incoming and outgoing troops was chaotic. The gurvani captains were still trying to regroup and counter-attack when my bit of tunnel alchemy overtook them.

The explosion was so powerful that a dozen gurvani had been blown clear into the surprised ranks of the Crinroc, far behind our makeshift wall. They welcomed the practice – they were starting to get bored. While some of the surviving gurvani still fought hard and furiously, our people were able to mop up much of the rest of the force before my battered body was returned to the Castle by my rescuers. No quarter.

But then the castle rejoiced, Tyndal told me, when they saw the triumphant return of the Spellmonger at the head of a column of reinforcements – they even chanted "Spellmonger!" as we rode in, and there was no doubt who they were talking about. Despite Garky's presence and demonstrated magical competence in the defense of the castle, when someone in the Bailey's said "the Spellmonger," they meant *me*. That proved to be a metaphorical burr under his saddle.

Penny and Terleman weren't alone. Plucky little Penny had brought *nineteen* itinerant warmagi, mostly young veterans of the Farisian Campaign, looking for trouble and hungry for a chance at a witchstone. Among them were some old friends, some acquaintances of note, and a few strangers. They all wanted irionite, and were willing to do just about anything to get it. They had heard Penny's message and word had spread among my former colleagues like a flux on a ship. Before she left Remere she had six eager hotshots ready to ride to the ends of Callidore (and they weren't far wrong) if it meant irionite. Her cousin

Planus (nice fellow, I'd met him) was green with envy that he could not accompany them. The rest were recruited along the way.

Her father Orisorio had insisted on sending a hundred mounted household troops as a personal guard – presumably to protect his little darling's non-existent virtue – led by a grizzled old one-eyed Remeran mercenary captain, veteran of a hundred campaigns. Pentandra had started out with another three hundred mercenary mounted archers from Faronal, but they were commandeered by the lord of Gans and not allowed to pass beyond the River Tarr. There was an invasion of the Wilderlands going on, he explained. He would have taken her company of guards, too, had they not threatened to attack

Penny brought the disappointing news that while no one else was riding to our rescue, the menace in the west had not gone unnoticed at the Ducal level. Goblins ranged in warbands all across the Alshari Wilderlands, as far east as Tudry. The ducal Warlord was finally taking an interest in the threat of invasion. Nice to know we weren't completely forgotten.

They shot their way through Mor Pass, noting that Mor Tower was now in possession of the gurvani – though many less gurvani than had previously occupied it, after the warmagi forced their way through the pass. From the moment they entered the Valley, they had been fighting one long running skirmish. Gurvani were everywhere. Only by stealth, superior skill, and timely illusion did they push on through.

Penny's band had stopped first at the Brandmount fortress and rescued the last nine hundred survivors, three hundred of whom were in fighting shape. A small guard was detailed to escort the wounded and civilians to Mor Pass while the rest of the troops pushed on to Boval Castle. It was uncertain whether or not they would be able to force their way through, but they had no desire to remain, and chose the chance at death on the road to death in the castle. Hard to blame them.

The smaller keep did not fare as well as we had, even though the force that faced them was a tenth the size of the army that besieged Boval Castle. Brandmount's walls had been breached repeatedly by siege engines flinging stones, and mobbed with wild gurvani troops. At first they were able to drive the invaders back at great cost, until they couldn't maintain the outer defenses and were forced to retreat further into the keep. Had Penny and her expedition not shown up when they had, the defenders could not have held out, for all their tenacity, for more than another week.

Koucey's brother had made it, though he was now missing his left hand and burdened with a nasty infection or poison or both. Zagor and a surviving fragment of the Gobarba Order, still singing hymns in devotion to a long-dead god, had survived. The Boliek sisters had not been so lucky; as hedgewitches it turned out that they were far better at curing gout than clobbering goblins. They weren't alone on the casualty list. The siege of Brandmount had been deadly, and the evacuation had been costly. Considering the odds they were facing, it was no minor miracle that anyone escaped at all.

I have to hand it to Penny. For someone who wasn't a warmage – who had, *literally*, never been in any sort of fight in her life – she had plunged into the heat of battle with a cool head and a good eye for carnage. Terleman told me, later, that she acted as if she had been disposing of troops and building strategies all of her life. She was no slouch tactically, either.

In a daring raid on the gurvani command post overseeing Brandmount's siege Penny had captured a shaman's witchstone, and with its power and some skillful tactics she led her people in through the lightly-manned siege lines to liberate the fortress.

After that, things get fuzzy, but there were some powerful illusions involved, some quick and efficient strikes by her guards, plus a commando-raid by the six warmagi who specialized in that sort of thing, on top of some inspired mayhem from Zagor, who showed what a lifetime of attunement to a witchstone could do for a mage.

The result of the daring plan was the destruction of the command structure of the besiegers, the glorious sight of their own infantry attacking and slaughtering their own artillery, and three more witchstones captured – all the while Penny led the column of survivors out through the lines. I almost wish I had been there.

Zagor had put the gurvani into a situation where they could either quell a magically-induced rebellion from their fiercest fighters or go after the fleeing humans. The confusion allowed Penny to lead them on a mad dash through more hostile territory to Boval Castle – only to save me and the besieged at the nick of time.

What a girl.

The castle was a little more crowded, now, but the breath of fresh hope everyone felt – not to mention the close brush with total destruction – gave us a good reason to be accommodating to the new arrivals. They wasted no time and pitched in with the defense right away. Within a day the repair work on the failed breech was under way and the sentries on the walls were doubled, with one of Penny's fresh veteran guards shadowing every two militiamen or mercenaries.

Those Remeran soldiers were for more than show. The luxury-loving Imperial-descended Remerans have an undeserved reputation for being effete cowards, but when it came to the fighting men from Pentandra's family estates, they were every bit as tough and adept at their art as the Wilderlords. Those dusky war-eyed bastards were as tough as anyone I'd fought with in Farise. Not that the goblins cared.

The goblin army was keeping its distance after their defeat at the breach, no doubt regrouping and preparing for yet another assault. Their numbers had not visibly suffered from either Penny's strike or my pyrotechnics – indeed, more troops were arriving every day. I didn't much care – being outnumbered fifty-to-one or five-hundred-to-one didn't really matter anymore. I was just happy to see a few more warm bodies manning the battlements, and they were happy to see some sturdier battlements to man.

But otherwise their arrival proved a bittersweet reunion. Many of the Bovali of the northern valley had not survived, and those who had made it had lost family and friends in the siege. Koucey and his brother were visibly moved to see each other again, though his brother was on a stretcher, too sick from his wounds to mount a horse. Peasant militiamen searched for news of relatives, and were often told the worst. There was much weeping in both joy and sadness.

The tower opposite mine was vacated and devoted to housing many of the new warmagi, led by Penny, while space was made in the inner bailey for Penny's guard and in the outer bailey for the surviving commoners from Brandmount Keep. Snug quarters, but it beat the alternative.

So it would seem as if we were rescued, this being the first sign of outside help.

But not really.

Penny filled me in on the military situation in the rest of the Duchy while I recovered from my exertions. We weren't the only ones getting clobbered, apparently. Comparatively large bands of gurvani had burst out past Mor Tower and invaded Gans, Presan and beyond. Even Tudry was starting to get raids on the outlands of the city, she reported. There were all the signs of a major invasion, and everyone was taking the idea seriously, now.

She also told me that His Grace, Duke Lenguin of Alshar, had been informed, and was feeling far more anxious about the other goblin incursions into his profitable lands north and south of Boval than our desperate plight. That was timber and iron country, after all, the basis for Alshar's mighty fleet.

Nor was he sitting on his hands. The duke had put out the call to his vassals to assemble his troops – a long, complicated and politically delicate process in a feudal government – and in the meantime he was hiring mercenaries and impressing peasants to fill in gaps. But things just weren't moving fast enough, and before any army of note could be brought to bear on the problem, the goblins were taking advantage of the feeble defenses of the Wilderlands.

The western Barony of Denal and the entire northern County of Locare were both now battlefields, though the invaders had nowhere near the numbers that were rapidly filling up Boval. The entire Duchy was arming, supposedly, but His Grace had already written us off as lost.

What was one little Wilderlands domain, compared to the rest of his realm? The navy needed timber and iron, not cheese.

If it hadn't been for Penny's noble bearing and absolute insistence (and her escort of powerful warmagi) she never would have been allowed beyond Tudry, much less gained entrance past the towers at the pass.

So we could expect no further help. That news had come as a crushing blow to some in the Castle, but for others – myself included – it was actually a relief to hear. The failed breach in the wall was just the most recent reminder that our siege was becoming more and more a losing proposition. If there was no relief in sight, and with battle elsewhere, now, how could we hope to survive? There was no way that I could see, not with a bucketful of irionite and a squad of adepts. Boval Vale was lost.

But how do you explain that that to the Lord of the Domain?

Sire Koucey was strutting around the halls and baileys of the castle like a proud little cockerel, as if he had pulled the Remerans out of his own purse and rescued his northern keep by himself. Not even the battered image of his younger brother on a stretcher, arm in sling, racked with fever seemed to have much of an effect on his outlook.

To hear Koucey tell it, the gurvani had gotten licked so badly that they were packing up and going home, right after they all lined up and swore eternal peace to the people of Boval Vale. While hope was a much-needed commodity around the castle, what he was doing went beyond good leadership – it was a blatant disregard of the reality. There are limits to faith, and he shamelessly crossed them and never looked over his shoulder.

Now, I admit, I was still irate over his very public blame of me for the breach; and after hearing how his ancestors conquered the province I was even less inclined to be deferent to him. But by claiming that salvation was at hand when it was clearly not was almost criminal. It was certainly irrational. Even Sir Cei, his trusted castellan, looked concerned, though he refused to speak an ill word against his liege. Sir Roncil had no such qualms – he quietly came to me with a pair of his chivalrous brethren and asked about my plans for escaping the situation.

But Koucey? He thought the day all but won.

Perhaps it was my commoner's upbringing, but while I had always been taught to be respectful and slightly in awe of the nobility, I was coming to realize that that relationship worked in both directions. When a leader you are sworn to respect and obey comes out and simply lies about things you know are untrue, and does it to your face, it is a fundamental betrayal of trust that destroys the peasant/warrior relationship. Huin the Tiller and Duin the Destroyer are brothers, in the pantheon. Duin is only elevated as a god of the nobility because he supposedly destroys only to protect or conquer. He does not seek to mislead his own people.

Similarly, when the folk of the Riverlands are faced with a dishonest, corrupt, or even openly arrogant lord, there is a long tradition of the peasantry rising in arms. That happens much less often in the Wilderlands, due to the different social structure (villeins and serfs are rare – most of the Wilderland peasants are freemen) and the sparser population. To my knowledge Boval Vale had never enjoyed a peasant uprising before, but every time Koucey crowed about our "impending victory" in defiance of the observable truth, I was becoming more tempted to lead one.

I had more important duties that morning. After resting and healing for a dozen all-too-brief hours, I had the responsibility for distributing the captured irionite to the warmagi who had risked life and limb to get it. More importantly, I had to instruct them on their use.

I'd begun to notice a strange feeling that had developed when using my sphere, a feeling as if reality itself was a little warped around me. Of course I worried about gurvani magic and the influence of the Great Ghost, or whatever he liked to be called (I had already taken the precaution of associating the two pieces of irionite that Penny's troops had captured with my sphere to shield it from gurvani influences) but I was starting to think that the effect was a product of just using the stone itself.

I consulted with Zagor about this, when he felt up to the conversation. He was still recovering from the siege at Brandmount and the difficult journey south. Seeing so many of his friends perish had been hard on him. But he was an invaluable research tool, as he was the only human being I knew about who had grown up in close proximity to it, and had mastered its control. I hated to put the man to use like that, after what he had been through, but I really didn't have a choice.

The problem with Zagor was he either knew a Tree Folk term for something – which wasn't particularly helpful – or he would just shrug, because he didn't have the vocabulary to describe what he knew. That being said, he was helpful in advising us on the basic attunement and use of the witchstones. He did agree that there was a 'special feeling' that built up when you used the stones overmuch, something to be avoided. It was one reason why he was stingy with its power, to avoid the addictive properties of irionite. He watched me pass out the stones with a certain wry amusement, and enjoyed the reaction of the magi as if they were children getting toys at Yule.

The nineteen warmagi, plus our homespun "magical corps," had assembled on the roof of the tower in a neat semicircle around me, everyone within earshot as I passed out the magical bounty.

There weren't enough for everyone, of course. Beyond the stones held by Tyndal, Garkesku, and Rondal, there were nine stones to go around, and nineteen warmagi (plus Penny) to wield them. I took a moment to inspect the eager wizards as I distributed the stones. Several I knew from Farise or working as a warmage myself. Some I was just meeting.

Professional warmagi are an odd lot. When you can make a good living as a trained mage pretty much anywhere in the Five Duchies, it takes a special kind of person to voluntarily give that up for the hard, violent – but lucrative -- lifestyle of the professional warmage. I guess warmagi come in two sorts: those who get off on the pure adrenaline rush you get from charging an enemy line, and those who lusted after the powerful forces involved in warmagic, stuff the average spellmonger or court wizard just doesn't use in daily practice.

Warmagi also differ from non-magical soldiers in that they have style. That is, they tend to go out of their way to make themselves individually distinctive in dress, mannerisms, and behavior in order to increase their reputations, which in turn leads to more contracts. For example, Garky was gaudy, even for a spellmonger. Most of these mercenaries had adopted garb that was sleek or deadly-looking – high-grade leather, ornamented armor, dashing accessories of polished steel and such. In general they're good dressers and adopt an arrogant attitude when they work. I suppose it stems from their unshakable belief that they are superior to any other soldiers in all respects.

Egotistical bastards. I was grateful for every one.

The seventeen men and two women assembled before me wore a variety of robes and armors, ranging from the menacingly stark to the outrageously ornate. Various personal liveries and family mascots were emblazoned on some; others focused more on clothes and accessories that made them seem more dangerous to the untrained eye.

A few, as I said, I recognized. Azar, a slim, tall young man dressed in tight-fitting black leather over loose black Farisian silks, had patrolled the occupied City of Farise with me only a few years ago. He was a deadly fighter, I knew from personal experience, the kind who doesn't see enemies, he sees obstacles to be overcome.

There was Wenek, a small, mean-looking little man with a tendency toward portliness and a penchant for plaid wools. I'd played dice with him a few times while we waited for work down in Barrowbell, and despite his scowling, gruff manner he was a pretty decent guy. His specialty was nasty offensive magics, the sort that make you start bleeding from every pore or turn the air in your lungs solid – he'd been in the thick of the Battle of the Tower, in another squad, and counted himself lucky to be alive.

I was very pleased to see Hesia, a girlfriend of Penny's who had a spectacular knack for disabling defensive spells, particularly the kind that strengthen fortifications. She was also adept at magically augmenting siege engines – indeed, she loved the things. She was standing up front, swathed in a flowing red robe chased with golden griffins.

Then there was Horka, whom the jongleurs of Castabriel have said is a grandson of Duin the Destroyer (on his mother's side), War Incarnate, a one-mage army invincible to any foe. I know this for a fact because I was with him when he paid the jongleurs of Castabriel to say it. He had a non-descript peasant's face and a quiver on his back that held a variety of wands. His mageblade was a foot longer than mine, and he had strapped daggers to every limb. Penny had mentioned that he had been plying his trade as an assassin and saboteur the last year or so in the eastern Duchies, adding a little dark spice to the various inheritance feuds that were the main entertainment there, some of which dated back to Imperial times. Off the field he was a good if somber companion. On the field he nearly lived up to his inflated reputation.

Terleman, of course, I knew from the Long March down the Farisian peninsula – I even bunked with him for a brief stint during the occupation. He's a good mage. Good war captain. Good friend. With absolutely no fashion sense.

He wore a pale yellow cloak and a tight-fitting blue leather pants under a shimmering hauberk of the finest mail I'd ever seen, heavily enchanted, and he wielded a powerful battlestaff that doubled as a spear. He had a jaw line like a mountain, and he was an adept soldier and decent captain. And he loves his work. Terleman was the type of mage who got into warmagic because he liked the powerful spells. His idea of a good time is watching stone battlements crumble to dust under a powerful aging spell. He's also one of the few warmagi I knew who took an academic interest in warmagic. He was writing a book on the subject, he bragged.

Mavone was another warmage with whom I'd worked, both in Farise and in a few freelance assignments. He was a genteel Gilmoran mage, softly-spoken but very subtle – not the type of man you want to cross. Of course one could say that about most Gilmorans, for whom dueling is as much a recreation as a heritage.

The others were a mystery to me, though I knew a few of them by reputation alone. But they were an impressive looking lot, even to my eye. What impressed me more was that Penny had been able to get such a large, deadly group of individuals to come to my rescue on such short notice.

They didn't come into this hopeless siege out of a sense of duty, compassion, or obligation – they wanted to get paid in irionite, of course. That was the only reason they were there.

When the word had gone out from Penny – who has a habit of exaggerating just enough to motivate someone to do what she wants – the warmagi who heard it had lined up from all over the Duchies. In one case the Magical Corps on both sides of a lagging territorial dispute in Kestalon had simply quit, refunded their employers' fees, and made for the rendezvous point together. That brought me four warmagi (Astyral, Curmor, Carmella – a specialist in castle construction and repair, and the only other female warmage of the group – and Rolof). Enough stories about the Mad Mage's defense of Farise had circulated to enflame the whole twisted little warmage community.

"Masters," I began politely, "and Ladies. My name is Minalan, and until two months ago I was the spellmonger for a little village not far from here. Before you start making jokes about smelling horseshit when I'm around, let me add that I am also a graduate of the War College and the

Inarion Academy, I put in my time in Farise, and for the last several weeks I have been responsible for keeping that horde out there at bay.

"So if you feel I'm a complete idiot, please keep it to yourself, because I might just blast you where you stand out of pure malicious spite." That earned me a chorus of chuckles, and several appreciative nods. You can't earn the trust of a warmage by being obsequious. But crediting them with common sense works. They were warming up to me.

"It doesn't take a military genius to see what the situation here is. I appreciate your efforts on our behalf, so far, and hope that you find the proposed compensation . . . *adequate*." That brought more giggles. "I remind you that by accepting these stones from me you are technically in violation of the Royal Censorate's Bans on Magic, and may be subject to professional and civil penalties. I'll also mention that there is a dearth of actual Censors in the Wilderlands, so your chances of being tracked down here are negligible . . . and any Censor would have to fight his way through that lot before he could attempt to question you.

"Now," I said, taking the big leather pouch with the unclaimed stones from Tyndal, who stood by, "There are not currently enough of these to go around, so we will have to share, at least until we can increase the supply."

There were grumbles in the ranks, and a few sour faces. "The good news is that there are more on the way. The bad news is that you will have to hack your way through a thousand gurvani and duel an enthusiastically patriotic gurvani shaman to get one." More wry chuckles.

"Now, before we begin," I said, withdrawing the first stone from the bag, "some ground rules. I have no doubt that you all are far, far better warmagi than I am. I am not here to debate that.

"I am here to tell you that, to my knowledge, I am the greatest living human academic authority on the subject of irionite since the recent death of Orril Pratt, in that I have had the most experience and instruction with the stuff, and you should listen to me for your own safety and benefit. Zagor, over there, actually has possessed a stone since childhood, and has received instruction in its use from the Alka Alon."

That impressed them. Any mage who has studied with the Alka Alon, even briefly, tended to be held in esteem by magi.

"While he has the experience to use it," I continued, "he isn't classically trained and may find it difficult to speak on the subject in terms we could understand. Nor is he a warmage, he's a hedgewizard. He has agreed, however, to sit in and assist in your introduction to the stones.

"We are dealing with potent forces, here, more than you've ever used in your lives. They are haphazard and dangerous. Already there has been one unintentional death and a vicious maiming due to the improper use of these stones."

That caught everyone's attention, and I gave a sketchy account of Urik's Rebellion, leaving out parts that would be embarrassing to Garkesku. The old man was still in a state of shock about the whole thing. I was hoping he would recover.

The rest of the lesson was similar to the one I gave to my original magical corps a week before, and so does not bear repeating. One item of note, though, was the dramatic proficiency the warmagi showed at using the stones.

While Garkesku and his boys had clumsily lobbed uncomplicated bolts of pure magical force at the hapless goblin infantry, this new bunch began sending a sophisticated variety of nasty offensive spells to rain down on our foe almost immediately. Augmented by the power of the stones, their attacks had a visible effect on the distant gurvani lines. We all watched with amusement through magesight as they practiced on living creatures.

In some places they were stricken with bouts of coughing, or oppressive heat, or a maddening screech that made it impossible to sleep or concentrate. The shamans on the day shift put up defensive spells in a hurry, but they didn't do much against the skills of the wizards. My new magical corps was used to evading such inconveniences, and they quickly came up with counterspells. They were like kids with new toys, trying out subtle variations of their favorite spells that were profoundly effective when powered by irionite. And I made everyone take turns on them. I let them play like that for two or three hours. Then I ordered them to do the more serious job of erecting a real magical defense over Boval Castle.

The thaumaturgical field ("dome of power", to the layman) that had surrounded it was reinforced in manifold ways as each warmage added his or her special spells to it. When they were done it was so strong and devious that it could be seen even without magesight. It would stop most regular magical attacks now and keep anyone from magical reconnaissance, too. Even arrows and missiles flung from siege engines had a hard time targeting anyplace significant within after they improved the defenses.

I put three men on harassment duty, making life difficult and occasionally dangerous to our foe by dropping lethal bits of magic in their midst, just to be annoying. That was a popular job, as they could try out theories and iterations of power on a real, live foe. I had two magi on surveillance duty at all times, scrying for minute movements in enemy troop formations and pinpointing the location of our opponents' witchstone-wielding shamans in the camps all around us. That last bit was important, because we planned to hunt them relentlessly. I wouldn't be happy until every one of them got a piece of irionite, as promised.

The rest of them I returned to their tower, where they could take turns practicing with their stones. Or sleep. Most of them slept.

Some didn't. Terleman, for example, wanted to talk strategy – particularly in light of the approaching force – not the huge army of gurvani, but the undead thing that led it. They had all detected the advance of the Old God's avatar, like the wake of a great ship, and worriedly asked me more about it.

I tried to be vague about my answer, but they could smell the bullshit and pinned me down about it. So I eventually admitted that this massive power was only days away from us, likely with another horde at his back, and regardless of what Sire Koucey might say our time here was limited. That troubled them, but these men were used to risk, even magical risk. They got back to work with a shrug instead of packing their bags like sane people. Like I said, Warmagi are strange.

After I dismissed the class I joined Penny on the edge of the wall where Tyndal had been thoughtful enough to provide a small and simple supper.

She was a bit older, more mature, than when I'd last seen her. She was almost twenty-one, she bragged, as she caught me up on gossip from our mutual friends. She looked as elegant eating cold rations in a siege as she had dining at the Academy Solstice Ball. She was still wearing her black riding leathers, but had added a rakish black mantle cut in a masculine style. Ordinarily that would seem an unnecessary fabrication. On her, it worked.

"It's a lovely group I've put together, eh?" she asked, one eyebrow raised as she poured the beer daintily into a mug.

"Comparatively speaking? I cannot argue with that. You saw what I had been working with. A spellmonger and a couple of apprentices. *'The amazing thing about a dancing bear is not how gracefully it dances—'*"

" *'—but that it dances at all,'* " she finished. "Agreed. Min, I'm so happy to see you alive I could bust." It was the closest to an admission of admiration I'd get from her. Like the warmagi, I accepted it graciously and gratefully.

"Same here," I nodded, smiling. "I can't believe that you actually came to rescue me."

"To be honest, I did it for the jewelry – like this lovely necklace," she said, touching the irionite bead that had recently graced the neck of the Black Skull shaman. "I've always been a sucker for jewelry." It was more powerful than the other pebbles, I'd determined, and while it might prove deadlier than other stones in the hands of other magi, she had earned it. "In truth, I came as quick as I could and would have brought more help if I could have. That Huin-be-damned little lordling! I had a crack unit of mercenary horse archers under contract, and he had the *nerve* to—"

"I know, I know," I said, putting up a hand to halt her tantrum. "That's just how war works, Penny. The rules are fluid. But you did make it through, despite all odds." That brought me to another point. "Look, as long as you have that pretty necklace, you'd better start learning to control your emotions. Witchstones have so much power that once you are attuned to a piece it will start powering even casual thoughts and emotions like spells."

"What do you mean?"

"If you get pissed off at the chambermaid once too often, you really *might* burn her down before you knew what was happening. You heard what happened to Urik. And then the servants will talk," I said, adopting the air of one of the old Imperial nobility, who still thought of gossiping servants as the epitome of evil.

"Yes, you are right," she admitted, after blushing just a bit. "We wouldn't want the servants to talk, now would we? But I think you'll find that I've mellowed in the last few years. A lot of that youthful impetuousness is tempered with mature wisdom," she added.

I didn't believe a word of it. "The difference is that before if you wanted to fuel a spell that could, say, burn a chambermaid alive, you had to make a conscious effort to raise that kind of power – you know that. Now, it's there around your neck just begging for a place to go. And it is very, very seductive. I catch myself using it even for things that I don't need to. I can see how it could become terribly easy to grow dependent upon it."

"Point taken. I can see that already. When we assailed the besiegers at the keep and I used one for the first time, it was exhilarating! I felt like an avenging goddess. And I'm not even a warmage."

"Exactly," I nodded, sagely. "You have to be cautious with the stuff. For your own sake, as much as other's. Remember what happened to Orril Pratt. He wasn't known as the Mad Mage of Farise because of his penchant for collecting rare art. The power of the stone drove him crazy. I wouldn't want to explain to your folks how you burned out your brain one day because you were throwing a fit. By the way, how *did* you sneak away from your folks as quickly as you did? I thought Daddy was being protective."

Penny chewed for a few moments, swallowed, and took much longer than she really needed to chase it with beer. She stared at me sharply the whole time, and I wonder to this day just what she was thinking. Finally, she sighed and said,

"Actually, it was my father who *sent* me."

That admission hit me like a thunderclap. I'd met Penny's father, Master Osorio, when I had stayed at her family's estate. He was the very picture of an old Imperial-lineage Remeran Practical Adept, which is what respectable professional magi are called in Remere instead of 'spellmonger'. He had sharp features he'd passed down to Pentandra and an impressive, neatly combed goatee. He never failed to dress in the most expensive fine silks and wore more gold jewelry than most women. He looked just like an archmage of old, though he acted like a social-climbing adept keen to expand his house and firm's interests no matter what. His magically talented little girl was his pride and joy.

Pentandra's older sister was un-Talented, the family disappointment. She was also incredibly beautiful, which I'm sure was fun for Pentandra.

But the admission just didn't sound like the Osorio I had met.. "Uh, has Daddy been drinking again?"

Penny giggled. "No, nothing like that. Actually, he did not *want* to send me, but he was compelled to do so by . . . the Order."

"Which order?" I asked, there being hundreds of orders organized for chivalrous, magical and religious purposes. There was even a mystical order associated with bakers, which my father had joined during his apprenticeship. They got together the day before Brigasday, and wore funny hats and drank a lot of liquor. I always loved the funny hats.

"The Order of the Secret Tower."

"Never heard of it," I admitted.

"If you had, it wouldn't be much of a secret, now would it?" she countered wryly.

"A good point. So why and how did the Order get your father to send you to come to rescue me? I didn't think I made that good of an impression."

Actually, Penny's Dad thought I was a decent enough fellow, and he respected my academic and professional capabilities, but he made a point during my visit to inform me, in no uncertain terms, that he had no desire to see his daughter allied with a common Narasi baker's son with few prospects beyond village spellmonger.

Her mother had been slightly less diplomatic. To her I'd always be *"that nice barbarian boy."*

"It wasn't you, silly. It was the allure of the *stones*. I guess I'm going to have to trust you on this, and by telling you what I'm about to tell you I am guilty of treason to the Five Duchies, violating the Royal Bans on Magic and could be marked for assassination by the members of the Order."

I glanced over the wall, where a hundred thousand gurvani were lurking just itching to see our bleached bones gaily decorate their ancestral homeland. "Ishi's pretty toes, I'm *really worried* about being arrested or assassinated right now."

She grinned, which made her look like a teenager again and brought back a flood of fond memories from school. "The reason that the Order of the Secret Tower is secret is because a few centuries ago it was known as the Imperial Collegium of Magi – the Princes Elector of the Archmage."

"Oh. Oh! Wait, I thought—"

" When your barbarian ancestors crossed the Vore and conquered the Magocracy," she explained, "it was one of only a few Imperial institutions to be banned outright by the Dukes. It was one of the main reasons the Censorate was created.

"For nearly four hundred years it has been punishable by death to be known a member. The Dukes thought that it had died out, but the Order has been kept alive in a few of the old Imperial families, mine included. We stay *very* quiet about it, taking a pretty passive role in politics. Mostly it's just for teaching some of the old family techniques in secret .

. . and watching and waiting. For the last four hundred years the Order has maintained a tight organization, but did very little beyond avoid the notice of the Censorate and throw regular secret parties.

"When I told Daddy about the irionite, he immediately convened the Inner Council of the Tower, and after due deliberation they authorized this fishing expedition – even funded it. Under the condition that at least one piece of irionite be returned to them."

That started my suspicions running rampant. While I appreciated the bailout, I was wary of secret groups of old Imperials plotting gods-knew-what kind of mischief with one of these stones. Perhaps it's the skeptical Narasi in me, but that just didn't sound like much good could come from it. There was still considerable resentment against my people by the Imperials, I knew – even though the two peoples had been regularly intermarrying for centuries – and I can't say I blamed them. While our occupation and usurpation of their country hadn't been particularly brutal, it had still been oppressive in spots. Particularly against the magi who had made our lives difficult out on the steppes.

But, hells! This was my country, too. I had been born here, not on some arid steppes to the north of Vore. I had no great love for the Five Duchies as a political construct, but I would hate to be called up to fight a determined group of disciplined magi with that kind of power at their disposal.

But then again I had just handed over more power than the whole Magocracy had been able to generate in its defense to a mercenary bunch of power-hungry young hellions, turning them loose on the world, so my moral judgment might be considered impaired. I'm sure the Censors would see it that way.

Who was I to judge? I was just trying to survive.

"Agreed," I said, finally. "I think we can work something out. Can we expect more magical reinforcements?" I asked, hopefully.

"No, not really. While the Council was generous, they were also cautious. If we get wiped out to the last man then they remained hidden from Ducal scrutiny, and no one will be the wiser. You have to understand how paranoid – justifiably, I might add – these people are, Min. They are masters at the long game. The Order traces its past back to Lost Perwyn, and has all the patience it needs."

"Great," I sighed. "Well, I don't see how I can say no, seeing as how you just saved our asses, and all. I still can't believe that Osorio risked his fainting flower of a daughter in a warzone in the Wilderlands."

"It wasn't easy, but Daddy is a professional – he couldn't pass up this opportunity. And it's not like I would have listened to him, anyway. Besides, you know how fanatical us Imperials can be about magic. We've been using it for nine centuries now."

"And I know how you used it on my ancestors to keep us in line."

"Fat lot of good it did us, in the end."

I couldn't argue with that. It was, in fact, an old argument between us. Instead I took a bite out of an apple that I wouldn't have paid an iron penny for at market and savored the over-ripe juices. I was ravenous. I looked forward to my next big meal, which wouldn't be until . . .

"Just thinking," I said, thoughtfully. "Did you have an idea of how to get back out, when you came into the valley?"

"This operation wasn't stifled by over-planning," she said, airily. "No, not really."

"So how *do* we get a few thousand humans past a few hundred thousand gurvani without them noticing?"

"Hey, I'm not a warmage. You barbaric types can figure it out," she answered, defensively.

"Just asking." That would be a problem, and one that would take quite a bit of finesse and subtlety. It would be a question of united strength and imagination of the new Magic Corps, no doubt. A corridor of flame a hundred feet high, leading to the valley's mouth? A million birds to fly us all over the mountains?

"By the way," Penny said, conversationally, trying to change the subject, "I had my valet bring my bags to your quarters, and told your serving girl to see to them. She seemed annoyed. I know that this isn't Remere, and these are not the best of circumstances, but you *may* want to have a word with her about her attitude. Or I will, if you'd like. I know you're squeamish about that sort of thing."

I stopped chewing and stared at Penny, an idiotic look plastered across my face.

Alya. *She was talking about Alya.*

The ramifications of Penny's arrival on a personal level suddenly leaped out from hiding and pounced on me, beating me about the head and shoulders. How does one do this? *Ex-girlfriend, meet new girlfriend – I'm sure you will get along famously.* It was a stickier diplomatic situation than a meeting of the Coronet Council.

"Uh, Penny, that *wasn't* my serving girl. At least not officially."

Her eyes widened as it dawned on her what I was saying, and, by extension, what she had done. "You mean to tell me that you are . . . *involved* with that girl?"

"Uh, yeah, a bit. Well, more than a bit."

"*You're blushing!*" she accused, grinning wickedly. "Oh, you dear, dear boy."

"I'm sorry, Pen, it's just been a long siege, and after the interrogation that your parents gave me I figured that waiting for you would be--"

"Goddess! You don't think I'm *jealous*, do you? *Me?* Min, you've known me for years! How could I be jealous of . . ."

"Careful! That's my girlfriend you're talking about!"

"Girlfriend. And I'm sure that she's a very sweet girl – and from your reaction, I can see that you have some deep feelings about her. I think that's great, Min. You're a wonderful catch, and whether or not circumstances pushed you together, I can tell by your reaction that you obviously care for her. The feelings are returned?"

"They appear to be," I admitted.

"I haven't any pretensions about you and me, and I have no desire to intrude in your affairs. I shall have my bags moved over to the other tower at once."

I regarded her with deep relief tainted with just a twinge of suspicion. Penny isn't usually this gracious about such things, but, a part of me reasoned, perhaps her post-Academy training *had* mellowed her a little.

Yeah, right, a little voice whispered in my head.

I nodded pleasantly and thanked her for her understanding, while simultaneously vowing to keep a close eye on her when she was around Alya. And now I'd have to explain things to Alya that, honestly, I didn't need to deal with right now.

Perhaps I did my old friend a disservice – after all, Penny's specialty was sex-magic, and she rarely formed emotional attachments with her partners. That had been one thing that had kind of bothered me, her cavalier attitude toward affairs of the heart. But then again most of Penny's affairs had less to do with her heart than parts further south.

I secretly hoped that I had been an exception (she seemed to have some kind of affection for me) but even for a lusty peasant lad such as myself Penny's sexual openness was a bit scandalous. My barbarian ancestors might have been lusty, but they tended to be sexually conservative, compared to the culture of the Magocracy.

But Imperial-style mores or not, Penny was still a woman, and women have a tendency to get territorial about the men in their lives.

Perhaps you might think it odd that I was dwelling on personal problems during a siege, but when faced with the prospect of fighting rabid gurvani and negotiating a truce between two strong-willed women who both had a claim on me, well, give me a sword and let the fur fly.

The gurvani are *far* more forgiving than a woman with hurt feelings.

*   *   *

The next night we struck back.

It was refreshing, being able to go on the offense, after dealing with siege towers, the tunnel, and various attempts to scale the walls. It didn't take much persuasion to get Koucey to agree to it – he was far too occupied with the recovery effort and settling the new arrivals in their posts to object when I suggested a raid. He muttered something about it being "good for morale" and continued his talk with the Quartermaster and the Castellan.

Calling it a military raid is kind of dishonest; this was nothing short of a bald-faced robbery. I had a gang of eager cutthroats who were acting like parched men fighting for a drink, so anxious were they to capture more witchstones. Our scrying sentries had located at least *two dozen* within a seven mile area, and the only thing standing between the warmagi and their prize were a few thousand goblins.

The gurvani never had a chance.

That first foray we split up into three teams of six men (or women) each. Each party would venture out against a reported cluster of stones, sneak or fight their way into the enemy line, duel magically with the possessors of the irionite, vanquish them, take their stones, and withdraw in good order, presumably doing much harm to the foe.

My first outing was pretty typical. We chose a spot about a mile away from Boval Castle, a farmstead that had become a kind of supply depot and field hospital for the goblins. While there were (reportedly) only two stones there, it seemed like a strategically important and vulnerable spot to hit. A good place for newly-powered warmagi to try out their spurs.

We used stealth spells to steal our way passed sentry after sentry, in full daylight, while the camps were sleepily alive with activity. I had Azar and Hesia with me, as well as three young noblemen from Gilmora, two of whom (Mavone and Astyral) had been in the amphibious landing in Farise.

We slipped through line after line of defenses clothed in a sophisticated illusion spell that made us appear to be a nondescript squad of goblin infantry on some errand. Hesia did a masterful (mistressful?) job of shredding the enemy wards without alarming anyone, and one of the Gilmorans magically distracted anyone who actually noticed us.

We came to the little cottage that I recalled used to be Goodman Houk's, but was now the centerpiece of an encampment vast in its own right. It took us little time to spread out around the house and prepare our spells according to the hastily made attack plan we had improvised.

The two stones inside the cottage were in the hands of shamans who had appropriated the cot as a command center. There were two bored-looking sentries outside the door, but otherwise security was generally lax. Magesight revealed two simple little wards and an alarm spell, all three of which Hesia dropped like a broken clothesline.

Attacking them while they were inside was not our first choice, so we lured them outside with distracting cantrips – screams, small explosions, that sort of thing – and then pounced on them.

Two of the Gilmorans cast paralyzing spells on the nearby sentries, keeping them out of mischief, while Azar and I calmly walked up to the shamans (they were the country-bumpkin variety, not Black Skulls), dropped our illusions, and quickly cut them down with our mageblades before they could react.

Hesia had thoughtfully dismantled their personal security spells before we went in and we slaughtered them like barnyard fowl in the confusion. In seconds we had their stones and in minutes we were moving as a group towards the next site even as the two befuddled sentries were trying to figure out how their bosses had gotten sliced up so viciously right there in front of them. I think their chances of promotion looked slim

While we trekked we had a grand old time littering the area with nasty little spells that were delayed by time or activated by proximity or sound or something. We cast warmagic spells of especial potency around their stinking latrines. Under the influence of the stone I was feeling giddy with power and just a hair sadistic, and I hope no one ever does that to me – I have no desire to have my arse burned off when I sit down on the pot in the morning.

The second attack zone was a little more complex, and involved an actual duel between two shamans and Azar, while the Gilmorans and I kept the guards off of his back and Hesia sheared off his defenses like fresh wool.

Azar was a wonder to behold when he was in action, plying his blade like a dancer's flag and pulling his warwands at tactically opportune moments. He blasted one foe's head clean off and impaled the other on his sword at the exact same time, a maniacal grin lighting up his face – for a moment I almost mistook him for War Incarnate, and then he sneezed, which kind of ruined the effect.

Luckily the attack had been vicious and sudden enough that it drew little attention until it was over. Hesia had a small burn on the outside of her thigh, but that was the extent of our injuries.

The final attack zone was much closer to the front lines, and centered on one particular stone. It belonged to the shaman who was apparently in charge of scrying our defenses, which made this as much a strategic strike as a robbery. With a delicate combination of distraction and misdirection, I was able to sneak up on the old fellow and slit his throat. It was almost anticlimactic, the way we stole his stone.

To make up for it, Azar and the Gilmorans trashed a hundred yard stretch of gurvani fortifications dug in around their perimeter. Bolts of fire, clouds of acrid smoke, chains of magical death – it was truly beautiful to behold, in a horrifying sort of way. We quit the field and headed home before the survivors were able to send for reinforcements.

That first night Azar made a point to carve the Ilnarthi rune for death in everything in sight, in an effort to instill an element of terror into the foe. The Ilnarthi tribes of the peninsula were savage warriors, and their script is reflective of their delight in brutality. The Farisian sentries did that to us, back in the war, and I know the sight of that jagged spiral made my spine run cold when I had seen it carved into a tree next to a tortured comrade.

The gurvani had no way to know what it meant, but neither had we. But leaving some obscure and vicious-looking mark like that helped with psychological warfare. That became our custom, in Boval Vale, and we didn't leave a fight thereafter without scrawling that dread symbol somewhere at the scene. From what I was able to learn later it had a similar discouraging effect on the gurvani as it had on ducal troops in Farise.

The next two nights were a nightmarish play of escalating violence, with our magi going out and hammering the enemy lines in terror raids, stealing irionite, and littering the fields with bodies of the dead, crazed and maimed. Each night we struck farther and farther afield, coordinating our attacks and using our best intelligence to strike where the goblin hordes were most vulnerable. We took a few casualties, but in general we were just too good for them. A well-trained warmage with a rock of green amber was almost unstoppable against any number of goblin infantry.

Horka, especially, went out of his way to increase his nightly body count, employing larger and more elaborate death spells. I was almost tempted to rein him in, but upon further consideration I decided that if there ever was a time to experiment with such wanton slaughter, this was it. I hope I won't be eternally damned for that, but then again I've warranted damnation for so much else that one atrocity, more or less, would do little against the weight of my soul in the afterlife. Besides, I was more concerned with strategy than I was with tactics. Fate – or whatever was in charge of my destiny – had put me in command of these lethal children. That was on Fate.

The raids were highly successful. After two nights, every mage in the Castle had his or her own chunk of irionite, with three to spare. Everything after that was gravy. And I was holding the gravy boat – those stones stayed in my quarters. Much to my dismay, I was apparently in charge.

To be honest, half of my relief at Penny's timely arrival had been at the possibility of turning over the responsibilities of command to someone more experienced. That didn't happen, though. Most of the warmagi were as young, if not younger, than I was, and the few old-timers among us were more than happy to work at my direction. They were far more used to taking orders than giving them. Even Terleman, who looks a lot more like an officer than I do and actually has talent for it.

I was astonished that even Penny was deferring to my judgment in martial matters. I was even more amazed to discover how many of my peers looked to me for real leadership. These sons of lords and barons followed the son of a baker without a quibble, our profession sanding away all but the barest vestiges of our original stations in society.

It kind of became official at a late breakfast in the Other Tower, as the barracks of the Magi had come to be called.

I was sitting down to polish off a huge plate of bacon and scrambled eggs seasoned with mushrooms and precious little else, when a squad led by a young tough named Rustallo returned from their mission. I don't know if the kid was drunk or tired or just filled with the uncertainty and idealism of youth, but he stopped in front of my table and bowed. I nodded back, confused (we tended to be pretty casual around the Magi Towers) and resumed eating. He then cleared his throat and addressed me.

"Captain Minalan?" he asked. I swallowed too hard in surprise – that was the first time I had heard that title used in conjunction with my name.

"Can I help you, Rusty?"

"Yes, sir. Me and the boys just got back from a little picnic, and we found some, uh, well, some things of value." He reached into his broad leather belt and took out a small cloth pouch. Upending it in front of me, he dumped a dozen and a half verdant stones on the table. Their color caught the dim light for a moment and my heart skipped a beat.

But the flash of green that bedazzled me was not accompanied by the mental tug I had come to associate with witchstones: these were raw uncut *emeralds*, not irionite.

A small fortune in raw emeralds – perhaps enough to buy an estate, or a poor barony, if I was any judge.

"Some chieftain of theirs was carrying it around his neck. I thought he might be a shaman, but they were just jewels." Rustallo sounded almost disappointed. "I guess they dug them up in their mines, away back in the mountains. Still, I didn't want to leave them there. *Some* people," he said, glancing accusingly back towards his mates, "wanted to keep them, but the war codes say that the captain of the unit is in charge of disposing of all loot. I suppose that's you."

I stared at the pile of pebbles that could buy my dad's village thrice over and considered the matter. Next to irionite, these were small beer, and considering the fact that they were nearly worthless in a war zone made this discussion almost seem funny.

But the lad did have a point. So far all the extra witchstones had been given over to me, now that every mage had his or her own. I did that for the sake of order and because my sphere was the only one able to remove the Old God's taint. It was only logical that other loot be given to me for re-distribution.

"I guess that is me," I finally agreed. "But maybe not. I didn't hire you, and while I did invite you, I never claimed to command over you. The war codes say that as mercenaries you get to elect your own leader. If that's me, fine. I'll divide up the loot. If not, get whoever you elect to do it. I don't want to be responsible for duels over who got what."

Rustallo looked around at his squad, then at the others in the room, another half-dozen or so who were just coming off watches on the wards and the scrying pools. They nodded to him.

"You're elected, Captain. Hell, we've been calling you Captain since we got here. Captain Spellmonger, sometimes. Didn't you know?"

I shrugged. "Nobody tells me anything – which makes me perfect for command, I guess. Okay, I'll split the loot." I divided the piles into roughly equal thirds. "One third goes to your squad," I dictated, "and one third goes to the rest of the unit. I take the last third. Sound okay to you? If not, call a meeting and elect yourself a new captain."

It was Rustallo's turn to shrug. "I've got no problems with that. Hells, they're just emeralds. We could find a whole barrel of them and they still wouldn't be worth one pebble of Glass." The youngsters had taken to calling the green amber they sought Glass, as the young and stylish often do.

I took my portion of the stones and tucked it away in my pouch. Should we ever get out of here alive, I vowed, I'd have some of them made into a necklace for Alya as a peace offering. She was just now starting to speak to me again after the argument we'd had over Penny's arrival. While I didn't think she was the type of woman to be bought off with jewelry, it couldn't hurt to try.

But that served as the only confirmation of my command I ever received. A couple of the boys had taken to wearing the jagged spiral rune of death as a badge of sorts, to set them apart from the regular troops, but apart from that and our living quarters, there wasn't much structural organization. I was too busy planning and plotting to pay much attention to those I was commanding.

But in the few short days the warmagi had been at Boval Castle they had coalesced as a military unit, with me as their fearless leader. I had expected my comrades from Farise to listen to me – or at least not to do anything too crazy without letting me know – but somewhere between raids I had earned the respect of the others, including these kids.

I didn't realize just how seriously they took this until later.

I had a hard time taking anything particularly seriously, since the Old God's arrival was becoming increasingly imminent. That was a well-known, if little-discussed fact around the Other Tower. Under my direction every mage in the castle took a turn on scrying and onwards, and there was no way that an irionite-enhanced mage could fail to notice that malevolent presence getting closer and closer. If the witchstones showed up like bright torches in the scrying pools, the Old God was like a blazing forest fire. The warmagi were currently happy to loot the enemy lines of irionite – the duels with the shamans were seen as pleasant exercise – but no one had any illusions about their chances against *that* terrible Power. Talk around the dinner table turned increasingly to packing and preparing to vacate.

And they didn't even know the *whole* story – the secret cave that was the focus of the enemy's attention and the major factor of the motivation of their morale: the birthplace of goblin gods that was in the heart of the hill upon which the castle sat. Nor did they know about the betrayal of the truce by Koucey's family.

They found out soon enough, though. The fourth evening I lead my squad back to the gates, just before dusk, only to find my apprentice skulking about in the shadows. He wore his mageblade and an expression of deep concern, though he tried to hide it behind a stoic mask. I handed him my warstaff and began to take off my weapon's belt when Tyndal stopped me.

"Master," he said, worriedly, "I tried to come find you, but they wouldn't let me. You must go see Sire Koucey at once!"

"What's happened?" I asked, concerned. "Another breach?"

"No, Master, Sire Koucey and Lady Pentandra had a falling out."

"Did she blast him?" I asked, my heart sinking. Damn her, I warned her about idle flashes of temper!

"No, Master!" he said, his eyes wide with fear. "Sire Koucey had her arrested. She sits in a cell in the dungeon beneath the castle, even as we speak!"

Chapter Thirteen
I Stage A Peasant's Rebellion

"Due to the unfortunate power of magic to corrupt the minds and souls of men, no mage, even should he enjoy noble birth, shall be allowed to hold lands outside of his home nor title above his station. Nor shall he become entangled in the territorial disputes of those whom the gods have placed above him."

- *The Royal Bans On Magic*

-

I found Sire Koucey meeting with a group of his cronies in the main hall of the donjon. They were clustered around the ornate chair – I couldn't bring myself to call a throne – in which Koucey sat, arguing and chatting and laughing and whispering amongst themselves. All of them, I noted, wore their blades, and more than half of them were armored.

There were two sentries posted at the door when we came in – Sire Koucey's regular men-at arms, I noted, not militia or mercenaries. I was not alone, myself – Wenek and Terleman had accompanied me, eager to see the show and willing to fight, if need be. They were both armed with mageblades and warwands, and both looked imposing in their way.

The glow of twilight was fading through the arrow slits, and a small fire was crackling to one side of the mammoth hearth. Koucey was enjoying a late supper of roasted capon, with a bowl of fresh fruit and cheese, along with an ewer of wine. I recognized the bottle – an old vintage from the south.

For no special reason, that pissed me off even more.

I pushed my way through that crowd of lackeys and stood directly in front of the seated lordling. He raised his eyebrows in that sarcastic way that even country lords affect.

"Yes, Master Minalan? You have news? You wish to see me?"

He knew *exactly* why I was there. He was trying to goad me. *Bastard.*

"Yes, Sire. I have heard disturbing rumors that I think must be addressed."

"Rumors?" he asked, pretending surprise. "And what rumors are these, Spellmonger?"

While not outright insulting, his tone was unpleasant in my ears. "It is rumored that the Lady Pentandra was lost within the castle, and found her way into the dungeon, and accidentally locked herself within a cell."

There was a general chuckle among the knights and squires, though my men were silent. Grimly silent. I was giving Sire Koucey a gift, here, if he was smart enough to take it. I was giving him a chance to let Penny out of the dungeon and avoid a confrontation.

"I had no idea such a rumor had been started! That's outrageous! Sir Cei," he said, calling to his Castellan, "Have it announced in both the inner and outer baileys that Lady Pentandra has been arrested for failure to obey an order of her rightful lord during a time of war. Let us put an end to these   . . . *rumors.*"

He hadn't been smart enough to take my gift. As Sir Cei scurried off to do his master's bidding, I did not move one muscle, though my eyes flamed, they tell me.

"My . . . Lord, if I might ask, just what order did Lady Pentandra disobey?"

"She refused to subordinate command of her troops to my officers. It is vital that we press home this timely advantage against our foes. With the mischief your men have been able to make amongst the enemy, we feel it is time to pressure them to quit the field. I have been preparing to mount an attack on their headquarters with an aim to capturing it. I have ordered all my forces readied for the assault. When I informed the witch of my orders, she refused to cooperate. I was polite, at first, but I had to insist."

"*Insist,* Sire?"

"She persisted in denying me what is mine by right. Worse yet, she demanded we begin preparations to *abandon* the castle and retreat, which caused unrest and alarm among the civilians. I had no choice to arrest her for her rebellion. I would do the same – or worse – for *anyone* who would impede our defense."

The old bastard was smug as he said it, as if he had come up with a brilliant solution to a difficult problem. With the greatest restraint I took another step forward, my eyes fixing on his.

"My lord," I began, with greatest deliberation, "the Lady Pentandra took *great* personal risk and expense, venturing incredible peril and spending her own coin to bring succor to us in our hour of need – *at our request*. We would all likely be dead right now if she had not come when she did. Leaving aside, for the moment, the fact that her family is a powerful one unused to such rough treatment, might I suggest that we do ourselves and our honor a disservice by imprisoning our agent of salvation?"

"Certainly not!" the old knight said, scornfully. "Should I ever meet her family I shall make all due apologies for any such perceptions. I *am* a gentleman, sir!

"But we are besieged at the moment, at war with an implacable foe, and I *alone* command here. I will *not* sit here on the eve of victory and be imperiled by the whims of one silly, obstinate *girl*, no matter how highborn or well-schooled! As a mage, she is not, in fact, ennobled, but a commoner as you all are. In truth, it was her noble lineage alone that stayed my hand from more dire punishment for her defiance!"

"And brought whatever shreds of hope of survival that we had crashing down around us!" I volleyed back. "Those men you have assumed would follow you as lord and war leader are *not* mercenaries, Sire Koucey, they are members of her family's household guard! They will not willingly follow the man who imprisoned their liege!"

"If they ever want to see their charge again, they had best do as I command! She is a hostage to their obedience. And your own."

"I wouldn't count on either, my lord," I said, quietly. "Such dishonorable behavior stinks before the thrones of the gods, who dislike the taking of hostages."

"You speak to me of honor, Spellmonger?" he scoffed, angrily. " This is outrageous! I *alone* am lord in Boval! Forget that *not!*" he warned. "All lives within these walls live or die on *my* word – including the lives of the 'Lady' Pentandra, yours, your apprentice, and your peasant slut!"

Oh, I wanted to incinerate him, as did the warmagi behind me. I could feel their loathing grow for the Wilderlord. "These are not meek men, my lord. They will not agree to such dishonorable tactics." I was at a good seethe, now. Imprisoning Penny was bad enough, but insulting Alya in the same sentence? There were sparks in my hair, it was said.

"*You* challenge *my* honor?" he asked. His brother, still pale from loss of blood and infection, drew his sword left-handed, as his other arm was still in a sling, and took a guardian position in front of Koucey. I could have kicked him in the knee and he would have fallen down. A few of the other Wilderlords also drew, though many looked worried and confused. Sir Cei returned, and witnessing the scene he seemed genuinely perplexed.

I did my best to stay calm and reason with the man. That doesn't mean I wasn't willing to provoke him. "Nay, Sire Koucey, *you* challenge your own honor by this deed. To make a man fight against his will by threatening to murder what he holds dear is as base a deed as any roadside bandit could boast of."

My own men had not yet touched a weapon, but I could feel a dozen spells snap into place around me. Sire Koucey stood, his own hand on his sword hilt, and glared viciously at me.

"And who are *you* to lecture me on the finer points of honor? A baker's son from the Riverlands with the lecherous habits of a goat! Perhaps you did serve in the wars, and your Talent as a mage is clear . . . but blood will tell, it is said. You can dress a goat in silks and a goat it remains! Remember your station, peasant!" he spat.

"And you remember your *lineage*, Koucey! Better the honorable sweat of flour and fire than the stink of treachery that lies on your House." Now I addressed the rest of the hall. "There is a reason there are a *hundred thousand* goblins outside the door right now, isn't there, Lord of Boval? A reason of which you are entirely aware?"

"Silence, you filthy little churl!" he said, his face awash in red anger. Now he drew his blade. I kept my mine sheathed on my back.

"Tell your men of the shame of House Brandmount, Koucey! Tell them how your ancestors violated the truce between the Duke and the goblins, slaying them under a flag of truce in an act of base treachery! Tell them how your great-grandsire slit the throat of the goblin witchlord after he had pledged peace on *his* word of honor! Tell them of your house's shame!"

"*Silence!*" he shouted. The tip of his sword was quivering. I did not relent.

"Tell them how his men slaughtered the females and cubs in their camps, camps where they were assured by the Duke that they were safe from harm! Tell them how your great-grandsire schemed to steal this land from them to raise his own station!"

"Peasant, silence or you will lie tonight in chains beside your bitch, and feel the axe on your neck at the dawn!" Despite his harsh words I could see the fear in his eyes. Not the fear for his life – he was a brave man, after all – but the fear of the *truth*. To men such as Sire Koucey their reputation is worth more than their lives. His brother looked even more stricken at my words – apparently the family's history had not been shared with him.

"*Tell them, you old fool!* Tell them where the treasure came from to build this very keep! The rents your farms pay you and your cut from the cheese merchants could not have paid for this keep in a thousand years. *Where did that gold come from?* Your House stole it, that's where! Your sires wanted this land because it held a horde, didn't it? The wealth of the goblin lords."

"My lord, is this true?" Sir Roncil asked, his eyes wide. Koucey said nothing. He wasn't quite angry enough yet. So I did.

"The truth? Your house was founded by *thieves and murderers*, Sire Koucey, and all your pretensions of nobility cannot change that. But your actions today have told you out, you arrogant old bastard! You've proven yourself as vile in the eyes of truly honorable men as your ancestors were!"

"*They were merely goblins!* They weren't *people*, so the codes of honor do not apply!" he argued, as much to his men as to me.

"They were innocent women and children, for all their black hair and yellow eyes! *No* code of honor allows their slaughter, not the Book of Huin nor the Book of Luin, nor the codes of chivalry which you cleave to! Not *any* code of war I have heard of.

"But gold is gold, and land is land, and your House wanted both – at the price of its honor. Not even base treachery would have mobilized a so many gurvani to invade the Duchy, though. They don't want their gold back. They want *revenge* . . . and something else.

"Revenge for the . . . the slaughter?" asked Sir Cei, distastefully. He might be a dour man, but Sir Cei was an idealistic knight. "It occurs to me, my lord, that such incitement may last more than a lifetime, and grow in the telling."

"Tell them, Lord Brandmount! Tell them the *truth!* That gold came from someplace special, didn't it? Not just a treasury, but a shrine, a temple holy to the gurvani, pillaged by your ancestors. The Cavern of Karumala, birthplace and bridal grotto of the Old God, their most *sacred* shrine. Somewhere under our feet is the real reason your men have died. They want it back."

"They shall not have it!" he declared, his eyes flashing with a fanatical sheen. "It was not holy – it was a den of stinking evil! My sires built this keep to *keep* them from it. It was thought that a strong military presence here would deter any future incursions into the Duchy, and keep the goblins in the mountains where they belong. They must not regain it, not while a single man in this vale draws breath!"

"So, how is that working out? It succeeded *brilliantly*, didn't it?" I said. To say my words were dripping with sarcasm would be dramatically understating the truth.

"For a hundred and fifty years it did!" he insisted. "And it will work yet! We were not ready for this, not yet, that is true. The castle was finished, and I was beginning to school my people into becoming warriors as my sires instructed. But the goblins struck too soon, and in too great a force! How did we know that they had these witchstones, or so many numbers? We should have had another twenty years before they could have rebuilt their armies, after the last war. And they should have forgotten about that pit by now."

"Your ancestors didn't think that they would still be pissed off after you killed their young and stole their gold and defiled their shrine?"

"They could be controlled, it was thought." His manner changed from angry to apologetic, but for the entirely wrong reasons. "Minalan, I didn't create this situation. I was born into it. But in reflection I agree with the policies of my fathers. The goblins had no need for this Valley. They do not farm or ranch. They are happier in the mountains. We have only taken what they could not properly use."

"It was their *sacred* valley, which housed a *sacred* shrine! *That's* what they used it for. How would you feel if one of them took a shit in one of Iniri's sacred wells? Spilled spirits in pious Ifnia's counting house? Or turned a temple of Trygg into a brothel? This vale was *hallowed*. Even the Tree Folk know this, and respected and honored it. To pillage a hallowed space, even of a god of goblins, is forbidden by the gods."

There were worried glances around the room from the rest of the Wilderlords. No soldier, and particularly not knights, want to be on the wrong side of the gods. Desecration such as Brandmount had visited on the gurvani was strictly forbidden under the codes of war.

"It was a *military* decision, not a religious one!" the Wilderlord insisted. "The Duke did not approve, at first, but the Baron didn't want a ready-made staging area for invasion left on his borders, not one the scrugs would defend so potently. *He* bid my House to take the valley, despoil the cavern, and slay its defenders. He pledged the vale to us as an independent domain in return. The Duchy and his barony suffered greatly in that war, and leaving an intact foe in a protected area was not the way to avoid a second one. So it was a military decision," he rationalized. From the faces of his knights, they looked unconvinced.

"It was a poor military decision, as it turns out," I observed.

"That cave is *evil,* I tell you! We *must* keep them from regaining it at all costs," he insisted. "It was where the horrors of the last war issued from. Undead! Terrors of the night! Even dragons, it is said! Left alone, in time they would have grown yet stronger, and unleashed them on us again. Building this castle was the *only* way to deny it from them. They must not be allowed to return to that vile place!"

He paused dramatically, and looked around the room for support. To be honest, his men were too confused and preoccupied to raise much of a cheer. Mine were like statues. During our heated debate not one had moved their position an inch.

"I don't think you have much of a choice," I said, sadly. "There are a hundred thousand gurvani outside your castle, now. But do you know what is out there? Do you know what's coming this way? The Old God of the gurvani is even now headed through the mountains!. I don't know what kind of super shaman he is, or even if he isn't the real divine thing, but when he gets here that massive army out there will be redundant. If the Old God, the Great Ghost shows the same magnitude of power as his priests, then one old man in one little castle won't stop him from taking whatever he desires."

"But we are more, now, than one old man!" Koucey insisted. "Can't you see that? With the power of the witchstones, and the additional troops, you and your comrades can rout this creature, whatever it is, and send these dogs back to their caves! Why can't you see that?"

"Because I know what I'm talking about, and you don't. Sure, we have irionite, and now we have trained warmagi who know how to use it. We *might* even stand a chance against that army, out there, although I hope

I never find out.

"But that . . . *thing* who desires back the Caverns of Karumala, who covets revenge on House Brandmount and all of humanity, that is headed this way is like a thunderstorm, Koucey. It's a big fat powerful magical force of nature, and even with a bucket full of witchstones I'd have as little chance against it as you would fighting a thunderstorm without getting wet."

"But we *must!*" he pleaded. "All of our hard work depends upon it! Can't you see that? We must defeat this goblin god, or all is lost!" His mad insistence finally had worked me to the breaking point.

"Whose hard work*, yours*? Your House's? The Duchy's? What about *my* hard work? I came here at your bequest because you needed a spellmonger, and that's what I wanted to be. I wanted to cure warts and sell love potions and maybe meet some nice miller's daughter and raise a family. That was the hard work I wanted.

"But I remember how eager you were to have me after our service in Farise. You set me up to get caught in an invasion and fight for my life. There are horrors in that cave? Well, perhaps we deserve a few, for letting ourselves be ruled by the scheming of petty Wilderlords who would lead us into death and ruin for the price of their broken honor.

"The truth is, I don't give a damn about your ancestors, your honor, this castle, or that cave. I'm fighting for my life and the lives of those other peasants you suckered into your bullshit cause." I sighed, tired of the posturing and the threats. "The truth of the matter, Koucey, is that I insist that you release the Lady Pentandra from her cell and I recommend, in the *strongest* possible terms, that you order preparations be made to evacuate the castle."

"Need I remind you that I still rule here? That has not changed. *That* is the truth of the matter, Spellmonger. My heritage aside, my worthiness aside, *I* am still lord here."

I laughed in his face. "And you think that really *means* something anymore? Who will do your bidding, oh righteous lord? Your lackeys here?" I said, all pretense of civility gone. "The mercenaries in the Inner Bailey, who took coin from my hand? The Crinroc, who have sworn an oath to their own gods to obey me? The peasants, who already look up to me? The warmagi, my comrades?"

I had briefly met with representatives of all four groups before I entered his chamber to let them know that there might be some political fireworks, while at the same time feeling them out on the matter. While no one wanted trouble (except maybe for the warmagi, who were pretty pissed that this hayseed lordling had imprisoned a popular fellow mage on such a pretext) but all four groups had given me unofficial pledges of support. They were all concerned about Koucey's inability to grasp the strategic situation adequately.

Koucey could count perhaps on his piecemeal mercenary outfits, his fellow nobles, and a few score of his regular household armsmen if it came to a fight inside the castle. I reminded him of the possibility of an uprising – every noble's worst nightmare – in a last ditch attempt to release Penny.

"You may be lord in name, Sire Koucey, but a lord who ceases to act as one deserves not the title! History is replete with such fools. Forget that at your peril!"

I felt hot. The air around me crackled and danced as stray bits of magic leaked from my sphere, through the primal part of my mind that gave it thoughtless form. It was becoming increasingly difficult to *not* exercise that dark part of my mind. With a single thought I could have erased this man from existence. It was tempting . . .

"So it comes to this," Sire Koucey said through gritted teeth, as he lowered his sword, but did not sheath it. I let him talk – I was silently arranging some last-minute spells while he spoke. "Base rebellion. I had *thought* that you were a loyal and worthy ally, Minalan. It was whispered by some that I placed too much trust in you, that you had designs of your own on my lands. That you used your vaunted Imperial training to becharm my people and turn their hearts away from me. I didn't want to believe it, but it is true.

"You lust not only for the loins of peasant sluts, but for my very seat of power, my lands and my sword. You will not be content with plying your trade honestly, serving a just lord; you will not rest until you are called lord in my place, they said. It has been suggested that the influence of the stones have made you mad, like poor Urik, and that you were using them to influence my people and turn them against me. I have heard the stories – the *true* story, not the tales you have had spread!"

"And what would *that* be?" I asked, amused. Well, perhaps not that amused. My pride does not rest on the foundation of my reputation.

"How your disgusting lusts drove you to work a charm on poor Urik, and how – under your influence – he turned against his own master and brother apprentices! How he paid for it with his life when you feared that truth getting out!

"Really?" I asked, my eyes narrowing. "I barely spoke to the lad, before that night."

"I know that you keep an agent of the enemy here to spy upon us – *that*, at least, will be taken care of. That stinking goblin dies within the hour. I have heard of the perversities in which you indulge in your tower, the sordid play you indulge in with your apprentice and your peasant whore. You speak of betrayal, but who betrays us now? Who betrays the laws of gods and men? With your vile perversions you might as well go throw open the gates and invite the Old God in yourself!"

"And just who whispers such jagged lies into your ears?" I hissed. "Who regrets my presence here so much – and feels so ungrateful for the life I've given him by my actions – that he wishes to see us all to ruin before his own reputation is damaged?" My eyes caught the movement of someone trying very hard to stay hidden in the far recesses of the great hall..

But you can't easily hide from a mage with a witchstone. Even if you have one yourself.

"Master Garkesku!" I called. "Come out and face me."

I kept my voice even. At first he hesitated, and I could see the debate whether to run or fight play out across his features. Then he came to some resolution, straightened himself and swaggered over.

"You rebellious upstart," he spat at me. He wore his irionite shard in a silken pouch around his neck, and a dagger at his belt, but made no move toward either one.

"This is the loyal man who spoke to me of your true inclinations," declared Sire Koucey. "A man with no incentive to lie!"

"He has every incentive!" I said, my voice filled with contempt. If he blamed Urik's accusations on my bewitchment, then he could escape blame for the disorder in his own house. And tarnish my reputation at the same time.

"As I warned you before, he is a rebel, my lord," he said to Sire Koucey out of the side of his mouth. "And he is dangerously willful. You were quite right to imprison his foreign bitch in your dungeon – perhaps the threat of losing her will keep him in line. Together they would have wrought even more mischief, even ruin, if I am any judge.

"Garky, you're mad!" I sighed.

"He speaks of madness? Such temerity! I once hoped the boy would look to me for guidance, become a protégé, if you will – he has some goodly store of Talent, after all. But I can see now that he is unpardonably corrupted. His morals and behavior is repugnant." He strutted between the knight and I, secure in the protection of the lord, and I prepared for an attack spell.

It didn't come. Garkesku wasn't a warmage, after all, he was a third-rate village spellmonger with delusions of grandeur. He was depending, I realized, on my willingness to participate in the politics of the situation. Despite his occasionally skillful use of the Art, magic wasn't something he relied on in a conflict. He was a small-time shopkeeper, using intimidation and verbal bullying to maintain his position in society, relying on magic for his status.

But he angered me – worse, even, than Koucey. I had put in Garkesku's hand enough power to rival the greatest magi in the Duchy, and he was resentful, not grateful. I raised my finger, and blue lightning crackled along its length. "You lying, chicken-fornicating old--"

"*See* the disrespect, my lord? From the first day he arrived in this vale he has treated me commonly, even basely. He was jealous of me and covets my power, so jealous that he was loathe to part with the stones for fear my greater experience with the Art would upstage him!"

Garkesku's eyes lit up just mentioning irionite – the power had a potent hold over the little man, I could see. "When at last he relented, he *still* refused to fully instruct me in their use, weakening our defense, so jealous is he. I did not want to level blame at such a time as we find ourselves in, but it is obvious that his misuse of his powers has put us all in jeopardy. Especially my poor young apprentices," he added, sorrowfully. "I suspect he used the youngest one damnably until the poor lad broke under the dishonor, and slew the eldest."

I kept my peace, and let him talk. Every moment that Garky spoke, he was giving me more rope to hang him with.

"Urik certainly showed no signs of disobedience, much less rebellion, until he was under Minalan's influence," he recounted. "Indeed, Urik was always a friendly and obedient apprentice. If his *other* habits are any measure, then I have no doubt that he attempted to seduce the boy, succeeded, and convinced the lad to strike out against me. He certainly makes enough noise with that slut – my chambers are directly below his, and the noise is interminable!"

"Are you even certain you know what you're hearing?" I taunted the old lecher. He ignored me.

"Minalan also failed to detect the breach in our walls – *or did he?* He brought a prisoner into our keep and has him treated like an honored guest. And then he has a troop of mercenary magi show up seemingly in the nick of time, gives these . . . warmagi what should belong to the domain, while he riles the peasantry to the point of rebellion over trifles!"

"That he has, Sire," Sir Cei agreed, his eyes narrowing.

I feel compelled to explain that last charge. A few days before this meeting I had been returning to the castle from one of our terror raids, only to be met by a delegation from the outer bailey.

It seems that Sir Cei, the Castellan, had ordered a supply of bacon originally intended for the rations of the common folk to be diverted to the castle garrison in the inner bailey. The bacon in question, a few hundred pounds, had originally been brought from one of the prosperous nearby farmholds, not purchased by the Castellan. The farmer in question had objected strenuously: either the bacon was for the people, or it was available for purchase by the castle garrison.

Sir Cei balked at either option, and turned the man away. The farmer had taken his problem to the Quartermaster, Sir Olve, and when the old knight proved unwilling to listen to his case, he brought the matter to the attention of the informal Council that governed the outer bailey. Before going directly to Koucey about it, they wanted *my* advice.

I considered the matter, then pointed out that the garrison stored a few supplies in a shed next to the stables, and that I knew for a fact that two barrels of beer were stashed there for the refreshment of returning cavalry. I then mentioned that those two barrels of beer were probably worth about as much as a hundredweight of bacon. As Sir Cei had been getting stricter with dispensing beer as supplies slowly dried up, they took this news gleefully, and, I realized, saw it as a suggestion that I condoned. Which, in retrospect, I did.

As I went by to check on Traveler that day, I watched them attack the shed and liberate the beer barrels over the objections of a young guard – a militia soldier of sixteen years – who was not about to draw his blade on such respected members of his community. The small mob took the two barrels – and *only* the two barrels – over to their encampment and began to have a party.

News spread quickly of the deed, and before long there was a crowd of very happy and defiant peasants gathered. Sir Cei came himself with four guards to fetch the beer back and punish the wrongdoers. An argument ensued. Sir Cei threatened to have them all imprisoned, whereupon twenty volunteers offered to stuff the four small cells under the castle – certainly the safest place to be in a siege.

Sir Cei changed his mind and threatened work details for all of them, and they just laughed. All of them had worked harder on repairing the breach than anything in their lives, and the thought of even cleaning latrines seemed like easy work in comparison.

Finally, Sir Cei made noises about having the perpetrators thrashed. That got everyone's attention; but the menacing mass of common folk intimidated the guards into inaction, and in the end Sir Cei himself had to retreat with whatever shreds of dignity were still intact while the farmers sang a rather rough little country drinking song about the stupidity of the nobility.

As the castellan left, red-faced, he looked to me for support. I just shrugged and went back to my quarters, eager for a status report and a nap. Hell, I had more important things to think about than bacon and beer.

It was a minor squabble, the sort of thing to expect from a group of regular people under enormous stress and the threat of dire peril.

Castle life fluctuated back and forth from mind-numbing fear to absolute boredom, and little episodes like that relieved stress.

But Sir Cei had obviously taken it wrong, reported to Sire Koucey, and when the Wilderlord heard about my little role in the incident, he had Sir Cei chew me out about it. I ignored him – Cei is a perfect Castellan, keeping everything running as efficiently as possible under duress – but that also means that he's a complete asshole most of the time.

In any case, Garkesku had apparently jumped on that as a sign of my rebellious nature, and got a complete agreement from Sir Cei. Garkesku is an asshole, too.

I let him continue. I wanted to hear every vitriolic word.

"I wonder just where his loyalties *truly* lie, m lord. As do you. By his own admission, he merely wishes to preserve his own neck. He has no interest in you or your interests, my lord, except his envy of your position. I expect that when the time was right he would do anything in his power to usurp your seat. Anything from a complex spell to a dagger in the back. He is *dangerous*," he hissed, "and letting him at-large to continue to make trouble is an unwise course of action. I suggest, my lord, that you strip him of his witchstone and have him confined."

"You just try it!" I sneered. "Come and try to take it!"

"That's what the 'lady' Pentandra said, as well!" noted Sir Cei, darkly.

"And did she give it up?" I asked, curious.

"Well . . . no." he admitted. "But she pledged not to use it to escape. She gave her word as a noblewoman."

I could see that Penny and I would have to have a talk.

"You are, indeed, rebellious, Minalan, and I cannot tolerate it," Koucey pronounced, a mocking tone of false sadness in his voice. "If you beg my pardon now, and surrender your witchstone to Master Garkesku, then I will only sentence you to exile outside of the walls. You may take your sword and your horse, but nothing else."

"Which brings us back to the matter of enforcement," I replied. "Are *you* going to try to take my stone from me? With my mates at my back, similarly armed? On the off chance that you survive such an encounter, are *you* going to be the one to explain to the warmagi and the Crinroc and the others how you slew their Captain? Or the peasant militia who has come to see me as a leader? Those troops are not loyal to you. Try to enforce your gracious sentence and it will be your own head that adorns a spike above the gate. Next to Garkesku's, of course."

"You *dare* threaten me in my own chamber?" Koucey asked, aghast.

"I *do*," I said, coolly. "I gave you full opportunity to release Lady Pentandra without losing face. I asked you, and when you said no, I insisted. This is your last chance, old man: *release her or I will tear this castle down stone by stone* and damn you and your cursed cave with every breath!"

Koucey's face twisted in anger, his eyes wide with rage at my threat.

"I've had quite enough of this, you promiscuous peasant bastard! You can join your slut in darkness until I decide to take your head. *Seize him!*" he ordered. Two or three men-at arms started to do so, as did Koucey's brother, when the first of my spells went off.

A long tendril of magical energy reached out and grabbed Koucey and lifted him about a foot off of the floor. His feverish brother suddenly found his sword too hot to hold, and the few others who had bravely and stupidly tried to execute his order were on the ground and writhing in pain. They were not being injured in any way, they just *hurt.* One of Wenek's favorite spells. I could almost hear him grinning behind me.

"If anyone else wants to try to seize me, they are welcome to try. No takers? Just as well. I've wasted enough valuable time with this foolishness. Let's take a walk, you and I, Sire. My men will stay here with yours to keep them company and avoid any . . . *unpleasantness.*"

Terleman had drawn his mageblade, which glowed brightly, while Wenek merely thumped his thickest warwand into his palm over and over again. They were sufficiently intimidating that I wasn't worried about them getting rushed by the knights and men-at-arms, even if I'd just essentially declared a rebellion. While Koucey hung struggling in the air, his sword dropped on the floor, forgotten, I walked straight up to Garkesku and looked him in the eye.

"I have *special* plans for you, Master Garkesku," I said, softly to his fear-stricken eyes. I reached out and plucked the pouch from around his neck. "You are stripped of my gift. You are unworthy of it. By all rights I could put a blade in your belly for the insult you have given me and no one would object – nor would you be missed. You are a disgrace to the profession. Not only could you not keep order in your own house – which cost you the lives of two apprentices – but you are dabbling in the dark magic of politics.

"You know as well as I that the Bans prohibit this. As a chartered mage of the realm, in the absence of a Royal Censor I have the right to burn out your brain, keeping you from ever casting a spell again. Or I could kill you in a duel for the insult you have given me.

"But I won't do either. Instead you may go for the rest of your life remembering the power that you lost the day you betrayed me. You will never again have access to irionite. You could have rivaled the finest magi of the age, Garkesku. Now you will never be anything more than a spellmonger, with only the powers within you at your disposal."

I turned on my heel and faced the still dangling Koucey.

"Come, my lord," I said gently. "Your rule here is ended, for now. I am in charge. And as my first act, let us tour your cellar."

*   *   *

The guards wisely stood aside as we descended the stairs to the cells under the donjon. I almost wanted them to start something that I could finish. I had a lot of pent-up frustration to be worked out.

We found Pentandra in her cell (the "nicest" of the four, as it had a kind of window in both the thick redwood door and also a vent above her), levitating about a foot off the filthy ground. There was a wry smile on her face as I made Koucey himself open the door. He did so quietly. I had tired of his babbling on the way down into the dungeon and quieted his voice with a spell, but his eyes still blazed in righteous indignation and his mouthed still moved in silent curses as he was compelled to do my bidding.

"About time you showed up," was all Penny said. She lowered her feet until they touched the floor, then stood up. "You took a lot longer than you should have."

"I was distracted," I said, as I embraced her.

"So what possessed the little runt to get rough with me?"

"Fear of losing his place to me. Garkesku and Cei – that's the Castellan – convinced him that I had designs on his miserable little fief, and suggested that he take direct command of the warmagi. He also didn't like the way you kept prattling on about us being all doomed, if we stayed at Boval Castle. Ironically, they put me into a position where I had to essentially take over and depose him to undo their mess."

"Idiots," she breathed. "It hasn't been a total waste, however. I've become well-acquainted with your friend Gurkarl. Charming fellow, for a gurvan. So what is all this about a sacred cave? It's fascinating. Gurkarl tried to explain it, but he doesn't know much outside of hagiography and propaganda."

"The Old God's cave, the Cavern of Karumala, is under this castle," I explained. "It's the most sacred of gurvani holy sites. As a matter of fact, we were just going to visit this lost wonder . . . weren't we, Koucey?"

The old knight's eyes continued to blaze, and his mouth worked rapidly. Thankfully nothing came out. I had had some initial misgivings about deposing the man, but the longer I dwelt on it, the better I felt about it. As long as I had my witchstone the chances of me hanging or being decapitated were acceptably low.

"You go to see the Sacred Cavern of Karumala?" came a gravelly voice from the next cell over. "Take me, I beg of you! Slay me afterward, if you so desire, but let my last sight in this world be to look upon it!" Gurkarl begged, his furry black hands protruding through the bars, beckoning.

"What do you think?" I asked Penny. She shrugged.

"Do you give me your parole?"

"Yes! Yes, a thousand times!"

"You will not try to escape?"

"Dragons could not drag me away from this holy place!" There was no trace of deceit in his voice.

"Okay," I said. I nodded towards Koucey, who objected silently but fervently. I arranged for him to get a little jolt of pain up and down his spine, and after enduring a moment of that he hurried to comply.

The massive wooden door squeaked open and Gurkarl bounded out, no worse for wear for his captivity that I could see. "I thank you Minalan. You are truly a credit to your species."

"It's nothing," I said, as graciously as I could. "Okay, Koucey, let's go to this place. Where is it?"

He looked at me blankly for a moment. I then realized what was wrong, and with a wave of my hand I dropped the spell that bound him.

"I had it sealed up behind a wall down here."

"Which wall?" He hesitated, and I raised my hand. He sighed and relented.

"At the end of the corridor. The original entrance was there. We built around it, and tried to destroy it, but no hammer could break the stone.

So I sealed it."

"Sounds like a magical cave to me," observed Penny, nodding her head.

"Lead on," I commanded him gruffly.

We found the spot, and sure enough it had been thoroughly bricked over. It looked like a mere blank wall, the end of a corridor. I got out a work wand – as opposed to a warwand – and traced a rough outline of a doorway on it. Using the power of the stone I pushed against the line, and in a few moments the blocks of stone tumbled away, revealing a dark and foreboding hole.

"A little light, Penny?"

"My pleasure." In moments a brightly glowing globe appeared between her hands, a perfect magelight, and with a shove it dove into the hole. Suddenly the interior of the cave was illuminated, and we peered in.

It was majestic, in a goblin sort of way.

The cavern was a roughly elongated oval about sixty paces long by forty paces wide, with a slight bend toward the center. The sides sloped gently up toward the roof, and crystals had been set at regular intervals, reflecting the glow of the magelight like a thousand tiny mirrors. The floor was mostly flat and covered in sand, but at the far end it sloped up, and toward the middle it was broken by a rock formation of some sort.

Every wall and the ceiling was covered by pictograms and hieroglyphs either carved or painted into the stone, and runic gurvani letters filled the space between them. As exhibitions of gurvani art go, it was impressive.

Some of the designs were obvious, like the gurvani thunder god, complete with stylized thunderbolt, leering down from a carefully painted mountaintop. Some were abstract to the extreme, lines and swirls that had no readily apparent meaning – it could have been some ancient language, I suppose.

The floor was littered with debris, most heaped into sorted piles. I could make out boot prints, perhaps of Koucey's father or grandfather, wandering the chamber from pile to pile. The cave had an empty feel to it, at the moment, but I could tell it had once been a center of activity and storage of important things. There was a cluster of little stone altars to my right, for example, that had obvious holes in them for some type of implements. There were spaces where objects had clearly rested for display in the past. Our goblin companion fell to his knees in awe.

"Gods of my fathers," Gurkarl croaked. "I am the first gurvan to view this cavern in almost two hundred years! Blessed am I!"

"When I was a boy," Koucey ventured, tentatively, "This chamber was filled with all sorts of foul junk. Much of it was gold and silver. There were many jewels. My father ordered it sorted. The valuables we sold to merchants. Some of the more vile creations were burnt. The rest we just left."

"It must have been impressive, once upon a time," I commented, stepping through the new-made doorway. I cast my own magelight to improve the illumination, and the shadows faded in its light.

"It was. Impressive and thoroughly evil. They sacrificed even their own kind to their foul gods. We found dozens of goblin heads in niches all along this wall, no doubt victims of barbaric sacrifice."

"Those were the heads of *my ancestors!*" Gurkarl snarled. "They were the kings and great shamans of the past! Their heads were placed here as a token of highest honor!"

"I've heard of the skull cult in the gurvani," Penny mentioned conversationally. "They believe the spirit of their ancestors reside in the head, rather than the heart."

"The custom is not limited to the gurvani," I replied. "The Crinroc have a cult of skulls, as do some of the other barbarian tribes in the Wilderlands and among the East Islanders."

"And like your Narasi ancestors?" she asked, eyebrows cocked jauntily. This was an old game that we played: she would advance the cause of Imperial culture, while I championed (weakly) the sometimes confusing customs of my people.

She was correct, in this instance. My forefathers had a fetish about collecting the severed heads of the Imperial soldiers who opposed them and stacking them in huge pyramids. And occasionally turning them into garish, ghoulish drinking vessels, so her comment stung a bit.

"Yes, actually, much like the head-collecting, horse-loving steppe barbarians . . . who toppled the Magocracy."

"A disgusting habit!" Koucey hissed bitterly.

"Depends on your culture," Pentandra shrugged. "The Cormeerans do some pretty icky things with their dead. They are considered an ancient and highly civilized people."

I walked over and began to examine the piles of cast-off ritual rubbish. The largest was mostly trash, bits of cloth and leather and bone, broken pottery and the like. I tugged out my blade and poked through it while Penny looked at another pile as Gurkarl gazed adoringly at the pictographs in the magelight.

Koucey stood near the entrance and pouted angrily. I wasn't particularly worried that he would start anything. I had dropped most of the control spells for him, but I had a few left that would snap back into place like a dog's leash at the first sign of trouble. He was behaving himself, for now, but I knew he would try something eventually.

I picked up two large pottery shards and fit them together. It was beautiful work, probably an oil lamp, with a primitive but vibrant design in vermilion and jet showing dancing gurvani figures and strange beasts intertwined. It spoke of a sophisticated culture, perhaps more advanced than where the gurvani found themselves today. I felt the faint remnants of the magic that had once inhabited them.

Gurkarl was right; this had been a reverent and holy place for many, many generations. Religious magic always has a certain feel about it, and this place felt like I was wading in it up to my hips.

I moved on to a charred and broken section of wood – some ancient shaman's staff, I gathered, from the shape and feel of it. There were no remaining spells, and it felt as if the entire thing had been expended in one last, desperate act of defiance. I pictured gnarled black, furry hands clutching the thing as the original owner fought to protect this shrine from defilement.

"Hey, what about these?" called Penny from one of the other piles. I dropped the shard of staff and came to look at what she had found. It proved to be a pile of parchment – well-cured animal skins, actually – covered with the runic gurvani language. In the absence of moisture and vermin – and perhaps because of the innate power within this place – they had remained relatively intact, though spots were burned here and there.

"Can you read gurvani?" I asked her.

"No, can you?"

"Nope. Gurkarl? Come here a moment, would you?"

The gurvan ambled over, a profound sense of contentment surrounding him despite the state of the temple. He halted at the pile and furrowed his brow at it.

"Holy books?" he asked.

"We were hoping you would know."

"I was a smith, not a shaman. I know my letters, but this is more than I can read. Without a lot of work," he amended.

"And you're not particularly anxious to provide aid and comfort to the enemy. I understand."

He shrugged his shaggy shoulders. "In a few days, it will not matter. The Old God is coming. The Great Ghost returns."

"Stop saying that!" Koucey howled from where he had slunk. "He is *not!* That is merely an evil heathen superstition! A damned lie to try to make us yield out of fear!"

The gurvan and I looked at each other, then at Koucey. "Well there is *something* coming," I said, slowly and deliberately, "and based on the magical power it has shown so far, it will flatten us like so many bugs, superstition or not." I turned back to the pile and Gurkarl. "Can you even tell me what they *might* be? I don't want to take a lot of trouble for your great-great-great aunt's gingerbread recipe. Well, I might, for the novelty value – my dad might be interested. But it would be helpful if I knew what they said."

He appeared to give it great thought, then nodded. "I will try. It will take me a while, and more light would be helpful." I raised my hand and another globe, smaller by half but twice as bright, came into existence over the pile. The gurvan grunted, then began sorting through the papers.

Penny moved on from the pile, more like she was eagerly moving through a busy market looking for a particular bolt of cloth than searching an ancient shrine for occult secrets. She didn't seem to be bothered by the ancient bones strewn about, or the musty smell of the cavern. I shrugged. Penny responded unusually in any situation. She had seemed perfectly content to languish in a prison cell, but I've seen her thrash a lazy serving girl for spilling soup and publicly humiliate tavern owners over the cleanliness of their establishments.

We continued poking around the cave noting a number of points of interest: shrines to gurvani gods, ancient stories told out in pictures, and plenty of magical enchantments written into the stone walls. There were strong sorceries still woven into the very rocks around us, I could feel. When I found broken and abandoned mining tools of human make I was able to verify that Koucey had sealed the place because he was, indeed, unable to destroy it.

That cave was a magical wonder. It was a fascinating study of gurvani magic and window on their ancient culture. I'd gotten mere glimpses of the subject before now, enough flashes of their magical methods during combat and the power of their enchantments on the goblin stones. I'd even started to recognize a few of their techniques, I'd thought, becoming familiar enough with them to perhaps find weaknesses. The magic in the cave thoroughly dismissed that notion as naive.

This was gurvani magic at its peak. The spells woven into the fabric of that space were complex tapestries of subtle spells, every bit as elaborate, ornate, and functional as the Imperial style of magic, in their way. Or, hell, I admitted to myself, as good as the Tree Folk's unique and potent system. The entire cave was a complex and delicate magical device with hundreds, nay, thousands of possible uses.

The runes so painstakingly painted or carved on the walls had bound within them intricate spells for working the weather, charms assisting the growth of crops, promoting fertility among the people, healing disease and wounds taken in battle, and appeals directly to the gods, from what I was able to determine with Gurkarl's help.

He might not have been a shaman, but he was knowledgeable enough to point out that spells for healing were held within the crystal formations, spells for religious initiation were worked into the walls in iron, and copper, the gurvani metal associated with fertility, was used to create a complex series of spells in the ceiling of the place.

I couldn't resist examining the place with a simple thaumaturgic essay, and either could Pentandra. What amazed me the most was how many of the formations seemed to have multiple uses. It rivaled the fabled Palace of the Archmage before my people ruined it, or the Tower of Gellmari at the peak of its power.

But it was also a terrible weapon. While I could not really say for certain, a good third of the spells about me had the sleek and deadly feel of warmagic. Some required living sacrifice – that much I could see – and some were so obscure and powerful that I classed them as martial by default. There were amplifiers and dampers and filters and all sorts of magical control mechanisms that would allow a little power to go a long way – and a lot of power to be devastating to their foes. Us, in other words.

I realized that a talented mage, if assisted with irionite, could be able to do a serious amount of damage to someone with those enchantments. A dozen or so magi who knew what they were doing would become unstoppable.

And the Old God had *hundreds* of shamans.

Was this, then, the answer to our prayers? This wonderful set of artifacts, this product of lifetimes of gurvani wizardry? Would it allow us to turn the tide and throw the Old God back into whatever crack he crawled from?

No, not really. This was goblin magic, and I knew nothing about it beyond basic arcane cognates and the occasional real-world experience. I considered it eagerly, though, just for some respite to the hopelessness I was feeling. The thought of using the cave to strike down the Old God, to drive his armies back and destroy him utterly was pretty appealing.

But I would have been a fool to mess around with a magical style I wasn't familiar with even as a trained thaumaturge with irionite. I couldn't even read or speak their language, and that would be essential if I was to understand the basics about how that cavern worked.

Sure, there were a few things that I was pretty sure I could use, given time to study them, like the spells for prosperity and fecundity and increasing the fish supply. But that dark tangle of warspells scared me. I would use them only in a suicidal rage.

"While you are down here," Koucey said, after clearing his throat loudly, "perhaps your brilliant mind could clear up a mystery." He walked over to a roundish hillock of rock that sloped up from the floor and into a flat, clear space on the wall.

"We always thought that this altar was used for a particularly cruel sacrificial death, hanging upside down while disemboweled, for example. But that never seemed to be right. There was no idol, see, in front of it. Just a circle cut into the rock, ringed by stones. Some of them were precious, and removed, as was the gold. But why would anyone sacrifice to a god of . . . *nothing?*"

"There were some old Imperial cults who worshiped in Rada, goddess of emptiness, back during the Early Magocracy's Decadent period," Penny offered. "It was stylish for a while, but she was never popular. Who wants to go talk about nothing all night?"

"I can't see this being a salon for the sophisticated courtiers of the Imperial nobility," I replied, dryly. "Of course, your folk did have some pretty depraved ideas during that period. No, Koucey is right." I studied the thing more closely, slipping up a more and more detailed form of magesight as I did so. As it settled over me, I was startled nearly into speechlessness. This was no ordinary altar. I did some cursory thaumaturgic essays and swallowed, hard.

I quickly came to the conclusion that the area around the blankness was also the center of what the Imperials call a *molopor,* or arcane spatial insecurity.

This is a complex subject which I'm going to attempt to paraphrase, so don't get upset if you don't understand it the first few times around. I know I had several sleepless nights wrestling with this concept back when I was taking Advanced Magical Theory during my thaumaturgy courses at the Academy.

Consider a piece of cloth. From five feet away, it appears solid, a sheet of fabric. From two inches away it becomes a rolling landscape of intertwining threads. Get even closer and it becomes something else entirely. No matter how sturdy the cloth, there are going to be places where it is weaker than others. Nor will it be uniform.

Take my sister's first piece of loom work, for example. In places the threads were so thick that they formed lumps, while in others the threads were so thin that you could see through them. Even the best pieces of storm-rated sailcloth will develop rips and tears along weak spots. And there are always weak spots, no matter how masterful the weaver. If you looked very carefully at a piece of cloth you could find the thinnest spot and push a needle or something right through it with very little effort.

Reality is like that cloth, except that it isn't flat, it isn't woven, and it isn't particularly cloth-like in any other way, save to poets and to weavers. But in this case it's a useful metaphor.

Without devolving into technical jargon, there are places where the very "fibers" of reality are so thick that magic has trouble working there. There are also places where reality is so weak that it occasionally rips and tears for an instant, and sometimes things slip through, tear, or other catastrophes occur. This was all theory, mind you, but it was theory backed up by centuries of thaumaturgical experimentation.

Lodestones had something to do with it, it was thought, as were the arcane mathematics of astrology, but the standing theory had been that it was possible to discover naturally-occurring "thin spots" in reality. The theory also suggests that if one had masterful control and access to a gargantuan amount of power, one could press a metaphysical "needle" through it. Why one would want to do this, except for the pure curiosity of it, is beyond me.

A *molopor* isn't really a thing, an event, or even a place, but it can be all of them. The thaumaturges of the Magocracy loved hunting them down and cataloging them, though why one would want to do this outside of pure curiosity is beyond me. There are variations. There are even regularly occurring, fairly stable *molopors* which seem to "move" and transform with the regularity of the planets and tides. A *molopor* is, first and foremost, an *extreme condition of reality*, and the truth is we really don't know shit about them, save how to occasionally identify them.

Some are famous, like the two called the Twins near a waterfall in Sabra, where strange bolts of fire sometimes shoot out into the river for no good reason, or the irregularly appearing thing out over the ocean the seamagi know as the Stormbringer because it was supposed to (surprise!) affect the weather. You can't move one, and they rarely move themselves, though it has happened.

There have been others recorded, but most were unstable, fleeting affairs that could rain fish on a town or create enigmatic patterns in wheat fields overnight, hang around for a few hours, days or weeks, then fade into . . . existence?

Simply put, a *molopor* is a weak spot that could, theoretically, be connected to any conceivable point, points, place, places, time or times in the universe.

Magic worked easier around the vicinity of most *molopors*, it had been suggested, due to the more plastic nature of reality in the area. Needless to say they are extremely rare and difficult to detect, and their very existence had sparked centuries-old controversies in erudite circles about the very nature of the universe. A stable *molopor*, and its equally immovable, anti-magical opposite, the *jevolar* (like the famous-to-magi one on the island of Unstara), was a natural curiosity.

This one was massive, compared to the reports of others I'd read. And it had been discovered by the gurvani and improved. If a "regular" *molopor* was a thin spot, then this thin spot had been reinforced. Consider it a grommet in the fabric of space-time. In effect, a portal to . . . where?

Or when?

Or . . . *what?*

The possibilities taxed my imagination, and I realized then why the Old God wanted the place back so badly. If the Great Ghost had as much power at his disposal as he seemed to, then this place would make him about as omnipotent as a deity could ask for. With power, the theory runs, you can use an arcane "needle" to traverse through (or around, opinions varied) the *molopor* to elsewhere. And possibly get back. With stuff.

A molopor this size, arcane reinforced as it was, had enormous potential, I realized. Here the Old God had a direct connection to worlds and planes of his choosing. It would take a lot of power and some seriously sophisticated spellwork, but he seemed to have an endless supply of irionite and an army of devoted – nay, fanatical – followers.

A pity he wanted to kill off my entire race. With this, he might be able to manage to.

"So," Sire Koucey asked after he had decided I had studied it enough. "What *is* it?"

I sat down in front of it and tried to remain calm. In the proximity of my sphere it could be quite dangerous to let the absolute fear that was rising up my gullet manifest itself magically if I was too close to it.

But the consequences were clear enough. I began to feel old, and tired, so *very* tired of all of this. Despair beckoned to me, inviting me to just give up, while anger and fear insisted that my tired body and my over-wrought mind do everything in its power to keep the Old God and the *molopor* from ever meeting. Somewhere in the middle they crashed, and there was little I could do about it. But at least a few more things made sense.

"It's a magical gateway to pretty much anywhere, if you can find a way through. I can't tell without a far better understanding of gurvani magic, but I believe that this portal, when activated, could lead to anywhere in the world. Or any other world. Or to a lake of fire, the bottom of an ocean, a poisonous hell, or to nothing at all. This hole in the wall surrounds a rip in reality, or something like that. When the Old God gets here, he will be able to use it to do pretty much anything he wants."

Koucey looked shocked. "Then we must destroy it!"

"Impossible."

"Nothing is impossible," he said, gallantly.

"Actually, destroying the *molopor* would be. You see, there isn't an 'it' to be destroyed. Even if you could disable the protection spells and bring this cavern down around it, it would still be here. You could flood it, burn it, hit it with a rock or pelt it with pillows, *it still would be there.* It will be here long after these mountains have eroded away. You can do anything to it because there's nothing to act upon. Just through."

"So it's dangerous?"

"Not on its own – I don't think. But yes, this *molopor* could well be our doom if Old Grouchy gets control of it."

"Then the Old God must be stopped!" Koucey announced, as if by will alone it could be accomplished. Plenty of noble fighting spirit left in the old bird.

"The Old God *cannot* be stopped!" Gurkarl called out from where he was crouched by the manuscripts. Penny returned from her snooping to see what all the commotion was about.

"Both of you *shut up!*" While it felt good to say it, my feelings fueled the desire. The silence spell that I'd used so recently on Koucey was back up, and extended to the gurvan as well. I shook my head when I'd realized what I'd done and started to take it down when I stopped. A few moments of peace would be welcome, I decided.

I didn't get it. Pentandra had overheard us.

"This is a *molopor*?" she asked, intensely interested, "Like the Twins?"

"Yes, it is. At least I think it is. A real, honest-to-gods stable *molopor*, augmented by ancient gurvani shamans to let them travel anywhere, and bring anything to them that they wanted. I think. Probably an artifact left over from the wars between the Alka Alon and the gurvani a few thousand years ago. By itself, that would be amazing. Put it together with the magic in this cavern, and it's a wonder how the gurvani ever lost *any* war."

"I think it could be that they forgot how to use it. Min, some of these enchantments are *thousands* of years old. I'm not a specialist in magical archeology, or even as good a thaumaturge as you are, but if the results of my tests are correct, the most recent spells used here were the ones devoted to fertility and prosperity, along with the war spells.

"Primitive tribal magic," I nodded. "It also explains why it's so easy to do magic in this vale. Not much in the way of resistance, thanks to this thing."

"Yes. But there are great works here that haven't been used in millennia, truly sophisticated spells. It hints at a much more sophisticated thaumaturgy than the shamanic magic they practice now. The gurvani seem to have had a pretty advanced civilization, once – but that was a *long* time ago, long before the Magocracy, even. Possibly before humanity came from the Void. I wonder if the Old God could date from that time?"

"It would make a lot of sense. But how, exactly? Time travel? With the *molopor* that would be theoretically possible – and it would explain why he wants it back so badly. Or perhaps he's just been asleep? There are theoretical stasis spells that would preserve someone in a time-free environment. Cerd Larne did some impressive experiments a few decades ago. Such a spell would not be beyond the ancient gurvani, if these enchantments are any example of their craft. And, of course, there is the possibility that he is just a regular old pissed-off deity of vengeance."

"Does it matter?" she asked, shaking her head so her hair flopped gracefully over her shoulder. "If he's coming here, we can assume for the sake of argument that it isn't for the mystical and cultural importance of the site. He's *after* that thing. So we had better decide if there is some way we can use it against him."

"It won't hurt to look," I said, grinning wryly. There was no reason that the *molopor* wouldn't react poorly to our examination and fry us in the process, but I was becoming so accustomed to fatalistic despair that I was unconcerned with the possibility – considering our situation, accidental death suddenly looked pretty appealing.

I turned back to the *molopor* and reflected on this force of nature that was neither matter nor energy, but mere potential. In magesight it barely registered. It didn't glow with the brightness of magic, except at the perimeter, it merely glowered darkly, a faint, dark purple disc hovering in space.

But the tracery of spells around the perimeter, which I assumed were designed to control the manner and type of magical force employed, made a brilliant and elaborate spider web that stretched the length of the cavern. I tried to trace the lines of control that emanated from the rim of the stone and gave up it up as futile a moment later. Gurvani magic was just too strange for me to recognize more than basic lines of force.

Finding the device was academically fascinating, and certainly strategically significant, I knew – *but how could I turn this to my advantage?* If I couldn't keep the Great Ghost away from it, was there any way I could use it myself to good effect?

I could try to open the portal myself, I reasoned, and by force of will alone have it transport me someplace safe, like under my parent's bed back home. Without the supporting enchantments the gurvani had used to refine its use, however, I doubted I would have the strength or the control to undertake such a potent spell. Thaumaturgy demands that a spell of that kind needs an abundance of both. And you don't mess around with something as powerful and unknown as a *molopor*.

More likely I would be killed in the attempt. The forces involved were titanic, and if I was already casting spells without conscious thought, then I wasn't nearly focused enough to even give it a try. There were limits to the capacities of my irionite, I knew, and we'd bump into those fairly quickly if we tried to use it. Not to mention my personal limits. That kind of powerful spell takes a toll on the mage, and the human body – not to mention the human mind – has limits.

But perhaps one of the other magi would have an idea about that. True, most of the warmagi were young and experienced only in war spells, but many of them had studied particularly arcane areas. Terleman might have some thoughts on it. I wish Sandoval was here – he was a great thaumaturge, almost as good as I was. But we had a wealth of talent to work with and I was hopeful. A meeting of the minds might produce a better answer, I reasoned.

My thoughts were interrupted by Penny, who was thoughtfully chewing her lip. I still found that adorable, despite my feelings for Alya. "Min, you mentioned something about *kirsieth*, that evergreen tree?"

"Yeah. My research shows strong support for the theory that *kirsieth* sap is the building block for irionite. Why do you ask?"

"Um, don't quote me on this," she said, carefully, "but I *think* I can design a spell that will actually activate this thing. And control it. That's the good news. But it depends upon whether or not we can generate sufficient power, and hold it for enough time. But if we did . . ."

". . . then we might be able to establish a kind of portal to . . . well, to somewhere else! Anywhere else!"

"Exactly," she sighed.

"Uh, that's bloody *great* news," I answered cautiously. "How much power are you talking?"

She told me, in technical thaumaturgical jargon. It was a lot. More than our individual stones were capable of, I was certain. There are other ways to manifest and augment power, though, as any good thaumaturge knows.

"Ishi's tits! Are you considering human sacrifice, then? That's about the *only* thing I know of that . . . If we had the power to . . . oh . . . I think I see what you . . . oh . . . well? . . . I guess . . ." I stumbled as my questions answered themselves.

"What seems to be the problem?" asked Sire Koucey. "Can't . . . do whatever it is without sacrificing babies?" he asked, curiously.

"That would be one way to do it," admitted Penny. "But it wouldn't be my first choice."

"Then what?" Koucey asked, insistently. Penny and I looked at each other, a long and searching look. Yes, that's what she was thinking.

I heaved a great sigh. This was going to take some serious explanation.

Chapter Fourteen

A Plan To Escape

"The greater magics in the history of the Magocracy were done with meticulous planning and a surety of the outcome that non-magi have come to fear and respect, yet some rites involve deplorable rituals that cut to the core of all human decency. The more lurid and outrageous the practice, from Necromancy to Prophecy to so-called Sex Magic, the greater the fear invoked in the layman. Therefore, as it is doubtful that these practices have any true arcane usefulness, the study and proliferation of these deviant rites shall be prescribed, save by sages and scholars who understand fully the dubious nature of these rites, under the guidance of the Royal Censorate of Magic."

- *The Royal Bans On Magic*

"Now tell me again just how *nailing your old girlfriend* is going to save all our lives?" asked Alya, with a sarcastic toss of her head. There was a blaze behind her eyes that made me uncomfortable. Hell, it *scared* me. I'd rather fight a squad of Black Skulls than face a wronged woman.

"It has to do with the nature of magical power," I tried to explain for the fourth or fifth time. "In order to open one of these portals, you need a truly *massive* amount of energy, properly tuned and augmented, more than even a highly trained group of magi could generate on their own."

"But you have *witchstones* . . ." she said, angrily. "I thought—"

"The irionite gives us a way of amplifying that power, certainly – I wouldn't even make the attempt without it. But even when we are using the stones they are not exactly producing arcane energy, merely amplifying the energy we send through them. If we want to open this portal, and keep it open long enough to do any good, then it will require every shred of power that we can muster. And iron control over that power, tuned properly and directed with incredible precision.

"Now I could lecture you for hours about the various ways to raise power. Drugs can be used, when you have the right ones in the right dosage and you know what you are doing. Chanting works if you have a few weeks and a devout enough group who likewise knows what they are doing, and we just don't have the time for that. A lot of tribes use dancing, but that takes years of practice to do effectively."

"I don't really see you as much of a dancer," she said. I didn't know if she was trying to be mean, or humorous, or both.

"You'd be surprised. No, there are only two ways that I know of to generate a tremendous amount of raw arcane power in a short period of time.

"Blood sacrifice works terrifically well, and is possibly how the gurvani who found this cave did it at first. But I don't see anyone volunteering, and, to be honest, I'm just not the kind of mage that can handle the ethical questions involved, never mind the fact that it's been banned since Imperial times. Death magic is a potent and dangerous realm, but it's one way to achieve our means.

"The other is by tapping into the opposite realm, the realm of creation and procreation – from the sacred fount of Life itself. *Enormous* amounts of power are available there, if you know how to capture it and make use of it. Every time a baby is born, there is a powerful release of arcane energy from that side of things, and occasionally it can manifest magically. I suppose if we had a few dozen pregnant women who could all go into labor at once, that might work – but there aren't that many here, and trying to arrange that kind of timing is just impractical.

"So that leaves banging your old girlfriend? I'm starting to favor human sacrifice."

"Well . . . yes. Sex magic pulls the same kind of power, but it's a lot easier to arrange and maintain. And sexual magic has other advantages, as well," I said, as enthusiastically as I could. "It can be sustained over time, whereas blood sacrifice is over pretty quickly. It doesn't leave a stain on the Otherworld, the way sacrifice does – or birth, for that matter. You have a lot more control over it. It can be more gently manipulated, making it easier to focus into the proper sphere. And, luckily, Pentandra has spent most of her professional career studying that particular branch of the Art. She's probably the world's foremost living expert on it. And I worked with her long enough to know what to do, myself."

"Yes," she hissed acidly, *"aren't we lucky?"*

"We are, when you think about it," I said, trying to sound nonchalant and matter-of-fact and reasonable. I don't think I was selling it. I noticed my voice was a little higher and squeakier than normal. "Of all the magi who could have come here, one of the top experts in her specialty landed in our laps just when we needed her the most. No one knows better how to generate and manipulate that kind of power. With her expertise there to support us, the rest of the group can deal with weaving the power to activate and control the portal."

"I just can't understand why you can't do *that* part," she complained. "Why can't she slut around with one of the other guys? I know for a fact that she has slept with at least four of them!"

"Because I was her study partner for *three years,* and not just a casual liaison. There's a big difference when you have two magi who know what they're doing, instead of one and a willing subject. And to be honest, we were a *great* team. No other partner has ever been able to raise as much power or with such control as I did, she said," I said, proudly.

"I bet she did! You men will believe *anything!*"

"She knows me, how I act and react, how to wheedle every last nuance of energy from a run," I said, weakly. "And I know *her.* Together we can build significantly more power and of the right kind than any two other magi present. And, if I do say so myself, we can keep it up as long as we need to."

"I'm sure you can," she said, icily. "You all say that sort of thing!" She stared at me for a moment, then, and sighed, her mask of the scorned woman crumbling to reveal for a moment the image of a scared young girl. "Look, are you sure there is no other way?"

"If there was, I would have thought of it by now. Hells, I'm not even guaranteeing that *this* will work. It's just our best chance of any of us getting out of here alive. We can't even send for more help through the Otherworld. Whatever else we tried, the barrier that the Old God has put up around us would keep it from working." For the last few days we had all become aware of a kind of arcane bubble – stronger than regular wardings – that had intercepted every attempt we'd made to even scry beyond the valley. And we had all noted that it was only growing in strength.

"But the molopor portal works – theoretically – in proportion to the proximity of the mage, and right now we are closer to it than *he* is. In three or four more days, though, it won't matter. He will be close enough to kill us a thousand other horrible ways. Probably by ritual sacrifice, to fuel spells to use the portal himself."

Alya was quiet for a long time, looking at her hands. "So you really *do* need to nail your old girlfriend to save us."

It was my turn to sigh. "I promise I won't enjoy it, okay? It will just be work. I'll be thinking of you the whole time," I added, with a little desperation. "Look, my love, we *need* to do this, we really do. It's our only possible means of escape – for all of us. If it even works. I'm sorry if you are upset by it – and I can't really blame you for that – but it needs to be done whether you like it or not. I don't expect you to stand next to us and cheer us on, but I had hoped that you would trust me enough to know that I wouldn't be doing this if I didn't *have* to. I just wish you would understand." Her eyes flashed.

"I guess it's just too much for a poor little ignorant peasant girl like me would understand. You've already taken over the castle – I hear

Koucey is confined to his chambers – and so I guess pushing aside some country wench that was warming your bed is pretty small game in the scheme of things!"

"I am *not* pushing you aside!" I said, raising my voice. "I don't lust after power, and don't pull that 'poor little peasant girl' routine on me! I – I *love* you, Alya. I'm awfully fond of Penny, and she's a wonderful friend and a great colleague, but I love *you*. This is just business. I want to spend my life with you, not her. I want you to continue to warm my bed, among other places, assuming that we don't burn out our brains in the process of doing this."

"That sounds like a load of --"

"*Enough!*" It was my turn to get a little emotive. She seemed to be purposefully exasperating. "Woman, I just pled my *undying love* for you, and you can't retract your claws long enough to listen to me? We are going to be dead in a week unless I do this! I've already risked my neck a thousand times for you and your people, and only survived because it amuses some capricious god or goddess to play with my fate like a toy. Well, fine. I can put up with all that, because I've found *you* in the bargain.

"Of course, you are too busy indulging in a jealous fit to realize that I'm doing everything I can – including nailing my ex-girlfriend! – to preserve what we have, and what we *might* have, together."

There were tears in her eyes. She walked sullenly over to me and I prepared myself for a slap. Instead I found her entwined in my arms.

"Just don't enjoy it, all right?" she whispered through her tears.

"I will do my best," I promised, holding her tightly. "I really wished you two liked each other. That would make all of this a lot easier."

"I guess that we would have run into each other eventually. She's a part of your life. But the whole 'I'm an Imperial Noble and a Mighty Sorceress' thing of hers really *gets* to me, sometimes."

I had to chuckle. "Yeah, it does, doesn't it? Me, too. She really is a nice person, when you get beyond that. Remember, she grew up in a crumbly old villa, raised by servants, schooled by the best tutors, and ignored by her parents until she developed Talent. She didn't have the advantages we did growing up – chasing each other with sticks, playing in the mud in the commons, making each other eat dog poop." That brought a ragged smile to her face, like a ray of sun through a thunderhead. "So feel sorry for her. But don't *hate* her."

"I'll try," she said, sniffling.

"I hope you will. Because you are right: she will always be a part of my life. I fully expect her to dance at my wedding."

"Minalan?" Alya asked, looking me in the face.

"What?"

"Uh, assuming we aren't dead any time soon, that may occur sooner than you planned. If you really *did* plan it, that is, and aren't just saying what a silly farm girl wants to hear."

"Uh, what do you mean?" I asked, troubled.

"I think I'm pregnant. I should have bled two weeks ago."

That was unexpected.

"Are . . . are you *sure?*" I asked, when the words managed to penetrate my whirling brain. The whole world stopped while I waited for her answer.

"Hey, aren't *you* a spellmonger? Usually you lot can check on this kind of thing? Magic, spells, charms . . . "

"Right! Yes, it's a pretty simple spell, a mere scrying technique, really, and--"

"Well, quit babbling and *do it!*" she snapped, frustrated. "I've been worried about this for weeks, and haven't been able to tell you. If I have to go one more day – one more hour! – I think I'm going to scream."

Pregnancy would explain why she was behaving more moodily than usual. My mind did its best to focus on the practical in the face of the deeply personal news, but it was suddenly having trouble. "Uh, yeah, sure," I said in a daze, fetching my sphere from its pouch on my weapons belt. She stood there expectantly (no pun intended) while I did the preliminaries. When I realized I was stalling I went ahead and did it, before she realized I was stalling.

In moments an image of her innards entered my mind. I was pretty familiar with anatomy, particularly her anatomy, and though I wasn't adept at the type of magics worked by hedgewitches and midwives, finding the swollen uterus proved easy. In magesight all of her body's energies centered on it. It took only a little more probing, a slight focus to my attention.

And there it was. A tiny, wormlike grub that would all too soon be the size of a standard-issue baby.

"Uh," I said, eloquently.

"What does *that* mean? Professionally speaking?" she asked wryly.

"Uh," I said again. "Uh, you are really, definitely pregnant."

"With *your* child," she added.

"Apparently," I said, my world spinning around me.

"If you have doubts as to the paternity I invite you to investigate them," she said, icily. "But whatever the princess says about me to the contrary, I haven't been with anyone but you since my husband died. The little bastard is *yours*."

"You sound pretty happy about it," I commented, stonefaced.

"I *am!* I wanted a child so badly. When my husband died, I never thought I'd get another chance. Until I met you. But I can see by the look on your face that this is not automatically a happy thing for you. Look, if this is a problem, then I can go my own way. Assuming that we live to the next full moon, that is."

"No! No, that isn't what I meant. I'm just stunned. And confused."

"And a daddy."

"Yeah, that's the part that is stunning and confusing me. *Trygg's toenails!* Why didn't you tell me sooner?"

"I didn't want to distract you from your work, so I didn't even mention the possibility before. But I vomited twice since yesterday, and I can suddenly smell like a bloodhound. This morning I broke down into tears for no good reason. So it seemed like a good time to bring it up."

"I'm glad you did," I said, not really even hearing my own words.

My entire personal universe had just altered significantly. Everything, from my recent usurpation of power to my long-shot scheme for rescuing us to my relationships with both Alya and Penny, was in flux; all of that shifted in perspective. Evil dark lords and goblin hordes and magic portals and traitorous wizards all faded into unimportance as the weight of the idea started to bear on me.

I suppose every man, when confronted with this situation, finds himself at a crossroad where one way leads towards acceptance, where you embrace the idea of fatherhood. The other way also beckons, that almost irresistible urge to put as many leagues between you and the mother and the lifelong responsibility as possible. And then, like a legal case, you are shown evidence for making that decision by the lawbrother of your conscience.

Perhaps it is a judge of your deepest character; perhaps it is a primitive reaction to an inherent biological condition, but every man, no matter how much he thinks he knows the answer before the question is asked, I think, has to go to the deepest corner of his soul to make that choice.

Interestingly enough, my arguments against embracing the pregnancy were mostly based on the normally sane fear of the unknown. I really liked, no, I really, truly *loved* Alya; there was no doubt in my mind, based on my short but intense acquaintance with her, that she would be a superlative mother to any child. What would this do to our relationship? Pregnancy and motherhood change a woman.

They also change a man. My own role as a father I doubted more. After all, who was *I* to be a father? I felt as if I had only recently stopped being a child myself. Mostly. Maybe.

What decided the matter, actually, was the briefest flash of memory from my own childhood.

I must have been about two, maybe a little older, sitting in the kitchen with Mama and getting in the way of her skinning some river tubers that I never liked. My youngest sister was also there, maybe helping a little more than she was destroying.

Suddenly, the door to the bakery burst open and my father was standing there, covered from head to toe with flour. He had wetted it into his hair, spiking it up in a grotesque mockery of horns, and twirled his beard into little floury ringlets like a white-gray thorn bush. In retrospect there may have been spirits on his breath.

It took me a frightened moment to realize that it was Dad, and when I did I still squealed. His eyes wide and maniacal, he began chasing me around the kitchen making growly noises every time I screamed. My heart raced, my eyes were whirling, and I was enraptured. But not nearly as much as he.

I remembered this moment vividly; I could smell the bread baking, the fresh green smell of the tubers, the taste of flour in the air. And I saw the ecstatic look on my father's face as he played Flour Monster with his only son.

And then for a frozen instant I saw *my* face under the flour instead of Dad's. I saw the same expression, same look of enchantment in my eyes. I could imagine perhaps what it was like to chase a two-year-old around, and then tickling them to death while your wife looks on with a smile warm enough to proof dough.

I took the road that I hoped led to *that*.

*   *   *

Alya's news had not stopped the world nearly as long as I would have liked it to. Around us the castle bustled with people going about under my orders.

While it was true that I had officially confined Koucey to his quarters, the rumor that I was going to have him executed the following dawn was not. Indeed, once he was made to realize that our position was untenable and that I had a better alternative than fighting bravely to the last man, he had become very cooperative.

While he was in his quarters a stream of messengers ran to and fro, conveying his bidding to his men. He had given his unconditional parole, agreed to cooperate fully, and to be honest I think he was happy to be relieved of the responsibility of over-all command of the castle.

The little rat Garkesku, on the other hand, was nowhere to be found. Not that we looked too hard. His remaining apprentice started haunting my quarters, and I kind of adopted Rondal as a result. He proved to be truly helpful, even if there was some friction between him and Tyndal. There was plenty of work for two apprentices, though, so that kept them from getting into fights.

Everyone else was as busy. If we were going to pull this off without disaster striking, there was a lot we had to do. I had three dozen peasant women stuffing and sewing a pile of cast-off clothes into a small army of dummies, which began filling up the guard positions on the battlements. A few of the younger warmagi were giving them slight magical dweomers to make them seem alive, at least to casual scrying.

I put the Castellan, good ol' grumpy Sir Cei, to work judging which personal items would be approved for travel through the portal. That caused a lot of squawking, especially among the peasants, some of whom thought of chickens and piglets as "irreplaceable goods." Sir Cei was perfect for the job. It took a fanatic to argue with the man once his mind was set. Only a dozen or so cases were appealed to my judgment, and with two exceptions I backed the crusty castellan's ruling.

The mercenaries were also grumbling over leaving behind horses and weapons that they had grown fond of. I gave them a little more leeway, but was still strict. I, myself, was not happy with the prospect of leaving Traveler here to become the main course at a gurvani luncheon, but as much as I loved that rouncey, he was still just a horse.

The Crinroc, too, were unruly about abandoning their possessions, though they were more pragmatic than the Bovali peasantry. They left their wagons and livestock, but were defiantly unwilling to leave behind about two hundred two-foot tall totem statues that had some religious significance. In the end I acquiesced. They weren't willing to leave them behind, and I wasn't about to leave the Crinroc behind.

Preparation for departure was just part of the plan. I continued the routine terror raids by the warmagi against the gurvani, for a couple of good reasons. While the remaining shamans had tightened up their operations and security, they were ultimately unable to stop my men from pillaging another four or five more witchstones. When that produced a couple of haphazard assaults on the gates in response by overeager goblins, I even allowed two brief sorties by the regular cavalry, a kind of last glorious run with their steeds before we left.

But going after witchstones was only part of the plan. Each warmagi raid left a trail of destruction in its wake and provided enough distractions so that my sabotage teams of warmagi were able to complete their own clandestine missions. These were designed to mess up goblin communications and logistics as much as possible. While we didn't have a chance against the Old God, there was no reason to leave his forces unmolested before he showed up.

And that factor was foremost on everyone's minds. The overbearing presence of the Old God on the horizon could be felt by nearly everyone with a shred of magical sensitivity. We could see past the mountains a few miles, to the extent his barrier allowed, but westward there was a shimmering in the air over the peaks the kind of distortion you get when there's a lot of ambient magic in the air. It became especially florid at dusk. So did the sense of oppressiveness. There was no denying that every dusk was worse than the previous one. While the approach of impending doom did little for morale, it kept everyone *extremely* motivated about his or her tasks. No one wanted to be here when he arrived.

Meanwhile, I stayed in conference with the team I had chosen to help us open the portal, direct it, and keep it open. We continued to meet in the Cave, itself, usually with Gurkarl helpfully providing translation of some of the gurvani texts that discussed the matter. He had been a model prisoner, almost one of the team, once we'd allowed him access. He was certainly no longer Shereul's creature.

He was almost smug about it. Since he had seen and dwelled in the sacred cave he had seemed to transcend the pettiness of the Old God's rampage, readily helping us with our plans as the best way to accomplish the goal of cleaning the valley of all *humani* influences.

The others were wary of including an admitted foe into the midst of our most secret councils, but I invited any of them to find a single spell on him that tied the gurvan to his former leaders. Besides, his gruff voice and odd accent concealed an offbeat sense of humor to our discussions that kept things cordial under tense circumstances.

The core team stood at seven, excluding Gurkarl. Penny and myself would be the energy providers; Carmella was the Transformer, controller of the various *apis* that we would need in the course of this spell – really a director of power and monitor of our physical bodies. Terleman helped design the specifics and would act as a back-up to Carmella or Delman or Taren, if needed.

Delman would direct our energy out to the other magi, who would then spin it up to reality-altering levels, before shooting it back through Reylan, who would act as a Converter, taking all of that raw power and building it into a coherent wave.

Then there was Taren, a mage not too much older than me, with whom I had studied briefly at the Academy. While trained as a warmage, Taren had been one of the few who had been so gifted that he was selected for advanced study at the War College instead of normal duty. He missed the Farisian Campaign entirely, electing, instead, to pursue his studies without being shot at. I don't remember being given a choice, but maybe I'm just not that good. Taren would be our Focus. He had spent the longest time at Inrion Academy, and that's where we were trying to go.

That might sound like an unusual choice of destination, but it made sense in a lot of ways. First, it was a place that most of us were familiar with. Many of us had gone to school there, so we knew it like a farmer knows his chicken coop. There was a lot of residual magic there, some going back to the Magocracy, which theoretically made it a bigger target for Taren to latch onto. While the distance was far greater than, say, one of the larger cities in Alshar, we couldn't really decide if distance had anything to do with it. I was pretty sure it didn't.

Taren had suggested attempting to anchor the other end of the portal – assuming we could activate it – to an old and crumbling memorial archway in one of the courtyards of the Academy. It dated from Imperial times, some benefactor of the school no doubt had it built to celebrate the glory of the Magocracy, or some crap like that. No one knew for certain.

But it was there, made a good theoretical anchor point, and should be mostly deserted. Taren said he found it a perfect place to study, and I fondly recalled one rare and memorable assignation I had there with one of the local girls from Towertown at the Midsummer festival. I never saw her again, and don't really remember her name, but I'll never forget that night. Others had similar memories to help reinforce the target so we aimed for the Academy.

It didn't take long to decide the most basic issues, like who did what. We played to our strengths as magi. The problems came in executing such an intricate spell. Imperial training covered the basics for what we were doing, but no one had tried anything like this, with irionite, no less, since the Magocracy fell. Not to my knowledge. We were improvising, making some pretty large assumptions, and hoping and praying a lot. And cursing. Not really textbook-standard thaumaturgy.

It took almost six hours just to hammer out the particulars for the spell. We did two rehearsals, using minor cantrips to stand for the more serious power we would generate, and made certain everyone knew their part.

There was the usual grandstanding and juvenile complaining that you get anytime you try to get more than three people to do one thing at a time, but then again these were highly motivated professionals with their own lives on the line. The tangible sense of doom that was only a day or two away, at most, gave us a sense of urgency to get this *right*. We would not have a second chance. The hour of departure was set for dawn the next day.

Not that you could really see the sun anymore. Shereul had darkened the sky, making Boval Castle a goblin playground all day and all night.

*   *   *

I awoke long before dawn the next morning with my face pressed into Alya's sweet-smelling hair. I restrained the impulse to make love to her one last time. As sweet as it would have been, it would have depleted me of my vitality prematurely. I settled for holding her and smelling her hair until I could brook no more delay.

"You remember what I said?"

"Yes, my lord," she said sarcastically as she pulled her shift on over her head. She'd taken to calling me that since I'd "usurped" Sire Koucey and "conquered" the domain. "Take your baggage through to the Academy grounds. Find some old codger named Master Hesclesti and give him your letter and journal. Then tell my story to the authorities, whoever they are. Wait for word from you for three fortnights, then take the small fortune you have given me and use it to get to your parent's house with Tyndal, along with the depressing note about how you are dead, so that they can take care of me and your unborn bastard."

"A little dramatic," I concluded, "but essentially correct. Tell my folks that I love them."

"You tell them yourself," she said, sliding up next to me for a last hug and kiss. "Now get down there and screw your ex-girlfriend for the good of the people!"

"Al-ya!" I groaned. "I thought you were past this?"

"No, seriously. Give her an inch from me," she said, swatting me on the butt. "Ring her bell hard. And a lot."

I'll never understand her. Or any woman. But *particularly* her. Perhaps that's why I had fallen so hard for her, and why leaving her standing there, pregnant and packing, was high on the list of the most difficult things I have ever had to do in my life.

I made my way down into the Cave and tried not to think about what I was going to do, else my doubts about our success would undermine the attempt. Once I got there, most of the others were already standing around, drinking hot cups of sweet mulled wine (the bastards had raided what was left of Koucey's cellar and been holding out on me!) and taking the herbs they would need to sustain them through the spell.

Penny had our little pharmacopeia laid out on one of the old altars for me to inspect before she dosed me: no less than six different powders and herbs prepared in various ways. Three of them I knew, the other three I took without comment. Penny knows her stuff, and I trusted in that.

While I waited for the drugs to take effect, I wandered around and talked to each member of each team, joking, laughing nervously, and double-checking that everything was prepared. That was as much as for their benefit as my own, I guess. They had formed as tight-knit a team as I could ask for in this last week, aided, of course, by the potent power of the witchstones and the fear of immanent doom. They were a good team – young, skilled, ambitious. When I had done all the reassuring I was capable of, I wandered over to the *molopor* soon-to-be portal and stared at it for a while.

Could we do this? *Really?*

There was no doubt that it had been done in the past. The gurvani records Gurkarl had translated were certain on that point. The horrors of the Goblin Wars, the strange beasts that were not native to this world, had arisen from someplace, and this looked like the place.

But could *we* do this? This was high magic, on an order that hadn't been attempted in centuries. I was proud and confident in my crew – I've never worked with better magi – but would the rest of the universe cooperate? The questions haunted my mind.

Could we activate this thing, direct it, and keep it open long enough for everyone to get out? Would I have enough strength? My future wife and child depended upon it.

Did I have enough resolve to save them? And everyone else? I had to. I would will them away on my own, if I could.

Did I suddenly have a *screaming erection so hard it could break rock?* Apparently I did, I noticed as I looked down.

"All right, everyone," I called, "get to your places. Goodman Pokey-Poke says it's show time."

Penny stretched out on the round cushion we had created as our staging area – and "staging," I realized, suddenly, was indeed the proper term. I was used to performing for Penny. I was not used to a well-informed and highly critical audience watching my every move, mundane and mystical.

Don't get me wrong, I'm hardly shy. About sex, that is. But this was *different.* The group would not just see my lusty performance, but they would also see the complex interplay of magic that would arise from it – the interesting part. I was more worried about their thaumaturgical criticism about that than I was my ability to physically perform. Besides, whatever Penny gave me had me stiff as iron. I couldn't wimp out of this if I tried.

But because of the way things were set up, if all went well then every single one of the refugees using the portal would end up seeing me, too. Literally thousands of people. That was a level of exposure I had never had to contend with.

Penny leaned forward as I was shrugging off my robe and gave me a quick peck on the cheek – the only kiss we shared. This wasn't about romance, this was business.

"For luck," she said, settling back.

"Luck is for cowards," I said, with mock-bravery. "We *real* men—"

"Yeah, yeah, mister, I've heard it all before. Let's get on with it." I appreciated her businesslike and professional demeanor. I tried to ignore her trembling.

We started out in the first of the Five Classic positions, with me on top. This is best for starting a brisk rise of power. I was handling the *apis* for the two of us – the concentration required is helpful for maintaining a consistent state of arousal over a long period of time, and First Position is the easiest one to hold an *apis* in.

The plan was for us to go through all five, then repeat. I clasped my irionite sphere in my left palm, and felt Penny do the same to hers in her right hand, and the moment we began to raise power the two were linked. I felt it run through me like a shiver, coalesce around the sphere, then jump over to Penny's shard. I felt a reciprocal jolt from hers, and I welcomed it into me to mix with my own.

All of this was more or less textbook (though textbooks on Sex Magic are rare), except that the power levels we were playing with were rising far faster than I had anticipated. Before we knew it, our personal reservoirs were filled, and it was time to begin the operation in earnest.

It was . . . unexpectedly intoxicating, like discovering too late that someone has poured triple-distilled spirits into your wine glass unexpectedly.

The connection between our two stones was even more intimate than the one at our loins. I could feel Penny's thoughts and emotions *through* the stone, without going through the medium of the Otherworld at all. The proximity of the *molopor* was not hurting, of course – I could sneeze down here and cast better spells by accident than an Eastern adept could do in hours anyplace else. I had the barest moment of panic that the power would be too much, but the confident look in Penny's eyes banished it instantly. I was far more confident in her abilities than my own.

"Prepare, Delman!" I called, though I never took my eyes from Penny's. Eye contact is very important in such a working. It facilitates communication at levels that even magic can't reach, and it gives you something to stare at. And Penny had pretty gray eyes.

When I heard Delman's assent, I silently questioned Penny about who should do the honors, and with the barest nod she let me take control. It was like pair dancing. Someone has to lead.

I shifted my weight slightly, shifted my focus minutely, and suddenly the reservoir of magic poured out of our combined bodies and minds, through the *apis*, and over to Delman, who used his own stone to parcel it up and hand it off to the others. It was a strain, I know – I was feeling it myself – but Delman was good in groups, and after the first couple of sloppy hand-offs he got more efficient. We got faster. The power began to flow in earnest.

After that time just kind of stopped for me. I was anxious, of course, but I knew my anxiety wouldn't help matters, so I concentrated on the task at hand. It was after our first position change that I heard Delman call out, "Here it comes, Reyman!" and I felt a slight shift in the power flow. I could also feel Reyman struggle with the first few transfers, but he straightened out quickly and began building his spell wave.

I continued to focus, feeling almost overwhelmed at the amount of power we were handling. It is indescribable, as if every cell in your body is singing at once. I saw those feelings reflected back at me in Penny's eyes and we both added a little extra capacity with our enthusiasm for the chore, like two little kids who found the sugar bowl unattended.

In this type of magic, the power is built on the male side by postponing orgasm while encouraging empowerment, while on the female side the power comes in sharp waves, tied to the duration and frequency of orgasm. Every time Penny had a happy moment there would be a resulting spike in power that was my job to complement.

"Keep it going, friends!" called out Carmella, who was doing an excellent job of monitoring. "Just one more link and we'll be there, I think!"

That was fine by me. My arm was getting tired. We were about to shift into Position Three when Reyman finally called out, "I'm just about there! Get ready, Taren!"

Our final mage in the working nodded curtly, and suddenly there was a sustained magical flash between Reyman and Taren as their witchstones leapt to life. Taren was stationed in front of the portal, which he had been studying nonstop since he found out about it (he was a brilliant thaumaturge, after all), and he did not move a muscle that I could tell.

He stood there, stone in front of his face, and waved his right hand as he plumbed the depths of the *molopor*. He had tried explaining his theory to me, but it was based on precepts that were in advance of what I knew and I was therefore lost very quickly. At least he *had* a theory. I had no idea how I would try to unlock the thing.

He must have been doing something right, though, because shortly the disk started to cloud in, a thick gray murky cover over the naked stone underneath. I saw glints of shapes and colors wade through it, and I found it fascinating to watch. Too fascinating. Penny slapped my face, hard.

"Focus!"

I grunted, and focused. She was quite right, of course. I had my job to do, Taren had his. There was no time for professional oversight, not when a moment's faltering could send the entire working into the chamberpot. I got back to business and redoubled my efforts.

It took far longer than I would have liked, and I won't lie and say I wasn't worried for a bit, but Taren eventually shouted, *"I've got something!"* Then, a moment later, "I have it! I see the arch! *I see the arch!"*

While we were all too professional to burst out in cheers or applause – which would have been counterproductive, if not disastrous – I could definitely feel the shift in attitude around the room toward hopeful optimism. One of the mercenaries who had volunteered for the assignment took a breath, made a sign with his hands, and then walked through. In seconds he stepped back through and was shouting excitedly, *It worked! I saw people! It worked!*

I could tell it worked, too. There was suddenly a warm breeze on my backside, and the smell of fresh grass, rather than moldy cave. A few seconds later, I heard the bell tower in the commons sound the afternoon call to chores.

We had done it. We had taken an ancient piece of alien magic and made it do our bidding. We had threaded a grommet in the fabric of reality, with my root acting metaphorically as a needle. Something this powerful hadn't been done by humans since the Inundation, if then. I really wish our spectators would have been more impressed with the subtleties of the working, but I guess ignorance is the layman's privilege.

Pentandra and I altered our work then, concentrating more on maintaining and sustaining the reaction, and not building more power. This was easier for me than Penny, in theory, as women have a natural inclination to increase the level of their climaxes. But then again, when it came to Sex Magic, Penny could screw circles around me.

As she regulated her climaxes I finally broke eye contact with her (in Position Three this is pretty easy to do) and closed my eyes, fine-tuning the stream. I almost didn't notice the busy parade past the bedstead.

The refugees were starting to file past, their arms full of their valuables or their children. I didn't see them, of course, but I could smell them, hear them, and feel their terror as they walked into a hole that wasn't there a few moments ago. They were being herded by the castle's men-at-arms, and overseen by Sir Cei.

Time tromped by like the feet of a thousand peasants – which were also tromping by – but I kept going. Twice Carmella came by and offered Penny and me water, for which we were grateful. Dehydration is one of the inherent dangers in Sex Magic, as the participants are often too distracted by the work to care about such things. But not *too* much – interrupting a spell because you need to find a chamberpot is amateurish and unprofessional, not to mention unproductive.

One by one they hurried through the portal. I didn't even try to keep count, although Sir Cei would shout a number out every now and then. I tried to ignore it and concentrate on doing what I was doing indefinitely.

Toward the end it was Alya's turn in line, and she broke step just long enough to kiss me on the ear before she was safely through. I thought Penny would have a hissy fit about letting a commoner distract me at such a crucial moment, but when I ventured a worried glance in her direction I was pleasantly surprised to see a warm, almost loving smile on her face. Heartened that my personal life may not be a total disaster after all, I focused my efforts and gave her a little extra for a few minutes.

We were almost ready to switch out of Position Four when Tyndal came by bearing a huge pack, trailed by Rondal with a similar one. Tyndal knew better than to interrupt me, but he drew his wand and saluted bravely before he left. Somehow I don't think Penny would have been as tolerant should he have kissed me like Alya did.

I'm not sure I would've been, either, come to think of it.

I should have realized that the line was almost through, as Tyndal was definitely at the tail end of it. Gurkarl was behind him, technically in Tyndal's custody, our one prisoner of war.

The rest of the Bovali followed, until all of the civilians were through. Then it was the garrison's turn. One by one the guards and sentries were pulled from their posts and replaced with the slightly enchanted dummies we'd prepared.

From a distance they should fool casual observation, as they would appear to "move" in small ways – shift weight, scratch their nose, rub their eyes – and to improve the effect we had several fires lit in the kitchens and the bailey. From the front lines and the scrying pools of the gurvani besiegers it should look, more or less, like we were all still here awaiting slaughter.

Finally, Carmella called out, "Sir Cei just went through, ladies and gentlemen! We have officially rescued everyone! Over four thousand people just saw your hairy, naked arse and Penny's boobs, Min!"

I felt elated. So did everyone else. And I wasn't tired at all – Ishi's tits, I was just getting *started*.

Which was good, because this was the part of the plan that was problematic. You see, it took a dozen of us concentrating intently to keep the portal open. It wouldn't *stay* open unless we kept at our tasks. So there was no way *we* could follow them through the *molopor*.

That fact had caused a lot of discussion. As brave and public spirited as my team was, none of us wanted to volunteer for a suicide mission, especially since we just got ourselves a horde of irionite.

So when the gate vanished that left us with very few options. We had discussed it far into the night, and the result was our second phase plan: cutting our way out of the Valley. While a thousand people may have a hard time sneaking past a quarter of a million goblins, twenty-odd highly trained and newly augmented warmagi shouldn't have near as much trouble.

Oh, it would be difficult, no doubt. Some of us would likely die in the attempt. But we were counting a number of factors in our favor, and this was one of them: after we let the gate collapse, we still had a full circle crackling with power to play with. Penny and I kept at it, but Delman and the others shifted the focus of the spell and its intention.

I had had the diorama we built of the castle brought down from my tower, and the moment the gate was gone several magi converged on it and started throwing around a *lot* of spells through it.

Most were simply nasty war spells, the type we had been using so liberally on the goblins in the last few weeks. Those were designed to put fear and discomfort into the enemy camp, which is always fun. Others were longer term, subtle spells that would be difficult to detect and remove, but would make life in Boval Castle less than pleasant for the new owners. Still others were specifically designed to cut a weak spot in our enemy's defenses, something devastating enough that we could exploit it to escape the immediate siege and cut out across the Valley like Korbal was chasing us. Which wasn't far from the truth. The mythical Demon God of the Mindens was mythical, and Shereul the Great Ghost was not.

After rescuing everyone else, the magi seemed almost relieved to have this opportunity. The team was like a bunch of teenagers settling down to their first dice game. It was the most fun they had ever had professionally. Being able to use warmagic spells without having to consider civilian casualties allowed the most talented of them to try out the truly outrageous spells that had always been interesting theory around the campfire, but were seen as impractical in reality.

Now they had a unique opportunity to experiment with the theory.

Chains of explosions erupted from every fire. Distractions and annoyances like dancing lights and foul odors hid truly lethal spells. Waves of terror and despair would be rocking the enemy camp. Giants made out of smoke, uttering horrible curses, emerged from the castle and spread terror. Their supplies would rot, bundles of firewood would spontaneously ignite, and water supplies would spring leaks. Whole encampments would suddenly faint, or vomit, or have amnesia. Fleas, molds, and fungus multiplied at an increased rate. Sandstorms of pebbles. Wild animals. Sudden bursts of lightning and thunder. Rusty weapons and rotting leather. Gouts of green fire jumping from soldier to soldier. We spared no indignity, no injury, no ingenuity to trouble the gurvani.

Of course, this also let the enemy know that something unusual was happening inside Boval Castle. While we were running the molopor portal, all of our power was directed within. Now everyone in the valley with the magical sensitivity of a rabbit would know that we were throwing our mystical weight around. It would only be a matter of time before the enemy would feel compelled to act.

"All right, happy couple, time for the big finish," Delman called with a grin. "If you two have had enough, now, you can, uh, do what you need to. A big burst would actually help, so ramp it up all you can!"

"Position Two?" I asked, with a grin.

"Just what I was thinking. Want a pillow?"

I won't bore you with the details, which would be of interest only to the aficionado and the vulgar. Suffice it to say that in another five minutes we culminated at a masterful peak, dwarfing the amount of energy that we had produced before. Then I finally – finally! – climaxed.

It was . . . indescribable. It sent shock waves through the net of spells and enchantments they'd cast, and for a few moments I was in a storm of mental confusion and fuzzy feelings, all tinged with the green amber. I think we both went unconscious for a while, because the next coherent moment I remember was Carmella shaking me awake, a worried expression on her face.

"Minalan?" she said, more of a statement than a question. "Come on, boy, *wake up*. It's over. It's *over*. *Minalan?*"

The pale green magical glow that had permeated my mind softly faded, and reality reasserted itself. Penny lay next to me, a dreamy, unearthly expression of absolute bliss on her face. I could still feel the hum of every cell in her body, hear their quiet whisper as they went about their metabolic business. She still blazed by magesight, and I had little doubt that we both stood out like a beacon in the Otherworld. She rolled over slowly, and her unfocused eyes stared in my direction.

"Damn," she whispered. "You are *good!*" I smiled. Just the affirmation I needed.

As much as I wanted to bask in the compliment and the attendant afterglow, my brain stubbornly refused to let go of the number of crises that would have to be dealt with to affect my eventual survival. I spared one last moment for pure appreciation and awe, and then sat up.

"I need some food, and some water, soon," I said, swinging my shaky legs over the side of the makeshift bed.

Penny groaned and turned over. "Just like a damn man," she muttered. "*I* need a towel. And a basin."

Carmella sighed and put a water skin into my hands. While I drank she fished a sausage and a hunk of Boval cheese out of a hamper. "Take it easy," she said gently. "You were out for at least five minutes. The Mountain Folk are still reacting to our mayhem, so we probably have a little while."

"Every second is precious," I grimaced. "And everything I've got is suddenly sore. Is everything ready?"

"As ready as it's going to get," Delman called. "There is a fifty foot high wall of magical green flame around the castle, and the scrugs seem to be keeping their distance, for now. I think they're distracted by what we threw at them. Every now and then someone will shoot an arrow at the barrier, but that's about it. No assault parties, no siege towers, just screams of defiance. They have their own problems right now," he grinned.

"Not for long," I countered. As much as my body wanted me to relax, as much as I wanted to enjoy the brief respite before an attack began in earnest, as much as I ached and parts of me were chafed, my soldier's instinct was telling me it was time for *action*.

"Get dressed," I said to Penny, who was curled up in a delicious-looking fetal position. "It's time to go."

"Just leave the money on the dresser," she said dreamily. "I'm going to take a bubble bath."

"Woman," I warned, "play time is *over.*"

"Oh, you are so *frustrating.*" She struggled half-heartedly into her robe. I stood, and reached for my own clothes. "Just like a damn man," she muttered.

Fifteen minutes later we were gathering in the inner bailey, checking our packs and leaving a few last-minute surprises for our friends the goblins before we moved out. There was, indeed, a green wall of flame that blocked out the horizon in all directions around the castle. It was impressive. I was saddling up Traveler – the revised plan had included a speedy retreat, and I was overjoyed that we wouldn't be parted yet -- when I felt a presence and heard a voice I wasn't prepared to.

"My congratulations, Master Minalan," said the quiet, tired voice of Sire Koucey from behind me. "You have saved my people. A small victory, but one I am pleased to have witnessed."

I jumped, still a little shaky from the ritual. "Sire?"

The old man stood there in his full armor, helmet on and visor raised. He looked worn and tired and . . . resigned, somehow. "Sir, not Sire, since you conquered my domain," he offered. "Just a landless knight, now."

"Sire, why didn't you go with them? Why didn't you escape? I mean, you can come with us—"

"I shall not abandon the land my ancestors fought for," he declared, softly. "While the honor of my House may be questioned, my personal honor is my own responsibility. I shall stay and be the last defender of my lands."

I started to call him a fool, and then realized that choosing death with honor was the knight's only chivalrous way out of the situation. Should he return to the Five Duchies as a refugee lord, a knight without lands and folk, he would be at best a laughingstock and an outcast, and at worst an ignoble mercenary condemned to die in unchivalrous obscurity.

This way, his brother could – in theory – continue the title and the family line without the blemish of dishonor on the House. But while his brother was carried through the portal on a stretcher, raving with fever, I didn't really expect him to survive much longer. His body had been through too much. Sire Koucey probably was going to be the last living scion of House Brandmount. Nobility works in weird ways.

Instead of rebuking him, I drew my mageblade and saluted him. He bowed in return, a slight smile on his face. "I also wanted to thank you for . . . doing what you did. I acted on the advice of poor counsel, I see now. Had I listened to Garkesku . . ."

We both knew what would have happened. I nodded. "Where is the little weasel, anyway? Did he escape with the others?"

"No one saw him go through the portal. But he may well have gone in disguise to avoid your wrath. That would be congruent with his character. Somehow I can't imagine that he'd stick around here all by himself."

"It would serve him right if he did."

"If you will indulge me – my lord – we have a last bit of business," Koucey said, changing the subject without comment. "We don't have much time. Here," he said, proffering a velvet sack, "are the jewels of my House. Rather than let the goblins make toys of them, I bid you to take them, sell them, and make provision for my people. My brother has already taken what gold was left in my treasury, but . . . if he does not survive, I trust you and Sir Cei to look after my folk. Included is the deed of title to Boval Vale, for what it is worth. According to the Laws of Luin and Duin, it is rightfully yours . . . but if you see fit to return it to my house, perhaps it will be of use someday when all of this," he said, waving to the destruction around us, "is passed. But first and foremost, see to my brave Bovali," he insisted.

"It shall be done, you have my promise," I said, taking the sack.

"Here also is a parcel of some of the more *interesting* artifacts that we took from the caves. They may well be enchantments that will prove useful in your studied. Perhaps they will even be of use in the coming war."

"They might at that." The basket he handed me had all manner of odd junk in it. None of it was gold or silver, but some of it was clearly magical . . . and some of it was clearly not. I looked forward to peeling it apart someday when my life wasn't in mortal peril.

"Next, I bid you to carry this letter to the Coronet Council. After Boval falls, it will not be long until the blight spreads throughout the Five Duchies – indeed, the Wilderlands is already under assault beyond our frontiers. This is my report, and my recommendation, as well as a truthful accounting of my House's acquisition of this land."

"I shall deliver it."

"Finally, here is a letter and a token to be delivered to Count Olode, Head of House Rieran. My wife's family," he explained. "A last farewell, is all, and the return of an heirloom from her dowry they count as precious."

"I shall see it done."

"Thank you, Master Minalan. I shall die easier knowing these things are attended to. Despite all that has happened, you are a brave warrior and a cunning wizard, and it has been a true honor to have fought next to you – both in Farise, and in my home."

I rested a hand on the old warrior's shoulder. Words were unnecessary. All of our acrimony was done.

"You had best mount," he said, at last, tears in his eyes. "I must see to my fate, and you to yours."

I nodded and began to do just that, securing the baggage to my saddle-horn, when I felt it.

A rumble. The ground began moving, as if an earthquake was thinking about happening. While that isn't uncommon in the Mindens, I didn't think it was a natural event. Traveler neighed in protest at the harsh vibration, and started to stamp, and I couldn't blame him. It's disconcerting when the ground refuses to behave like it should.

"Uh oh," I said sagely, and looked around. I settled on the west for a direction to look at, because that is where the rumble originated. Above the green flames, above the peaks beyond, I could feel, more than hear, the disturbance.

From the west, the direction of the Old God's approach, I could see a dark cloud, blacker than any storm cloud. There was a noticeable change in its signature.

Something had changed. Something knew that it was being thwarted. Something had suddenly decided to expedite its journey.

The Old God was coming, quickly.

And I could tell Shereul the Great Ghost was *pissed.*

Chapter Fifteen

The Dead God's Judgment

"When faced with your imminent death, the wise man reaches into the depths of his soul, grabs his sword, and does what is proper. The gods have a way of treating you like a two-penny whore on payday, but at least you might face the experience with the faintest bit of dignity."

\- *Minalan the Spellmonger*

\-

Everyone froze for just a moment, while we figured out what was happening. Part of it was obvious – at least to me, and I wasn't the smartest one there.

It was clear that the great gurvani shaman, Shereul, the one who had been secretly been building an army for a century, the one who had planned and plotted the recapture of Boval Vale, the one who had been journeying through far mountain passes for weeks, now, with an entourage and an army, had suddenly left them behind and was now speeding – through the air, probably – *straight toward us.* Our time was up. We were trapped inside the castle while certain doom approached.

Everyone froze, and then everyone moved at once. Some tried to mount, some tried to hurry their preparations, some came to the conclusion that there was just no possible way to flee in time and tried to make their peace with the gods. One thing was certain: that thing, whatever it was, would mow us down before we crossed our own ward of flames.

That's the conclusion I came to, at least, and so I calmly led Traveler back to a post and tied him up, then retrieved my warstaff and mageblade from my saddle and walked back to the center of the deserted bailey. If I was going to die, it would be on my feet, fighting. I tried to put on my best defiant sneer.

I wasn't surprised to feel Sire Koucey at my shoulder, sword in hand. He couldn't feel the approaching malevolence, but he could read a crowd.

One by one my team assembled around me, each one of them preparing spells and clutching witchstones, some drawing swords or doing feats of martial magic in preparation for our last stand. Irionite flashed all around me.

Pentandra joined us late; she had figured out what was going on before she came out. I realized that her hair was wet and smelled of aromatic Eastern soap – *the evil witch had found time to bathe*, while I still smelled like a wharfside bordello the day after the fleet came in. I suppose there are worse ways for a man to die. I felt her fall in line on my other side as the rest of the warmagi filed in, and for two solid minutes we all just stared at the sky and cast preparatory spells, prayed, and waited. None of the gods we invoked bothered to show up. Wise of them.

One of the kids (Rustallo, I believe) was starting to make jokes after the pregnant pause stretched on uncomfortably. That's when I saw it.

I wasn't sure exactly what it was, so I hung five or so nasty offensive spells and three good defensive spells that I had prepared to welcome it. Mine were pretty straightforward. Some of the others, I could feel, were pretty elaborate.

"So, at last, our Fate approaches," Koucey murmured fatalistically.

"I hope it ate its biscuits this morning," Azar said, dismissively. "I'm feeling rowdy." I ignored it. We all knew what was going to happen.

"Talk first, or hit it with something?" asked Penny, quietly.

"You're asking *me?*"

"You're the Captain, my Captain. Once the sex was over, you're in charge again."

Crap. As if I didn't have enough to worry about.

"Let's talk first," I decided.

"Why?"

"I thought I was Captain? Because it might give me time to think of something better to do. Right now, I can't remember my own name."

"It's Minalan. Captain Minalan the Spellmonger. Lord by right of conquest of Boval Vale. The Spellmonger. Captain Minalan the *Great.*"

"Now you're just getting silly."

Someone began loudly offering prayers to some divinity. Or it could have been an incantation. I wasn't really paying attention. I was looking up.

You could see it far off, at first, a speck of bright green in the absolute center of the dark black cloud. It illuminated the clouds around it with the pale green glow as it descended with all the speed of a shooting star. It was a terrible thing to behold, an utterly unnatural thing, and I again debated myself whether making a stand was a better idea than blind flight. That thing was moving fast, and was heading right for us. I feared a collision.

As it approached the bailey it slowed down rapidly. Instead of crashing with a thunderclap it floated down like a hawk preparing to catch a hare – not a pleasing mental image when you are feeling very much like a hare. The glow intensified, until it outshone the light from our own protective wall. It snapped through our wards like threads, and came to a stop about four feet above the ground, twenty paces ahead of us, until I could almost make out what it was. And wasn't.

It wasn't a goblin – at least not all of it.

It was a sphere, as wide as a large pumpkin. A sphere of clear, flawless irionite. It was a sphere so translucent that you could see the mummified skull within. The mouth was open in an eternal rictus of pain and rage, and the eyes were sunken and dead – but there was no mistaking the feeling of intelligence that it radiated. The skull was *alive*. There was a being inside that aberration of nature.

Aberration it was – I could feel just how deep an impression on reality it made, as potent in its way as the molopor had been. As it approached us slowly, it sent sheering waves of distortion just by its very existence.

The Great Ghost. The Old God. The Dead God. Shereul, the super-shaman. All of those names fit. It was dead, no doubt about it – undead, really. It was clearly the skull of a gurvani shaman, mummified and preserved within the green amber. And gave it all the power a human god could ever dream of.

I would have wet myself in fear if I hadn't been so damn dehydrated.

I understood a lot, now. This had to be the head of Shereul, the great shaman slain by Koucey's ancestors in an act of treachery. Shereul, whose head was removed from the pike they had staked it on and spirited away by the survivors – I could even see the exit wound in the top left of the fossilized skull. His shamanic disciples had apparently taken it deep into the mountains, far away from humans, and somehow had embedded it in the largest chunk of irionite that had ever been.

And then they had somehow awoken him up from the dead, determined to do its bidding. And the bodiless head wanted *revenge*.

What were you doing in the sacred cave? came a powerful thought in my head, in a hideous parody of my own voice. It was beyond spooky.

"We were allowing our people to escape," I said, bravely.

You defiled the sacred cave with your filthy humani *feet.*

"Hey, I wiped my feet before I went in. It was messed up like that when I got here," I explained.

You used the artifact. You call it a molopor.

"Yeah, well, you kind of gave us no choice. You put up barriers around the Valley."

Such is my right. I am reclaiming the valley for the Targa gurvani.

"I'm not disputing that," I agreed. "And we helpfully depopulated it for you."

The Targa gurvani are not pleased that they will be forced to postpone their vengeance.

"There's a lot of people disappointed with how things have worked out."

This was not going exactly as planned. I expected to be dead by now, killed in a powerful magical attack. The fact that I was not – yet – gave me a certain stupid confidence in what I was saying. What did I have to lose? "I acknowledge that the men who took this vale did so by treachery, committed acts of murder and pillage, and destroyed a valuable religious center. But the people who live – lived – here now are not the ones who did that. Those men are dead. Take back your valley, your sacred cave. Keep the castle, if you want. No extra charge. But leave us in peace."

These are the descendants of those people. Their line bears the stain of their ancestors' crimes.

"Then leave that for their own gods to deal with."

I am a god.

"A metaphysical subject for another time. But even if you are a god, you are the god of the gurvani, not of men."

The gods of men seem slow to respond.

"I've noticed that myself, recently. I'll speak to the monks about that, if I don't meet a human god myself some day. But the fact remains: you are *not* a god of men." I was on shaky theological ground here, I'm sure. Theurgy is a fascinating subject, in its way, but not my specialty. It occurred to me that I might be able to ask the gods shortly in person, after I was dead, but for the moment I wasn't. I didn't know what I was doing, but what I was doing was working, if I wasn't dead. We were talking. Even negotiating, if you wanted to look at it that way. Perhaps there was a faint, faint hope that we could reason with it.

I am the god of the Valley now. The humani gods are forever banished. The defilers of our sacred cave need to be punished.

Now we were in dangerous territory.

"They have lost their homes. Many have lost their families. Their lives will be chaos for the rest of their days. They will suffer nightly the dreams of their experience until they die. There will be hunger, and suffering. Simply killing them would have ended their pain," I reasoned. "From this they can never recover." Not a good time to talk about the resiliency of the human spirit.

They are beyond my reach for the moment. Let them suffer. But you *are still here. And you,* he said, turning the globe incrementally so that the dead eyes stared at Koucey, *are the descendant of Sir Brandmount.* It was a statement, not a question.

"I have that honor." Said Koucey in a strong, proud voice.

Your sire's face was the last thing I saw in my old life.

"It was war," Koucey said, simply. "He did his duty, as he saw fit. He was commanded to do it."

Your line owes me a debt for its treachery.

Koucey didn't say anything. He also didn't lower his sword, for all the good it would do him.

"It was *war,*" I repeated, when the silence grew too long. "And this man was not even born then."

It matters not. His line owes me a debt. So he owes me a debt.

"What could he possibly give you? He has nothing. All that he had, you took from him."

There was a short pause. *Not all. He has his life. He owes it to me.*

"Killing him would end his suffering, too," I offered, trying to buy the man a way out. "Whatever crimes his sires committed, he, himself, was only guilty of defending his people and his lands."

His people. My lands. Yet I will not murder him. Instead he shall serve me until his last heartbeat.

"Never!" Koucey said defiantly, and started to charge. He looked splendid in his armor, his device on the breast of his surcoat, every inch the Wilderlord knight prepared for battle. The fathers of his House would have been proud of him. "I will die before I serve you, foul beast!"

Me? Not so much. He was a damn fool who was going to get us all killed. Insulting the undead goblin head wasn't going to help. But Koucey followed the insult by charging, sword swinging.

"No!" I shouted, and immediately began to fire a spell from my warwand. It was the least lethal of the ones I had hung. It was a short but powerful stunning spell, the kind of thing that's great for knocking over a cavalry squadron. I had it ready before Koucey had taken five steps, but I was too slow: the Dead God had reached out with his mind and took over control of Koucey's body. My spell passed him harmlessly, though it gouged out a small crater in the earth behind him.

"Let him go!" I shouted, smoking wand in hand.

He belongs to me, now.

"I said, let him *go!*" Koucey's legs moved jerkily until he was standing to the left of the globe. I tried to think of an appropriate spell, but I had nothing.

"Milord Captain," called Carmella, warningly, "is it not best that he live out his fate?"

"I agree, Min," added Penny quickly. "He knew what might happen when he stayed behind the evacuation."

"I can't allow that," I said, sternly, and advanced to within three paces of the Dead God. What the hell was I doing? This was worse than facing the incarnation of death. As I approached I got to see a little more detail of the undead goblin's face within the sphere of green amber. It was grotesque – just what you would imagine a two hundred year old fossilized and partially decomposed head of a goblin who died by violence might look like. "Let him *go*."

He is mine, the voice said in my mind. It was disconcerting how it was no louder, now that I was close to it. *Stand away.*

Instead I stared intently at the sphere, committing every detail to memory. "He does not deserve this," I stated.

You are correct. But this is the worst punishment I can bestow. He deserves a thousand times worse.

"He is a good man who has done nothing but defend his people!"

He is scion of House Brandmount. I knew his great-grandsire. I spoke with him for days, before he murdered me. He shares his sire's face. He himself has hunted my people and kept them away from the sacred cave. He has prevented the fulfillment of the prophecy.

"What prophecy?"

Shit. There was a prophecy. That could complicate things.

Centuries ago a great shaman, Ula-telec, prophesied that we would lose the Valley to the unclean, and that all of my people would be in danger. The time was called the Exile, and it came to pass. Ula-telec also prophesied that the Great War would come, and for four generations all would be in chaos. All is doomed, he said, until the One gurvan who sees the Cave first after the Exile leads his people through the war and into a greater Peace. I am the fulfillment of that prophecy. I alone shall lead my people to wipe yours back into the Void.

Uh, oh. Genocidal prophesies, a maniacal undead god, a potent mystical portal – this was all leading someplace. The Dead God was to be the savior of his people, because he would be the first gurvan to see the cave after the Exile.

Only he *hadn't been.* Gurkarl had that honor. *And Shereul didn't know that.* That had to be significant, somehow.

"Well, we wouldn't want to stand in the way of the fulfillment of prophecy," I said. "Why don't you just let the knight go, and we'll be on our way?"

He belongs to me. His fate has been spoken. His life is forfeit. To the end of his days shall he serve me.

How much was I willing to push this? Enough to get us all killed for the life of one man who was prepared to die anyway? A man who had insulted and betrayed me? Before I answered my own question, I decided that it would be best to know exactly what the stakes were.

"If you take him, you would let the rest of us pass in peace?"

He owes me a debt. I am deciding if you do, as well.

"What the hell did *I* do?"

You slew my captains, killed my shamans.

"They invaded our homes. It is the right of every being to defend their homes."

And it is the right of every conqueror to cleanse the lands of the conquered.

"You might find that more difficult than you think," I said, starting to get pissed off a little.

The Dead God laughed, inside my head, which was eerie when I could see his unmoving "face" through murky green amber.

Those pebbles you clutch are meaningless. They are the merest slivers of my power, cast-off and given to the least of my servants..

"But they no longer answer to you," I pointed out.

It matters not. A hundred times as many would be useless against me. You are no threat, Spellmonger.

"How did you—?"

I can see inside your minds as well as speaking to them. For all of your vainglory, you are little better than a village witch. A pawn of your betters. You are no match for me. From inside your own eyes, I see. I know what spells you have prepared. Useless.

"Let's hope we don't have to find out. I want safe passage for all of us, outside of the Valley."

I want the last two centuries of suffering and exile to not have occurred. It appears we are both doomed to disappointment.

"Perhaps. I thought you hadn't decided if we owed you a debt, yet."

True. If I decide you don't, then I will grant you a quick death. If I decide you do, then your agony will encompass weeks before you are sacrificed to me.

That was a cheery thought.

"Then you realize what I'm going to have to do."

I look forward to it. It should prove entertaining if naught else.

"Last chance," I warned.

You try my patience.

"Attack!" I yelled in what I hoped was an impressive and inspirational voice, and loosed my two most powerful hung spells at once. I could feel everyone else's going off all around me, in what was the largest sudden release of magical energy I had ever been involved with in my life.

Nothing happened.

I don't mean that we didn't hit him, or that it didn't have an effect. I mean that time stopped, and suddenly I was standing in a forest of statues. And I wasn't alone.

Around me, in front of me, a line of diminutive figures had suddenly appeared, each one holding a gnarled branch that doubled as a powerful magical implement – at least as potent as any wizard's staff I'd seen.

The Tree Folk had arrived.

*   *   *

While I can't honestly say that they were the last folks I expected to see, they weren't high on the list.

I knew that the Alka Alon had been watching us, monitoring the situation as we dwindled away under the goblin onslaught. They were too good at magic not to notice that abomination, or all of the activity in their front garden. I had thought that they would have stayed away, quietly slipped out of the valley while they could – that's what I would have done.

I did not honestly think that the Aronin would pitch in, else I would have tried harder to gain his alliance earlier.

But there he was – he and a dozen or so of his "court." They picked their way across the courtyard, as normally as you could ask. It was everything else that was askew.

My comrades were in various stages of flinging spells at the sphere, their arms raised and their mouths open. Sire Koucey was hanging in mid-air, frozen, a blank look on his face. Even the birds in the air were still, hung as if suspended from strings. The sphere wasn't moving, either. Not that it moved much before. Everything was frozen.

Penny was an elegant statue with a look of grim determination on her face, hands gracefully outstretched in mid-spell.

Carmella had a mixture of fear and excitement on her face as she mouthed the trigger of her own attack. Terleman and Wenek were charging, mageblades flashing. Taren was shouting a war cry, Hesia was flinging something from her staff . . . but all around me, everyone was petrified. Suspended in the moment.

Except for me.

"Huh? What . . . ?"

"Minalan the Spellmonger," the priest-king called, and stepped gracefully across the pockmarked courtyard as if he was out on a nature hike. "It is good to see you again."

"Uh . . . yeah. You too, my lord Aronin. I take it you were in the neighborhood?"

"We have been watching you for weeks, now. We knew you would provide us an opportunity to strike."

"You *did?* I did?" I asked, confused.

He gestured toward the malevolent sphere. "We knew the Abomination would seek to engage you personally. Sharuel has a thirst for vengeance too strong to do otherwise. It kept him distracted. You kept his army at bay for weeks longer than he had planned. – and longer than I had expected, for a human mage. We knew you would mount a defense. We had to wait for the encounter before we struck at the Abomination."

"Why?" I asked, openmouthed. "Uh, a couple of weeks ago, we might have had a chance, with your support. But now?"

"Because as much as it troubles me to say, the welfare of your people was not our foremost thought. It pleases me mightily that you have found a way to preserve them. We did not expect you to make use of the *molopor* so readily."

"I didn't think the Alka Alon were able to be surprised."

He broke into a smile that was overwhelmingly good-natured and calm, under the circumstances. "Surprise is a novelty we don't enjoy often. It happens rarely. And when it does, it is noteworthy. We waited for the right moment, the moment when he was distracted, and his defenses were canted towards human magics, before we chose to attack."

I looked around. "Well, glad we could oblige. Um, how are you doing *this?*" I asked, gesturing around.

"This close to the *molopor* such songspells are simple for those who have studied them for centuries. In essence, we have slowed time. It was one of the few things we did not think he would expect or be able to counter."

"So . . . you have a plan?" I asked, hopefully.

"We do. We will surround the Abomination and weave a web of energy around it such as hasn't been attempted in living memory – and the memory of *my* folk, not just you ephemerals. This is not the first time this has happened."

I stared blankly. "Beg pardon? You mean, magically reanimated goblin heads aren't the novelty I suspected?"

"The gurvani have never tried this, but the technique occurs in nature. You are aware, of course, that irionite is the result of *kellisarth* sap crystallizing?"

"Yes . . . I suppose." I could see how it would happen, from a theoretical perspective. The glowing green globe that wanted to see all of humanity wiped off of Callidore was proof of the concept.

"Occasionally an insect or small animal gets entrapped into the matrix. When that happens, the creature's Will can re-assert itself, only magically. The enneagram of its self awareness is frozen, but accessible with sufficient power. The poor creature is usually driven mad, of course, unable to escape its essential nature, but unable to realize the potential it enjoys.

"We call such aberrations *kulnuara*. They often go on to cause much destruction and havoc, and have to be brought to bay."

"So how do you defeat a . . . *kulnuara*?" I asked. "Please tell me it's a simple and trivial piece of conjuration."

The Aronin shook his head sadly. "It is exceedingly difficult, even when the animal involved is simple. Sometimes armies of my folk have been sent against the beasts, and been slain before they were able to control it. In this case, we face someone who knows what they are, who knows how to sing magic, and who revels in their power. This is no ordinary *kulnuara*." He looked at the sphere, the first time I ever saw one of the Tree Folk truly look grim.

"The three usual ways to counter a common *kulnuara* are to sap its power utterly, to bend it against itself until it can no longer hold the strain, or attack the integrity of the physical object itself. We shall attempt the second measure. The power is too great to attempt to draw it off, and the sphere is quite massive. Should we manage to break it open there will likely be enough crystal left within the skull to counter any further moves we make. So we shall turn its own power against itself."

I sighed. "This should be fun to watch."

"No, Spellmonger, you shall not be here to witness our battle." The way he said it left no room for doubt.

"We won't survive the fight, I take it. Well, I expected no less."

"You misunderstand. Your presence here would be a . . . *distraction.* And we have further work for you to do."

"I beg your pardon?"

"Someone who understands what is involved *must* organize the defense of Men, Spellmonger. Else the human world will be destroyed, as the Shereul the Dead God gains power. You must go to the Councils of Men and tell them what you know. You must organize your dukes and lords into a defense against his armies, most of all. Your magics are crude and elementary, and they must be strengthened and organized against the gurvani tide, else Man will be washed away from the shores of Callidore, just as my own folk will likely be."

"You sound like you aren't planning on winning this contest."

"Yet it must be fought. We must be prepared, our two peoples. This is the first step. We must find a way to destroy Shereul. This is not a certain thing. It bears much risk.

"It is . . . very powerful. Far more than we anticipated. And his stunted enneagram shows little sign of fading, fueled by the power of his irionite casing. The Abomination is . . . far more potent than we anticipated," he said, sadly. "We may well fall before he is defeated.

"But even if we are victorious, there is still the matter of his misguided hordes, who loathe my folk for the past wrongs they perceive almost as much as they do yours. Should the Dead God fall, his followers will be leaderless, weaker, but still very destructive. They will come after your people until they are ground to a halt. Defenses must be erected against them, lest your fractured nations fail the challenge of their vengeance. Win or lose, this great army will issue forth from this valley as your folk left the sky . . . and they will drive the *humani* in front of them. Those who are not killed or consumed. Thankfully, your folk rejoice in battle, and the effort will be celebrated by the survivors in song and story."

"That is not the kind of song or story I like."

"They will offer no quarter, and will slaughter or enslave every human they encounter, we believe. They will bring forth flame and steel, and magics most terrible. They will brandish weapons not seen in ages of Men. They will seek to turn the weak-willed to their bidding, and use Man's own power against him. If you value your race, a great line of defense must be erected against their assault. And that is if we are victorious. It is *your* charge to see to that."

"Why would anyone listen to *me?*" I asked, raising an eyebrow. "I'm a spellmonger with an illegal shard of irionite! The first Censor I see will kill me!"

"Because you will make your case with such passion and conviction that you will crush any opposition. You will provide such a great and noble example of humanity and nobility that thousands will be inspired to defend human lands."

"More foresight?" I asked, hopefully.

He shook his head. "Nay. You just seem like that pushy kind of man."

"Ishi's tits. Thanks," I said, weakly.

"You will not be unaided. Your friends here will follow you unquestionably. And there will be others. As you work, the lore of your ancients will prove helpful. Perhaps alliances with the other Alon will sprout. My own folk will do what we can to aid you, but you, alone, should be sufficient to rally the human lands for this crisis."

"You have a pretty high opinion of my abilities, Aronin. And an imperfect understanding of Ducal politics."

He shrugged – which looked strange on him. Their shoulders were so narrow. "As you did here, we use what we have available."

"I . . . *see*. Okay, I'm not going to argue the whole escape plan, because I've wanted to flee this place for weeks. But . . . how about my people? The other warmagi?"

"All shall be rescued. They will be needed in the coming days. All save *that* one," he said, nodding toward Koucey.

"Why not the lord of Boval Vale?"

"He is trapped within a powerful song, Spellmonger, one which we shall not have the strength to breech while we struggle against the Abomination. Lord Brandmount was a good and noble man, and I have watched him grow since he was a baby in this vale. But his life will be forfeit in this struggle. Knowing him as I do, he would not object to the sacrifice."

"You know Sire Koucey?"

"I have lived in this vale more than eleven lives of men. I have seen him grow from a babe to an old man. There is little that happens here I do not know."

"Well, you're probably right. He is a noble sort of cuss. He wouldn't mind dying, not if it helped end this menace. But it's hardly the glorious death of a Wilderlord in battle. So . . . how are we getting away?"

"Here," he said, sketching a circle in the air about ten feet across. The magic from his little wand was palpable. "In other times I might open our Ways to you, but this close to the molopor a more effective song beckons. In a few moments this portal will open and lead your people outside of the valley. Not as far as you did with the *molopor*, but beyond the greater invasion, and out of harm's way."

"Great. I really appreciate it."

"You will earn your passage. This spell of time will fade shortly, and when it does you *must* lead your men against the sphere, just as you had planned. You must keep it distracted a moment while our songspell comes into play. Only then you will flee."

"And you?"

"I will fight. Perhaps I will die, but I must make the attempt. That is what an Aronin does," he said, looking toward Koucey sympathetically. "In our own way, we are as dedicated to our cause as your Wilderlord is to his position. My guardianship is important, but this takes precedence. For once this Valley was a holy place, even before the gurvani adopted it. Amadia is but a remnant of that age of wonder. What the Dead God would turn it into would defile even the memory of that time."

"Why don't you just move on, escape with your people?"

He smiled faintly. "My people left Amadia weeks ago. My daughter Ameras led them away, and will inherit my traditional responsibilities as guardian when I am gone. The leaders of the other kindreds of my folk will not be pleased with this, of course, for they may see it as an abrogation of my responsibility. It is not. Ameras knows her duties. This valley is my home. Like Sire Koucey, I would rather die than see it turned into a dead wasteland."

Even the Alka Alon were, in the end, stubborn villagers when faced with inevitable doom that threatened their home. "I . . . I don't know what to say. I almost wish I could stay and help . . ."

"Nay. You *must* leave. You and your people are destined to be the core of a great new army, an army that can beat back this tide. An army that you will lead. The gods themselves will follow you, if you let them. It must persist, and persevere, and fight until there is no more danger from our cousins. You *must* lead them, Minalan. No one else. Only you have the talent, will, and capacity to do what needs to be done. You and your children shall become the founders of a great line, should you succeed."

That was good news. Except I didn't want to lead an army. I wanted to settle down and make babies. Not for the first time I considered how little my wishes mattered to the will of the rest of the universe.

"There is more. When the time is ripe, in its fullness, you will seek out my daughter Ameras, who even now seeks a place of refuge for the rest of my folk. I have given to her certain . . . things that may assist you. Arcane secrets, you would call them. Things the other kindreds of the Alka Alon would not grant you, even in the most dire of circumstances. Things from our past, things that nearly destroyed us, once, and imperiled our place on Callidore. She has agreed to act as my messenger in this. Her word will hold great weight in the councils of the Alka Alon. Seek her when you can find no other way."

"Again, you're not sounding optimistic."

"I wish that I could be, Spellmonger. But I fear I will never see my daughter again in this life."

"I'll . . . I'll tell her you said hello," I said, which was a stupid thing to say but I was long past the influence of inspiration.

He smiled. "Please do. Now prepare yourself, for you have a long and difficult journey ahead."

"Thanks, Aronin. May Briga guide your magics."

"And may Trygg keep you and your new family safe in your travels," he responded amiably.

"Wait, you know about Alya? And the baby?"

"As I said, I know of everything that happens in this valley. Are you now prepared? Our time is nearly at an end."

Hells no! I heaved a great sigh and raised my wand and staff. "I suppose," I lied, though I didn't know how I could become more prepared. While we had been talking more Alka Alon had gathered around us. His folk formed a loose ring around the malevolent green sphere, and were establishing a net of power around it with strange and beautiful, yet warlike songs. With a nod that they, too, were ready, he closed his eyes . . .

And suddenly the world came back. It went from near silence, with not even the sounds of wind or trees rustling, to a loud, explosive chaos. I bellowed the release mnemonic on my own spell and sent them towards the sphere, and then followed with another as fast as I was able.

"Every ounce!" I screamed into the magical tempest. "Hold nothing back!"

"Wha--?" someone near me shouted, as – to him – a ring of Tree Folk suddenly appeared between us and Shereul, hands outstretched, wands ready, their web of magic instantly in place. They continued singing, a beautiful, soulful song the words of which I couldn't make out.

I fired another spell instead, the last of my prepared offensive charms. Then I shouted encouragement to the others and watched that section of space that was our getaway.

Trying to keep my eyes on three things at once was difficult, but I managed to spot the . . . call it a dull area in space, exactly where the Aronin has sketched it. The reality around the edges thinned out until they melted into a grayness – and then formed a lovely picture of a forest glen where none had a right to be.

"Time to go, folks!" I called. "Prepare to disengage and follow me!"

The sphere was shaking and vibrating as the Tree Folk adepts spun web after elegant web around it. As soon as it would throw one of them off, another soon came back and added more bonds of power. It kept him from laying waste to us all, which was all right with me.

My people were throwing an impressive amount of magical energy at the sphere, but it was hard with so many Tree Folk in the way. I screamed at them to withdraw and retreat through the sudden portal. They listened, when they realized that the focus of the Dead God's attention was not on us.

One by one they fell back, and as they did so I motioned them through the portal. Penny even grabbed Traveler's reins and took him through.

I stayed to witness the battle as long as I was able to. Some of his folk fell, but not the Aronin. Not until the last. I felt compelled to watch as long as I could, even though Pentandra was screaming for me to step through the portal before it was too late. I was reluctant. The Aronin of Amadia's brilliant attack and willful sacrifice should be witnessed by someone, after all.

The last thing I saw before I stepped through the shrinking disk was his face, focused in concentration and determination, with just a hint of laughter and desperation thrown in, as he unleashed a fresh wave of magic against the Abomination of the Dead God. I suppressed the urge to run to his side and add my feeble powers to his against the eternally screaming goblin he faced. But Pentandra grabbed the back of my tunic and pulled me through the portal.

Then I was gone.

Chapter Sixteen

Escape From Boval

"Every ending is a new beginning. Or at least that's what we keep telling ourselves to keep from killing ourselves with drink and self-pity."

— *Minalan the Spellmonger*

The only thing you could charitably say about the little village of Duprin was that it didn't have much of a goblin population.

The Aronin did the best he could, I'm sure, under very difficult circumstances. We were well outside of the Dead God's malevolent influence, but we were also in one of the most backwoods fiefdoms in all of the southern Alshari Wilderlands. Still, the local folk – all three hundred of them – and the local lord, who was a country knight, welcomed the coin we brought. We needed all sorts of supplies if we were to make the long journey towards civilization, and we probably flooded Duprin with more hard currency than they'd ever seen in their lifetime.

The people of Duprin were a little disconcerted at first by twenty-odd warmagi appearing out of nowhere. The local priestess of Trygg was called in to verify that we were not, in fact, demons of some kind, and after getting a clean bill of metaphysical health from the old biddy, we started spending like sailors. Food, horses, saddles, tack, and wains – we needed just about everything. We were almost nine-hundred leagues away from the rest of the survivors at Inarion. But we were also over two hundred fifty leagues away from Boval Vale.

We wanted some rest. The last few days had been heady, busy, and exhausting. Doing magic, even augmented by the stones, takes a lot out of you physically and mentally, and without a good rest we would have eventually fallen out of our saddles.

Oh, we could have re-energized ourselves magically, but that way lies madness: the likelihood that we would soon grow dependent upon the stones was too great. A couple of days taking it easy at Duprin before we moved on were just what we needed. Rumors of goblin invasion north of here were already starting to filter in, but we didn't spread them. We had more important things to do. Like sleep.

Late in the second day Penny and I met up for a late breakfast or early lunch at the tiny, nameless inn at the heart of the village. The fare was simple and rustic, a thick venison stew with tubers and grain, some passable bread and some cheese we passed up in favor of some of the last Bovali cheese that would ever be produced.

But the beer was excellent, and I had several mugs. Penny ate as daintily as she would have at court, whereas I mostly just shoveled it in as fast as I could chew.

We were comparing notes about our big spell, our typical post-coital post-mortem, when she put her hand on mine, stopping me in mid-thought.

"Min," she asked. "What do we do now?"

"Huh? Well, I'm thinking about a pie. I smelled blueberry pie. I love pie," I avowed. "It's in the blood."

"No, you idiot! Not lunch! I mean, what do we *do*, now?"

"Well, after we get our supplies together and enough horses that won't fall over dead under a saddle, we'll take the East Road to Veronal where we hire a barge, then go south along—"

"You're completely hopeless, you know that? I mean what do we do now, about the Dead God? Shereul! The Great Ghost!"

"Oh. Him. Right. Run. Hide. Fight. What else *can* we do?"

"We have to raise the Duchies against him," she declared quietly.

"We can turn over some valuable military intelligence to the proper authorities. What they do with it isn't our concern. Or our responsibility, no matter what the Aronin said. They're Dukes and Counts. I'm sure they'll think of something. Besides, we're *magi,* remember? We're prohibited by the Bans for interfering with politics."

She shook her head and stared off into the forest. "No, all of those old rules, they'll be thrown out after this."

I made a face. "You can't throw out the Bans! They're the only magical regulation we've had for four hundred years! The Censorate won't let you!"

"Nonetheless, they are outmoded and archaic," she quietly insisted. "They *will* be overturned. Between the irionite and the Dead God, the Bans aren't going to work anymore. More, we'll have to use our influence to push the Coronet Council to take a comprehensive approach to this invasion."

I shrugged. "Duke Lenguin of Alshar is mobilizing his troops at the summer capital at Vorone, I hear. I assume the Ducal Court Mage has been informed. There will be a meeting. What more could they do?"

She rolled her eyes. "You can be so *dumb*, sometimes."

"Yeah, barbarian peasant, remember? Dumb, ignorant and fiercely proud of it?"

"That's part of the problem," she said, her mouth full of apple. "You're looking at this from a peasant's point of view. Oh, you can see it from a professional's standpoint, too, I suppose, but your reaction is pure peasant."

"I like peasants," I defended. "They're cute. And uncomplicated."

"Don't we all. But a peasant looks at the world as if he has little choice, and little chance, to change anything outside of the village level. If a crisis occurs, his first inclination is to find a lord to help or blame. Looking towards the nobility for guidance and leadership."

"Aren't the nobility supposed to be our guides and leaders?"

"Yes. But they are such mostly because they take the initiative to lead. When an intelligent peasant takes that kind of initiative, they either kill him or raise him to the nobility. The point is, peasants look to nobles for leadership, policy, and guidance. Where do you think the nobility turns?"

"The gods?" I supplied. Hells, I didn't know.

"Thank the gods they don't!" Penny said, rolling her eyes. "Theocracies are hell. A sign of a diseased culture. For who speaks for the gods but the temples? And the temples have their own agendas that have little to do with the gods.

"No, the nobles look to each other – to themselves. They agitate and conspire and plot and plan. They may have good intentions or ill, be competent or incompetent, but they have put forth an effort to use their power and resources to advance the causes they choose to serve."

"I thought they just spent rent money and ran the courts."

"And the military, and the bureaucracy, and a hundred other things, if they choose. Or they can sit in a castle and play checkers and wait to be bred. But if they excel, it is because they put forth the effort and forged ahead to do what needed to be done."

"And the dirt-farmer tenant or serf who cuts yet another acre of farmland out of the swamp, he doesn't?"

"It's not a matter of effort, Min. It's a matter of resources. The nobles can make themselves rich, true, but what does that wealth represent?"

"Jeweled daggers and crystal chamber pots?"

"Those are symptoms. That wealth is power. Oh, they have the power of their position, of course, the special considerations. But the difference between Sir Turdfoot of WhereEverTheHellsWeAre and ambitious Count Sparky, High Counselor of the Exchequer is that Sparky was able to use his estates and money to gain power, while Turdfoot scrapes by not much better off than his peasants."

"So wealth is power. You aren't telling me anything I don't know. If you have the wealth, you make the laws."

"No," she said patiently, "if you have the *power*, you can make the laws. That is, you can make policy, codified into law. Money is one form of power, but there are others. And power isn't static, it's fluid. It changes form based on the situation. If things got dire in the Castle, under siege, which would have been more powerful: the noble with a sack of gold, or the peasant with a side of beef?"

"If the peasant could hang on to the beef," I grumbled.

"Exactly. Military power is another kind of power, a very blatant kind. But it isn't absolute. The realm suffers when it's run by pure military power. What other kinds of power are there?" she asked, the patronizing tones rising in her voice.

"Uh, the power of . . . well, you mentioned the temples."

"Yes, that's right, the temples can wield great power, for they can motivate the masses to ignore self-preservation in the name of a holy cause. They have moral power, as well, ideally. But most are run by petty people with odd ideas about a civil society."

"So . . . you said money, so I guess trade is out."

"Nope," she said, shaking her head. "Trade is different. Trade is money on the move. A noble can sit on his fat ass in a castle and collect rents, and accumulate power that way. But he can't exercise that power until he spends the money. On crystal chamber pots, sometimes, but mostly on the upkeep of defenses, the maintenance of his men, buying arms, armor, horses, a thousand other things that have to go from one end of the world to the other. This wonderful, lamented cheese, for instance. In Remere it costs almost a hundred times what it cost in Boval. Who do you think took the difference?"

"The cheese merchant. And the carter."

"Actually, about two dozen people had their hand in the transaction, I'd guess. Including all the nobles who taxed it along the way, and the people who maintain the roads."

"So what? Cheese is power, too?"

"*Trade* is power. The cheese stops rolling . . . all those people lose their cut. If they lose their cut, they complain."

"So *complaining* is power."

"Yes, actually, it is. When you complain that your trade isn't working, you motivate your nobility to do something about it. Or else the mercantile interests will arrange for there to be a noble in place who will."

"So cheese power trumps military power?"

"You are rutting impossible, you know that? Trade is great power. All those people along that route are going to exercise their power to complain – or, in extremes, withhold taxes – until they put enough pressure to get something done. The more efficient the trade, the more money is made, the more power it exercises."

"What about magic? You Imperial types saw it as all the rage, once."

"Magical power is real power, too," she admitted. "But not the way you think it is. The Magocracy ruled as an imperial power because the magical and the military made a potent combination, and allowed the mercantile interests to go pretty much where they wanted to and make a lot of money. Magic gave them an edge, of course, but it was in technological sophistication that led to a higher standard of living and afforded them such power."

"Until we Narasi barbarians came along," I said, proudly.

"No, actually. We were doomed before then. Magic was a potent force only if it was *used*, and when that idiot confiscated all of the irionite and dumped it in the waves over Lost Perwyn, he shackled the very thing that gave him power."

"But he kept plenty of irionite for himself," I countered.

"But the Magocracy was not designed to run on any one house's talent – or one man's. Magical power can only be used as a tool of real power when the situation is such that mere military or commercial means of influence are ineffective. That war in Farise you can't shut up about, for example."

"Wasn't that the last remnant of the Magocracy?" I asked, teasingly.

"Shut up. Orril Pratt was the last great Imperial mage outside of the Bans. But his temporal power was entirely situational. He was the power behind the Doge, who was a merchant prince. Pratt was only able to exercise power because he had irionite and could harm the mercantile competition – the Duchies.

"Similarly, the Archmage only held temporal power because he could use his magic against the heathen barbarians and keep them on the steppes where they belong."

"Yeah, how's that coming?" I asked, innocently.

"Shut up. Magical power is usually situational. The problem was that the Magocracy was designed to run on several Houses competing good-naturedly for the privilege of power by virtue of what service they could perform to extend and secure trade routes.

"When the competition got too rowdy and a magewar broke out, the Archmage was supposed to intervene and use his power to compel the combatants to work for the benefit of the Magocracy. He wasn't supposed to have *all* the power.

"When the Imperial house claimed a monopoly on the last few shreds of irionite, the great magical houses were all hopelessly subordinate, and so they didn't even try to help the defense of the Magocracy the way they should have. Without the power to protect trade, or the will to use it, magical power became a weak footnote in the collapse of the Magocracy, instead of its savior."

"Conquest of the Magocracy, you mean."

"Shut up. The point is, you take away the barbarians on the steppes and the pirates that threaten shipping, and the Magocracy ceases to have power based on magic. Unless you count the magic of bureaucracy."

"A dark and evil force if there ever was one," I added helpfully.

"And that is my point. The game has shifted, and suddenly some idiot peasant spellmonger has been given a tremendous amount of power. And because the Dead God has entered the picture, your magical power suddenly *means* something: the ability to protect trade routes and suppliers."

"I thought we were saving the world from ancient evil goblins?" I asked, confused.

"We are," she agreed. "For the mercantile interests."

"Oh. Is that good? And how do I have all this power again?"

"Okay, I'll try to use small words. Look at it this way: with the troops the Dead God has on hand right at the moment he can easily assault Alshar and overrun the Wilderlands. By this time next year he'll control at least half of the Duchy, probably more. And even with every sword in the realm riding at his bidding, the Duke will still lose in nearly every battle – every battle where there isn't an augmented warmage or six. Warmagi armed with witchstones. You have the irionite. *That's* power."

" *'Pol-i-tics,'* " I sang, reminding her of the Bans against such things.

"You want to know about politics? Here's a lesson: when Sir Cei and the rest of the survivors are able to finally present their case to the Duke and his council, there will be days and days of discussion in court about how reliable the accounts of such traumatized backwoods nobility and rustic peasants are.

"Obviously, it will be said, they are over-stating the matter, embellishing on the truth in order to advance their own goals. Never mind that all those people just lost their homes and appeared at Inarion out of thin air – that won't matter. What will matter is that the Ducal bureaucracy, which creaks along like frozen honey in the best of circumstances, will dig in its heels and do everything it can to ignore the truth in favor of the *status quo*."

"Penny, they aren't that stupid," I said, shaking my head.

"Wanna bet? Min, the only difference between the Ducal Council – or the Coronet Council, for that matter – and a shoemakers' guild is that the shoemakers will probably have a better organization and less political consideration on their side. Other than that, you have the same issues you have in any organization: everyone trying to protect their piece of the pie at the expense of everyone else."

"So it all comes back to pie . . ." I said, sagely.

"Pay attention!" she demanded. "The Ducal Council will hem and haw while the local and regional lords in the West get slaughtered, as they try to take on the goblins piecemeal. By the time the hordes are at the Vorone they will slooooowly start realizing that they are in trouble, mostly because their tax revenues are down over last year. Then they will start to creak into action, but not very efficiently. They will argue and debate and compromise for political expediency, when by all rights they should appoint a war leader and get to business. Else there will be Four Duchies next year."

"That seems overly pessimistic," I noted.

"It's overly realistic, actually," she sighed. "This is simple. If you had any familiarity with Remeran politics . . ."

"Okay, for the sake of argument, let's say you are correct, and the Duke's people won't be able to get their heads out of their asses. What the hells can we do?"

"We can take our case to them. Convince them. First the Duke of Alshar, then the entire Coronet Council. Or better yet, the Duke of Castal, Rard."

"Because I'm so damn cute and persuasive . . ."

"No, because you are in charge of the most powerful magical strike team ever assembled, and Rard is looking to expand his influence beyond Castal. His wife is the sister of Duke Lenguin, and they both want more power. By all accounts they are utter opportunists. That gives you a certain degree of leverage. You have the only stone that can break the Dead God's influence over other captured shards That gives you a unique power. How many stones do you have left, unclaimed?"

"Um, about nine," I admitted.

"And those give you significantly more leverage. Each one is worth about a barony, in mundane terms. You'll give those stones to magi who can make a difference, won't you," she said – a statement, not a question. I answered anyway.

"Well, yeah, I suppose. I'm sure the Duke can find—"

"Screw the Duke!" she said, bitterly. "You don't understand how power works – *political* power. The Duke sets *policy*. He approves laws. He sets style. He hires other people to enforce his decisions. He keeps the realm safe. That is the sum total of his power. To set policy he listens to advisors. He must have laws proposed if he is to approve them. He needs direction before he can appoint the proper people to execute them. That includes the Court Wizard and all the other Ducal posts.

"And that means he needs wise counsel – and in this situation, you are surely the wisest counsel he can hope to hear from. So we go forth boldly and demand an audience, tell it like it is, and then use your accumulated influence to convince him to form policy to our liking."

"And that would be . . . ?"

"Raising the Duchies! Ishi's tits, you're dim! Every single Duchy will have to send troops, weapons, supplies, magi – you name it, we'll need it. This is going to be a long war. That's the best-case. Worst case, Alshar is Shereul's new summer home, and the Eastern Duchies get to fight against him at half-strength – and lose."

"Pen, even at full strength we'll probably lose."

She sagged. "I know. But we have to try. And you're the only man who can do it."

"What about Terleman?" I protested. "Or you, for that matter?"

"We've all pledged to follow *you*."

"You did what? Who did? Follow who? When?"

"Sorry you didn't hear the announcement," she said, dryly. "We had a meeting while you were sleeping the night before last. Every one of us knows what is going to happen – apparently we're smarter than you. And after all the discussion it was decided that our best hope – the Five

Duchies' best hope – lay in getting behind a single leader and pushing him into a position of power."

"How the hells did you manage *that?*" I asked. "They can't agree which shade of blue the sky is!"

"Let's just say it's because I'm so damn cute and persuasive, and leave it at that."

"Penny . . . !" I said, warningly.

"Calm yourself. I didn't need to do much persuading. We all have a good handle on the situation. It was unanimous. In fact, they swore an oath."

"Great, now we have oaths. What kind of oath?"

"Oh, one I stole from Imperial times. It's based on the oath that subordinate magelords swore to the Archmage."

"So . . . Spellmonger to Archmage. And here I was, trying not to be ambitious."

" 'Based on'. And, well, yes . . . but they are just as concerned with the situation as I am. And despite all of the wonders of witchstones, they are *scared*. Scared of the power that they hold in their hands . . . and scared of the potential temporal power it suddenly implies. Not to mention scared of that nasty green ball full of undead goblin and what it portends"

"I'm sure they'll work through it."

"Why are you being so difficult, Min? I'm serious. They don't want to go back and get shuffled off to a bunch of meaningless skirmishes. Nor do they want to go to war with the Censorate. They have power, they realize, but it becomes greatest when they act as a united force. And they have no idea what to do with that power once it is realized. They need someone to make policy."

"They're bright. They'll think of something," I assured.

"It's not going to work that way, Min," she warned. Then she bit her lip. That's a well-known danger sign with Penny. "I've been talking to the others . . . they *want* to follow you."

I stopped eating. "What did you say?"

"They want you to lead them. *In battle.* Against the Dead God."

"So this is what irionite poisoning is like," I observed airily. "The bad craziness sets in. Pen, what happened during the siege, it was fun, but it's *over*. We're rescued . . . or something. No one's trying to kill us at the moment. I don't need to lead – I can't lead. I don't have any official standing – anywhere. I mean, I have my license, but . . ."

". . . but you 'prefer the life of a simple Spellmonger', I know. That's what I'm getting at, Min: you won't be able to be a simple spellmonger anymore. The next year will see one major loss after another, and before you know it the Coronet Council will be screaming for yet another mass call for troops to fight the invasion. They're going to need warmagi, especially, and specifically *us*.

"But what happens if we just linger, waiting for someone to do something smart while the bodies pile up? What happens when the

Duchy decides to take possession of the irionite, place it under the protection of the Court Mage? Or the Censorate confiscates it all and puts everyone to death? The peasants you think are so cute will get screwed. As do the warmagi you've been so valiantly leading. They get drafted or shafted, and they don't like either choice.

"So they want you to keep doing what you did in Bovali. Those were special rules, true, but *they worked*: they want *you* to keep the conscience of the stones and control their distribution and use. It's the only way they can trust each other with them. If you have claim, a claim that they all would enforce, then no one person can try to stir up trouble without bringing the wrath of the whole group down on them. That was the way the Magocracy was supposed to work.

"They won't listen to me," I protested, alarmed at what she said.

"They all agreed to the oath, that the stones are yours and they are forfeit on your word. When we go before the Ducal Council, and the Coronet Council, they want *you* to speak on their behalf, work in their interest. They want you to be their leader, their lord, their captain. Now, you can stand around and wait to get drafted again, or we can be pro-active and work to set this up the way we want it to go."

" 'We?'"

"Us warmagi," she explained. "Oh, not me, not really – I'm a theorist and thaumaturge, not a warmage. But I have a vested interest in this, as well, and I have my jobs to do. Everyone does, they just don't know it yet. It's our job to convince them. Your job – but I'll support you in that. And we'll all back you. We pledged to put ourselves under your command, offer you counsel, obey your orders, and give our lives in your service. Over oaths like those sworn to any other lord."

" 'Lord', now. That's great. Any thoughts to robes and silly hats?"

"That's still in committee. Seriously, Min, we *have* to do this."

"Penny, we don't have to do a damn thing!" I insisted. "Much less fight this war. I know I don't want to—"

"And when did the gods start paying attention to what you wanted, Master Spellmonger?"

"Point taken. Okay, I appreciate the vote of confidence, but find another lackey. I've got better things to do."

"Better than saving the Five Duchies?"

"In point of fact, yes."

"Like what?"

"Like raising my kid in peace. And not leaving he or she an orphan."

"You don't have any—" she stopped, and her eyes got wide. "*Oh, Min!*" she gasped. "You? And . . . um . . ."

"Alya?" I offered. "Yes. Just as I was explaining to her why it was necessary to have long, passionate sex with my ex-girlfriend when she told me. I checked. She's pregnant."

"And you're sure it's . . . yours?" she asked, suspiciously.

Anyone else and I would have blasted them where they stood. But this was Penny. I took a deep breath. "Alya has been a widow for over a year. I'm the first man she's had relations with since her husband died. So . . . yeah, I'm sure."

It took a few moments for her emotions to settle – and there were a lot of them flying around behind those pretty eyes. "I don't know what . . . are you happy about this?" she asked, hesitantly.

"Actually," I admitted, "I am. I'm ecstatic. Busting out with pride. Looking forward to daddy duty, as it were. And scared spitless, but I hear that will pass."

"Min, I . . . I'm sorry! Congratulations!" She had tears in her eyes.

"Thank you," I said, sincerely. Then she got mad.

"Why didn't you *tell* me?"

"I just did!"

"Sooner!"

"We were going to be dead, remember? And before that I didn't want anything to distract you from your work. So I thought I'd wait for an opportune time."

She sighed. "I guess you did. Okay, you're having a kid. Great! That should give you even more reason to want to defeat the Dead God."

"Sure, I don't want him – or her – to grow up in thrall to the short and fuzzy set, but that doesn't mean daddy has to go to the front lines."

"You won't be on the front lines," she said, shaking her head. "You are too valuable. You'll be in charge– which means I'll be running the hard parts. We're going to need a full lab, and a supply of—"

"And where is all of this going to come from?"

"The Duchy. Or Duchies. It doesn't matter, actually. Let me handle that end of it. You just figure out how to win the war."

"While raising kids?" I asked sarcastically.

"What you do in your spare time is no business of mine," she assured. "Look, Min, we need a strong leader, an adept, and a warmage. You're all three."

"I'm a rutting spellmonger, Penny!" I exploded. "I'm nothing special!"

"You're THE Spellmonger, you idiot! You hung on at an undermanned castle against twenty times the odds with nothing but a piece of irionite, guile, and some talented apprentices. *Any one of us*," she said, indicating all of the warmagi in the party, "would have packed it in early and buggered out. You persevered. You even won – kind of," she admitted.

"Not getting killed is a victory?" I asked, discouraged.

"Against the Dead God? Hells, yes!"

"Okay, okay, I concede the point. But if I agree to do this, it has to be real. *I'm* leader. No one else. The moment you guys don't like what I'm doing, throw me out and let me go home. Those are my conditions."

"Done. Min, I don't think you have a clear idea what kind of hold you have over these people."

"Nonsense. Sure, the peasants thought I was great, but these are my professional peers –"

"Who all insist that you are the greatest among them. Deal with it."

"That is such a load of—"

"Deal with it!" she repeated. "Look, there will be plenty of room for Alya and your kids in whatever gloomy old tower they give us. And wherever it will be will likely be safer than anywhere else. So just shut up and be our fearless leader for a change, will you?" she asked, annoyed.

"Oh, all right," I muttered. "Do I get to wear a silly hat?"

"As silly as you need it to be," she agreed. *"You're* the leader."

Crap. *I really was.*

The End

Make sure you check out Book II of the Spellmonger Series:

WARMAGE

ABOUT THE AUTHOR

Terry Mancour lives in Durham, North Carolina with his beautiful wife and three precocious children. He attended from the University of North Carolina at Chapel Hill pursuing a degree in Religious Studies, had a succession of crappy jobs, spent three years in exile in Greenville, North Carolina, and had more crappy jobs before he became VP of Broad Street Coffee Roasters, which was closed four years later due to no fault of his own.

He has written more than twenty books, many under pseudonyms, including the 1992 New York Times Best Selling Star Trek: Next Generation novel *Spartacus,* and two sequels to H. Beam Piper's 1967 classic sci-fi novel, *Space Viking*, *Prince of Tanith* (2011), and *Princess Valerie's War* (2011).

The sequel to *Spellmonger, Warmage,* was also published in 2012, and the third book in the series, *Magelord*, was published in 2013. After that came *Knights Magi, High Mage, Journeymage* and *Enchanter.*

He is a frequent contributor to a variety of websites on a number of topics, and has written all sorts of stuff that he doesn't want to mention here because they are largely too boring. A lifelong sci-fi fan and uber-geek, he has indulged in every nerdy stereotype possible over the years, yet remains remarkably cool except to his children. And what do *they* know, anyway?

Write the author at tmancour@gmail.com

Visit the author's blog: http://terrymancour.blogspot.com/

WARMAGE – PREVIEW

Chapter One:

The Slaughter at Grimly Wood

Grimly Wood, Late Summer

I surveyed the battlefield at Grimly Wood from horseback, looking out over the heads of the formations of infantry and the clusters of light cavalry, hearing the sounds of a thousand suits of armor rattle and hundreds of horses complaining about their burdens. I looked toward the distant line of the foe, barely visible in the mists and shadows that haunted this dour little land, and I had but one thought:

I really had to pee.

I should have gone earlier, I knew, but I was too worried about the battle to take the time. That was understandable: it was the first battle in which I was in command of the Ducal forces, and I was as nervous as a virgin on her wedding night. I had gotten little sleep the night before, and when I was awakened by my trusty servant an hour before dawn to hear scouting reports, I was still too busy to tend to my personal needs as messengers came and went and decisions had to be made. I'd managed to eat couple of camp biscuits with a rasher of bacon washed down with a big mug of weak beer but that was as much food as I'd managed – and now that beer was haunting me in an increasingly uncomfortable fashion.

I should have gone before I donned my armor, because once you put it on there's no easy way to pee without removing a good portion of it.

I had even stopped when that last chain skirt was being strapped around my waist and *almost* went, but then Captain Rogo had come with important news about the scouts, and I postponed it again.

By the time I mounted Traveler, I realized I was in dire straits.

I should know better. I'm not just some petty lordling elevated to command through favoritism or accident of birth. I was a trained warrior, a master wizard, and a veteran warmage of the bloody Farisan Campaign – not to mention a survivor of the hopeless Siege of Boval Vale.

I knew I was risking certain distraction and possible illness, a condition the healers call "belly rot" – what happens when a man's intestines or bladder is full when he sustains a wound to the lower abdomen. One of the first things they teach you in Basic Infantry Training (which, despite my magical profession I had been obliged to endure) is to "lighten your load" before you step onto the battlefield.

This was a particularly important battlefield, too, and a particularly important battle. It wasn't a decisive engagement, really, but a sustained skirmish which we were almost certain to win. But what happened on this battlefield and how would set the course for the many, many battles to come, I knew. This was the first time that the encroaching gurvani were being faced with a foe who not only expected them, but who knew what they were dealing with.

This lightning-fast campaign was but the opening salvo between two titanic powers: on our side was the massed professional military aristocracy of the Five Duchies, stout warriors with bright swords and snorting steeds and the favor of the gods (or so we told ourselves).

On the other was the gurvani horde of thousands – *hundreds* of thousands, actually. Gurvani were known as the Mountain Folk in some places, scrugs in others, but they were usually known as goblins – 'gurvani' was the name they called themselves. The average specimen stood four to five feet tall, covered in black hair, with a face like a terrier crossed with a pig.

They're as smart as most human beings. They use iron and practice warfare. They have a tribal culture that sticks to the mountains or remote valleys. Ordinarily gurvani were peaceful, or at least not warlike. Their warrior societies spar with each other to solve inter-tribal disputes. A few tribes raid human settlements to steal chickens or a pig or a bushel of potatoes, but for close to two hundred years even that was rare.

Until now. Now they were led by a kind of super-shaman. The ancient undead head of a defiant shaman who led the last major war between my folk and theirs, to be more precise.

His name had been Shereul (spell it how you will) when he was alive. Two centuries before he had led the last major organized resistance to human settlement of the northwest of the rustic Duchy of Alshar, where it abutted the Minden Range. He had lost several battles against the Alshari knights and their shining lances, and sued for peace.

At a truce meeting between him and the knights, he had been betrayed and slain in the sacred valley of his people, so that we could settle their lands. To add insult to injury, they chopped off his head and put it on a pike while they systematically cleared out the sacred valley of the goblins by slaughtering everyone in sight. Since then, the gurvani had been dispossessed from their sacred valley and their sacred caves and Shereul wasn't very happy about that.

Now he was just called the Old God or the Great Ghost by the goblins (we called him, more accurately, the *Dead God*) and he wasn't *just* undead – which would have been interesting enough, thaumaturgically speaking. He was also encased in a perfect sphere of a peculiar kind of green amber, known to scholars as *irionite*. It's absolutely rare, a translucent stone that shimmers like an emerald in the sunlight and is lighter in your hand than you'd expect. It's magically potent – actually, that's an understatement. It's magically *profound*. A tiny shard a centimeter wide can give most magi almost unlimited power. I've got a perfect sphere of it three centimeters wide, which makes me an extremely formidable warmage.

But irionite not only animated Shereul's thoughts, the huge mass of the stuff encapsulated his entire brain, giving the Dead God truly divine levels of magical power. How powerful? Just his existence is enough to threaten the nature of Reality itself in his proximity. Using that power he had secretly raised an army of almost a million gurvani back in the depths of the Minden Range and then launched a genocidal war on us.

I guess I shouldn't leave that part out. It's pretty important. It's why I was here, about to slaughter a bunch of hairy goblins at a misty, rocky little fief in northern Alshar called Grimly Wood. It was late summer, now, almost autumn, and as I sat on my horse and tried to distract myself from my over-full bladder with reflections of my life and its purpose, I couldn't help but realize that it had been an eventful summer. Hells, it had been an eventful year.

The previous autumn I was a spellmonger in a quiet mountain village called Minden's Hall, in a peaceful little valley stuffed full of happy peasants and contented cows, far to the west. I was doing a pretty good job of curing warts and casting love spells and making hens lay more prodigiously, while trying to forget about my service in arms, when the Dead God decided the time was right to launch his *very* inconvenient genocidal horde of goblins on an unsuspecting humanity – and he picked Minden's Hall for the honor of first slaughter.

And the first item on their agenda was the conquest of the blind valley of Boval Vale in which I was living. It had once belonged to them, had some deep religious significance to them, and was also the *perfect* staging area for a wider war against the scourge of humanity in the Five Duchies.

Shereul wasn't just relying on his magical innate power and half a million goblins pouring in from secret mountain caverns to conquer us; he had also given to an elite corps of magic-using gurvani shamans shards of irionite chipped from his sphere. Each one made the shaman the match of any warmage. Luckily their skills were crude. But their enthusiasm and the sheer power of the stones left the control of Boval Vale never in doubt. The local lord, who had some inkling that his generously large castle would someday have to defend against vindictive goblins his ancestors had betrayed, conned me into staying to protect the villagers and defend his indefensible fief from the inevitable conquest.

I fought like hell those few desperate weeks. I won my own little chunk of Irionite, endured a siege, and met some magical Tree Folk (non-humans, like the gurvani. Unlike the gurvani, they generally don't want to kill us), found a girlfriend, knocked her up, founded an elite unit of irionite-augmented warmagi, led numerous covert missions to harass our besiegers, led a peasant's revolt against the rightful lord of the Vale, and ended up saving almost everyone using a powerful spell through a mystical tear in the fabric of the universe fueled by a four-hour long session of magically powerful sex. With my ex-girlfriend.

Of course, I couldn't escape through a portal that I was holding open, so I got stranded at the castle with my warmagi comrades and only narrowly escaped with my life, mostly because the Tree Folk figured I needed to warn the Five Duchies about what we were about to get pounded with.

And that's how I spent *my* summer last year. As I said, it was eventful.

Ishi's tits, I had to pee.